TEMPTING THE WARRIOR

She stood naked in the stream, her hair hanging down her back, long and black with water. Her skin glowed and sparkled, radiating the silvery luminescence, glistening wetly.

Tristan braced himself with one palm on a fledgling trunk as the sight before him nearly drove him to his knees. Haith's arms were outstretched as if to embrace that far away, glowing moon, the profile of her breasts pushing against the night. The swell of her hips and buttocks, the gentle curve of thigh, twisted his guts as she bent at the waist to scoop the water over her pearly body once more. She stood again, flinging her hair in a wide arc and sending tiny diamond droplets flying about her.

And then she turned toward where Tristan stood on the bank, her lips parting in a smile of invitation.

Tristan heard his own growl of desire coming as if from some forest wolf. He splashed into the stream, the cold water rushing around his boots, caressing his calves, and stood before her. He panted not with exertion, but with a wild hunger and need . . .

<u>BOOK YOUR PLACE ON OUR WEBSITE AND MAKE THE READING CONNECTION!</u>

We've created a customized website just for our very special readers, where you can get the inside scoop on everything that's going on with Zebra, Pinnacle and Kensington books.

When you come online, you'll have the exciting opportunity to:

- View covers of upcoming books
- Read sample chapters
- Learn about our future publishing schedule (listed by publication month *and author*)
- Find out when your favorite authors will be visiting a city near you
- Search for and order backlist books from our online catalog
- Check out author bios and background information
- Send e-mail to your favorite authors
- Meet the Kensington staff online
- Join us in weekly chats with authors, readers and other guests
- Get writing guidelines
- AND MUCH MORE!

Visit our website at
http://www.kensingtonbooks.com

The
WARRIOR

Heather Grothaus

ZEBRA BOOKS
Kensington Publishing Corp.
www.kensingtonbooks.com

ZEBRA BOOKS are published by

Kensington Publishing Corp.
850 Third Avenue
New York, NY 10022

All Kensington titles, imprints, and distributed lines are available at special quantity discounts for bulk purchases for sales
promotion, premiums, fund-raising, educational, or institutional
use.

Special book excerpts or customized printings can also be created to fit specific needs. For details, write or phone the office
of the Kensington Special Sales Manager: Attn. Special Sales
Department. Kensington Publishing Corp., 850 Third Avenue,
New York, NY 10022. Phone: 1-800-221-2647.

ISBN 0-8217-8006-9

First Printing: March 2006
10 9 8 7 6 5 4 3 2 1

Printed in the United States of America

For Cody
I will love you forever, my best boy.
Thank you.

For Mary Frances Johnson,
who was proud of me.

And most importantly,
for Tim, my warrior.

PROLOGUE

October 1066
Seacrest Manor, England

"The lord is dead, my lady. England has fallen."

The soldier knelt before Ellora, Lady of Seacrest, in respect and exhaustion. The crude metal rings of his mail were packed with damp and drying mud, and he stank of cold and filth, despair and sweat.

"Lord James is dead?" Ellora asked in quiet disbelief. The soldier simply nodded his head as he remained in the supplicating position. "How do you know this? Look at me!" she demanded, struggling to keep her hands clasped in front of her and not strike the young man, clearly already beaten.

The soldier raised his head, and immediately Ellora saw the reason for his avoidance of her gaze: a wound ran the left side of his face, from the leather coif at his hairline to wrap around the bottom of his ear. His left eye was missing, a sagging flap of ragged skin the only covering for the empty socket. His gray lips twisted in agony when he spoke.

"I was the first at his side when he fell," he said. "His body follows me to the keep."

Ellora looked across the great hall to the wooden portal, still ajar from the soldier's stumbling entry. Already she could hear a rising din from the bailey beyond, the shouts and wails of the serfs left behind in the village. Clattering footsteps swelled behind her as the keep's servants raced from other chambers. Many had seen the approach of the soldier heralding the return of Seacrest's men, and all were anxious to have news of their loved ones.

Without further word, Ellora stepped around the soldier and walked toward the portal as if in a trance. Servants flowed around her and out the door like muddy water, heedless of their lady's state. Beyond the wooden palisade, villagers swarmed over the gentle slope away from the town and toward the band of fifteen or so men that approached. Fifteen men returning from the nearly two hundred who had departed on King Harold's behalf what seemed only days ago. Fifteen men, most limping and stumbling up the knoll, around a core of the most able-bodied, who dragged behind them a large bundle on a crude pallet. The fastest villagers and servants soon reached the group, and Ellora watched frantic women rush from man to man—grasping arms, peering into faces, searching for their own.

Ellora's eyes fixed on the pallet, and she left the safety of the doorway, making her own way to meet the group.

I am a widow, she thought over and over as she neared them. *My husband is dead.* Her brown eyes remained dry, her posture erect, her footsteps slow and measured to the death knell ringing in her mind: *Dead. Dead. Dead.*

The clutch of soldiers bearing the litter breached the wall of the town and dragged their burden to rest at their lady's feet. The men who could, knelt.

"My lady," the largest man of the group said. He was

Barrett, well familiar to Seacrest and Lady Ellora as her husband's first man and friend. "He fought well, to the end of the thing." A bearlike paw swiped at his huge face, from black, shaggy mane to thick beard. "'Twas an arrow that found its mark between his ribs. He did not suffer."

Ellora stood as if frozen, eyes fixed on the bundle. She heard Barrett's gently spoken words, but was unable to respond as the sight of the pallet filled all of her senses. Swathed as the body was in rough brown cloth, only the outline of Lord James could be detected, save for one dirt-streaked hand which had slipped from the litter and lay upturned on the moist, packed earth.

The soldiers who remained with their charge moved back a respectful distance, save Barrett, who was loathe to leave his sire's side even in death. The big man merely turned his eyes to a distant point on the south horizon to award the lady a modicum of privacy. It was as if he still watched for the enemy.

Ellora knelt by the litter and hesitantly reached for her husband's hand. It felt cold and heavy, clasped in her own warm flesh. The thick fingers lay stiff against her palm, and she lovingly stroked his hand from fingertip to wrist, rocking back and forth. The bailey was unnaturally quiet but for the soft sounds of groaning and sobbing. A sudden sharp breeze swept the knoll, pressing the gray kirtle to her thin body and blowing back the veil from her blond plait. Ellora pulled Lord James's hand to her breast and raised her face to the wind, closing her eyes and inhaling the crisp autumn tang—a taste of winter's chill soon to envelop Seacrest. A single tear escaped from beneath her eyelids, its hot trail soon frigid in the breeze.

Barrett stepped closer. "My lady?"

Ellora's eyes opened. Her gaze returned to her husband's

now outstretched arm and fixed on a thin band of color wound around the exposed sleeve of his undershirt.

"My lady," Barrett began again, "shall we move him to the hall?"

A ribbon, Ellora thought, tentatively touching the sky blue band. She ran a finger under its edge and tugged it loose, revealing a length of mud-mottled silk embroidered with the letter *C* in a thread of the same hue.

Ellora dropped James's arm as if it were afire, the ribbon still twined through her fingers. Her chest felt completely empty of air, no breath could be stolen from the breeze to fill her lungs. Her stomach was liquid; her eyes, stone.

He had taken her to battle.

A great gasp finally filled her, just as black dots began to cloud her vision. Ellora looked up into the concerned face of Barrett, and her body trembled as she spoke.

"Yea. Take him to the hall."

Ellora followed her dead husband as he was dragged on the litter into the darkness of the hall. The ribbon from his arm was crumbled into her fist, and as his remaining men positioned James before the hearth, Ellora's gaze went to the stone steps leading up along the right side of the hall.

"Nay!" The wail echoed from an upper chamber, freezing the servants and soldiers in their movements.

Ellora, too, paused at the sound, but just briefly before coming to stand at the bottom of the stairs. Her hand snaked out to jerk back a servant woman who rushed to mount the steps.

"My lady, please," the woman pleaded, daring to grasp Ellora's wrist. "Let me go to her. She does not—"

Ellora raised her hand and struck the woman across the

face. The servant quieted immediately, and Ellora shook her in a demand for her attention. "Where are the children?"

The woman gestured up the stairs with the hand that she had pressed to her mouth as another round of wails rained down upon them.

"Hear me well," Ellora warned, drawing the servant closer to her. "Go to the children and keep them until I come for you."

"But, my lady, Minerva—"

"Minerva will want to be with her mistress." Ellora released her grip on the woman with a shove toward the stairs. "Now go, and do as I say, or I will cast you from here and to the Normans who surely will descend upon us all soon."

No sooner had the maid scurried up the stairs than a blur of blue and fiery red descended, colliding with Ellora and clinging to her.

"Ellora! Ellora," the woman sobbed, grasping fistfuls of the lady's kirtle. "Tell me they lie! God's mercy, 'tis not so!"

"Corinne." Ellora held the red-haired woman away from her by her shoulders, and her hard brown eyes bore into searching, liquid blue. She swept an arm toward the hall behind her. "See for yourself what your wickedness has cost you."

Corinne looked past Ellora's shoulder, and her eyes found the still covered form of the Lord of Seacrest. She shoved Ellora aside and stumbled across the hall. Tripping and falling in her haste, she crawled the remainder of the way to James's side. Corinne's hands clawed at the makeshift shroud, and when the lord's face was revealed—eyes open, unseeing—her scream rent the air like lightning in the blackest night. She pulled the cloth down further and was rewarded with the sight of a jagged arrow shaft, splintered where it had been broken off, resting firmly in the lord's left breast.

Corinne collapsed onto James's chest, her hands cradling his face, fingers clutching his dark hair. Ellora approached from behind to stand over the prone figures of her husband and onetime friend.

"Nay, your wickedness has cost not only you, but us all." Ellora threw the wadded ball of ribbon at Corinne. It hit her gently and tumbled to the floor. "You bewitched him to the point that he could not fight." She spread her arms wide and seemed to address the entire hall with its few, grieving occupants.

"The greatest warrior in all of England! Champion of Harold and the crown! No sword of any Welsh nor ax of any Viking could injure him! Entire bands of thieves dared not approach Seacrest for fearing the wrath of its lord."

"And now! Now—" Ellora dropped to her knees and grasped Corinne by her red locks, turning the woman's sobbing face to her. "What is this? A tiny splinter of wood has laid him low. What of Seacrest now, Corinne? What of our welfare or the welfare of my daughter and yours when the Normans come? Will you cast a spell to protect us? To protect all of England from William's barbarians?" Ellora released her grip on Corinne's hair, letting her head fall once again to James's chest.

"You've killed him," Ellora whispered. Then louder, incredulously, "You red-headed bitch! You've good as killed us *all!*" She stood and looked at the faces staring openly at her. "Why do you stand there?" she shrieked. "This sorceress has killed your lord and master! Seize her and have her hanged!"

The eyes of the onlookers widened in shock at her words, and some looked away at the sight of their lady, so obviously crazed with grief.

"Nay? Then I shall do it myself." Ellora's eyes searched

for a weapon, and finding no steel at hand, she grasped a log from the cold hearth. Lifting the heavy object above her head, she readied herself to bring it down on Corinne's exposed back.

"Ellora!" A woman's strong voice rang out and was quickly joined by a young girl's shriek.

The log was snatched from Ellora's grasp as Barrett stepped from the shadows. He cast the weapon aside and enveloped Ellora in his massive arms when she would have thrown herself on Corinne. The lady's strength quickly left her then, and she sagged in grief and shame, clinging to Barrett and sobbing.

A girl of twelve summers ran to Ellora's side, yellow plaits flying, and was included in Barrett's embrace. Across the hall, the gray-haired woman whose voice had called out moments before nestled an even younger girl in her skirts. The child struggled against the kind hands that held her and broke free, running to Corinne and kneeling beside her.

"Mother, what is wrong with Papa?" the girl asked. When no response came, she touched Corinne's shoulder. "Mother? Is Papa sleeping? Why does he sleep in the hall?"

Corinne's only response was to grasp her daughter's hand, and the older woman came to stand over the pair.

The child looked up. "Minerva, what is wrong with Papa?"

Minerva dropped to the rushes. "Oh, Haith. My wee faery," she murmured and cradled the child's face in gnarled fingers. "Your papa's soul has left this earth to join the spirits."

"Papa is dead?" Haith pulled away from Minerva's touch to look more closely at her father. Corinne was still draped across his chest, and a low stream of murmurs issued from her.

Haith reached out and tentatively fingered a lock of her father's hair and then froze, her gaze flying to the older girl.

"Bertie?" she called. "Bertie, Papa is dead!"

The blond child turned her head from Barrett's waist and, seeing her half sister's uncertainty, scrambled free and stumbled to Haith. The two girls entwined themselves with each other there on the rushes and stared at their shared sire.

"'Tis alright, Haith," Soleilbert soothed, rocking the girl, junior to her twelve years by four. "Papa is in Heaven now with the saints and the angels."

"But what shall we do without Papa, Bertie?"

"'Twill be alright," Soleilbert insisted through her tears. "We still have our mothers and Minerva."

During the girls' exchange, Minerva had gathered several items from the kitchen on a tray, and she now returned to Corinne's side. She crumbled pinches of herbs into a small wooden bowl and spoke in low tones. Water was added from a pitcher, and a dash of salt. The old woman withdrew her eating knife and inserted its tip into the bowl's contents, making vague outlines on the surface of the water.

The small audience of villagers and soldiers, Barrett included, discreetly left the hall as Minerva began her practice. The sound of her prayers as she lifted the bowl high above her head started Ellora out of her grieving reverie.

"Nay!" she screamed, rushing to Minerva and slapping the bowl from her hands. It clattered and skipped across the floor, splashing its contents on everyone left gathered around James. "You will bring no more evil into this hold with your witchery!" She flung an arm in the direction of her dead husband. "Have you not done enough already?"

Minerva rose to face Ellora, her eyes blazing. "How

dare you say any in this keep would harm Lord James! The body must be cleansed and his soul blessed to leave!"

"Then it shall be done by a priest," Ellora said, not backing down, "not a godless heathen."

"And just where do you think to locate a priest, my good lady?" Minerva stepped closer, putting herself nearly nose to nose with Ellora. "Perchance you have not noticed that the only friar of Seacrest didna return with his lord's men? Shall we sit and wait while James's body rots before our eyes?"

"Be gone from me," Ellora said through clenched teeth. "Take your things, and those of Corinne and her bastard,"—she looked pointedly at Haith, still clutching Soleilbert—"and be gone from this hall."

"Mother," Soleilbert gasped, "do not say such things!"

"Ellora, I warn you," Minerva said, "you go too far."

"Nay." Ellora shook her head. "This is overdue. You should never have come to Seacrest all those years ago, and now, the one who held you here"—she looked again at James, and her voice quieted—"is no more."

"This is Corinne's home as well as yours."

"No more!" Ellora insisted.

"We will go." The soft words drove between the two women like a wedge of iron. Corinne raised her head from her lover's chest, and her features seemed to have aged a score of years in the past hour. Minerva and Ellora looked at her in shock.

"I know my presence has been a burden to you, Ellora," Corinne said, "but it wasn't always so. In honor of the friendship we once shared, we will set out on the morrow." Her fingers still gripped James. "There is no one for us here now."

"Corinne," Minerva said, "James would have wanted us to remain. We needn't do this."

"Very well," Ellora said as if Minerva hadn't spoken. "On the morrow is soon enough."

"Mother, nay!" Soleilbert cried, clutching Haith to her. "Do not make them go!"

"What's happening, Bertie?" Haith asked, her small face ashen.

"Would you give us leave to perform the blessing?" Corinne asked stiffly.

A sharp nod was Ellora's only answer, but she stepped forward to grasp both Haith and Soleilbert by their arms. "I am taking the children from here," she said. "They need not be witness to such things."

"Nay." Corinne reached out and grasped her daughter's other arm. "Haith stays." She mustered all of her strength and won the tug of war. Haith screeched and reached for Soleilbert, who was jerked to her feet by Ellora.

"I shall return, Haith," Soleilbert called as Ellora led her up the stairs. "Do not fear."

Haith retreated closer to the hearth and sat alone, her small arms wrapped around her knees.

Minerva rushed to Corinne's side. "Have you gone mad?" she asked the woman, who was slowly salvaging the spilled herbs from the rushes.

"Minerva, trouble me not about this," Corinne said, crawling around Lord James and stretching to grasp the errant bowl. "We would serve no purpose here but to increase the grudge Ellora bears me. 'Tis better we leave now."

Minerva moved again to Corinne's side to assist her and plead her case. "Where would you have us go? Scotland? Winter is nigh, and the land crawls with Normans. Two women and a small child traveling alone would make easy game for soldiers." She grasped Corinne's wrist. "We would be lucky to starve."

"Mayhap," Corinne said and shook her arm from

Minerva's clutches. "But we have beasts to carry us and supplies aplenty to see us to our journey's end." She beckoned to her daughter.

Haith grudgingly approached and pressed Corinne's arm. "But, Mother, Bertie will not be able to find me in Scotland."

"You will find new friends, my love," Corinne whispered and smoothed back the hair from her daughter's forehead. "Mayhap you already have cousins waiting to play with a wee faery like you."

"I don't want cousins," Haith said. Her wide blue eyes, so like James's, filled with tears for the first time that day. "Bertie is my *sister.*"

"Sh-h-h." Corinne drew Haith to her bosom. "I know. But we must go. The gods will aid us in our journey."

"The gods doona aid fools," Minerva muttered. Then in a gentler tone, she said to Haith, "Faery? Have you a prayer to send to the ancestors with your papa's spirit?"

Haith's sobbing quieted a bit, and she nodded.

"Then lay your hand on him during the blessing and speak to him." Minerva smiled. "You can whisper if you wish—he'll hear you."

Haith moved from the circle of her mother's arms and scooted to James's side. She laid her small head on her father's forearm and slipped a tiny hand into his. Haith squeezed her eyes shut as Corinne began to speak.

"With great love do I commit the soul of my beloved husband, James, Lord of Seacrest, to that gentle place the gods have reserved him . . ."

Haith took in the blackness behind her eyelids and spoke with her mind. *Papa?*

The earthy smell of burning sage reached her nostrils, and she breathed deeply. Her mind searched the blackness for her father, unsure of what his spirit would look or sound or feel like. Corinne's and Minerva's voices faded behind her concentration.

Papa, can you hear me? 'Tis Haith. Please, Papa, Mother would take me away from here and away from Bertie. Oh, why must you be dead? I fear Scotland and the Normans, Papa. Minerva says we shall starve!

From the blackness of her subconscious, a pinprick of light appeared, as if a tiny ember had been struck. Haith concentrated on that spark with all her might. *Papa? Is that you?*

The pinprick grew to a dot, which grew to a flame and then a yellow-gold blaze, as warm and bright as sunshine. A black outline appeared in the center of this sun and grew larger as the blackness of Haith's mind became an open meadow of sweet grass and the outline took the shape of her father.

James came striding through the waist-high grass, smiling and holding his arms open wide. Haith ran to him shrieking with joy.

"Papa, you came!" She launched her small body into his embrace and buried her face in his neck. He smelled of warm sunshine and hay, and his prickly black beard brushed her cheek.

"Think you I would not?" James chuckled and squeezed his daughter. "Oh, Haith, I love you so." James carried Haith down to the grass with him, and together they lay under a blue sky.

"What shall we do, Papa, now that you are dead?" She eyed him suspiciously. "You don't *feel* dead anymore."

James laughed aloud, and the sound seemed to fill the meadow and Haith's heart. He tickled her ribs, and she giggled.

"I don't, do I?" he agreed. "I think 'tis because to you, I still live." His blue eyes sparkled like jewels, and the gentle smile never left his lips even as he spoke his next words.

"Haith, love, there are many trials that you will soon be faced with, and I want you to listen closely."

Haith nodded and smiled despite the ominous words. She had never felt as content as she did just then, lying in her father's arms and listening to his rumbling voice.

"Soon, strangers will come to Seacrest." He cocked his head as if listening, but Haith heard only a bird, and perhaps the distant thunder of a summer storm. "Nay," James amended, "they have already arrived."

"Who are they, Papa?" Haith asked, tracing lazy circles on his chest with her finger. No arrow marred its wide expanse.

"Normans."

Haith stilled and looked into her father's eyes. His face was serious now. "Will they kill me, too, Papa?" she asked, her chin trembling.

"Nay, love. Nay," he assured her and crushed her to him. "But there will be great sorrow for a time." The distant thunder was closer now. "You must not fear."

"Bertie said the same," Haith ventured and eyed the sky for signs of clouds. There were none.

"Bertie is very wise, is she not?" James smiled again and held his daughter from him. "There is not much time, love. Pay close heed."

"Yea, Papa."

"Do not become separated from Minerva. She is very wise as well, and will protect you with her life, but you must heed her, ken?" he asked. At Haith's answering nod, he continued.

"Haith, you were a gift from Heaven to me and your mother. Our love for each other is very strong and special, and 'tis what created you."

"Magic?"

"Of a sort," James said, hurriedly now. "Because of that special love, you are special as well. Mayhap at times, 'twill seem you know not what to do. Listen to your heart. Pray. Follow your instincts. Learn all that Minerva will teach you, and you will have your answers in time."

"What of Bertie?" Haith asked.

James chuckled. "Yea, Bertie will teach you things as well. You will never be far from your sister, love. You will grow old together."

The thunder sounded again, and James sat up, drawing Haith with him. The tall grasses waved over their heads.

"But Mother said we—"

"There is no time, love," James said. "Do you understand all that I have told you?"

"I think so, Papa." Haith frowned. "But you have said naught of Mother."

"Your mother and I will take care of each other." James stood, bringing Haith with him. The wind picked up, tossing their hair, his black, hers red. He gestured behind her, and when she turned to look, the keep of Seacrest, previously absent, had appeared in the distance. Haith gasped—huge, black thunderheads hovered over the keep.

Haith felt the warm pressure of her father's lips on the crown of her head and his strong hands heavy on her shoulders.

"Go now, love, and find Minerva," he said from behind her. Lightning pointed at the old wooden hold as if to reinforce his command. "Tell Bertie I love her as I do you." She felt the brush of his lips at her ear as he whispered, "So much."

His hands left her shoulders, and Haith spun around to encounter thin air. She looked across the meadow in terror to see her father standing atop a far knoll, the opposite direction of Seacrest.

Lightning and thunder burst from the stillness with what seemed to be the fury of Hell, and Haith flung up an arm to shield her eyes. The wind gusted like a cold blanket, buffeting her small body, and she screamed, "Papa!"

James's form was small in the distance, but when he spoke, his voice was as clear as it had been a moment before. "Run, Haith! Run to Seacrest! *Go now!*"

Haith spun on her heel and ran. The wind increased and whipped her hair across her streaming eyes to stick to her cheeks. She scratched it away and ran harder as thunder and lightning raced to meet her. The skies burst just then, and rain poured down in heavy, waxen drops that threatened to drown her.

As Haith neared the familiar portal to the great hall, she slowed her pace and chanced a final look behind her at her father. Her breath was being torn from her small lungs, and her head suddenly hurt terribly. Squinting through blurry eyes, she could barely make out the shape of her father and now, of another form that seemed to glide across the meadow toward him. Haith glimpsed flowing red hair and arms that reached for James.

"Mother!" Haith screamed, and then the lightning struck, and all was very, very black.

CHAPTER
1

April 1075
Greanly Manor, England

"Hold!" the bearlike man shouted. He stood in the center of a lowered drawbridge, barring the way to Greanly, although the formidable black iron portcullis had been lowered behind him. "State yer business for coming to Greanly and those of the men who ride behind you."

Tristan turned to grin at his companion, who brought his black horse even with Tristan's gray destrier. His dark-skinned friend stared at the huge man and sighed.

"Must things always be difficult?" Pharao asked, irritation tingeing his words.

"It seems so," Tristan chuckled. "At least I know my possessions have been secured in my absence."

"*I said,*" the keeper of the bridge growled, "state yer business or prepare to meet my friend here." He gestured with the huge battle-ax he held.

Tristan noticed the man's boulderlike biceps, which flexed as he raised the ax, and knew that he would be an asset to his new holdings if only because of his brute strength and loyalty to the village. A warm spring breeze raced around the knoll where the keep was perched and ruffled with some effort Tristan's sweat-darkened blond hair.

"It smells wonderful here, Phar," Tristan said, stretching his arms wide and then dismounting with a groan. He touched his toes several times, twisted this way and that, and bounced on the balls of his feet.

Pharao, still astride, sniffed the air. "Indeed, 'tis fragrant. Quite refreshing after London's stench."

"I'm warnin' you for the last time," the guard said eyeing Tristan warily. He raised the head of the ax to his other hand, gripping it tightly across his chest when Tristan completed his stretches and approached the drawbridge with a smile.

Barrett flexed his fingers on the ax and shuffled his feet indecisively, his gaze flying between the foreigner who remained on the black horse and the man who so boldly approached him.

To charge him or no? The stranger was smiling, and his clothes were of noble cut—surely he was no highwayman come to rob the fledgling castle, especially with his comrades riding so far behind. Simply a weary traveler seeking supplies?

On the other hand, he still had not answered the questions asked of him. Indeed, he had cheerfully all but ignored them. Was he sly and daring, thinking to take Barrett by surprise? The breadth of his shoulders and thickness of his legs indicated strength enough to prove a worthy opponent.

The blond man strode to the edge of the drawbridge and peered over the side to the moat below. Turning his back to Barrett, he busied his hands at a hidden task.

"Pardon me," he said over his shoulder.

Barrett knew that a decision had to be made. For the protection of the castle, he would strike now and see if the foreigner would answer questions later.

With one giant step, Barrett was behind the blond man, raising his ax above his head. Suddenly, a fiery sensation numbed his hands, and the ax fell harmlessly to the drawbridge behind him. Barrett grunted and held his hands in front of his face to see tiny black flecks embedded in the heels of both palms.

"What the—" He looked quickly to the dark man, who was idly swinging a small leather pouch by its strings in a lazy circle and shaking his head. The sound of water being poured from a ewer echoed under the bridge, and Barrett's head swiveled to the blond man in shock.

"Ay, now!" he said, offended. "There's no need to be pissin' off me bridge."

Tristan retied his chausses and turned once more toward the gate. He smiled and gestured up to a small stone cubicle jutting from the side of the castle wall. "That's where it all goes in the end, does it not?"

The guard rubbed his still stinging hands on his chausses and glanced at the garderobe indicated. "'Tis rude, any matter," he grumbled.

"My apologies," Tristan chuckled with a small bow. "I fear 'tis an affliction I incur when traveling long distances astride. Excuse me, but you seem to have dropped your ax."

"Who are you?"

"I am Tristan D'Argent, wayward Lord of Greanly."

The guard's eyes widened to the point that they nearly came loose of his skull. He quickly fell to one knee and bowed his head. "My lord," he sputtered. "Forgive me! I did not know."

"Do not trouble yourself about it, er—" Tristan paused

and stared pointedly at the large man who still knelt before him. "Your name, good man?"

"Barrett, my lord," he said, rising and bowing at the waist. "Sheriff of Greanly." The big man flushed. "That is, until you decide otherwise, of course, m'lord."

"Well met, Sheriff Barrett," Tristan replied. "'Tis plain that you do your duty well, guarding my home until I arrived. I commend you."

Pharao had dismounted and appeared at Tristan's side. "He should have struck sooner."

Tristan was used to the curious stares his friend received, and Barrett reacted no differently as he took notice of Pharao's pock-marked face, turban-wrapped head, and white caftan.

Pharao returned the appraisal. "Were we highwaymen, you would be dead at this time."

"Do you think so?" Barrett faced the bold stranger and crossed his arms over his chest.

"Sheriff Barrett," Tristan said, "my first man, Pharao Tak'Ahn. Phar, Sheriff Barrett."

Pharao sniffed as his eyes took in the woolly beast of a sheriff, while Barrett merely grunted, perhaps remembering the sting from the man's sling.

Tristan looked from one man to the other, his broad smile indicating his enjoyment of the situation. "Well then," he said, "I am eager to see my new home. Shall we call for the portcullis to be raised?"

Barrett tore his gaze from Pharao. "Certainly, my lord." He turned and called up the stone wall that rose high above the moat, "Raise the gate, you stinkin' louts! Lord Tristan has arrived!"

The unlikely trio of Tristan, Pharao, and Barrett strolled about the bailey at their leisure while Tristan's men poured through Greanly's wall. Amidst the sounds of stamping hooves and shouts among the soldiers, Barrett gave his new lord a tour of the grounds and village that lay within the recently constructed walls.

Greanly was magnificent. Commissioned by the king to be built after his army had destroyed the old wooden town, the construction had taken serf and skilled craftsman alike nearly six years to complete. The keep and outer walls were formidable stone edifices, boasting square turrets that pointed to the heavens and massive battlements along the wall walk. The village spilled out from the hold and was large enough to accommodate a bustling berg of several hundred, with structures for every imaginable occupation required in a holding of Greanly's size. In all, it reminded Tristan of some of the more vast estates in France, and pride filled him as he realized that this place was now his home.

Tristan had doubted he would live long enough to take possession of his new demesne when he had accepted Greanly's charge. The years since William had come to power had been filled with the task of quelling uprisings from outlying factions, putting Tristan and his men at constant war with one band of rebels or another. It had been a hard life, one filled with the threat of death at every turn. That Tristan had survived the years of bloodshed to finally come to this reward—a home of his own and soon, a new bride—was a miracle in itself. He pushed the unsettling emotions he felt aside and returned his attention to the sheriff, who had by now brought him and Pharao full circle in their tour.

"Very good." Tristan approved wholeheartedly of the layout of the town and nodded as he gazed around the open bailey. His men had arrived, and were busying themselves in the new stables, where a pair of harried young boys assisted with the equipment and settling of the horses. Besides Barrett, the stable lads, and a handful of village men, the keep and grounds were deserted.

"Do you wish to continue into the hall, m'lord?" Barrett gestured toward the grand stone edifice that dominated the center of the bailey. "I'm sure you could use a bit o' food and a skin to brace you from your journey."

"In a moment," Tristan said, taking in the vacant cotter's dwellings, the empty granary, and the evenly green sod surrounding the public well. After the spring rains, the bailey's interior should have been a churning quagmire, not have the neat appearance of some London picnic area. The few cottages he and Pharao had passed as they had neared Greanly had been vacant as well, and the fields had lain fallow, lush with milkweed and thistle, when the planting season was well underway.

Where were his serfs? Why hadn't his crops been planted?

"Sheriff Barrett," Tristan began, "might I ask where my villagers are?"

Barrett shuffled his feet and cleared his throat. "We're them, my lord. Er, all us here," he indicated the few men and boys in rough serf's garb attending the soldiers with a grand sweep of his arm, "are in your service."

"Impossible," Pharao said sharply. "William would not have commissioned a holding for my liege that was without serfs to provide for it. Greanly was said to be a prosperous berg under Harold."

"That is so," Barrett said, standing taller and looking down at Pharao. *"Before William,* Greanly's people numbered in the hundreds. The horde burned the old keep to the very ground and murdered the old lord and his entire family. Destroyed most of the village, too." He looked to Tristan, almost in apology. "Those who survived had nowhere to go, my lord."

"I am well aware of Greanly's history, Barrett," Tristan

said. "Lord Nigel of Seacrest was charged with taking in the displaced villagers until the new keep was constructed." His eyes narrowed in speculation. "Reports of Greanly's completion reached me this past summer in the Northlands, and Lord Nigel himself sent word that Greanly's villagers prospered."

"Aye." Barrett nodded and smiled.

Tristan sighed and grasped the bridge of his nose between thumb and forefinger. The dull ache behind his eyes threatened to blossom into a full-fledged attack.

Pharao looked around the deserted bailey. "They do not appear overprosperous to me."

Barrett again nodded. "Oh, aye, they prosper. Just not at Greanly."

"Then where?" Tristan bellowed, losing the last shred of patience he possessed.

Barrett flinched, startled at his new lord's flash of temper. "Why, at Seacrest, m'lord."

"Sheriff Barrett," Tristan said in a measured tone, "why do my people remain at Seacrest when their town has been rebuilt to magnificence? Surely they knew their lord's arrival was imminent and still the fields lie unplanted, the storehouse, empty."

Barrett grimaced. "They fear you, m'lord. 'Twas the rumors that done it." He winced when Tristan cursed but continued. "There's been talk of the subdued villages along the Scots border. The people call you William's Hammer."

The slight crease in Pharao's forehead was the only evidence of his outrage. "Lord Nigel was duty-bound to see to the welfare of my liege's people. He should by now have ordered them to return and prepare to serve."

"Indeed," Tristan muttered. "He was paid handsomely to foster their care."

"I have spoken to Lord Nigel about this very matter,

my lord," Barrett said, his shagg⟨...⟩e solemn. "'Tis the reason I'm here meself."

"What did he say?" Tristan asked.

"Well,"—the giant scratched his head in thought—"said he wasn't going ter take no orders from the likes of me and that if I cared so much for Greanly, I could live there." His smile was broad. "So here I be."

Tristan closed his eyes and sighed. "What did he say about the *villagers?*"

Barrett flushed. "Oh, aye. He says he couldn't afford the serfs to leave Seacrest with planting season drawing nigh and no lord to rule them here." Barrett paused as if searching his mind for a solution that would bring back his new lord's good humor. "Perhaps when you wed the lady—"

"Very well, Sheriff Barrett," Tristan interjected. Although he spoke calmly and graciously once more, there was an undercurrent of danger surrounding him. "My thanks for your service and your attempts to return my errant flock to me. Come."

Tristan turned and strode to the hall, where he flung open the giant doors and disappeared inside. Pharao and Barrett stood for a moment staring after him, Pharao looking exasperated and Barrett clearly at a loss. Both men began following their lord at the same time, the sheriff lumbering solidly along beside Pharao's unique, gliding stride.

"Are you always so addlepated?" Pharao asked in disgust.

Barrett shrugged his massive shoulders and glanced at the dark-skinned man.

"Do you always go about in ladies' clothing?"

CHAPTER
2

"Minerva!" Haith bellowed toward the back of the cottage. The little boy sitting on the stool before her squirmed impatiently, twisting his leg and trying to free it from her grasp on his ankle. The gash on the bottom of his foot ran diagonally across the arch and had been left untreated for several days. The wound had festered, leaving the underside of the foot swollen and blazing red. The boy eyed the open door to the cottage and squirmed again.

"Ham, please be still," Haith said distractedly. She then growled, tossing her red plait over her shoulder, *"Minerva!"*

Minerva shuffled through the doorway from the other of the cottage's two rooms, looking thoroughly disgruntled. Her wiry hair stood frazzled from her head like an ancient halo, and her shrewd black eyes glistened with impatience. From the small room behind her, a woman's groaning could be heard.

"Well?" the old woman demanded. "What is it?"

"Could you hand me the onion poultice?" Haith gestured to a small earthen jug located amongst many similar jars on a topmost shelf. Dried herb bundles hung from the ceiling of the healer's cottage, and a pot boiled enthusiastically over the fire, emitting an aroma that was both pleasant and tangy.

The moans from the back room turned into a shriek.

"Get it yerself, you lazy chit," Minerva said. "From what I see, 'tis wee Ham's got foot trouble, not you."

"If I release his foot, he'll run," Haith gritted through clenched teeth. She looked at Ham with forced sweetness. "Is that not so, Hammy?"

"Yea." The eight year old nodded with vigor. "I'll hop out of here on one leg if I have to." He smiled fiercely back at Haith.

"See?" Haith cried as Minerva sidled closer to look at the boy's foot.

"Ah," Minerva said, leaning closer to Ham's face. "I'll tell you now, lad, if you so much as twitch yer nose before Haith gives you leave, we won't trouble ourselves with a poultice at all." She straightened, and Ham's large brown eyes went to the sickle-shaped blade Minerva lovingly stroked on her belt. "We'll just have off with it then."

"I-I-I-" Ham stuttered. He broke gaze with the old woman and looked at Haith, his small face earnest. "I won't move."

Haith caught Minerva's sly wink as she returned to the screaming woman in the back of the cottage. "Would you quit screeching like a sylkie and just push the babe out, Mary?"

Haith gave Ham a final warning look before retrieving the jar of poultice and plucking some fresh herbs from a bowl of water. She resumed her place in front of him, and he obediently replaced his heel in her lap.

"Thank you," Haith said and smiled smugly. She took the handful of leaves and rubbed them between her palms until they were a damp, crumbly mass. "Ham, this will burn a bit, but 'twill keep you from feeling the wound when I drain it."

Ham's eyes grew even rounder, but he remained still. "Ow-w-w!" he howled when Haith ground the herbs as gently as possible into the sole of his foot.

"Tell me what is about in the hall today," Haith said, seeking to distract the boy as she readied her small blade. "I saw riders this afternoon, strangers."

Ham spotted the instrument and quickly squeezed his eyes shut and gripped the seat of his stool. "They come from Greanly," Ham said stiffly, "for Lord Nigel."

Haith swiftly drew the blade up the center of Ham's wound, satisfied when the boy did not flinch. Thick, yellow pus tinged with streaks of red oozed from the cut, and Haith gently prodded the flesh with her fingertips to aid the excretion of the poison. She continued conversing with the boy.

"I did not see Barrett among the riders," she said, reaching for a brazier that contained a small pot of warm water. She dipped a clean rag into the pot and then wound it around Ham's foot. The boy sighed in relief and opened his eyes, animated by the soothing comfort.

"Nay, not Barrett," Ham said, an eager glint in his elfish brown eyes. "Soldiers."

"Hammy, there are no soldiers at—" She stopped abruptly as she realized what the boy's description of the riders meant.

"Yea," Ham said, nodding. "Lord Tristan has come to Greanly."

Haith said no more for several moments as she quickly but carefully unwound the rag from Ham's foot and finished the dressing with the onion poultice and a clean bandage. She also said a short prayer over the boy.

"There you are." Haith gently removed his foot from her lap. "I know the weather grows warm, but find a shoe and keep it on so the dressing remains clean. Stay out of the stream and the tannery, and see me three days hence that I may check it, ken?"

"Yea." Ham nodded and glanced at the door.

Haith smiled. "Be gone then."

As the child limped out of the cottage, Haith rose and began tidying her supplies. Her mind raced.

So, William's Hammer has finally arrived, she thought. *He's come to claim his prize after nearly ten years of terrorizing England. Would that I could have seen his proud face when he arrived to an empty castle.*

A final, ear piercing screech came from the back room, followed by the feeble wails of a babe. Mary, herself come to Seacrest from Greanly those many years ago, had borne the child, her and John's fourth in as many years since they'd wed. The pair had not been many summers older than Haith when they'd arrived with Greanly's surviving villagers, and no one had been surprised when John took Mary for his wife.

The thought of marriage quickly turned Haith's reminiscing to concern. Soon after Lord Nigel had claimed Seacrest for his own—and Ellora and Soleilbert along with it—England's new king had sought a strong alliance among his lords. Nigel had promised his young stepdaughter to Tristan D'Argent, favored knight of the crown. Eager to please his king, D'Argent had accepted the betrothal by proxy and had promised to claim his bride when Soleilbert was of age and Greanly had been rebuilt at William's command.

Now Greanly stood once more, this time a stone homage to one of William's fiercest champions, and his return meant that Haith and her half sister would be separated.

You will never be far from your sister, love.

A sudden cold breeze caressed Haith's cheek, and she

froze, every nerve in her body attentive to her surroundings. A flash of pain, nearly blinding in its intensity, seared her temples, and she raised a trembling hand to her face.

"Haith," a weary voice called from the other room, breaking Haith's reverie, "come see the babe."

"I'll be but a moment." Haith blinked back tears. The pain had vanished as quickly as it had come, leaving gooseflesh in its wake. She shook herself to chase away the uneasy sensations and busied her hands gathering dried raspberries and hot water for a tea—Mary's afterbirth was always stubborn.

"What am I to do now, Sister?" Bertie whispered urgently, her gaze flicking to Haith's for but an instant.

The two young women sat side by side in a corner of the hall, conversing under the guise of doing needlework. Haith glanced around for signs of eavesdroppers before addressing her sister.

"In honesty, I do not know," Haith said. "Have you any word from Lord Nigel?"

"None," Soleilbert replied. "Although I do know Lord Tristan's message made mention of me. Mother has no news either, save that Lord Tristan will soon visit Seacrest to collect his serfs and his"—Bertie gulped—"betrothed personally."

"He cannot *collect* you, Bertie," Haith said. "You're not yet wed."

"I warrant I will be soon enough," Soleilbert said around a biscuit she crammed in her mouth, the third since she and Haith had sat down to stitch. She swallowed and then continued. "What if he beats me? I would wager Lord Tristan is not called William's Hammer for naught. 'Tis rumored he is a fierce warrior with a quick temper."

"If he beats you, 'twill only happen once," Haith vowed, accidentally pricking her finger at the thought of any man abusing her sister. She popped the stinging digit in her mouth briefly and then pointed it at Soleilbert to emphasize her words. "If ever he strikes you, you must send word to me immediately. I would ride to Greanly that day and relieve him of both hands."

Soleilbert giggled, her rounded cheeks flushing merrily, and Haith was glad to have soothed her sister's anxiety, even if only for a moment. Soleilbert grew solemn again and produced another biscuit from beneath the piece she was stitching. She swallowed the morsel with a loud gulp and looked down at her lap.

"What if he will not have me?"

Haith froze in midstitch and looked at her sister in shock. "Bertie! How could you say such a thing? Any lord would be honored to have a maid as sweet and pretty as you for his lady."

"My shape, Haith," Bertie said, her voice low with uncertainty. She swept a hand down the soft rolls and fullness of the body contained in her kirtle. "And do not deny it," Bertie warned. "I know I am overlarge. Think you I am deaf to the jests at my expense from the men in the village?"

Haith winced.

"And the womenfolk, too," Soleilbert added. "Many times their barbs are more painful."

"Soleilbert,"—Haith set her stitchery on the floor and grasped her sister's hands—"you are the most beautiful woman I know—in mind and physical beauty." Haith lowered her head until Soleilbert met her gaze. "There is no one more loving or kind or loyal, and you must never set your worth at what ignorant people may say." She squeezed Bertie's hands. "They do not know you as I do."

Soleilbert's eyes shimmered with tears when she reached for her sister, and the two embraced. "I will not go without you."

"Sh-h," Haith whispered. "Fret not about matters we do not yet face. We will do so when we must."

"What have you done to upset her now?" a strident female voice asked.

The girls broke apart, both swiping at their eyes, to see Lady Ellora glaring at them. To worsen matters, the demonic-looking Lord Nigel stood at the blond lady's side.

Haith rose from her chair. "Good eventide, my lady, my lord. We were but discussing Soleilbert's imminent wedding."

Nigel smiled at Haith, an exercise that caused one of his slender black eyebrows to arch suggestively. It had the maddening effect of turning a gesture of friendliness into a disgusting leer. His eyes raked her body from head to toe, and as usual, Haith felt naked under his gaze.

"Perfectly common, I would think," Nigel said. "Women do tend to worry about their wedding, particularly the wedding *night*." His despicable eyebrow rose even further at the innuendo. "Perhaps you were giving her advice?"

"I doubt it not," Ellora sniffed. "In any matter, you have no leave to discuss such intimacies with my daughter." She dismissed Haith with a wave of her hand. "Be gone from here and back to your hut and that hag you keep. The lord and I wish to speak to Soleilbert about a family matter."

"Mother, please," Bertie implored, "I would have Haith stay. She is family to me."

Ellora's lips thinned. "I will not argue that point with you again, Daughter—"

"Cease this prattle," Nigel said. " 'Tis of no real consequence whether the wench hears." He turned to address

Soleilbert as Ellora brushed by Haith to claim her recently vacated chair, giving her a wicked look as she sat.

"Stepdaughter," Nigel began, "as your mother has informed you, Lord Tristan of Greanly has come at last to claim his keep and his bride." He looked pointedly at Soleilbert, and his mouth was a grim, miserly slash. "He shall arrive at Seacrest at the end of a fortnight, at which time the nuptials will be planned and the details of your removal to Greanly resolved."

At those words, Bertie pulled a handkerchief from her sleeve and held it to her quivering lips. Ellora patted her daughter's hand, and Haith could only look on, helpless, as Nigel ranted.

"I would remind you that your behavior at the feast is of the utmost importance." Nigel ticked off his orders on his slim fingertips. "You will not disgrace me with your emotional outbursts or hysterics. You will be agreeable to any terms set forth that eve, and you will *abide by them fully.*" He paused and fixed Soleilbert with a firm look. "You will not offer comment unless addressed directly, at which time your opinion shall be reflective of mine alone. Do I make myself clear?"

Soleilbert nodded, unable to speak lest she sob, and Haith's heart reached for her. Nigel bowed slightly to Ellora.

"My lady, if you have something to add?" he offered with a sweep of his hand and a meaningful look. At Ellora's answering nod, he assumed a leaning position against the near wall behind mother and daughter. Haith watched him furtively and cringed inside as he leered at her. She wished for a moment that she had taken the escape offered earlier by Ellora, but then dismissed the thought as cowardly and disloyal to Soleilbert.

"Daughter," Ellora began with a hesitant smile, "although the thought of marrying and leaving your home troubles you, you must do your best to impress Lord Tristan." She paused, her eyes flicking away from Soleilbert's face and fixing on a point above her daughter's head. "That being so, from this moment until you are wed, I have instructed Cook that you are only to receive one trencher each day. The tidbits you wheedle from the kitchen are to cease as well."

Soleilbert raised her eyes to look at her mother in shock. "You would starve me?"

Haith's blood rose to her face, hot enough to singe her skin. At Nigel's next words, however, her embarrassment for her sister turned to outrage.

"I sincerely doubt you will starve, Stepdaughter," he smirked. "I think we would all agree that you have flesh enough to sustain your strength for several months, much less a few weeks."

To Ellora's credit, she had the grace to blush. Soleilbert let out a strangled cry and ran from the hall, fleeing up the stairs. Haith quickly turned to follow her, but was jerked back by Ellora's grasp on her elbow.

"Leave her," the older woman said. "She will understand in time that 'tis for her own welfare."

"How could you?" Haith demanded, shaking her arm free.

Ellora's expression hardened. "Do not question my motives where Soleilbert is concerned, you bastard wench." She moved closer to Haith and sneered, "You would keep her fattened and shackled to you rather than see her flourish as a lady of her own manor." Closer still she came, heedless of Haith's clenched fists and rising ire. "Are you jealous, slut? Hm-m? Do you disguise your envy as concern and covet her noble match?"

"You are unworthy to be called mother," Haith said.

Ellora withdrew slightly, and her face took on a look of bewilderment before being replaced with rage. "You are a whore's whore!" she screamed and raised her arm to strike.

"Control yourself, my lady." Nigel chuckled, encircling her wrist with slim fingers. Haith was sickened to see an amused look on his devil's face.

Ellora screeched and twisted in Nigel's grasp. "Unhand me so that I may teach this slut the manners she lacks!"

"Cease!" Nigel shoved Ellora toward the stairs. "See to your daughter."

Ellora stood indecisive, her eyes clearly betraying her anger at Haith, as well as her fear of her husband.

"Do as I say, Ellora," Nigel warned. "I will deal with this piece myself." He glared at Haith, but she was unmoved. She dreaded not his anger, only his lechery.

"My lord," Ellora acquiesced through tight lips and curtsied to Nigel, but her gaze showered furious sparks at Haith. The lady turned and fled up the stairs.

Nigel grasped Haith's elbow, and she flinched at the unexpected touch. "Allow me to accompany you to your own hearth, my lady," he said, a glint in his black eyes.

Haith shook free. "Do not trouble yourself, my lord," she said and made her way toward the portal.

"I insist." Nigel resumed his hold on her and escorted Haith into the night-darkened bailey.

As Nigel led her farther from the keep, Haith looked around the deserted grounds with unease. "M-my Lord," Haith stammered and gestured behind her with an arm, "my cottage—"

"Silence," Nigel said sharply as he continued dragging Haith along toward the stables. "I know where your cottage lies. There are matters I wish to discuss with you in private."

CHAPTER
3

Once inside the stable, Lord Nigel released Haith's arm, and she stood in the aisle, rubbing the spot where his fingers had gripped her. She watched him stroll leisurely to the nearest stall and stroke the head of a curious steed.

"If it pleases you, my lord," Haith began when Nigel remained silent, "I would hear the matter you have need to discuss with me. Minerva waits."

Nigel continued to ignore her, and Haith's discomfort grew. The only sounds to be heard were the gentle huffing of the beasts around them and the muted laughter of men in a nearby cottage. The floating notes of a lute wafted on the breeze, stirring the rich, earthy scent of the quiet stable, and Haith understood how alone she was. Finally, he addressed her.

"Haith, 'tis well understood that you and Lady Soleilbert have a strong bond." Nigel scooped a handful of sweet grass and fed it to the horse.

"Yea, my lord," Haith agreed, confused. This was the private matter Nigel wished to discuss? "Although our mothers were not the same, Bertie has always been sister to me."

"I also know," he said, brushing off his slim hands and turning to face her, "that the thought of Soleilbert leaving Seacrest troubles you. You would be left behind."

Haith nodded cautiously but did not reply. 'Twas no secret that Ellora detested the very sight of her. What unnerved Haith was how closely Nigel's words echoed Haith's recent concern for her own welfare after Bertie had gone.

Nigel strolled past Haith, chuckling at her silence, and the spicy scent of him caused her stomach to churn. He seemed quite comfortable, taking distracted interest in his surroundings.

"What would you answer if I should say that there is a way for you to accompany Soleilbert to Greanly?"

Haith blinked in surprise. "My lord? You would hand my guardianship to Lord Tristan?"

"Nay," Nigel said, offering another horse food from his hand. "You would remain my ward, but 'tis possible that you could accompany your sister to see her settled." Nigel paused and turned to look at Haith, his mouth crooked in a sly grin. "Especially if 'twas rumored you departed Seacrest at the offer of a betrothal."

When Haith only stared at him, he continued. "Donald the smithy returns to Greanly this night. He has need of a wife."

When the meaning of Nigel's words finally sank in, Haith gasped. The image of the squat, toadish man with the burned face and heavy brow filled her mind's eye. A transplant to Seacrest many years ago, Donald had taken up his trade alongside the resident smithy. Haith remembered that he was widowed, his wife having supposedly succumbed to influenza two years past, although Haith and Minerva had doubted the cause of her death after seeing the frail woman's body covered in black and green bruises.

"My lord,"—Haith cleared her throat in an attempt to steady her voice—"I have no wish to wed Donald."

Nigel's laughter was indulgent. "Of course not. Your betrothal would merely be a ruse."

Haith watched Nigel warily as he brushed off a small wooden stool and perched upon it as if it were a throne. He continued.

"Haith, I have been faithful vassal to William these many years. 'Twas I who secured Seacrest for him, I who willingly fostered the people of Greanly in my own hold, and I who managed the construction of the new keep." Nigel's eyebrows rose and he waved a beseeching hand in Haith's direction. "'Tis only just that I be rewarded accordingly, do you not agree?"

Haith's disgust at Nigel's greed threatened to twist her mouth into a disbelieving sneer. "My lord, 'twas my understanding that William compensated you for your service."

"If you consider a few coins and paltry tracts of worthless swamp compensation, then yea, he has compensated me." Nigel snorted, and his eyes grew cold. "Seacrest rots before our eyes, Haith. While I have labored here tirelessly, that pup D'Argent has done naught but ride about the countryside. Many of Seacrest's villagers have intermarried with Greanly's—what will become of us when our population is decimated?"

Haith bit down on her tongue. Seacrest's deterioration was due in whole to its lord's lack of care. Nigel preferred to fritter away William's stipend on frivolous personal luxuries, like the rich tunic he now wore, rather than to see to the upkeep of his demesne. Haith surmised his concern for the departing villagers was due only to his unwillingness to lose William's monetary support.

"Forgive me if I speak out of turn, my lord," Haith said after she had regained her composure. "But did you not foresee this problem when Greanly's charge was granted to Lord Tristan?"

"'Twas no matter then," Nigel scoffed. "When the betrothal agreement was reached, D'Argent was to remain in the king's service for many years. I did not expect him to live to see Greanly's completion. That he has done so only proves my suspicions of his unworthiness."

Nigel stood, clearly growing more agitated. "It should be I who takes possession of Greanly! D'Argent is undeserving of such a gift when I have cared so well for its villagers!" His fists clenched, Nigel closed his eyes and drew a deep breath. Once again in control, he turned his wicked gaze on Haith. "The bastard will be outraged that his serfs have not returned to serve him, and why should they?" Nigel's expression grew suspiciously wide-eyed. "William's Hammer is a cruel, bloodthirsty savage."

A chill chased up Haith's spine, and her voice was hushed, incredulous. "Then why provoke his anger?"

"His anger will matter naught if Donald succeeds in the task I set him to this night." At Haith's bewildered look, Nigel expounded. "The only way for me to gain Greanly is for the king to become displeased with his man or for D'Argent to die."

Haith felt the blood leave her face. "But what of Bertie?"

"What of her? Should D'Argent die, Soleilbert is young. She will again have chance to marry." Nigel approached Haith with a pointed stare. "Do not concern yourself with her welfare. Your only thoughts should be of gaining me the information I seek to ensure D'Argent's death should the smithy fail tonight."

Fury and fear boiled up inside Haith, and her chest heaved. "I will not be a pawn in your game, Lord Nigel.

Bertie is my sister, and involvement in this treachery would mean destroying any chance of happiness for her."

"I surmised you would have reservations," Nigel said and stepped closer to lift a lock of flaming red hair and rub it between his fingers. "And so you have another choice."

Haith stepped back quickly, the movement tugging her hair from Nigel's grasp. He advanced.

"Ellora may despise you, Haith, but I have grown quite fond of your—how should I say?—*spirited presence*. You may, of course, choose to remain at Seacrest,"—he circled around behind her, and Haith could feel his hot breath on her scalp—"as my mistress."

Haith's insides froze, her breath suspended in her throat.

"I have need of an heir, Haith," he whispered. "Ellora's womb is as prickly as her demeanor, and my seed finds no purchase there to grow a child."

"I will not," Haith said through clenched teeth.

"Answer not in haste," Nigel advised, drawing her plait from over her shoulder to hang down her back in a long rope. He stroked it hand over hand as he spoke. "You are of noble blood, Haith. Our child would be heir to Seacrest, mayhap even Greanly should my plans succeed. You would want for nothing." He paused in the handling of her hair. "I do not wish you to be so near Donald and away from me at Greanly. Indeed, I fear for your safety should that be your choice.

"But understand that those I have spoken tonight be your only choices." He grasped her shoulders and turned her to stare hungrily into her eyes. "After Soleilbert is gone to Greanly, Ellora will not abide your presence here without my command. I will see D'Argent's downfall, and you will aid me or pay the cost. As I see it, we shall both profit."

Haith fought the urge to break from his hold and run.

She knew Nigel could feel her shivering, and she loathed herself for her fear. She had to escape, had to get away.

"My lord," she whispered, "I cannot choose—"

"Sh-h." Nigel placed a finger against her lips. "I do not ask for your decision this night. But think on it well in the coming days, my sweet. I would have your answer by Lord Tristan's arrival, if indeed he does not already lie dead at Greanly." He leaned closer until Haith could feel his breath against her mouth. "In which case, we shall . . . *renegotiate* our agreement. I do you a great honor in giving you this choice, lovely Haith. Should it suit me, I could take you right now."

"Nay!" Haith jerked back, but Nigel's hands held firm.

"Fear not, my lady," he grinned and dragged her back to him to press her body fully against his. Haith's stomach churned. "You will yield to me willingly when the time comes." He pressed his lips to hers, and Haith squirmed until he released her. She stumbled backward and scrubbed at her mouth while white-hot tears filled her eyes.

Nigel chuckled. "I doubt you will get the same courtesy from Donald." With that, he gave a mocking bow and spun on his heel to exit the stables.

After Nigel's departure, Haith slid slowly down the rough wooden boards of the stall behind her. Her body jerked with horrified sobs as she came to sit on the dirt floor. Her lips burned from his touch, and her skin seemed to want to crawl from her body in disgust. She took deep, dragging breaths of the musky stable air to try to center herself.

But visions flew through her mind, thwarting her attempts: Bertie's angelic smile; the smithy's wife's dead, battered body; Nigel's vile grin as he slid against her. Throughout the images that flashed through her consciousness, Ellora's damning phrase, first aimed at Haith's mother and now at her, twined shrilly.

Whore. Whore. Whore!

Panic overtook her, and Haith's sobs escalated until she lay completely prone on the hay-strewn ground.

It was an easy matter for Tristan to breach Seacrest's gate unnoticed after his messengers had been admitted into the bailey. He left his mount some distance away from the keep with Pharao as guard and approached on foot in common garb. Taking advantage of the stir created amongst the guards and villagers at any word from Greanly's new lord, Tristan slipped into the milling crowd and observed at his leisure in the heavy afternoon light.

The snippets of conversation he overheard were as enlightening as they were disheartening. 'Twas clear to Tristan that word of his exploits as one of William's favored peacekeepers had reached his displaced serfs and had instilled a sense of fear and resentment among the people. While stories of his work with the uprisings in the Northlands contained some truths, many tales were bloated with exaggerations and outright lies of cruelty and mistreatment.

"'Tis said he burned every village to the ground," he overheard one stout village woman say to her neighbor. "Never even gave 'em a chance. Killed most of the menfolk and planted William's bastards from Scotland to London."

"Aye," the woman's companion agreed, continuing with, "'Tis also said he rides with a devil who can see the future."

Tristan hid his smile at the woman's reference to Pharao and stored the quote away to relay to his friend later. He was about to move on through the crowd when further comments stopped him.

"Lord Nigel has word that he's a defiler of women, as well as possessing unnatural appetites for young boys."

One of the women gasped, and Tristan felt hot color rise from beneath his rough shirt and creep over his face.

"I'll not go back to Greanly to serve that monster, I vow," the woman hissed. "How's he to tell who's from Seacrest or no?"

Tristan moved from within earshot of the women, his temper rising. As he walked through the bailey, his ears abuzz with gossip, his patience grew weary of Lord Nigel's stewardship of his people.

" 'E's only got one eye."

"—takes his bath in pig's blood."

"—ruthless tyrant. Lord Nigel says—"

"—have us all starved or murdered—"

"Lecherous, perverted—"

"Born without any bollocks. S'why he's so—"

Tristan steered away from the bulk of the commotion to skirt the wall of the village and gather his thoughts in private. Now he understood his people's reluctance to reestablish their homes under his lordship. 'Twould seem Nigel had grown accustomed to the burgeoned workforce now occupying Seacrest, as well as the generous stipend allowed for their care by William. No doubt Nigel looked upon his bursting storehouses and thriving keep with a gluttonous eye and schemed to retain Seacrest's new wealth at Tristan's expense. The rumors could only have originated from the lord himself, as most serfs never strayed from their home villages their entire lives.

The beginnings of a plan formed in Tristan's mind, and he strolled aimlessly through the outlying cottages, refining his thoughts. A young lad had just hobbled past on a bandaged foot when a woman's bloodcurdling scream filled the air. Curiosity teased him, and he slipped quickly to the nearby cottage from which the cry—and the boy—had come.

Tristan's head edged around the crude window of the hut and the sight that greeted him caused his heart to stop—a woman's back, slim and lithe, with red curling locks tamed back by a leather strap. Her hands were busied with a task on the table before her, and she seemed oblivious to the cries that now flowed like water from somewhere at the rear of the cottage.

Tristan thought the shapely woman looked oddly familiar, and he shook his head to clear the sudden buzzing that plagued his ears. He imagined he could almost smell the clean scent of her from where he crouched. He tried to dismiss his unease by making light of the situation, and thought to himself that the woman must be deaf not to cringe at the wails that crescendoed from beyond her. He chuckled halfheartedly.

The woman in the cottage stilled suddenly, and her head came up, alert, listening, and giving Tristan a fleeting glimpse of her porcelain profile. He quickly ducked below the opening in the wall. Gooseflesh covered Tristan's arms, and he realized that the warm beauty could hear after all.

A thick voice, replacing the earlier cries, wafted through the window over Tristan's head. "Haith, come see the babe."

Tristan cautiously crept upward to the window again, in time to see the woman shake herself much in the same manner as he himself had. Then she spoke.

"I'll be but a moment."

The sound of her voice seemed to pierce Tristan's skull. His breath seized in his chest as he stumbled away from the cottage, gasping in the waning afternoon light. He braced his shoulder against another hut's rear wall and struggled to steady his breathing. *That voice,* he thought wildly. *'Tis her!*

It cannot be, another part of him argued. *That woman is a dream, a nightmare even. The woman you saw is merely a villager with red locks and slim build. It means nothing.*

But the voice . . .

Tristan's head hurt madly. A sheen of icy sweat blanketed his face, and his legs felt weak with the exertion of simply standing. His blood roared in his ears, echoing the pounding surf just beyond Seacrest's walls, prompting his eyes to scan the nearby dwellings for a place of refuge.

The stables were a mere fifty paces away, and seemed to glow with the sun disappearing behind them. The dark opening yawned like a hungry mouth waiting to devour him, but 'twas the only shelter to be found.

And he needed shelter desperately.

Tristan staggered toward the stables, shielding his eyes from the light that radiated from its outline. His skull felt as though it would split at any moment, and he paid no heed to the amused calls from the village men he passed.

"A wee bit early in the eve ter be gettin' a fat head, ain't it, lad?"

"Perhaps he seeks a fair maid to soothe his pains."

"Aye, well, the only ones he'll find in there gots four legs to wrap 'round him!"

Once inside the darkened haven, Tristan let out a sigh of some relief. His vision remained blurred and sun-blinded, but the frantic tattoo of his heart had slowed somewhat. He stumbled down the main aisle to a rear stall, blessedly empty and freshly supplied with hay.

Tristan collapsed face down in the pile as the floor spun wickedly under him. His eyes closed, and her voice came to him even as he sank into unconsciousness.

Save me, Tristan, the woman in his dreams cried. *Save me, I'm dying.*

CHAPTER
4

Tristan woke some time later to find the stable draped in darkness and his head feeling sore and swollen. He pushed at the hay beneath him and rolled over. Tristan stifled his body's impulsive groan when a man's voice pierced the blackness of the stall's interior and the sounds of a scuffle followed.

"I doubt you will get the same courtesy from Donald," the man said. Tristan heard footfalls exiting the structure and then muffled weeping. He gained his feet with great care, in deference to his pounding head, and felt his way along the boards to the stall's opening.

Though night had fully fallen, the bailey's moon-drenched landscape could be seen through the far opening, flooding the first half of the stables in white-hot light. At first glance, Tristan thought himself alone and attributed the earlier sounds to a trick on his ears played by the beasts housed within. Then, a glint of copper-reflected moonlight caught his eye. Protruding into the aisle was a single, curling lock of red hair.

Cautiously, he moved toward that still lick of color, his

fect gliding soundlessly over the littered floor. As he neared the half-wall that concealed the lock's owner, he heard the quiet mumblings spoken when one thinks oneself alone. Not wishing to startle her, Tristan eased around the corner and dropped to his knees beside the woman he had seen through the cottage window—he remembered she had been called Haith. His head instantly cleared, seeing her lying pitifully in the moonlight. Her hair, escaped from its plait, fanned around her in a brilliant arc, mindless of the filth and muck it brushed against.

The woman's sobs quieted, and she became perfectly still, as if she sensed his presence, but she did not look up.

"Please, my lady," Tristan breathed, enchanted by the slim grace of her shoulders, the delicacy of her exposed neck. "Is there naught I can do to ease your sorrow?"

Slowly, she raised her head from her folded arms, and when her eyes met Tristan's, he saw that she still wept. The woman drew a shaky breath and stretched out a hand to him as if in wonder.

"I thought you were a dream," she whispered.

Tristan shook his head dumbly, his eyes drinking in the sight of her face. He reached out his own hand to clasp hers, and a slow, heavy hum traveled the length of his arm.

"Nay," he replied, "not a dream." Their joined hands held suspended between them, and he saw tears slide down her cheeks like tiny, wet jewels. "What can I do?" he asked, frantic in some unexplainable way to comfort her.

"Take me in your arms."

The words were barely audible, but to Tristan's ears, they seemed a shout. No sooner had the request passed her lips than Tristan jerked her to him, pressing her heart to his own and wrapping her firmly in his embrace.

A bolt of lightning shot from the night sky and lit up the bailey beyond as if it were midday. Horses reared and screamed in fright, but the display went unnoticed by the two people folded together on the ground. Tristan's palm cradled the back of Haith's head, and her sobbing ceased even though her fingers clutched greedily at his back.

"Sh-h," he murmured. "All is well. I have you now."

"You will not allow it," she said into the rough tunic that covered his chest.

"Of course not," Tristan replied, unknowing and uncaring as to what he promised. Every nerve in his body felt her pressed to him, and his heart beat in rhythm with hers. He knew only that he would perform any duty, battle any foe should she ask it of him. The weight of his feelings should have been unbearable, but instead, Tristan felt free, as if he were flying. "You have nothing to fear."

As Tristan continued to hold and rock her, Haith's body became more relaxed, limp. Her breathing grew measured and slow, and a glance at her face confirmed that she had retreated into slumber.

Tristan's mind whirled with joy and confusion. His thoughts twisted and tangled together dreams with reality. This was the woman in his dreams, of that he was sure. The woman whose voice and face had tormented and favored his sleep for ten years was no spectral image, but warm and flesh and in his arms.

I thought you were a dream, she'd said. Had she, too, known of his existence, known they would meet? What of the man who had left her moments before—a husband perhaps? A lover?

Tristan's arms tightened around Haith's form. No one would have her but him, he vowed silently. He would not have her within his reach after ten long years of searching only to hand her back to some village slop. He calmed himself with some effort, and a steely resolve came over him.

"No matter the cost, love," he whispered, unaware that he spoke aloud. "Be it a man that stands between us or a king, I will keep you with me always. Always." He pressed his lips to the crown of her head.

"My liege!" The frantic whisper broke Tristan's reverie, and his head jerked toward the sound of the voice.

Pharao stood just inside the stable doors. "You must come quickly," he said, ignoring the very obvious fact that his lord sat on a stable floor in serf's garb holding an unconscious woman. "The messengers were nearing Greanly when they were overtaken by a band of men."

"Highwaymen?" Tristan asked, trying to stay focused on his man's words.

"Nay," Pharao said, stepping fully into the moonlight. "Villagers of Seacrest. They seek you with ill intent."

Tristan glanced at Haith, lying peacefully in his arms, then back to Pharao.

"Have they gained entry to the hold?"

Pharao shook his head. "Foolish Englishmen. They number little more than a score and have set up camp outside the walls." He spat on the ground. "They think you afraid to face them."

Tristan sat in thought for a moment, then stood carefully, lifting Haith in his arms. "Then I shall return to greet them properly. Give me but a moment."

Tristan ignored the quizzical look on Pharao's face and moved back down the aisle to the empty stall. He lowered himself and Haith to the ground and straightened her gown and smoothed her hair.

"My lady," he whispered, "if you hear me in your dreams, heed my words. I know naught about you, your kin, even where your hearth lies, else I would take you there now instead of leaving you in these rude accommodations." He thought about the man who had caused her tears earlier, and his brows lowered into a frown. "Or mayhap I would not."

"I must leave you now, but only for a short time. Hide from your tormentor here if you must, but I pray you, do not go far. I shall return for you."

Haith whimpered in her sleep and moved restlessly. Tristan lowered his face to hover above hers and filled his lungs with her scent. "I swear it." He gently pressed his lips to hers, stood quickly, and was gone, leaving Haith to her dreams.

Pharao had boldly risked discovery in his search for Tristan by leaving the horses only a short distance away from Seacrest's wall. The two men easily evaded the drunken guard and raced on foot to mount their steeds. Once astride, the pair turned north toward Greanly.

"Who leads them?" Tristan asked, raising his voice over the pounding hooves. "Nigel?"

"Nay," Pharao answered. " 'Tis merely a mob of village men led by one of their own." Pharao spurred his horse, as he lagged behind Tristan by a head. "The lone messenger who escaped had not enough time to discern their reasoning."

"I have an idea as to why they seek me, but their reason matters not." Tristan's eyes squinted against the rushing air, and his jaw hardened. "They seek me, and so they shall have me."

Nearly two hours of hard riding later, Tristan and Pharao topped the final rise to Greanly to see its grand stone turrets rising out of the night mist. The two men halted their blowing mounts and surveyed the scene before them. A smattering of dying campfires glowed weakly against the west side of the keep where nearby Greanly's abducted messengers were bound together.

Tristan's blood boiled. The day's events had left him in a whirlwind of confusion, and his body longed for release lest he go mad from the strain. Vengeance for the trespass incurred would be delivered this night.

Tristan turned to Pharao, who sat still and silent by his side. "Phar, can you gain entry to the keep by means other than the drawbridge?"

Pharao thought for a moment before answering. "I can."

"Then do so. Once inside, command Barrett that the drawbridge be lowered and my audience admitted to the hall."

Tristan expounded further on his plan, and Pharao nodded. Soon, the dark man was afoot and moving swiftly through the night toward the castle. While he waited for his orders to be received and carried out, Tristan's mind returned to the woman he'd left behind in Seacrest's stable. An endless string of unanswered questions wound itself around his brain until his thoughts were hopelessly tangled and choked.

Was it his destiny to be wed to a common village girl after his lifelong struggle to gain his present station? Being a bastard of noble parentage had laid a heavy burden on Tristan from an early age, and each reward had come well earned many times over. Was he now to deliberately disobey William, his friend as well as his king, by refusing the match made for him? And what would be the consequence of that action? To once again be forced from a home he had barely come to live at? Stripped of his fledgling title and exiled with his common bride?

He had no family to speak of—the father who had denied him now long dead, and the mother who had sent him away out of shame lived in France. Tristan had neither seen nor heard from her in over twenty years. Perhaps she was now dead as well.

There had been a time when Genevieve D'Argent had paid handsomely to care for her ill-begotten progeny— Tristan still remembered with vivid clarity the jingle of the coins contained in the small pouch delivered by his mother's servant. However, as soon as the messenger had turned on his horse, the old woman who was to be his guardian had pocketed the coins and cuffed Tristan on the head.

"Get from here, orphan," she'd growled, shoving Tristan hard from the doorway of the city apartment and into the narrow street. "I need no more mouths to feed, especially not one that belongs to a noble's bastard."

Tristan had merely looked at the hag with hurt confusion in his ten-year-old's eyes. Although his mother had said this woman would care for him, some instinct warned young Tristan against fingering the heavy blue stone in his pocket.

"Madame," Tristan sputtered, "my mama bade me stay with you until she comes for me."

The hag reared her head back and cackled. "You stupid little fop," she said with a sneer. "She's not coming for you—she sent you away to be rid of you! Now, get from here before I set my hand to you again." She stepped forward menacingly.

And a crying Tristan had run.

Tristan shook himself from the wretched past he'd conjured when he saw the drawbridge to Greanly lower. Men in the enemy camp stirred and approached the small band of soldiers who appeared from within Greanly's walls. Although Tristan could not hear the exchange, he was confident that his men now followed the orders relayed by Pharao, the only family Tristan now had.

When the last of the would-be aggressors had filed through the gate, Tristan nudged his destrier forward at a leisurely pace, Phar's mount following obediently. He was no longer a frightened lad to be so easily turned away. A wicked, hard smile lifted the corners of his mouth but did not quite reach his eyes.

No one, he vowed, would ever send him from what was rightfully his again. Nigel's minions had come to Greanly seeking William's Hammer, and Tristan planned to grant them their wish.

CHAPTER
5

Haith awoke in the same stall as Tristan had in much the same manner, swathed in confusion and with her head pounding. Her eyes, accustomed to the dark through sleep, focused on the beamed and thatched underside of the stable's roof.

She remained still for several moments, trying to remember the events that had led her to her current position. Her eyes blinked as her mind worked and she recalled Nigel's ultimatum. Haith replayed her encounter with the evil man until the point that she'd collapsed in despair, then she bolted to a sitting position in the prickly straw.

The blond man in her dreams! He'd been there, spoken to her!

Haith scrambled out of the straw and staggered to her feet, grasping the rough half-wall for support when her world tilted sharply. She stumbled down the aisle, looking frantically around her, behind her, but he was nowhere to be found.

"Nay," she whispered. "Nay, nay, nay!"

She burst from the stable into the moon-drenched yard, turning in circles, searching the dark shadows.

He was here, she insisted to herself. *He held me in his arms and promised to protect me. He held me until I—*

"Asleep." The word was barely audible to her own ears, but the reality of it brought Haith to her knees on the hard-packed earth. She stared up at the full, buttery moon as if she might glean the reasoning for her madness in the glowing disc. "I slept. He was but another dream."

The stars twinkled down from heaven as Haith sat alone in the midnight quiet. A breeze chased dust around the yard in tiny dervishes, and Haith shivered. She should have known better than to believe, even for a moment, that Minerva's talk of soulmates held any truth. 'Twas all useless, superstitious nonsense.

A rustle from behind caused Haith to quickly turn her head, hoping against hope that she would see a tall, blond man, broad of chest and with blue, smiling eyes.

But 'twas only an owl come to roost on the stable's roof peak.

"Who-o-o," it called.

"Well, certainly not you, Willy," Haith muttered.

The owl hooted again, flapped its wings as if in irritation, and swiveled its head toward the north end of the bailey.

"Oh, very well," Haith sighed. She rose slowly, not bothering to dust herself off. "I'm coming, Minerva."

Haith pushed the cottage door open with a creak to find Minerva sitting comfortably by the hearth, mending needle in hand. The small brown owl Haith had seen on the stable roof was now perched daintily on the windowsill, and he eyed Haith with apparent smugness. Minerva glanced up from her mending.

"Well, good eventide, lass," Minerva said with a bite in her voice. "Glad I am ye finally decided to come home."

The owl hooted quietly.

"Och, aye, Willy. Forgive me." Minerva grasped her needle firmly and bent at the waist to touch it to the dirt floor between her feet. She drew a long, straight line away from her, pointing toward Haith and the open door, causing Haith to step quickly to the side of the portal.

Minerva straightened in her chair and stomped one foot. Immediately, a tiny mouse raced from beneath her chair, along the line she'd drawn, and out the door. Willy swooped across the small chamber and through the portal in swift chase. Minerva resumed her mending with pursed lips.

Haith closed the door after the owl and sat in the closest chair at the small wooden table. She folded her arms on the work-smoothed surface and rested her face in the hollow created. After a moment, Minerva loosened her pinched mouth.

"Kindly tell me when next you plan to stay with your sister all night, Haith," she scolded. "Some folk have want to seek their beds while the moon still shines."

When she received no biting retort, Minerva looked up to see Haith's stooped shoulders.

"Sweet Corra, lass," Minerva exclaimed, stuffing the mending into a corner of her chair and rising to join Haith at the table. She sat and laid a gnarled hand on Haith's head. "What troubles you so? Not my tongue, I'll wager."

Haith shook her bowed head and sniffed.

"Then what?"

Haith drew a shuddering breath and, without raising her head, explained Nigel's offer. When her tale was told, Minerva's anger exploded, and she popped out of her chair, her agility belying her age of over three score and ten.

"That randy jackass!" she hissed. "I've known 'twould come to this eventually. What a tricky bastard he is!"

The flame in the hearth shot up the chimney in a shower of sparks but went unnoticed by the two women.

"Thinks he that you, a lord's daughter, would gladly aid his treachery when you have the beauty and station to pair with any titled lord in the whole of England?" Minerva gestured wildly as she spoke, and the flames in the hearth danced accordingly. Haith merely shrugged, her head still bowed.

"Nay!" The old woman bellowed the answer to her own question. "And he picks the worst one of the lot to align you with—*Donald*." Minerva strode to the hearth and spat into the flames as if the very mention of the name sickened her. The flames glowed bile green. "That hoary murderer."

"Nigel knows I would not choose to betray Greanly's new lord with Donald," Haith said, her words muffled.

Minerva shook her fist in the direction of the keep. "Aye, he thinks you will eagerly climb into his bed to bear him a bastard!" The flames in the hearth shot skyward again, filling the small hut with loud cracks and pops.

Haith raised her head slightly. "Minerva, please, have you a wish to set the cottage roof afire again?" She let her head fall back to her arms.

"Och," Minerva muttered and waved a hand toward the ceiling before again taking her chair at the table. The sound of a steady rain soon beat comfortingly on the roof. Minerva continued, "You'll nae lie with a married man, Haith. I know it."

"And why not?" Haith demanded. She sat up in her chair fully and addressed Minerva with red, swollen eyes. "Mother did as such."

" 'Twas different with your papa, lass. You know—"

"I know naught," Haith interrupted, "but that I am a bastard from a union between my mother and my father, who was wed to Lady Ellora."

"You doona ken, girl. Your papa was—"

"My mother's soulmate," Haith supplied wearily, clos-ing her eyes for strength. "I know the tale well, Minerva, and it grows older and thinner with each telling. 'Tis the Buchanan's curse, and I, for one, will not be bullied by some ancient witchery."

Minerva opened her mouth to rebuke Haith's harsh words but closed it as she noticed a change in the girl's face.

"You've seen him!" she whispered.

"Seen who?" Haith asked in exasperation. She opened her eyes and saw Minerva's rapt attention. "I don't ken."

"You ken," Minerva said, her voice still hushed. "You've seen your soulmate. Did he come to your dreams again? You've not spoken of him since you were a girl."

"And I do not wish to speak of such nonsense now." Haith rose from her chair. "I've had a trying day, and would find my bed for what little darkness is left of this night." Haith strode past Minerva to the rear doorway of the hut but froze in her steps at the old woman's next words.

"Och, my poor faery," she said softly. "He's nae dream. He's as flesh and blood as your papa was."

A chill raced up Haith's spine, and she squeezed her eyes shut against the tears that welled there. "Good night, Minerva."

Tristan tossed his reins to a stable boy waiting just inside Greanly's wall and strode across the bailey toward the hall. His anger was in check, but just barely. His blue eyes, normally as clear and bright as a summer's day, were now dark and opaque, like the night sea churning east of Greanly. His right hand clenched and unclenched the air, aching to grip the familiar hilt of his sword.

As he neared the portal, he heard the commotion of

the score of Seacrest men gathered inside. Voices were raised in anger and confusion, and snippets of their demands trampled the heavy mists that covered the ground.

"Where is the cowardly bastard?"

"Yea, bring out the thief of our good town!"

The shouts were met with roars of agreement and more of the same as the men became bolder *en masse*.

"I'll slit his bloody throat meself!"

Tristan saw a glimmer of white dance toward him, and Pharao emerged from the shadows bearing Tristan's sword. Tristan belted on the weapon with a word of thanks. Pharao merely nodded, pointedly ignoring the rising din from the hall, but his eyes, too, shone black.

"Are the soldiers readied?" Tristan asked.

"They but wait for your signal."

"Give it now."

Pharao disappeared as silently as he had come.

Tristan entered the hall casually, as if nothing at all were amiss. He strolled around the cluster of what he guessed at a glance to be twenty-five men, mostly younger, and full of righteous indignation. They blocked his view of the lord's table, so he skirted the group and went toward the ale barrel where he filled a horn. He stood and watched the group as he sipped, listening to their outrageous proclamations. The few soldiers Tristan had bade show themselves were stationed sparsely along the chamber's walls and, per their lord's instructions, behaved as if made of stone; they neither acknowledged their lord's entrance nor moved to subdue the rioters.

A squat, toadish-looking man seemed to Tristan to be the head rabble-rouser of the group. He was so bold, or so foolish, to have perched his wide, flat bottom on the lord's table, from which he was now addressing his followers.

"I'll tell ye, men," their leader roared, a wicked-looking burn scar freezing the right side of his face. "We would be right to gut this Lord Bastard and throw his body into his fancy moat!"

The cheer that arose only served to encourage the man further.

"'E's no *lord*," he sneered. "'E's a thief and a murderer. Where are all the poor blokes what came to live here against Lord Nigel's advice?" He looked pointedly around the hall, eyes bulging comically to prove his point over the murmured assent of the men. His eyes fell on Tristan, lounging against a wall and still nursing his ale.

"You there!" the trollish man shouted, pointing a stubby finger in Tristan's direction. "You live here?"

Tristan set his horn down and nodded, strolling through the crowd of men who parted for him. Many of the invaders slapped his back as he passed through, commiserating with him on his sad misfortune. Tristan stopped just short of the lord's table, where the leader eyed him from head to toe with a malicious grin.

"Well, where is your mighty lord now?" the man asked, his arms spread wide. "Does he cower in some chamber in fear for his life?" He threw back his head and laughed, a disgusting, hoarse sound. "Probably curled beneath some poor stable boy, I'll wager."

The men around Tristan burst out laughing, but the noise soon dwindled to chuckles and then nervous clearing of throats when Tristan's face remained stony. His eyes looked upon the poor excuse of a man before him.

The inciter looked around indignantly when no more encouraging barbs were offered to support his tirade. Finally, he fixed Tristan with an exasperated look.

"Well then, where is he?"

Tristan stepped forward until he towered over the odious man.

"Right now, he is considering how to kill the lumpy piece of shit sitting on his table."

The bulk of Tristan's men dressed in full chain mail and with battle weapons drawn filed into the hall as if on cue, quickly surrounding the stunned gathering of trespassers. Good Sheriff Barrett was among them, dressed in his usual garb, with his great battle-ax laid casually over one shoulder.

"Ay!" the squat man cried and looked nervously around Tristan's broad form. "What's the meanin' of this?"

Tristan grasped him by the front of his filthy tunic and, with a mighty tug, flung him into the midst of the men where he fell to the floor and skidded to a stop on his considerable backside.

"Throw down yer weapons, lads," Barrett bellowed jovially, strolling up to stand next to Tristan. "No sense in any bloodshed now, is there?" His eyes fell on a slim, chestnut-haired man who stood among the defeated group looking thoroughly bewildered. "Hello, John. How's the wife?"

"Er, well. Very well, Barrett. My thanks for asking."

Some of the men readily dropped their weapons, while others stood in confusion during Barrett's exchange with the villager. Their eyes shifted from Tristan, to the soldiers, to their recently dislodged leader, who was just beginning to rise from the floor.

"I'll do you for this, you bastard," he growled at Tristan as he gained his feet. He reached for the long knife at his belt, and the men clustered around him quickly drew away.

"Now, Donald," Barrett said to the man as if admonishing a young child. "Don't be foolish."

Tristan held up a hand to silence the sheriff, his steely gaze never leaving the newly introduced Donald. "Let the man have his chance, Barrett," he said. " 'Tis what he came for, after all." Tristan smiled coldly at the man wielding the knife.

"As you wish, my lord," Barrett said, stepping away respectfully and turning his attention to the closest of the Seacrest men who was still armed, albeit with a ridiculously small blade. "You there," he said, advancing toward him with his palm out. "I'll be takin' that now."

Donald glanced around furtively at the men between glares at Tristan. "Think you to slaughter us all without a fight?"

"The only men at Greanly heretofore intent on slaughter," Tristan reminded him and advanced, "were yours, by your own admission."

Donald's eyes grew slightly wider as the realization hit him that this new lord had overheard all that he had said. A look of unease crept over his twisted face, but he shook it off, replacing it with bravado. Donald lunged at Tristan with his dagger drawn.

Tristan easily sidestepped the clumsy but powerful thrust and swung his broadsword from its hilt to bring it down across his opponent's passing shoulders. Donald crashed to the rushes with a grunt, rolled, and then gained his feet with amazing agility for a man of his size. His face reddened with embarrassment, and he faced Tristan in a readied stance.

"Only a coward would try to best an ill-equipped man," Donald wheezed. "My blade is no match for yours."

Tristan raised an eyebrow. "I asked not for this fight— your poor choice in weaponry shows not only your lack of skill with it but your ignorance as well." Tristan eyed Donald from head to toe. "You were confident that a blade so small could defend an arse such as yours? Tsk-tsk."

Around him, Tristan's men chuckled, and Donald's complexion grew apoplectic around the constant paleness of his scar.

"You're afraid to face me on equal terms," Donald tried.

Tristan threw back his head and laughed long and

heartily. The sound echoed eerily in the now silent hall, and small beads of sweat danced down Donald's temples. Without a glance, Tristan tossed his sword into the waiting hands of Pharao, who had appeared in the hall as if conjured. Tristan beckoned to Donald with small movements of his hands.

"Come then."

Donald lunged again, and again Tristan dodged the blow. A powerful sweep of his leg brought Donald to the floor, where he rolled under the table and came up on the other side. Tristan advanced, and the two circled the massive oaken slab.

"I'll not play with you all night," Tristan warned. "Have you the will, make your move now."

"Coward!" Donald shouted, circling away from Tristan. He glanced around at the remainder of his men, who watched the exchange with expressions of unease. "Take him down, lads!"

But the men remained motionless, surrounded by Greanly's soldiers. They glanced from each other to the huge blond man stalking their leader.

"Oh ho! What is this I hear?" Tristan asked lightly, blocking each of Donald's attempts to evade him by skirting the table. "What of gutting me and throwing my body into the moat?" he taunted, finally coming to a stop and stepping onto the table with a mighty stride. He hopped down directly in front of Donald. "Yonder moat waits."

Donald arced his blade at Tristan's heart with a strangled cry but looked in shock at his empty hand as the blow was deflected and the knife clattered to the table. His face paled, and he lunged to retrieve the weapon. In the blink of an eye, Donald's right palm was pinned to the table, the hilt of a slender eating knife plunged through the meat of his hand and sank deeply into the thick tabletop. His scream split the tense silence.

Tristan seized Donald by the throat and drove the man to his knees, his right hand still anchoring him to the table. Tristan leaned down.

"Who sent you?" he demanded, releasing his grip just enough for the man to form words.

"No one."

Tristan's fingers tightened until veins stood out clearly on Donald's forehead and the man gurgled and clawed at his throat with his one free hand. Again Tristan relented.

"Who sent you? Tell me!"

The sounds that issued forth from Donald's bruised throat were garbled, the single name he spoke nearly unintelligible. Fear shone brightly in his eyes. Tristan released him fully with a shove and a sound of disgust. He retrieved his eating knife and, with only a cursory glance at it, tossed it into the blazing hearth. Donald, now untethered, crumpled to the floor, clutching at his crushed neck with his bloody hand and eyeing Tristan as if waiting for the death blow to be dealt. Tristan ignored the beaten man and turned to face the hall.

"Does any man here have any further quarrel with me; is there any who wishes to do me harm?" he asked, arms spread wide in invitation, looming.

The few men who still held blades dropped them to the rushes with a clatter. Tristan turned to Barrett.

"Imprison them," he commanded, and the soldiers quickly moved to obey. To Pharao, he added, motioning toward Donald, "Put this one in a cell alone. When I have regained my temper, I will speak with him privately." He eyed the man's dripping hand as Pharao hauled him to his feet. "Bind his hand, and if the wound festers before I have my counsel, cut it off."

Soon the hall was empty. Tristan retrieved his sword from where Pharao had deposited it against a rear wall and dipped another horn of ale. He stood for several moments before the hearth, sipping and refining his thoughts in the silence. His muscles burned with unused energy, and his jaw twitched in barely controlled rage. His body, his pride, cried out for him to go to the dungeons and cut out the hearts of all of Greanly's would-be invaders, but his mind argued that choice with the reality of William's wrath. No, he would deal with Nigel's lackeys as Nigel himself had—he would use them as pawns to gain his desires.

The flames danced before him, and a vision of fiery red curls filled his mind. He remembered that the name Donald had been spoken to Haith by the man in the stables, and Tristan wondered that he had not recognized the noble diction right away. Only one man had the power to threaten villagers in such a way, and that was their lord. And there was only one lord at Seacrest.

Nigel.

What could he have threatened her with, and what part did Donald play in his schemes? The mere thought of the graceful beauty anywhere near that disgusting mountain of flesh had Tristan gripping the horn of ale until the sides cracked, which he only took notice of when he felt the wetness in his hand.

He would solve this riddle, he vowed, and win the lady. On his terms and with William's blessing, or he would die trying. Lord Nigel's demise, Tristan surmised, would come about regardless.

CHAPTER
6

"Ow, Sallie! Not so tight," Soleilbert cried, her fingers flying to her offended scalp. Bertie's maid merely slapped at her lady's hand.

"Be still, my lady. 'Tis nearly done."

Haith lounged across Bertie's bed, idly pulling the silky yellow scarf that matched her sister's ensemble through her hands. She'd watched Soleilbert's transformation into the festive finery with awe. Bertie's heavily embroidered kirtle shone like the sun, and the creamy underdress boasted slim sleeves and delicate stitching at the neck. The maid applied the finishing touches to the plait that encircled Bertie's head and held out a hand for the scarf. She attached it expertly and then stepped back to admire her handiwork. Haith scrambled off the bed to join her.

"Bertie, you look magnificent!" Haith breathed, circling her sister and touching her gown and hair. "You will bring Lord Tristan to his knees, I vow."

"It matters not to me," Soleilbert said sullenly, shrugging away from her sister's touch. "I feel like a huge yellow cow." She moved to gaze out the chamber window.

Haith exchanged raised eyebrows with the maid, who quickly excused herself and exited the room. Haith went to stand at her sister's back, wrapping her arms about Soleilbert when she would have moved away.

"Bertie, what troubles you?" she asked gently. "Are you fearful of meeting your future husband?"

"Nay," Bertie sighed. "And yea. Oh, Haith!" Soleilbert turned into her sister's arms. "I don't wish to marry because I don't want things to *change!*"

Haith patted Bertie's back. She could not argue the fact that their lives were indeed about to change drastically, especially if Nigel had his way. Haith pushed the thoughts of the evil man away.

"I know, Sister. But I shall visit often," Haith said and leaned back to look into Bertie's round, unhappy face. "And you may enjoy being a lady of your own household. Bertie, you can have babies!"

Bertie sniffed and shook her head. "I care not. I've never met him, and I've heard terrible things about him." She glanced up at Haith accusingly. "And you won't even humor me enough to cast the stones!"

Haith grimaced. She'd heard many of the rumors about William's Hammer that were circling the village, especially since a group of Seacrest men, one that included Donald, had gone to pay a visit a fortnight ago and had never returned. There had been no word from Greanly, an oddity that Haith thought should have alarmed Nigel. To the contrary, the lack of news concerning his men's welfare seemed to have left Nigel pleased and even slightly amused.

But not even for Bertie would Haith take up the nonsensical divination practices of her mother or Minerva.

"Do not judge him until you meet him yourself," Haith said. "Your opinion is the only one that matters."

"Won't you stay this eve and dine with us?" Bertie's eyes turned pleading. "I beg you, don't leave me to face him alone."

Haith withdrew and began picking up the clothing that was strewn about the chamber. "I'm afraid not. Your mother has banned me from the hall. I should not even be here now."

"Mother," Soleilbert said in disgust, "has been unbearable of late."

"She's merely upset that she will soon lose her only child."

Soleilbert huffed. "Nay. She's worried the Great Lord Tristan will take one look at me and flee. Perhaps you could cast a binding spell for her tongue?"

Haith straightened with a bundle of clothes and, despite herself, laughed. A headache had begun to manifest itself behind her eyes, and Bertie's half serious jest eased it slightly. Since that night in the stable, Haith had been on edge. Sleep had been given the most perfunctory of nods, as the torment of her dreams was too much to bear. Minerva was so convinced that Haith was having visions of her soulmate that twice she'd discovered tiny dream sachets filled with fragrant lavender and mint beneath her pillow.

And on top of everything else, Nigel's ultimatum loomed large. Tristan D'Argent was to dine with the family this very eve to seal the betrothal, and Haith had no illusions that Nigel had forgotten the deadline he'd imposed for her decision.

Haith drew a deep, silent breath. Soleilbert deserved her attention now, and she vowed to try to comfort and encourage her as best she could, while ignoring her pleas for magical intervention.

"Then you must not think about your mother one whit this eve," Haith advised.

Soleilbert merely wrung her hands and stared out the window. "'Twill be impossible," she said. "She watches my every move like a hawk."

"And that you cannot change," Haith replied, dropping the bundle of laundry on the bed and moving to Bertie to take her hand. "But you *can* try to enjoy Lord Tristan's company." Haith gave her sister's hand a little shake to draw her attention. "And when the night has ended, I shall sneak to your chamber and you can tell me all."

"What if he truly is a beast?" Soleilbert asked.

Then the choice I have before me shall be that much easier, Haith thought to herself. To Bertie, she said simply, "We shall think of something."

Haith made her way down the steps into the great hall where below her the room was a flurry of activity. Servants rushed to and fro, scrubbing the already gleaming tables, rehanging freshly beaten tapestries, and sprinkling fragrant herbs onto the fresh rushes. Delicious smells of roasting meats wafted through the rear portal from the kitchens, and Haith's stomach growled.

When was the last time she'd eaten?

Lady Ellora stood in a far corner of the hall, deep in conversation with Lord Nigel, when Haith caught her eye. Ellora's lips thinned, and she glided quickly across the floor, Nigel following lazily behind her, as Haith rushed to make her escape.

She was not quick enough.

"Why are you still here?" Ellora stepped into Haith's path, arms crossed over her bosom. "Think you to catch a glimpse of my daughter's betrothed so that you may play the whore?"

"I am taking my leave now, my lady," Haith said, not wishing to enter into another battle of words with Ellora, especially since Nigel was nearly upon the pair. Haith turned to move past Ellora when Nigel called out.

"Haith. A moment of your time, I pray."

Haith halted in her steps, fighting back the dread that wanted to creep up her spine and strangle her. Surely he would not bring up this thing in Ellora's presence.

"My lord?" Haith composed her expression and turned to face him. She could see that Ellora watched her from a short distance away, eyes narrowed and flicking uneasily between her husband and Haith. Nigel paid no heed to his wife's proximity, save for lowering his voice.

"The hour draws near when I would have your decision," he said, his eyebrow rising with his smirk. "You have not forgotten?"

"Nay," Haith answered nervously, glancing around the hall for eavesdroppers.

"Ah, good. You have made your choice then."

"Nearly, my lord. I need but a little more time."

"I have been most generous in allowing you these past weeks," Nigel admonished. "Is the choice so difficult between an ogre and a lord?"

Haith said nothing, and she kept her eyes downcast lest he see the disgust she held for him.

"Shall I make your decision an easier one?" he asked almost kindly.

"My lord?" Haith looked up, unable to control her desperate hope that perhaps Nigel had changed his mind.

"As you know, Donald left for Seacrest a fortnight ago with a group of men to . . . er, greet the new lord." Nigel smiled as if the statement amused him. "Perhaps Lord Tristan was . . . *displeased*."

Haith remained silent, wary. Nigel's words made no sense.

"He has not returned," Nigel expounded.

"Forgive me, my lord, but what bearing does that have on my choice?"

Nigel chuckled and reached out to trail a finger down the side of Haith's face. "It cannot be said that you hie to Greanly to marry a dead man, my sweet."

Haith jerked her head away. Nigel's leer pierced her kirtle, and the heat of it sickened her. Her thoughts whirled inside her head like caged birds, seeking escape. Within Nigel's proclamation, there was a way out for Haith, and that she stood in the hall before Ellora and a room filled with servants only prompted her hasty decision.

"I shall seek you this eve," Nigel said and began to stroll away.

Before her nerve could leave her, Haith called out loudly, "My lord." Her voice echoed, its volume unnecessary in the quiet busyness of the hall, but it had the desired effect of drawing the attention of all within.

Nigel halted straightaway and pivoted on his heel, a wary expression on his face. "Yea, Haith? Is there something you wish to speak of in private?"

Haith's gaze flicked to Ellora. "Nay. Here will do." She took a deep breath and raised her voice even further. "I have decided to accept the betrothal offer from Donald the smithy."

Outraged gasps filled the hall, and a servant girl dropped a tray of earthen jugs, their crash resounding in the aftermath of Haith's proclamation. Unintelligible murmurs raced among the serfs.

Ellora pushed her way through the gaping throng. "Get back to work, all of you. This is no concern of yours."

Nigel's expressive eyebrows twitched furiously above his darkened complexion, and he calmly but quickly approached. "Is that so?" he asked menacingly, keeping his voice low and a smile on his face. "You think to outwit me, do you?"

Ellora appeared at his side, color high in her cheeks. "What is the meaning of this nonsense, Haith?" She turned to her husband. "My lord, did the smithy offer for the slut's hand?"

Nigel's jaw bulged as he gritted his teeth. "Yea, my lady. Before he departed for Greanly to welcome Lord Tristan." Although he spoke to Ellora, his eyes never left Haith.

Ellora frowned and looked at Haith. "Well."

Haith took the opportunity to plead her case with Ellora. "If it pleases you, my lady, I would take Minerva and leave for Greanly this night to inquire of"—Haith gulped as her stomach churned—"my betrothed's welfare."

"Of course." Ellora peered into Haith's eyes as if trying to discern some mystery there. "Do the other villagers depart, then so shall you. But I warn you,"—Ellora cocked her head—"should you try to jeopardize Soleilbert's marriage, I will personally see you exiled."

"You needn't worry, my lady," Haith said, hoping she spoke true. "May I go now?"

At Ellora's answering nod, Haith fled the hall and ran for her cottage, leaving the noble couple staring after her.

Ellora turned to her husband. "That was quite unexpected," she said, the crease of her frown still present between her eyes. "Although Soleilbert will be pleased, I'm sure, to have the chit so close. Why did you not tell me, husband?"

"As you said yourself," Nigel said, turning to walk away, "'twas unexpected."

The band of men that approached Seacrest some time later did so with a small measure of unease. Seacrest's keep rose up before them, crowning the jutting cliff over the water that gave the demesne its name. The proud, ancient timbers of the wooden hold seemed more organic to the surrounding countryside than the massive stone of Tristan's Greanly. Its population having more than doubled over the past several years, hundreds of twinkling lights betrayed the fact that Seacrest was near to bursting its seams with the bulk of Tristan's village.

Which, it seemed to Tristan, Lord Nigel was loathe to be quit of. Not to mention the healthy royal stipend Seacrest's lord received as long as he remained their protector.

The imprisoned Seacrest men had been eager to reveal their lack of understanding about their disastrous mission to Greanly, regaling Tristan with the rumors that had been circulating for nearly a year about the new lord and his cruelty. They had sheepishly confessed that most of the tales had originated from Donald the smithy, but where he had acquired his information, no one seemed to know.

Now, most of the men were free to roam the town as they chose, and the biggest complaint was the absence of their families. Donald, however, remained imprisoned. While his confession in Greanly's hall had been most freely given under threat of death, he now refused to impart further knowledge of Nigel's machinations. Instead, Donald spoke endlessly of sending for his betrothed, a mystery woman who no one knew of and who Tristan doubted even existed. He wondered what manner of woman would willingly accept a beast such as Donald for her husband.

Tristan seethed beneath his cool exterior. The finery he'd donned for the occasion was not to impress his own unknown betrothed but was chosen carefully for Lord Nigel's benefit. He was anxious to meet the bold bastard and take his measure. Tristan wanted to be certain that his enemy recognized it was not some pampered, stripling noble's lad he connived to rob, but a warrior, secure in his own vast wealth and royal favor in William's court. A man his equal or better who would not accept the treachery dealt him easily.

And of course, there were his thoughts of Haith. He knew now that she was not some common wench but the daughter of Seacrest's old lord, James. The news had left Tristan stunned and somewhat confused—'twould seem that mystery surrounded the woman on all sides, and Tristan wanted nothing more than to unravel her secrets himself. He knew not how he would find her again once he arrived at Seacrest or how he would convince her to leave, but he was determined that Haith would accompany him away from Nigel this very night.

The horses danced and huffed impatiently, sensing the town nearby and with it, the promise of oats and relief from the burdens they carried. Tristan reined gently, and his steed obeyed. He surveyed the group that accompanied him one last time: Barrett and Pharao flanked him, and John the crofter drew a humble nag even with the good sheriff's. Twenty soldiers, accompanying as guards, surrounded the group, and Tristan's standard cracked in the stiff twilight breeze. Following the band were two score more battle-seasoned soldiers leading a train of empty wagons, soon to be filled with Greanly's allotted portion of Seacrest's stores. Should Nigel resist allowing Tristan access to the staples, the soldiers were primed for combat. His company was tense, silent. Wary.

Tucked neatly in Tristan's belt were the betrothal contract and the royal decree releasing Nigel of Greanly's stewardship. He lightly fingered the hilt of his broadsword and the cool surface of the D'Argent sapphire that adorned it. Armed with these weapons, Tristan urged his stallion to Seacrest.

* * *

Hidden away in their cottage, Haith and Minerva dined on the meager stew that was to be their last meal at Seacrest. Neither wanted to discuss the matters that weighed on their minds, as all that needed to be said already had been. Haith had relayed her bold decision to Minerva, and the old one had met the news with quiet resolve. There was no other choice to be made, and so the pair was silent.

Haith rose to clear the table of the barely touched meal, and Minerva chanced a glance at the worried face so much like her dear Corinne's. The old one's eyes were then drawn to the crude window, framing the pitch black of a sky deep in new moon, and she heard the riders approaching like distant, ominous thunder.

CHAPTER
7

"Lord Tristan, welcome to Seacrest." Nigel crossed the hall with a pronounced swagger and offered his hand.

Tristan valiantly denied himself of the urge to grind the effeminate bones of the slender palm he held into dust. Still, it gave him no small satisfaction to see the carefully concealed wince on the other man's face.

"Lord Nigel,"—Tristan released the misshapen hand with regret that it was still intact—"at last we meet."

"Allow me to present my wife, Lady Ellora."

Tristan bowed to the tall blond woman, who curtsied and eyed him warily.

"Welcome, Lord Tristan."

Nigel rubbed his hands together as if in anticipation and drew to his side a very large, very brightly attired young woman. "My stepdaughter, Soleilbert." He prodded the girl toward him, and for a moment, Tristan thought she might swoon.

She looked up furtively from her curtsy, giving Tristan a glimpse of the saddest brown eyes he'd ever seen. Quickly, he bowed.

"Lady Soleilbert,"— he took her hand and gently brushed his lips across its back—"'Tis my pleasure to make your acquaintance."

Soleilbert flushed becomingly but did not smile. Her answering, "My lord," was barely audible.

Nigel looked confounded, but only for a moment before gesturing toward the center of the hall. "Lord Tristan, the meal is nigh ready. If you would—"

Nigel's words were cut off as sounds of a small scuffle just beyond the hall doors reached them. Sharp, hushed voices were heard, followed by a great thump. A moment later, one of the grand double doors opened, and Barrett and Pharao jostled each other through the portal and approached their hosts.

Barrett bowed to Nigel almost grudgingly, but he gave his respects freely to Ellora. "My lady," he intoned.

Although Ellora would not curtsy for one as common as Barrett, her face relaxed noticeably. "Barrett," she said, "it has been many months. I hope all is well for you at Greanly."

"Aye, milady." Barrett grinned. "Although a bit quiet of late," he said, then quickly addressed Solcilbert as if to thwart any reply. "Lady Soleilbert, how lovely you look this eve!"

"Barrett, 'tis good to see you again."

Tristan was intrigued to see the girl's face, which until a moment ago had been so glum, brighten with a smile that sparked warmth in her dull eyes. Her image was transformed into sunshine and then transformed once again as she beheld Pharao. Her mouth dropped open, and her eyes widened in amazement.

Seacrest's hosts were silent as they openly stared at Tristan's friend.

Tristan cleared his throat. "May I introduce my first

man, Pharao Tak'Ahn," he said. "Phar, Lord Nigel; his lady, Ellora; and Lady Soleilbert."

Pharao bowed at the waist to those he was presented to, but his eyes, Tristan noticed, were strangely fixed on Lady Soleilbert alone.

Ellora seemed to notice as well. She stepped slightly in front of her daughter, drawing a frown from the girl as her view was blocked.

Nigel cleared his throat. "Shall we be expecting any more guests, Lord Tristan?" His tone carried a hint of impatience.

"Nay," Tristan replied easily. "My soldiers will see to themselves. Although we tried to persuade John to join us, he was eager to see his wife and family."

"John?" Ellora asked.

"Yea, John the crofter," Barrett offered. "He's fit in well at Greanly."

"Is that so?" Nigel asked.

"Yea," Tristan said, "and glad we are to have him." He eyed Nigel for signs of discomfiture, but the man was stoic.

"'Tis well, then. Your men are most welcome at my table, Lord Tristan," Nigel said. "But let us talk of the matters of towns and weddings"—he smiled pointedly, and Tristan was growing annoyed with the way the man's eyebrows seemed choreographed with his speech— "after we dine. Shall we be seated, gentlemen?"

Nigel offered his arm to his wife, and Tristan took Soleilbert by the elbow, leaving Barrett and Pharao to follow.

As they moved through the hall, Tristan stared coldly at Nigel's slight form, his anger barely kept in check behind the polite façade.

Unnoticed by his liege, Pharao's eyes never left Soleilbert's gently swaying form.

And no one at all paid heed when Bertie glanced over her shoulder to return his appraisal.

Used to meals made in camp and the crude fare prepared by the inept men at Greanly, Tristan grudgingly enjoyed the sumptuous food at Nigel's table: a roast boar, creamed peas, bread pudding with dried apples and raisins, spiced pears, herring in a rich stock, and sweet meats completed the feast laid before him, accompanied by a robust red wine.

Ignoring all but his stomach, Tristan ate his fill. He enjoyed the meal even further after surmising that part of it originated from the labors of his people. Around him, discussion of trivial matters flowed, mostly among Lady Ellora, Soleilbert, and Barrett, consisting of uninteresting town gossip until Ellora mentioned Donald. Tristan now listened carefully to the lady's chatter.

"Our smithy grows old and weak," Ellora said with regret. "With Donald now at Greanly and soon to wed, I fear Seacrest will likely be without that craft."

Soleilbert's head popped up. "Donald is to marry? But who—"

Tristan noticed the sly half-smile that played about Lady Ellora's lips. "Never you mind, Soleilbert. You shall find out soon enough as Donald has returned to his home." The remark was a blatant allusion to the fact that Soleilbert would soon be the mistress of Tristan's keep.

Barrett snorted most impolitely. "I'm sure you can have the blightin' troublemaker back."

Immediately, Nigel's head jerked, keen interest on his face. "Donald fares ill at Greanly?"

"Nay, nay." Barrett's eyes, full of regret, flicked to Tristan. "Donald and me's just never got on." He glanced at Soleilbert. "Ain't that so, Lady Bertie?"

"'Tis true." The girl nodded and shyly addressed Tristan. "Why once, Barrett became so incensed with Donald that he threw him—"

"Soleilbert!" Ellora hissed. "That is not proper discussion for a meal!"

The table grew awkwardly silent after Ellora's rebuke, and although Tristan felt sympathy for the girl, he was relieved that Donald was no longer the topic of conversation. For some reason, he felt it important not to reveal that the smithy remained imprisoned.

Lord Nigel, on the other hand, had apparently decided that the time for small talk was over. He stood, wiping the corners of his short, black beard daintily, and picked up his chalice.

"Lord Tristan," he said, gesturing with the vessel, "if you are inclined to move to a more comfortable area, we shall get on with the arrangements."

Tristan acquiesced with a nod, and he, too, rose from the table. He caught the pointed glance from Nigel to Ellora, and so expected the lady's excuse before she spoke.

"I beg your leave, my lords," she said. "My daughter and I have want to refresh ourselves while you discuss these matters."

"Of course," Tristan said, bowing from the waist. He caught Soleilbert's eyes flitting to Pharao.

Barrett and Pharao politely stood at Ellora's and Soleilbert's departure, and Pharao's normally serene face, Tristan noticed, had developed an expression of intenseness.

The men moved to a pair of ornate chairs arranged before the hearth, and Nigel looked to Barrett and Pharao in annoyance.

"If you would excuse us, Barrett and, er—" Nigel began, "*Pharao*, is it?"

"I stay with my liege," Pharao stated, his expression once more intact, arms folded solidly across his chest.

"All is well, Phar," Tristan assured him. "Barrett, with Lord Nigel's permission, perhaps you could show Pharao the grounds of Seacrest."

"Marvelous idea," Nigel said enthusiastically. "Barrett has my leave to go where he would."

"My liege?" Pharao looked at Tristan, a question in his eyes.

Tristan nodded curtly.

"Come on then, Pharao, you great beast," Barrett muttered. As they reached the portal, he said, "My God, you'll scare the villagers to death."

Nigel seated himself comfortably and gestured for Tristan to do the same. "So, *Lord* Tristan," he said, the slight emphasis on the title coming out as a sneer, "how fare things at your new demcsne?" He brought his chalice to his lips, and Tristan saw the slight curving of a smile only partially hidden by the rim.

"Let us not play games, *Lord* Nigel," Tristan said easily and smiled to himself as the man's demeanor became guarded. "I am not as dense as you apparently believe."

"I don't understand," Nigel said warily, but his posture remained relaxed.

"You sent men to Greanly with false rumors in their ears, whose intent was doing me harm." Tristan leaned forward, an earnest expression blanketing the hard planes of his face. "Did you think I would kill them, winning you favor with the king?"

"You have been misinformed," Nigel began. "Why would I wrong a man to be allied with me through marriage?"

"I am no fool, Nigel," Tristan's voice rumbled with barely controlled rage. "I know that you expected either my death or the deaths of the men you sent to Greanly that night. Had your simple scheme succeeded, there would be no wedding. 'Tis possible that William would have stripped me of my title and lands were I unable to prove your treachery."

Nigel's face relaxed, and the smug expression returned. "I think perhaps you have been too long at war, D'Argent. Do you suspect every man of deceiving you?"

"Nay." Tristan pinned Nigel with the twin daggers of his gaze, relishing the moment before he revealed his best evidence. "Only those whose sins are confessed by others."

Nigel carefully set his chalice down on a small table, and his eyes became hooded. "The men sully my intentions toward you with their talk?"

"Nay, not *the men*. One man." Tristan rose to stand at the hearth, his back to Nigel. "You overestimated Donald's loyalty."

Tristan heard Nigel rise from his chair. "That toady bastard," he cried. "What lies has he spoken?"

"He has spoken enough." Tristan turned to face Nigel. "I should kill you where you stand," he said quietly, thoughtfully, and was pleased to see Nigel blanch under his swarthy skin. The slimly built fop stepped casually behind his chair.

"I have done you no wrong, Tristan D'Argent," he insisted, pointing a bony finger. "And I will not take lightly these threats against me."

"'Tis well you don't," Tristan said. He reached into his belt and withdrew the papers tucked carefully beneath. He unfolded one and tossed it at Nigel, such that it sailed through the air to rest on the chair before him. "'Tis the royal decree releasing Greanly's people from your keep."

Nigel's eyebrows rose, and he glanced down at the paper, although he didn't pick it up. He looked back to

Tristan in disbelief when he continued. "I am collecting my people, and we depart this night."

"Ah, but they'll not go easily," Nigel said, his voice doubtful. "Your reputation has preceded you."

"The people know naught of my reputation, save the lies that you have perpetrated. Any matter, they are my property and will do as I command, or they will pay the price." Tristan's gaze never wavered from Nigel's shocked face. "As will you if you interfere."

"This is the manner with which you thank the man who has so generously cared for your bequeathment?" Nigel's animated brows drew downward, and his face darkened. "With accusations of treachery and insults?"

Tristan ignored the questions.

"I depart with Greanly's villagers who would go with me this night," he reiterated. "The ones who do not will soon follow. By now, my men have begun loading Greanly's share of Seacrest's stores, and what we cannot carry, we will return for."

Nigel's mouth gaped. "I have given you no leave to enter my stores!"

"'Tis not your leave that I require," Tristan said, waving a hand to William's document. "Although you did bid my sheriff to go where he would."

"You shall pay dearly for this," Nigel seethed, realizing his mistake. He gripped the back of the chair he stood behind.

"Give my regrets to Lady Ellora and Lady Soleilbert." Tristan drained the remaining wine in his cup casually and set it down on the table with a satisfying thunk—'twas good wine. He strode toward the portal.

"D'Argent, you will not dismiss me! What of the betrothal?" Nigel cried at Tristan's retreating back. "'Tis of royal decree as well!"

Without stopping, Tristan tossed a crumpled parchment

over his shoulder so that it landed in the rushes without a sound. Nigel stood transfixed as Tristan opened one of the massive oaken slabs and left, the hall echoing its slam as he exited.

Nigel swung the chair he held into a grouping of tables with a high-pitched yell, sending splintered shards flying.

Right now, he thought, *that bastard pillages stores belonging to me, and I can do naught to stop him.*

Any who would heed Nigel's command to stop Greanly's wagons from departing would surely be outmatched by the seasoned soldiers and slaughtered. Although Nigel cared little for the commoners' lives, without soldiers and serfs there would be no one to provide for the noble's keep. The population would suffer enough should D'Argent succeed in luring some away.

Nigel picked up his chalice and drained it, tossing the intricately carved pewter piece into the hearth with a loud clang and a shower of sparks.

"My lord?" Ellora appeared on the steps, a perplexed look on her face. "Is aught amiss? Where is Lord Tristan?"

"He is gone, thanks to your stupid, hulking daughter."

"What do you mean?" Ellora descended the stairs and retrieved the wadded parchment to which Nigel pointed as if in answer. She quickly scanned the paper and looked to her husband in shock. "He has broken the betrothal? But 'tis by William's own hand!"

"I know that, you stupid bitch!" Nigel's arms flailed about him as if he were having a fit.

Ellora flinched as if she had been struck, but continued her query out of desperation. "Has he given cause?" she pressed.

"I know not the reasoning of a thieving bastard such as he," Nigel roared and closed the gap between he and Ellora. He reached for her and shook her violently.

"Perhaps he desires a woman smaller than his horse and less dense!"

"My lord," Ellora pleaded, struggling to break free. "Please release me."

"Or perhaps he has heard of your failure to conceive and fears his wife would be barren as well." He shoved Ellora from him and sent her crashing into a nearby table where she clung. "Is that not the reason you were cuckolded in the first place? Because you could provide but one worthless girl child?"

"Please stop," Ellora whimpered as he advanced on her, his fists clenched.

"Nay," he growled and grabbed his lady by her hairpiece, tearing the fine linen veil and eliciting a cry of pain as he jerked her face near his. "Nay, I'll not stop and let some green bastard who licks William's feet for his favor lay waste to all I have worked for."

He shook her by her hair again and, with his other hand, grabbed her throat. Ellora's head tilted up against her will until she gazed with fear into Nigel's blazing face.

"D'Argent said naught about breaking the betrothal this night, but I know he will petition William. And if it is by fault of that sow you call daughter that we lose our wealth, I will personally"—he shook her once, hard, for emphasis—"*personally* flay the lard from her myself." Nigel shoved her away again, and this time, Ellora fell, gasping, to the rushes.

Nigel stormed to the hall door but paused before exiting to address his wife, who now lay sobbing. "I have further business to attend to this night if I hope to salvage this alliance. If you value your life, you will not seek me."

Unable to speak, Ellora merely kept her eyes averted while her husband left the hall. Black, thick hatred for Nigel boiled up inside her until she was nauseous, and she beat her balled fist against the hard-packed floor in impotent rage.

Slowly, she gained her feet, sore and tense and unbelievably weary. *All my labors,* she thought, *all of the years spent refining Soleilbert's skills for her to be so casually refused.* The feeling was all too familiar to Ellora, and her pride spasmed under the sting.

She looked down at the mangled parchment still clutched in her fist. Carefully, she unfolded the paper and smoothed the wrinkles from it across her bosom. Unless the betrothal was repudiated by the king himself, Ellora knew that Tristan was bound to make Soleilbert Lady of Greanly or he would be stripped of his worth.

But even should the king somehow allow Tristan to dishonor her daughter in such a manner, Ellora vowed that she would not.

CHAPTER 8

"Must we leave immediately?" Mary asked of Haith. "'Tis so sudden."

The women stood in front of Mary's and John's home at Seacrest, where John, Barrett, and a dark-skinned foreigner helped strange soldiers load the family's possessions into a wagon. Already, the cart bulged with other villagers' belongings.

John was the one to answer his wife's question, pausing on his way back into the cottage. Although the torchlight emphasized the fatigue etched on his features, his eyes gleamed.

"Aye, Mary," he said, "Lord Tristan wants to get us all out from under Nigel while he's here to protect us."

"Protect us?" Haith asked. She wondered what manner of man this new lord was to take such quick measure of Nigel's evilness. Perhaps she would have a chance to protect Bertie and herself after all.

John shrugged. "Dunno, milady. But I trust him." Mary's slim husband rejoined the moving operation with an enigmatic grin.

Haith was left confused and concerned by John's comments. At this hectic pace, the villagers, Haith and Minerva included, would be quit of Seacrest within the hour, leaving no time for farewells. Haith's thoughts were of Soleilbert and how she would find a way to reach her and explain before the wagons departed. She dared not enter the hall after her earlier confrontation with Nigel. She thought to perhaps enlist Mary for the task, but the woman was already moving away, calling out instructions.

"Ay, there! Don't set that chair upon my crocks, you great lout!"

Minerva appeared suddenly at Haith's side, holding the bridle of their ancient nag, who carried the satchels and sacks of their belongings tied to its pommel.

"He comes," the old woman whispered, taking hold of Haith's arm in an urgent grip. Her eyes were black as the night curled around them and sparkled with something akin to excitement.

"Who?" Haith asked, but then believed her question answered when she saw Nigel striding across the bailey toward them.

Fear instantly gripped Haith's insides, causing them to twist in panic. Did he plan on preventing her leave of Seacrest? Would he deny their bargain? She turned to flee but found Minerva's claws clutching her tighter.

"Minerva, release me, I pray!"

"Nay, faery!" Minerva's grip was strong, urging Haith to hold her place. "He must know—"

"Nay!" Haith twisted away and bolted from Minerva's reach. She ran, dodging between the cottages, heedless to Minerva's calls.

"Come back, Haith! You'll nae be safe!"

Haith ran until she reached the bailey's great wooden wall and could run no further. She spun left, then right, trying to quickly determine the best direction in which to flee. To the left lay the stables, but the thought of being trapped in that dark interior with Nigel once more was unthinkable. Haith ran to the right, deeper into the village.

Her frightened scream pierced the starry night when Nigel stepped from behind a building and grabbed Haith, dragging her against the rough wall with him.

"You think to escape me, sweet?" He chuckled while she writhed in his arms. "I cannot allow that. Your very life depends on my charity now, Haith, and I would be repaid for your deceit."

"I owe you nothing." Haith spat the words in his face. "By your own word do I leave Seacrest this night. You gave me a choice, and I chose! Now release me!"

Haith's sound reasoning was rewarded with the backside of Nigel's hand.

"You owe me *all,* bastard whore, and I'll take it now."

Nigel fell on her despite her struggles, knocking them both to the dirt. Although his build was not bulky, his muscles were sinewy and lean, and he easily pinned Haith's hands above her head while he fumbled for the hem of her tangled gown. Haith screamed when his hand brushed her bare leg, and Nigel swiftly silenced her again.

"Call out once more, and I shall kill the hag. Do you ken?" He wagged a finger under her nose as if she were a child. Blood trickled teasingly down her nose and chin.

Haith nodded gingerly, but when Nigel tugged once more at her skirt, she grasped at any possibility of escape.

"Greanly," she croaked, her throat constricted with tears and shame and hatred. "You need me there."

"What?" Nigel froze and looked closely into her face.

"Donald's welfare is yet unknown. I-I will send you word of Lord Tristan's plans." Haith tried to pull down her skirts by sliding along the ground, but Nigel held her firm. "But only if you release me now, without harm."

"Is that so?" he asked, as if her answer was some sort of new, interesting language.

Haith didn't trust her voice to speak, so she merely nodded. At her answer, Nigel's head dropped in thought, and for a moment, Haith hoped he would release her. She bravely found her voice.

"Will you honor your word, my lord?"

When Nigel raised his eyes to bore into Haith's, she saw not resignation or defeat in them, but pure, oily black evil. His voice was smooth, and he even smiled slightly, one eyebrow arching into a malicious peak.

"Of course I will honor my word."

Haith breathed a small sigh, but her relief was short-lived.

"However, because of your earlier trickery, I am not so convinced you will keep yours." Nigel's eyes flitted over Haith's pale face. "I will release you to D'Argent so that you may do my bidding. But know that if you renege on our deal this time, sweet Haith, I *will* kill you."

Nigel leaned down and ran his tongue along Haith's cheek. She tried to turn her head aside, but he merely moved closer, his hot breath seeming to penetrate her very skin as he spoke. "And to show you that I do not make idle threats, you will not go without first giving me my due."

Haith had not noticed Nigel's success in undoing his chausses, and now, fear flooded her like an icy river as he threw himself against her. His hips pushed at her forcefully, frantically, as his one free hand struggled to eliminate the thin underskirt separating them.

Haith screamed with all of her might when she heard the rending sound of her undergarment being torn free and Nigel's cry of triumph. She shrieked until her voice broke and flailed wildly with her legs, but it was of no use. Nigel quickly adjusted himself, and she felt something pointy and hot pressed at her most private part.

But then Nigel was no longer atop her; instead, he was sliding down the bailey's rough wall some lengths away.

Haith scrambled backward, sobbing hysterically and still screaming while pushing her skirts down. Minerva was at her side, gathering Haith into her arms and rocking gently.

"All is well, faery. I have you now," she crooned. She smoothed Haith's sweat-dampened locks from her face. "He didna breach you, did he?"

Haith shook her head and buried it deeper into Minerva's wrinkled neck. "How did you find me?" Her teeth chattered a rattling tattoo of fear.

"I didna find you, lass," Minerva said softly. *"He did."*

Haith turned her head to see who Minerva had named as her rescuer and saw a huge man, magnificent broad sword in hand, standing over Nigel's crumpled, moaning body.

Blond hair ruffled in the breeze. Blue eyes pierced Haith's heart with an icy fissure of recognition.

The man in Haith's dreams stood not twenty paces from her.

"Minerva, I must be mad," Haith murmured before she sank blissfully into the chasm of unconsciousness.

Haith awoke still cradled in Minerva's arms and to the sounds of her singsong chanting. The dark alleyway between the furthermost cottages and the outer wall was unusually bright. During her faint, a host of Greanly and Seacrest men had arrived bearing torches, and the din from angry shouts bounced wildly off the close space.

Mary rushed to her side, her babe in her arms. But even as her friend knelt in the soft dirt, Haith pushed away from Minerva and leaned forward to see the commotion beyond.

A large group of men blocked most of Haith's view, but—there!—rising a head above the crowd, he glanced at her.

Her heart clenched and expanded with joy such as she had heretofore only known while sleeping. He was real! That fateful night in the stables, he truly *had* come to her, had sworn to protect her, and he had returned!

Haith stood unsteadily, ignoring Minerva's and Mary's concerned voices and gentle hands. Slowly, she made her way toward the group, her whole being reaching out and concentrating on the man in their midst. Her gaze transfixed, the sights and sounds going on around her muted—unable to touch or deter her.

As she neared, the crowd quieted and parted easily for her. The village men either stared openly in shock at her appearance or respectfully averted their eyes. Her kirtle was torn and muddy, and the blood around her bruised mouth and cheek was drying to a numb crust. She ignored them all, the morbidly curious and the sympathetic alike, approaching her target.

When Haith stood not two paces from her savior, she stopped and stared dumbly up into his hard, angry face. A warm, tingly band of energy seemed to wrap around the pair as her hand slowly rose as if of its own accord and reached out—

"Look at the whore." Nigel's voice cut through the gossamer web woven around Haith, and she started, dropping her hand and spinning in fright to where he stood nearby. "Now she throws herself at you, D'Argent. Do you see now that I speak the truth?"

Haith looked bewildered between Nigel's red, glaring face and this man—D'Argent's—stony, unreadable visage. Was Nigel accusing her of instigating the near rape?

But wait—*D'Argent*? That was—

Barrett interrupted Haith's tumbling thoughts when he shouldered his way easily through the mob to face Nigel, his boulder-like fists clenched. "You're a filthy liar!" he roared, causing Nigel to retreat a step in surprise at first, then approach the mountainous man with brazenness.

"I'll see you hanged for speaking to a lord in such a manner," Nigel said.

"Yer not my lord anymore," Barrett said, completely unconcerned by the threat. The sheriff pointed at the blond man, who watched the exchange closely but spared not a single glance for the bedraggled woman about whom the pair debated. "I've sworn my fealty to Lord Tristan, and with him's where me loyalty lays."

Haith's small cry of dismay went unnoticed as Nigel looked taken aback, but he did not back down from the sheriff.

"You beggardly outcast! You have no business in a matter between lords."

"This wee gel"—Barrett swept his yard-long arm in Haith's direction—"would never throw herself at any bloke, much less the likes of you. I knew her mum and sire well, and Minerva, too, and she was brought up right."

"She was *brought up*," Nigel sneered, "by a whore mother, and then a hag sorceress who was cast from the keep by my own good wife."

A murmur rippled through the crowd as Minerva appeared near Tristan's side and slunk menacingly toward Nigel.

"You sully my Corinne's name?" Minerva said in an eerie whisper. "You know naught of which you speak, Lord S-s-snake."

"Get from me, witch." Nigel's voice cracked slightly. "I shall deal with you and your whore later."

"Nay!" Minerva shouted in Nigel's face, causing him to flinch and reflexively raise his hand to strike.

Minerva's skinny arm shot out to encircle Nigel's wrist with a gnarled hand, and immediately, Nigel cried out in agony. The crowd of men stepped back with murmurs of alarm and fright as Seacrest's lord fell shaking to his knees in the grip of the frail-looking woman.

"Holy Christ!" he screamed shrilly. Tiny wisps of smoke curled from his arm where Minerva gripped it. "In the name of God, release me, you devil's spawn!"

"You gave the child an offer of betrothal, and she accepted!" Minerva leaned closer to peer into Nigel's face, and he squeezed his eyes shut in terror and pain. The smell of roasting meat wafted through the bailey. "You nae longer hold dominion over her by your own words, and we shall leave Seacrest this night."

"Go then!" Nigel roared, throwing his head back, his spine curving unnaturally. Sweat streamed down his pale, drawn face.

Haith came out of her stupor with a start. "Minerva! Hold—you're killing him!"

The old woman released Nigel's arm as easily as dropping a stick, and the lord stumbled to his feet and backed quickly away. Haith rushed to Minerva's side, urging her away from Nigel, but she would not be moved.

The crowd gasped in amazement as they saw the blackened and bloodied strip of flesh encircling the lord's wrist.

"Bride of Satan!" Nigel cried, cradling his tortured arm, heedless of the tears shimmering in his beady eyes. "You have scorched me with your hellish fire!" He spun toward the crowd of uneasy onlookers. "Seize her!"

But no one stepped forward to obey their lord.

"The rot on your arm shows your true heart," Minerva accused and raised a gnarled finger to point at Nigel.

Crone of ages, Mother and Maid,
Beware to all whom evil aid.
For the ill you spread comes back to thee,
Three times three times three.

Nigel's face took on the pallor of moonlight, and he remained rooted to the spot, unable to drag his eyes from the tiny old woman who had singled him out. From the crowd, whispers of "a curse" tingled in his ears, and some of the men genuflected.

"Go to hell." Nigel's voice shook.

Minerva threw back her cloth-covered head, and laughter burst from her like a silvery font. Her mirth was Nigel's undoing, and he fled the alley, sending some of the townsfolk gathered there scattering, too. Those who remained watched the strange nobleman, Barrett, Minerva, and Haith with uneasy curiosity.

With Nigel gone, Haith turned to Tristan, and the truth of her situation settled around her like a dense, dirty fog. "You are Tristan D'Argent, Lord of Greanly?" she asked, searching those eyes she knew so well from dreams.

"Yea," Tristan's deep voice rumbled. He returned her appraisal, but instead of wonder, he watched Haith as one would behold a deadly, but beautiful, viper. "And you are Haith of Seacrest, Lord James's daughter."

Haith slowly nodded assent, and her throat constricted as if trying to prevent her words. "You are my sister's betrothed."

Tristan's lip curled in disgust. "And you have bound yourself to the man who would see me dead."

CHAPTER
9

Haith struggled to keep pace on foot with the broken-down nag that carried Minerva. Her thin leather slippers, many seasons worn, seemed more of a burden than a relief. With each step, they successfully caught the tiniest and most jagged stones underfoot and ricocheted them toe to heel within their confines. Every score or so of strides she took, Haith was forced to stop and remove the offending pebbles before hobbling quickly to catch up once more.

The moon was invisible in its downward descent toward dawn, draping the land in the blackest pitch. Haith was not the only weary traveler among those on the dark pilgrimage to Greanly. Mothers tried in vain to quiet fussy children, rudely awakened for the unexpected journey. The older children walked when able, and those who were too small to cover long stretches or who grew too weary to continue were hoisted in front of those who had room on their horses. Several soldiers' laps were already claimed by sleeping children, and Haith envied their cozy perches as well as their innocent, youthful slumber.

The haphazard departure had produced a motley caravan of hastily piled wagons, animals, and people—those brave enough to come after the terrifying incident recently enacted in Seacrest's bailey. A few more than one hundred villagers traveled in the midst of Greanly's soldiers, not even a third of the original refugees belonging to Greanly either by birth or marriage.

Several wagons, filled to the brim with grains, animal feed, salted meats, kegs of ale and wine, butter and cheese—a small portion of Greanly's share, but as much as could be transported at once—led the caravan. Barrett rode alongside the lead wagon with the dark man called Pharao. The foreigner had met her eye a number of times thus far, and Haith sensed a cool contempt behind his hooded lids.

That contempt apparently stemmed from the similar demeanor of the man's liege. After Tristan's reference to Donald as Haith's betrothed, the lord had stalked away to join his soldiers, leaving Haith in Minerva's arms, hurt and still largely in shock. The glimpses she had caught of Tristan since had been one-sided—he paid her no heed whatsoever—and Haith marveled that this was the same man who once held her so tenderly in the stables.

Haith felt as though her heart had been ripped from her body.

In the span of a few short hours, every aspect of her life had changed drastically. The man she longed for, had dreamed of almost nightly since she was a young girl, was to wed her beloved Bertie by royal decree. Haith, a lord's daughter fully recognized by her father, was now trapped in a farcical betrothal to a violent, grotesque laborer. Haith had left the only home she'd ever known to flee Nigel, and in doing so, had quite possibly sentenced herself to a slow spiritual death.

I never even got to say goodbye, she thought to herself

as the heaviness of her burdens descended on her fully. Not to Bertie to try and explain that she would see her soon, nor to her mother and her cherished Papa at their graves on a knoll overlooking Seacrest. There had been no time. All that Haith now owned was contained in a few rough sacks tied to Minerva's saddle.

And perched on that very saddle, Minerva sang as if on her way to a London fair. The cheery Scots melody about a faery and her mortal mate grated on Haith's already worn temper.

"Minerva, I beg you," Haith pleaded, stumbling across a rocky pothole, "cease your noise. 'Tis not a journey to be making merry about."

"And why not?" the old woman asked easily. "You have found your soulmate, and even now we follow him to our new abode." She swiftly broke into another rousing verse.

Haith looked around hastily to see if any nearby travelers had heard Minerva's proclamation and stumbled again, this time falling on all fours. Fatigue and sorrow paralyzed her, and instead of once again scrambling to her feet, Haith remained crouched in the dirt. She struggled to stem the flow of tears that threatened by squeezing her eyes shut, but it was of no use.

Minerva stopped singing abruptly and wheeled her nag to stand over Haith's prone form.

"Och, lass, get yourself up," she admonished. "We doona want to lag behind now."

"I cannot," Haith whispered.

"Lady Haith,"—Rufus, a village man, stopped to kneel—"can you continue?"

"I fear not, kind Rufus," Haith said shakily. "I'll just rest here a while before I go on."

Soon another villager paused to inquire about Haith's

welfare, as did a group of folk in a wagon. Then another. Soon, nearly half of the party had stopped.

"M'lady, shall I carry you?"

"We shall carry her together."

"Perhaps she could sit atop a wagon?"

Haith tried in vain to be heard above the conversation. She knew that the longer they stood idle, the more likely it was they would draw their lord's attention, something Haith could not face in her present state.

Minerva, too, waved away their concerns. "She'll be fine in a moment. Go on with you."

The villagers remained unconvinced.

"Her slippers are filled with blood."

"M'lady, let me—"

"Take my arm, m'lady."

Haith felt the earth rumble beneath her palms as two gigantic hooves appeared on the ground before her. She raised her head up, up, up the lean gray muscles of the horse's forelegs to the face of the man astride it. He looked decidedly furious.

"Is aught amiss?" Tristan demanded.

Rufus volunteered helpfully. "M'lady's feet gave out on her, m'lord. She can walk no further."

Tristan's nostrils flared, but he remained silent, creating an awkward tension within the group of travelers gathered 'round Haith. Rufus cleared his throat self-consciously under his lord's murderous glare, then moved to take Haith's arm.

"Let me carry you, m'lady," he offered, starting to pull Haith to her feet.

"Unhand the wench," Tristan said abruptly, causing Rufus to drop Haith's arm. Haith fell to the hard ground once more with a small "oof."

"My lord?" Rufus asked in bewilderment.

"She will walk on her own, or she shall be left behind,"

Tristan commanded. "We are not yet halfway to Greanly, and I will waste no time on those who cannot keep up."

Haith blinked in shock at the harsh words issuing from Tristan's finely molded lips. His gaze fell on her, and Haith wanted to shrink into oblivion for her weakness. But there was to be more.

"From this moment forward, none shall refer to this woman as 'my lady,'" he declared. "She has pledged herself to a commoner, and thus loses all privileges of noble regard." Tristan's glare met the widened eyes of all those gathered. "She is one of you now, and will be treated as such."

Rufus and the other villagers shuffled their feet and murmured in confusion and embarrassment for their lady. The group feared their new lord as an unfamiliar ruler, yet they were loath to obey his commands.

With her eyes fixed on Tristan's sturdy, supple boots, resting easily in the fine stirrups of his saddle, Haith's temper rose. How dare he humiliate her in such a manner in front of her people for not keeping up while he himself sat comfortably astride? And stripping her of her respect and title because she had made a choice to save Soleilbert and Ellora from humiliation, as well as to protect herself from Nigel's lechery! What of his vow to protect her? Alas, it seemed he was intent on doing just the opposite by declaring to the good pilgrims the betrothal forced upon her. And he seemed determined to enforce the agreement.

Well, sorry for him, Haith thought. Tristan's manner of speaking to her nearly made her treacherous pact with Nigel more bearable.

Haith mustered her remaining strength to once more stand. She faced Tristan boldly, and even in her present state of dishevelment, her posture was regal, her chin tilted arrogantly. Her heart gave a tiny squeak of protest as all tender feelings for this man she knew only in her dreams were set ablaze by her burning anger.

Tristan's horse danced backward nervously when Haith rose before him, drawing a confused frown from Tristan as he quieted the beast.

Haith dismissed the prancing animal with nary a glance as her eyes were only on Tristan. When she addressed him, her words were of Minerva's native tongue.

"And you, my fine lord, are naught but a headless, braying ass who goes about not knowing he spews shit with every word."

The majority of the villagers quickly broke rank, most hiding smiles behind coughs and fluttering hands. Tristan's brows drew together, his glare alternating between Haith and Minerva, who sat calmly on her nag, smiling serenely.

"What say you, wench?" Tristan demanded of Haith, his complexion growing ruddy.

Haith ignored his question and hobbled off in the direction of the other villagers as gracefully as her bruised feet would allow.

Tristan turned to Minerva. "What did she say?"

Minerva reached across the gap separating her from Tristan and patted his thigh. "Not to worry yerself, m'lord. She said merely that your words are wise and she will do her best to please you." Minerva turned her nag around and clucked gently, leaving Tristan alone on his horse.

"Why is it that I do not believe you, old woman?" he muttered, shaking his head.

Tristan's eyes picked out Haith's slim back as she leaned on a village man's arm, and for a moment, he was struck with a pang of regret. Feelings that had been absent for many years tormented him cruelly once more: uncertainty, remorse, humiliation. Loneliness.

Perhaps I should have fled with her that night in the

stables, he thought as he spurred his mount forward. Or sought her before meeting with Nigel because in truth, he knew not the full details of her betrothal arrangement.

But he did know that having her so near was giving rise to a longing as intense as that he had last known as a boy, alone and abandoned on the streets of Paris.

If he could not persuade William to break the betrothal to Soleilbert quickly, Michaelmas could very well find Tristan shackled to the sister of one he could not forget. Haith by then would be Donald's wife and under his rule at Greanly, placing her forever within his reach but untouchable.

Just as in his dreams.

CHAPTER
10

Haith slumped in a chair in the front room of the large cottage she and Minerva were to share at Greanly. The dwelling had been constructed for the express purpose of housing a healer and her supplies, the forward-most room having walls lined with shelves and racks and pegs. The massive hearth took up an entire wall and had iron accessories embedded in the mortar to hold pots and kettles. There was a separate oven for baking, a large plank bench for creating and mixing remedies, and several newly built, sturdy wooden chairs.

Minerva danced around the well-equipped chamber with glee despite the stiffness in her limbs from the long journey astride.

"Oh, faery!" she exclaimed, dancing over to Haith and clutching the young woman by her shoulders. "Is it nae the loveliest cottage you've ever set eyes upon?"

Haith pulled away in irritation. "Yea, Minerva. 'Tis grand."

"Och, lass," Minerva tsked, "why do you mope so?"

"Why do I mope? Are you mad?" Haith stood abruptly,

tossing the bundle of her possessions on the workbench. Dawn had risen hours ago, and the cottage rooms were awash in bright light.

"I've been sent to this place to betray my sister and destroy the one who you claim to be my savior!" She paced the room like a cornered fox, running her fingers through her tangled curls. "Lord Tristan has humiliated me at every turn, although his reason I know not."

"Mayhap he was merely surprised at Nigel's plan for you to marry."

"Merely surprised?" Haith spun to face the old woman. "He forbid the villagers' use of my rightful title, then proclaimed me weak and unworthy!" She stormed through the rear doorway only to reemerge seconds later and continue her tirade.

"He's Soleilbert's *betrothed*," she raged, her blue eyes flashing like lightning on the sea. "Could he not have imparted that tiny bit of knowledge to me a fortnight ago?"

Minerva's ears perked up. "You've spoken before last eve? You did not tell me this, lass."

Haith sighed heavily and closed her eyes, willing patience into her words. "I thought he was but another dream."

"I knew it! I knew it!" Minerva resumed her merry jig from earlier. "He's the one for you, faery!" The woman clasped her hands to her age-flattened bosom. "You stopped speaking of him so long ago, I feared you had lost him forever.

"But now,"—Minerva glided to the bench, smiling gamely—"I know that the runes spoke true! He is the man you will marry, Haith."

"Have you not heard my words?" Haith joined the woman at the bench and began jerking items from her bundle. "He is betrothed to my *sister* by William's own hand!"

"Bah," Minerva scoffed, carefully setting tiny crocks filled with her precious salves along a shelf. "'Tis no matter, that. Bertie's nae meant for him. I've seen it meself."

Haith opened her mouth to ask Minerva what exactly she meant when a sharp crack caused her to jump. She watched the old healer walk calmly to the broom that had fallen across the cottage's threshold and right it. Haith's lips formed the words silently as Minerva spoke.

Lady Corra, your warning is set.
May our visitors be well-met.

No sooner had the simple rhyme found flight than Greanly's sheriff appeared in the doorway, his huge bulk blocking the view of the bailey and beyond.

"Ho, Minerva," Barrett called and poked his shaggy head inside the cottage. He spied Haith trying valiantly to tidy her bedraggled appearance, and after glancing over his massive shoulder for onlookers, he gave a sharp bow. "Lady Haith."

"Good morn to you, Barrett! Enter!" Minerva waved the sheriff in while she returned to her unpacking. "I'd offer you a bite to ease the journey we've had, but"—she chuckled and swept a mostly empty shelf with her wrinkled palm—"I fear our larder has yet to be stocked."

"Yea," Haith added, still smarting from Barrett's covert attempt at homage. "'Twould seem our good lord has forgotten to provide sustenance for his new tenants." She scowled and began assisting Minerva in her task.

"Oh, nay, m'lady," Barrett said hastily, shuffling his large feet. "'Tis what I came to tell you." He eyed the object Minerva had just removed from a sack warily—a colored jar filled with what looked suspiciously to be small eyeballs.

"Well, get on with it then, man," Minerva demanded

and shook the jar in his direction. "These won't be jumping out at you."

Barrett flushed. "Er, aye. The wagons from Seacrest are being unloaded now, and the lord says to come and get what you'll be needing for a day or two to hold you over. The rest'll be divvied up when all's put to rights in the stores."

Haith grabbed a recently emptied sack and a woven basket. "Our thanks for the word, Barrett. Minerva, I'll get what I think we'll have need of and bring it back."

Haith was moving toward the door when Barrett blocked her path.

"Nay, m'lady," he said, holding up his hands with a sheepish grimace. "The lord bade me fetch you to the hall right away. He wishes to speak with you."

"Does he now?" Haith replied in a deceptively calm tone.

"Aye." Barrett nodded. "Right away."

"You may tell *Lord Tristan*,"—Haith poked a finger somewhere beneath Barrett's sternum with each word, backing the burly sheriff through the cottage doorway—"that I have more pressing matters to attend to at this time. Should he desire to speak with me—"

The pair were now in the open air of the bailey, and drawing numerous stares from villagers. Barrett looked around him helplessly as Haith's temper found flight.

"—he can very well *request* my presence like a civilized person, although I know that may be difficult for him."

Behind Haith, Minerva moved to the doorway of the cottage and leaned against the frame, her hand to her mouth to cover her smile.

"Furthermore," Haith continued, "until he sees me wed and I in truth can no longer be called 'lady,' it would bode well for him to treat me with the respect of one equal to his station and not *bid* me to his audience as if I were some *serving wench!*"

Haith stood nose to chest with Greanly's sheriff, her cheeks high in color and her bosom heaving. Barrett stuttered and fidgeted with his discomfiture.

"Er—very well, m'lady," he stammered. "I shall surely tell him."

Haith nodded once and then spun on her heel in what she assumed was the direction of the storehouse.

"Lady Haith?" Barrett called to her back.

Haith spun around, bringing her hands to her hips and sending her sack and basket swinging. "Aye, Barrett. What is it now?"

The sheriff raised a hand to wiggle one finger covertly in the opposite direction. "Er, the wagons . . ."

Haith flushed and stormed past Barrett in the direction he'd indicated. "Thank you."

"Not at all."

Tristan leaned back in the lord's chair with a sigh of exhaustion. He'd been without the comfort of his bed for two nights, and the stress of recent events had put him on extreme edge.

Which was exactly the reason he'd sent the sheriff to retrieve Haith. His words and behavior during last night's journey haunted him, and he wished to repair in some way the damage his shock and dismay had prompted.

But damn it all! How could she so casually bind herself to the wretched Donald? Especially when Tristan had promised to return for her, to protect her? Did his word count for naught? That night in the stables had been so tender between them, as if they were two halves finally made whole. Yet she could not trust him with her troubles at Seacrest.

Last eve, something had whispered to him to walk down that alley at Seacrest; it was as if Haith had called to him. When he'd seen Nigel sprawled atop her, the shock of it had rooted Tristan's feet to the dirt before the trained warrior in him burst forth with a vengeance. He'd flung the slight man from Haith with one hand and drawn his sword to end the viper's life right then.

But he had been stopped by the sound of her sobs, distracted by her very presence, looking so much like the vision in his dream.

Tristan, save me.

And then the words she had actually spoken before his intervention had registered in his rage: *Will you honor your word, my lord?*

Tristan bolted upright in his chair as another possibility occurred to him. The night in the stables, he had been drawn to that place and had awoken to her presence. At the very moment of their embrace, Donald and his lackeys had been foolishly descending upon Greanly. Mere coincidence?

And then, last eve, when Tristan had somehow been led to intervene on her behalf, had it been planned thus?

Her claim of ignorance of his identity seemed real enough, but in truth, what did he know about the woman? That she was not at her beloved sister's side on what should have been a momentous occasion struck him as odd. Why did Haith not live in the family keep, instead living in a hovel with the village healer? Nigel himself had said that Lady Ellora had banished her, but for what reason?

Treachery?

Was this red-haired vixen who haunted his dreams and stirred his blood a conspirator with Nigel against him? Had he delivered the very enemy into his home?

Tristan's thoughts were disrupted when Barrett

entered the hall and approached with his usual lumbering gait.

"My lord," the sheriff nodded, "I've returned from your errand."

Tristan grinned. "I see that, Barrett. Where is she?"

"Er, well"—Barrett dropped his gaze—"she wouldn't come."

"What?"

"Forgive me, my lord, but,"—the sheriff unwillingly met Tristan's glare to explain—"Lady Haith said that she was going to get supplies for her an' Minerva and that 'twas more important than speaking with you, er—" He cleared his throat. "—at this time, that be."

"You jest." Tristan's blood pounded in his temples as the headache he'd been fighting stomped across his skull.

"Nay, m'lord. She also said that 'til she's wed, she expects to be addressed as 'lady' and treated like it, too."

"She did, did she?"

"Aye."

Tristan steepled his fingers before his lips. "And at this moment, she fetches supplies from the wagons?"

"Aye, m'lord."

Tristan rose and stalked past Barrett, his footsteps echoing like thunder in the hall. He flung open the heavy oaken portal and strode purposefully in the direction of Greanly's storehouse.

He had no trouble picking out Haith's unique form from among the villagers gathered around the wagons. Her coppery tresses glinted in the morning light, and the faces of his soldiers doling out goods were smiling and jovial in her presence.

Several of the clustered villagers saw Tristan's angry approach and discreetly moved away from who they guessed was his intended target. Because Haith was unaware of his advance, her head jerked around in shock when Tristan's hand gripped her arm like an iron band and dragged her away from the crowd.

Haith emitted a high-pitched scream as Tristan pulled her roughly in the direction of the keep. Her sack of grain and basket of turnips tumbled to the dust.

"Unhand me!" she shrieked, flailing her free arm at him.

"Shut your mouth, wench," Tristan growled and walked faster, causing Haith to stumble. He jerked her aright and continued without a glance in her direction. "You would be well-advised not to disobey me a second time."

Up the steps and into the hall he continued, dragging her by her arm. Once inside, he released her and bellowed to the few serfs milling about at various chores.

"Out!" he roared, one long arm indicating the open portal.

The villagers dropped the tasks at hand and quickly filed out the door. So incensed was Tristan that he almost missed Haith's near escape, trying to slip behind Barrett amidst the departing crowd.

"Not you," Tristan clarified, hauling her from the fleeing queue. He slammed the door after the last person had passed through and turned to face Haith.

"You have but mere minutes to explain your behavior, wench, before my temper overpowers my charity."

"I have naught to explain to you," Haith retorted with her nose in the air and moved toward the door.

Tristan stepped before her, barring her escape. "You forget that I am lord here," he said darkly, "and you will do as I command."

Haith's anger dissipated like smoke in the breeze, and she gulped audibly as she realized her predicament. Alone in a strange hall in the presence of a very large, very angry, and very forceful man. Her mouth was suddenly dry as sand, and she stared up at Tristan as he continued to speak.

"Why don't you begin with how you and your lover plan to have me killed?"

CHAPTER
11

Haith's mouth fell open at the statement. "What did you say?"

"You heard me, Haith."

Her stomach flipped over at his use of her Christian name, and for a moment, she was distracted by the sound of it on his lips. But the memory of his accusation soon flooded her with fear. How could he be so close to the truth?

"Yea, I heard you," she replied. "Have you been drinking?"

Now it was Tristan's turn to look perplexed. "I know not how that is an answer to my question, but nay, I have not. Do not play games with me, wench."

"'Tis no game. Only a drunkard or an idiot would have concocted such an accusation."

Tristan's nostrils flared. "You call me an idiot?"

"You yourself have eliminated the only other possible explanation!" Her desperation made her bold. "If my plan was to see you dead, I could have very well accomplished that task in the stables."

"Aha!" Tristan shouted. "You *did* know my identity!"

"Nay!" Haith's voice rose to match his. "I merely meant to show you how ridiculous your reasoning is!"

"You would do well to provide a better explanation than a wanton display in a horse stall."

"Wanton display?" Haith blanched. She had meant to distract him, not to incur his contempt. "I asked not for your company that night—you offered it."

"Because I thought you a maid in distress," Tristan shot back. "If you were not, then explain your weeping! What were you about that night in the stables?"

"Perhaps I should pose the same question to you, *Lord Tristan,*" Haith countered, bringing her hands to her hips to still their telltale trembling. "Why were you sneaking about in the guise of a commoner within a town not your own?"

"That is none of your concern."

"Then neither is it any of yours why I sought solace there. *Alone,*" she added. "You've called me whore twice in as many moments, and now I would take leave of your presence." Haith moved to pass him, but again he blocked her.

"You have given me no answers." Tristan's hands gripped her arms, and he glared down at her.

"I heard no question worthy of response."

Tristan's hands tightened, sending throbbing shock waves into Haith's shoulders. "I am lord here, and you will obey me. 'Tis not your place to judge my questions worthy or no."

Haith averted her eyes in stony silence. With every word, Tristan only cut her more deeply. How could he suspect Nigel's plan? And into what jeopardy would Soleilbert's future be cast if he discovered the truth? Indeed, what would Haith's own fate be for aiding Nigel? She vowed to spare herself further injury or incrimination by refusing to speak.

"You will not cooperate?" Tristan asked. When Haith failed to acknowledge him, his mouth became a tight slash. "Very well. Perhaps you will be more comfortable in the company of your fellow traitor."

Once again, Haith was dragged along behind Tristan, but this time, their destination lay deeper within Greanly castle. A new spiral of fear sizzled up Haith's spine, pushing pride aside and prompting her to speak.

"Where do you take me?" she asked as he pulled her down a narrow stone stairwell.

"To join your beloved."

His pace gave her no further opportunity to question him as the passageway became darker and more narrow. A clammy chill began to curl its misty fingers around Haith's ankles. Torches dotted the stone walls intermittently, and their flames danced maniacally in the breeze created by Haith's and Tristan's passing. From up ahead, a brighter glow shone, and sounds of shouts and angry curses reached Haith's ears.

"Barrett!" a scratchy voice called out from the recesses of the lit chamber. "You walking mountain of shit! You'd better have me some victuals!" A sharp, metallic clang echoed in Haith's ears, and the voice grew more insistent. *"Barrett!"*

A moment later, Haith was standing in front of a stone wall that boasted an iron-grilled window and an oaken door with matching bars. Donald the smithy sat like a great toad in a far corner of the cell, hunched on a crude pallet. The stench emanating from the small chamber hit Haith like a blow, and she recoiled from the opening, her hand flying to cover her nose. Only Tristan's firm grip stayed her from fleeing.

"I've brought you a visitor, Donald," Tristan said, his amicable words belying the disgust and anger in his voice.

Donald's eyes grew wide at seeing Haith at the

window, and he struggled to stand, grasping his right arm, which ended below his elbow in a bandaged stump. The breeze elicited by his staggering rush to the opening increased the putrid fumes tenfold, and Haith felt that at any moment she would retch.

"Haith," Donald gasped, "does Lord Nigel accompany you?" The grotesque man's remaining hand grasped the bars that separated him from Haith.

Haith could not speak, so she merely shook her head and squeezed her eyes shut against the stinging fumes. She tried in vain to seal her nose more tightly with her hand.

"Nigel won't be coming for you," Tristan growled, earning a snarl from Donald. "I simply thought you'd enjoy some time with your betrothed." He inclined his head toward Haith.

"Oh, that's very humorous, my lord," Donald sneered and backed away from the window, his eyes flicking nervously to Haith. "Certainly we'll be married right away now that I'm *crippled and imprisoned!* Next time, why don't you bring down a sack of coin and a leg of veal to dangle in front of me, you great bastard!"

"Oh, my God," Haith breathed into her hand. The sight before her sickened her nearly to the point of paralysis. While at Seacrest, where she was faced directly with Nigel's lechery, it had been an easy matter to forget the vile nature of the smithy. But now, faced with the quivering, sweaty bulk of the man, all Haith could think of was escape. "Please," she murmured. Swallowing her pride, she leaned into Tristan. "I beg you, take me from here."

Tristan turned icy eyes to Haith, and his tone was one of false surprise. "You do not wish to visit the man who is to be your husband?"

Haith shook her head. "Nay. Please, my lord, do not do this." She felt the tears welling up in her eyes, but could not stop them. Surely he would not leave her alone with Donald in this damp hell. "He is not—"

At that moment, Donald rushed the wall, flinging himself against the bars with a roar. Haith screamed in fright, then found herself shoved partially behind Tristan's wide back while Donald shouted at her.

"Shut up, you bitch!" Donald gripped the bars with his hand. "Nigel sent you here for me—you're to be *mine*!" He looked to Tristan with a twisted snarl. "Put her in here with me."

"I take no orders from you," Tristan said coolly, and Haith could feel the deep rumble of his voice where her hands gripped his tunic. "Give me the information I seek, and perhaps I will release you."

Haith gasped involuntarily at the suggestion.

Donald merely grunted. "I got nothing to tell you, you great git. She's mine by Lord Nigel's own word."

"Very well." Tristan shrugged, and Haith readied herself to fight him with all of her strength should he move to unlock Donald's cell door.

But to her great surprise, Tristan merely turned, taking Haith's arm before advising Donald a final time. "You would do well to remember, however, that Nigel is at Seacrest and 'tis more likely you'll rot before he comes for you." He started back down the corridor, pulling a shaking Haith along behind him.

"Haith!" Donald screamed until his voice cracked. "You're mine, me foine lady! There's an agreement, and you better stick to it if you know what's good for you!"

Tristan tugged Haith up the stairs, helping her this time when she stumbled in haste and exhaustion. When Donald's voice became too distant to hear, he stopped and leaned her against the stone corridor, staring intently into her tear-streaked face.

Haith stared back at Tristan with puffy, burning eyes.

"Please, you cannot release him," she pleaded. "Donald is a savage, and he would—"

"You did not enter into this betrothal willingly?" Tristan interrupted her.

"Nay." Haith shook her head and hiccoughed. "'Tis true I had no choice, but—"

"Why, Haith? Why would Nigel see you wed to a commoner when to make you a noble match would benefit him?"

Haith became more agitated when Tristan would not release her. His probing eyes unnerved her, and she feared she would accidentally misspeak. She struggled to move away from him.

"Nigel mustn't find out that Donald is imprisoned. If he does, he will come for me." Her voice shook with the tension she felt. "And I will not return to Seacrest!"

Tristan held firm. "Calm yourself, Haith. If I am to help you, you must explain to me exactly what danger Seacrest holds for you."

Haith ceased her struggles and looked at Tristan with all the sadness she felt. "You of all cannot help me."

"Yea. I can." Tristan slowly brought a hand to her cheek and gently brushed away a tear with his thumb, skimming the bruises she'd received from Nigel's hand. He then lowered his head and kissed her there tenderly.

For a fleeting moment, Haith let the touch of his lips sooth her. Then she turned her head, denying herself the forbidden comfort. "Do not be kind to me, Tristan. My only concern must be for my sister."

Tristan took her chin gently and turned it to face him once more. He lowered his head until his lips hovered over hers. "'Tis not your sister who concerns me."

He kissed her then, gently as if he feared she might bruise from the light touch. Haith's eyelids fluttered closed, sending a single teardrop sliding down her face to melt into the seam of their joined mouths.

Tristan raised his head a scant inch from Haith's face. She felt the nearness of him with her entire being, reveled in it, her eyes closed and her lips slightly parted. She sighed.

"Haith," he said, rousing her from her reverie. "We have much to discuss."

"Yea," she breathed, lost in the shimmery glow of his kiss, before realizing what she said. Her eyes popped open. "I mean, nay. Mayhap when you are married—"

"Sh-h," Tristan whispered, drawing a finger across her lips. "The betrothal will not stand. I plan to petition the king for its dissolution."

Haith shook her head vehemently and opened her mouth to speak, but Tristan thwarted her attempt once again.

"Nay. We will untangle this web together, Haith. But not now." He drew her away from the wall with his arm across her back, and they continued through the corridor until he led her into the hall.

"Barrett will accompany you to Minerva for your care. Seek your bed, rest." He stopped in the center of the great room to stare into her eyes. "When you rise, seek me here, and we shall talk. Will you do as I ask?"

Haith searched his face for a long moment, as if seeking her own answer there. "Yea," she said finally. She longed to pour out the fear and anger and regret in her heart to Tristan and be rid of it once and for all. But if she warned him of Nigel's plans now, to what future would Bertie be cast?

At that moment, however, Haith could only comprehend the closeness of Tristan. His broad chest was mere inches from her cheek, and his body heat radiated from him like a gentle sun, his blue eyes darkened with intensity. The urge to touch him was overwhelming.

She reached out her palm and placed it on his chest over his heart. He felt so solid and strong and *real*. Mesmerized as she was, the truth wobbled on her tongue.

Tristan covered her hand with his own, giving her the courage to ask, "You will not disappear again when I wake?"

"Nay." There was no hint of amusement on his face. "I'll not leave you again." And to Haith's thrill, as well as her dread, he lowered his head to kiss her once more.

Tristan's intention had merely been to comfort, but when Haith raised her arms to encircle his neck and draw him closer, the comforter turned into the one in need of solace. The taste of her against his mouth was like water to a man dying of thirst, and he drank of her. He took from her, longing to fill the great, empty place inside of him; to begin to plug the aching void left by too many years of war, too many years alone and without love. Years when he'd had only his dreams of her for sustenance.

With Haith in his arms, Tristan felt the weight of loneliness lift and his fatigue vanish and be replaced with a pulsing, warm light that encircled them both. His mouth tugged at her lips, and she answered his request willingly. Her hands cradled his head, fingers tangling his hair and skimming lightly along his jaw.

Tristan's embrace drew her gently closer still until their bodies bowed with their nearness. His splayed hands on her back pressed her to him as if they would melt to form one being.

A startled gasp within the hall broke the spell of their kiss, and both their heads turned to seek the interloper.

Ellora stood in the hall's open doorway, her outline in dark contrast to the sunny bailey beyond.

And behind Ellora, eyes fixed in shock on the sight before her, stood Soleilbert.

"Haith?" Soleilbert stepped around her mother, who tried in vain to shield her. Her eyes were wide with shock, and hurt confusion clouded her sweet face. "What is the meaning of this?"

"Bertie! I—we—" Haith sputtered, her cheeks flaming.

"I told you, Daughter,"—Ellora rushed to Soleilbert's side—"I told you 'twas her very nature to take that which did not belong to her! She is a slut, true!"

"Lady Ellora," Tristan growled, "I bid you still your tongue from such slander while in my household."

"Yea, quiet, Mother," Soleilbert added. Her tone was unnaturally sharp, eliciting a surprised look from Ellora. "This is between me and my sister."

Bertie closed the gap between herself and Haith and tentatively took her sister's hand. "Haith, tell me true— was Lord Tristan forcing himself upon you?"

Haith's eyes scanned the faces fixed upon her, and she suddenly felt very, very weary. To lie to Soleilbert would not only betray their relationship further, but would also dishonor Tristan and belittle what had moments before passed between them. Haith took a deep breath.

"Nay, Bertie." Her words sounded overloud in the hall. "The embrace you witnessed was consensual."

"Embrace?" Ellora squawked. "You looked as if you would devour each other whole!"

"Mother!" Soleilbert spun around. "If you cannot keep your silence, then be gone! This matter does not warrant your comment!"

"Do not speak to me in such a manner, Soleilbert! 'Twas your failings that led to—"

Haith's temper overrode her shock, and she stepped between mother and daughter. "Bertie has done no wrong here, Ellora."

"I have no need of your defense," Soleilbert said coldly to Haith. "I see firsthand how you would protect my interests."

"Enough!" Tristan's firm tone brought an uneasy silence to the three women. He turned to Haith. "Lady Haith, I beg you, take your leave while I see to the settling of my *unexpected"*—he glanced at Ellora—"guests."

"My lord," Haith pleaded, "please, I would speak to Bertie."

Ellora did not bother to hide the contempt on her face. "My daughter does not wish to hear more of your lies, I'm sure."

Tristan held up a silencing hand. "Nay. Now is not the time for discussion while emotions run high." He turned to take Haith's elbow but then seemed to think twice. Instead, he held out an arm to indicate that she should precede him to the door.

With a final, longing glance at her sister, Haith complied, waiting at the door for Tristan with a bowed head. Tristan opened the portal to find Barrett sitting against the keep's wall. The big man lumbered to his feet.

"Barrett," Tristan said gravely, "accompany Lady Haith to Minerva with my request that she rest until I send for her."

"Aye, m'lord." Barrett nodded, not even raising an eyebrow at the title of respect Tristan had returned to Haith. "My apologies for not warnin' you about that." He waved a giant paw in the direction of the hall beyond.

"'Tis no fault of yours," Tristan said, dismissing the need for excuses. "Greanly is chaos now. I am confident that once things have been properly settled, 'twill not happen again."

"Aye, m'lord." The sheriff's face relaxed. He stepped forward to take Haith's arm lightly. "Come, m'lady. You look 'bout dead on yer feet."

Tristan watched Haith's retreating form for only a moment, noting with a pain in his heart her bruised and dirtied appearance and stooped posture. He'd found her once more, miracle of miracles, and she had not willingly bound herself to another as he'd feared only hours ago. He had to struggle to keep the hope of it all from clouding his wits.

However, as much as he would prefer to send Ellora of Seacrest and her daughter back to Nigel without a thought for betrothal contracts or royal favor, Tristan knew that the situation must be dealt with if he was to have any secure future at Greanly.

He closed the door and turned to face the two women staring daggers into him, and Tristan knew the greater battle still lay ahead.

CHAPTER
12

After falling into an exhausted slumber under Minerva's loving ministrations, Haith dreamed.

She was in a strange hall filled with beautiful music and people who danced in raiments of magnificent splendor. Around and around, couples twirled and spun each other, laughing and smiling in their pleasure. The exotic tune surrounded Haith like a cool sigh, and she began to notice the faces of the guests who flew past.

Nigel and Ellora; John and Mary—she already with child again; Donald and his corpse of a wife, still smiling through her rotting, battered face; Haith's mother and father, an ethereal glow about them; Minerva and Barrett, an unlikely couple considering their difference in sizes. Haith's heart lurched as Tristan and Soleilbert whirled past, their feet a blur as they kept time with the increasing tempo of the frantically gay melody.

Haith's feet itched with the urge to join the fun, and they tapped in time with the staccato beat until she noticed that the smiles on the faces of the dancers were fierce, grimacing parodies of cheer. The beat of the music increased even more, and the tune took on a screeching, pained harmony that prompted Haith to cover her ears. The dancers before her fought valiantly to keep time with the ever quickening pace, and like marionettes, they jerked and flailed wildly, beads of sweat clearly standing out on their frozen masks of joviality.

"Stop the music!" Haith shouted in the dream. She rushed forward to intervene, only to crash into the cell wall now holding her captive. She pressed against the window, gripping the iron bars until she thought her fingers would bleed. "Stop the music! It's killing them!"

"You cannot stop what is not under your control."

A man's deep, melodious voice spoke within Haith's head, and her eyes instinctively flew over the dancers, seeking the source of the words. On the far side of the hall, sitting on a raised dais, was Tristan's dark-skinned companion. Pharao glowed resplendently in his white robes, and although his mouth did not move, his velvety brown eyes bored into Haith's, and she knew 'twas his voice she now heard.

"When you struggle against what is meant to be, you only succeed in breaking your own spirit."

"Can you not see what is happening?" Haith screamed at the serene onlooker, who was seated like royalty. "'Tis not possible for them to continue this way! They will all die!"

"That is not so," Pharao calmly replied, his eyes never leaving Haith's. He waved a hand over the crowd between them. "Can you not see? Some are already dead."

Haith observed with horror that many of the dancers now flung their dead partners along in a macabre attempt to complete the set. Lifeless, bloodied feet dragged the floor, and heads lolled back on shoulders, jarred by each frantic step.

"Make them stop!" Haith shouted, futilely jerking the

bars that contained her. Tristan and Soleilbert whooshed past her again, their faces frozen into angry, silent screams.

"But they dance for you," Pharao cajoled. "As long as you observe, they will also remain."

"I cannot go," Haith sobbed. "I am imprisoned!"

"Nay," Pharao replied softly. "If you but look at what lies behind you . . ."

Haith spun around to look to the rear of her cell. Where a wall had been only moments before, a perfect square of daylight now lay beyond, framing an oddly familiar knoll in the distance. She turned once more to the hall in her dream, only to see that even more of the guests had expired and now lay on the floor, twitching grotesquely.

She slowly backed away from the barred window, and the music quieted. She took another step back, and the pace slowed by half. As she continued her retreat, Pharao's image grew smaller, but his voice did not diminish.

"There are lessons for us all," he advised. "A choice must be made, and by you alone. Once cast, the decision will rule the futures of many."

Haith suddenly felt cool grass and soft earth beneath her bare feet.

"Do you dance or no?" The voice came from behind her this time, but when she turned, the meadow was empty. She spun again, only to find that the hall and her stone cell had vanished, leaving in its place miles of vacant, rolling hills.

Haith turned in a circle, frightened. There were no people, no birds or bees buzzing lazily over the tall grasses. Not one cottage or even a single tree dotted the mesmerizing landscape of green, pressed closely to the painfully blue sky. No clouds, no wind, and although the scene was bright as midday, no fiery sun sizzled. The silence weighed on Haith until her eardrums felt as though they would burst.

"Hello!" she called, her voice not traveling across the wide expanse but blaring back into her face as if she had just spoken into a chalice. She winced and tried again, cupping her hands around her mouth.

"Is there anyone here?" Her voice sounded flat, and Haith's fright nearly consumed her. Her heart raced, filling the ghastly world of the endless meadow with its heavy, ominous beat.

Fear froze her in place, and she sank down on her heels, grasping her knees and shaking. She could draw no breath, her lungs as porous as lead, and black dots swam before her eyes. Haith opened her mouth, willed the mad scream to issue forth, but no sound came.

She was alone.

Tristan was in a very foul mood.

After sending Haith to her rest, he'd returned to Ellora and Soleilbert to discover the meaning behind their unwelcome visit, even though all he wanted to do was to be alone and think. Perhaps sleep as well, for by now he functioned purely on his warrior training. Instead, he found himself offering the mother and daughter the grudging courtesy of seeing their trunks deposited in guest chambers, sending Greanly's hastily installed manor staff into a frenzy. Without having had time to settle his demesne into a town proper, Tristan was already entertaining.

To make matters worse, Pharao had passed through the hall not long after Haith's departure and had seemed greatly put out by some unknown issue. Tristan's first man had always had an easy demeanor, so Tristan was befuddled by this brooding silence and knew not how to approach his friend.

The women finally settled into their chambers for a

rest, the hall's flurry of activity slowed, and Tristan set out to join Pharao in the wide field just outside Greanly's wall. He found Pharao standing shoulder to shoulder with Rufus, recently of Seacrest, both men gesturing with their hands to the fallow lands before them.

"Good day, my lord," Rufus called hesitantly at Tristan's approach. Tristan surmised his own display of temper toward Haith on last night's journey had the messer uneasy about the new lord's good will.

"Good day, er—Rufus, is it?" Tristan asked.

"Aye, m'lord." Rufus stood taller, apparently pleased and surprised that the lord of Greanly recalled his name. He'd lived at Seacrest nearly ten years, and Lord Nigel had only referred to him by his title of keeper of the fields.

"Pharao."

"My liege."

The two men stared at each other, silently communicating— one wary and tired, the other carefully concealing irritation. After several moments, Rufus obviously grew uneasy standing within the cloud of tension.

"Well then," he said, shuffling his feet and squinting at the sky. "Better I get back to settling in so's I can get an early start on the morrow." He paused before leaving in deference to Tristan. "Unless my lord has another task he wishes to set me to?"

"Nay, Rufus," Tristan said. "Pharao's words are mine, and if he is satisfied with the plans made, I am also."

"Very well, my lord." Rufus bowed slightly to the men before hurriedly taking his leave.

"You have something to say." Pharao made the statement without looking at Tristan, but staring over the empty fields.

"I only seek to know what troubles you," Tristan offered, mirroring Pharao's posture. "We have always spoken freely to each other, and I would that you share the cause of your ire."

"You betray the lady," Pharao said simply.

Tristan's brows creased in puzzlement as he searched for the meaning behind Pharao's words. "You speak of Lady Soleilbert?"

"Aye." Pharao's nostrils flared, the only outward sign of the anger inside him. "She saw you with the other. The one for whom you would refuse her hand."

"How do you—" Tristan didn't bother to complete the question. Discerning events from which he'd been absent was quite an annoying talent of Pharao's. "'Tis true, Phar. I have no desire to be bound to Soleilbert. I plan to petition William for my release from the contract as soon as Greanly's immediate affairs are resolved."

"You want the other." Pharao's words were clipped. "The woman you see in your slumber."

Tristan had no reply for that comment. "Phar, I don't understand. You are angry that I desire a woman other than the one who would tie me to Nigel? Pray tell, do you wish me dead?"

"The lady has not wronged you."

"'Tis true, and Nigel's treachery does not fault Soleilbert. My refusal of her hand is not of a personal nature."

"Is flaunting your desire to bed the lady's sister of a personal nature?" Pharao's voice rose slightly.

Tristan's longtime friend was sorely testing his already ragged temper, and he struggled to understand.

"Have a care, Pharao," Tristan said in warning.

"I would say the same to you, my liege," Pharao said, still not looking at Tristan. "You may not yet know it, but the bond between the sisters is strong. Their life energies are tightly entwined. Wrong one, and the other would gladly kill you."

Tristan thought a moment, the sweet-smelling, lively

breeze combing his hair. "I hear your words, friend, and give you mine to tread carefully."

The men stood in silence for several moments, as if digesting what had just passed between them. When Pharao finally spoke, his tone did much to erase the earlier tension.

"Your woman is betrothed to Donald. Should Nigel discover he is imprisoned, will he not send for her?"

"He may," Tristan mused. "But Nigel will soon learn that his requests mean nothing to me. She will not return to Seacrest."

"I would not be so certain, my liege," Pharao said smoothly. Before Tristan could reply, he added, "Perhaps we could send the Lady Mother in her place."

Tristan chuckled. "Perhaps we will do just that, Phar." He clapped his hand to Pharao's shoulder. "Seek your bed, good friend. There is much to be done on the morrow."

Pharao nodded slowly. "Indeed. Good night, my liege."

Tristan turned and strode heavily up the slope toward Greanly, leaving Pharao alone in the meadow. He knew not that his friend had no desire to seek his slumber, that he did not wish to return to that great princely throne and preside over the dream ball.

In truth, Pharao was afraid.

Soleilbert sat alone in the foreign chamber assigned to her at Greanly. Her eyes were dry, but her insides roiled with confusion. She knew not what to make of the scene she and Ellora had stumbled upon in the hall.

Her sister and her betrothed, embraced in a way Bertie had never before witnessed and so oblivious to their surroundings that it had taken Ellora's voice to draw their attention. Had Bertie truly been betrayed by the only one who she thought loved her?

And what of her sister's appearance? Haith's face had borne the mark of a heavy hand, and her gown had been torn and muddy. Had the journey to Greanly been so arduous? Although Bertie had found the ride tedious, it had not been physically challenging astride.

Had the beast made her walk then? And beaten her? Bertie saw the way Haith had limped when she left the hall, and the bruises told their own tale. Perhaps not Lord Tristan then, but Donald. She still could not believe that Haith was betrothed to the disgusting man, even though Ellora had sworn 'twas true.

Bertie rose, unable to sit with her thoughts, and paced the chamber, wringing her hands. She had come to Greanly with her own agenda of saving Haith, but was now unsure of exactly what evil to save her from. It had all been so clear last night. And now, instead of offering her sister comfort and understanding, Bertie had taken on a demeanor akin to Ellora's. The thought made her shudder.

Walking to the window and looking down, Bertie saw Minerva exit a cottage with a basket over one arm. The old woman glanced up directly to where Bertie stood and walked on, ignoring the hand Bertie had raised in greeting. She let the hand fall to the windowsill self-consciously.

Was this to forever be her lot in life? Relegated to an upper chamber with a generous view of life below her? She could see the glow of Haith's and Minerva's windows clearly, and she imagined the occupants themselves would be visible if they were to pass by.

I do not belong here, she thought, and the idea of it rang soundly true.

Bertie missed the familiarity of Seacrest. She had no desire to wed Lord Tristan or to become Lady of Greanly. 'Twas clear that he felt the same but she was not saddened by his lack of care. Soleilbert surmised Tristan's reluctance stemmed not only from her sister's kiss but also from something to do with Nigel. Seacrest's lord had acted stranger than was usual for nigh a year, meeting with the more unsavory villagers in secret.

Mostly Donald, Bertie suddenly realized.

And then there had been the betrothal feast disaster.

Something had been alluded to in the conversation, but Soleilbert could not call to memory what exactly had been said. She'd been too distracted by Pharao Tak'Ahn's presence at her table.

As if conjured with a mere thought, Pharao appeared in the twilit bailey below her window. For several moments, the two simply gazed at each other.

And then he was gone, disappearing into the hall without even a wave of acknowledgment.

Bertie flopped onto the bed with a muffled cry of frustration. She stopped her display quite suddenly as a thought occurred to her. Ellora lay safely ensconced in her own chamber, Nigel was at far away Seacrest, and Pharao had just entered the hall below.

Bertie's mind raced ahead of her doubts, leaving her no time to become fearful. If she could avoid Lord Tristan, she might finally be able to be alone with this strangely exotic man who stirred her in ways she did not understand. She rose from the bed, straightened her skirts, and patted her hair.

Halfway to the chamber door, she stopped. What in the world was she doing? What would she say to him if even she saw him?

Good eventide, Sir Pharao. Would you mind terribly if I stared at you until my eyes fall out?

Good heavens!

Bertie turned back to her chamber, then spun again and stalked back to the door. Courage had never been an overabundant quality of Soleilbert's until last night, and she vowed to hang onto it. She grasped the handle and yanked before she could change her mind yet again.

Pharao stood so close to Bertie's door that she nearly ran into him in her determination. She gave a squeak of surprise and then quickly backed up a step, dumbfounded by his presence.

Pharao bowed deeply at the waist. "My lady," he said solemnly and rose, locking his deep brown gaze onto the trembling woman before him. "May I be of service to you?"

A shiver raced up Bertie's spine, ending at the raised hairs on the nape of her neck. She felt his gaze on her, intensely hot, and there was no hint of humor or ridicule as his eyes roamed her body.

Nay, 'twas almost as if he looked upon her with desire.

Strange sensations traveled just beneath Bertie's skin, prompting her to wonder just what lay under those ever white robes he wore so confidently. She shook herself mentally, pushing such lurid ideas away. But they proved stubborn, encouraged by Pharao's full lips and lushly rimmed eyes.

This is madness, a tiny voice whispered somewhere in her befuddled mind.

Bertie stepped back from the door.

"Please," she whispered. "Come inside."

CHAPTER
13

Haith awoke in the misty predawn light, her body covered in icy perspiration. For a moment, she lay unmoving, staring up at the strange ceiling. Her ears strained to hear a sound, any sound. She'd been trapped in the silent meadow throughout her lengthy slumber, and part of her wondered if it had indeed not rendered her deaf in the waking world.

But there—the clang of metal on metal from afar, the squawk of geese, a shuffling from the next room. Typical sounds of a village starting a new day, but the clarity of it all made Haith nearly weep with relief.

She flung the covers back and sat up, running her hands through her damp curls. Her body felt sore and stiff, and her head pounded behind dusty, swollen eyes.

The skin covering the doorway between the cottage's two rooms fluttered, and Minerva's head appeared.

"Good morn to you, faery," the old woman chirped. "Come out to break yer fast, and be quick about it. We have much to do today."

The curtain flapped shut again before Haith could reply,

and she groaned. She knew 'twould be impossible to concentrate on menial chores today. Haith had to seek out Bertie and try to repair the damage of last night, or at least explain as best she could. There was also the looming task of facing Lord Tristan once more and discovering what they all were to do now.

The thought of him brought back the memory of his kiss. Recalling it, Haith's headache lifted even as guilt assailed her.

Why, why? Her thoughts tumbled and twisted around the complex circumstances in which the occupants of Greanly now found themselves. She tugged her only other gown over her head as yesterday's clothing was beyond all repair and hastily plaited her heavy mane until it hung to her waist in a thick rope.

Haith ducked through the doorway to see Minerva flitting about the room. Two cauldrons were already brewing in the hearth, and the tangy scent of freshly torn leaves teased her nostrils.

Haith went straightaway to the newly constructed shelves and rummaged through the pouches and jars. She finally found the dried willow bark her throbbing skull screamed for and tore off a small strip, washing the bitter piece down with a dipper of water. A steaming bowl of cereal awaited her on the table, and Haith's stomach twisted with hunger.

Minerva waited until Haith was into her meal before speaking.

"When do you seek the lord?" She stirred a handful of seeds into one of the pots and sniffed appreciatively at the result.

Haith snorted. "I think he is the very last one I should keep company with today." She swallowed the food in her mouth. " 'Tis Bertie I must first concern myself with."

"I disagree, faery."

"Don't you always?" Haith took another bite. "You know what occurred at Bertie's and Ellora's arrival yesterday—"

"Aye."

"And Donald's reaction to my presence at Greanly."

"Mm–hm-m." Minerva brought a mortar and pestle to the table and joined Haith. She ground a pinch of some dark root into fine powder. "It answers many questions, does it not?"

Haith dropped the wooden spoon into the empty bowl with a clatter and looked at the old woman in shock. "Answers? Nay, Minerva." She shoved the bowl away and rested her head in her hands. "There are no answers— only a score more questions."

"'Tis simple, Haith," Minerva breezed, adding another pinch to the earthen bowl. "Tristan is here; you are here. Your wait for each other is over."

"Tristan. Is. *Betrothed.*" Haith spoke slowly as if to one of feeble mind. "To my *sister,* whom I love dearly. What am I to tell her?" Haith rose abruptly and cleared her dishes as she mimicked. "'Oh, Bertie, if you don't mind, might I have your intended? I've dreamed of him all my life, and he kisses quite splendidly.' I think not."

"Why? Bertie loves you and only wishes for your happiness."

"As I do her." Haith retrieved more willow bark. "Even if William would allow it, which he won't—"

"You doona know that."

"—Which he *won't,*" Haith continued, "am I to send her back to Seacrest with Ellora and Nigel to live as an old maid? Bertie has kept herself from marrying for several years while awaiting Tristan, and she is now a score and two. Who would have her?"

Minerva's eyebrows rose. "I'm surprised that you think so little of your sister's worth as a match, faery."

"'Tis not her worth I doubt," Haith said, exasperation

tight in her voice. "'Tis the lack of eligible partners! If Bertie wished to marry one besides Tristan, she would have to journey to London to make a match."

"You doona know that. Stir that pot."

"Stop saying that!" Haith grabbed a long wooden spoon to perform the chore. "Besides, I know not Lord Tristan's intentions."

"Pray tell."

"His *intentions*," Haith replaced the spoon on a hook. "Toward me, toward Bertie. And what are his plans for Nigel? Donald? Not even half of Greanly's villagers have arrived. William expects an alliance between his lords, and thus far, 'tis not going well." Haith sighed and walked to the window, pulling her long plait over her shoulder and staring up at the keep. "I know not his plans nor his heart."

"There is a way to find out." Minerva rose from the table and added the ingredients she'd prepared to the other cauldron. "Cast the stones."

Haith swiveled her head to toss a cold look over her shoulder. "I will not. That nonsense was for you and Mother, not me."

Minerva opened her mouth to speak, but Haith cut her off, pointing a finger menacingly. "And do not say 'you doona know that,' because I do."

"I was merely going to suggest," Minerva said smoothly, lifting her stubby nose into the air, "that if you willna cast the stones, then you should go to the keep. Seek Lord Tristan yourself, and have your answers."

"Yea," Haith murmured "I shall go to the keep." *But not to seek answers from Tristan,* she thought to herself. She strolled to the door. "Send for me if you have need," she called over her shoulder before closing the door after her.

Minerva sighed heavily and shook her head. "Ah,

Corinne," she said to the ceiling. "Your daughter is of you, no doubt." The old healer was on the second verse of a rousing Scots ditty when a rap on the door sounded.

"Enter," Minerva called, beginning to gather ingredients for her next concoction.

Barrett's shaggy presence soon filled the room, looking highly agitated.

"Ah, Barrett, what brings you again to me humble door?"

"Where is Lady Haith?" he demanded, folding his frame nearly in two to enter the rear room and calling loudly enough to shatter crockery. "Lady Haith! Are you about?"

"Hush now, you giant oaf," Minerva scolded. "Think you if she was within, she couldna hear your great bellerin'?" Minerva's brow creased as Barrett emerged from the bedchamber, his face stricken.

"Where is she, Minerva?"

"Why, she left not a moment ago on her way to the keep. You should've passed right by her."

Barrett shook his head. "I just came from the keep." He turned to leave the cottage, but Minerva halted him with a hand on his massive forearm.

"What's amiss, Barrett?"

"Donald's escaped," he said gravely. He continued as Minerva's eyes widened in fear. "He killed his guard mayhap just before dawn and is nowhere to be found. Lord Tristan has reason to believe that Donald seeks to do Haith harm."

"Sweet Corra, help us," Minerva breathed. "She'll not have gone far. Let us go."

Haith emerged from the privy some distance behind the cottage just as Minerva and Barrett went in the direction of the stables. A hand clamped on her upper arm and swung her about, bringing her face to face with Donald.

"Don't scream," he warned as he dragged her behind the privy, away from the bailey's prying eyes.

Haith's insides roiled with the nearness of him. He pulled her closer, and the hot stench of the rotting flesh of his arm seemed to wrap around Haith's skull. She boldly pushed against Donald's chest, and to her amazement, he released her. She realized that it was she who had the upper hand in this situation—with one scream, she could alert the village to Donald's presence.

"Now that I'm free, we have work to do, you and I." He chuckled softly, his rotten breath causing Haith's stomach to churn painfully. To her dread, he moved a half-step closer. "I believe you have some information to impart."

Haith's mind raced. "But I've only arrived yester morn. There has been no time to glean anything of import. And even if I had,"—she raised her nose slightly in the air—"I've decided I have no wish to aid Nigel."

Donald's brow lowered. "Is that so?"

Haith looked pointedly at the squat man before her whose complexion was taking on a violet hue. "It is. And you would do well to follow my example. Tristan will search for you, no doubt, and kill you when he finds you. If you fail in your allegiance to Nigel, you will surely meet the same fate at Nigel's hands. Your only hope is to flee."

"Understand this, you uppity bitch," Donald growled, leaning in so closely that Haith could see the slight twitching in the skin beneath one of his eyes. Some of her bravado left her then, and she drew back against the privy wall. "Lord Nigel is not the only one to gain if his plan succeeds—he's promised me a station within Greanly's hold for my aid, an' I'll not have you mucking it up for me. I don't want to be pounding iron for the rest of my days, you pampered slut."

"You're a fool. Nigel is a liar and will never keep his word." Haith's chin lifted as she recalled the humiliation that Nigel had put her through on her last night at Seacrest. "He uses you to do his dirty work."

"'Tis my business then, and not for you to be concerned with. Now shut up and listen." Donald held her back against the privy wall. "Should I tell Lord Nigel that you have *changed your mind*," he sneered, sending tiny drops of spittle flying onto Haith's face, "he will send for you, as is his right."

"I will not go back to Seacrest." Haith's words were strong, but her voice was unsteady. She knew Donald spoke the truth.

He ran a stubby finger slowly up Haith's stomach and between her breasts, stopping at the hollow at the base of her throat and cupping his small, meaty hand around her neck. "What do you think will be your punishment for betraying him, hm-m?"

Haith swallowed, the motion causing Donald's grip on her throat to tighten. He seemed to smile at the fear that she knew shone in her eyes at the mention of Nigel meting out punishment to her.

Donald released his grip on Haith's throat slowly as if he regretted having to do so and withdrew. "If you indeed wish to escape Nigel forever, you will give me the information I seek."

Haith's breaths were fast and shallow as she stared at the odious man before her. "I could scream right now. You would be found out."

"Then do so if you wish." Donald spread his arms in invitation. "And I will relish telling Lord Tristan of your alliance with Nigel. You forget I'm in the perfect position to play both sides of this farce."

Haith's mind whirled with the choice before her. Already, Tristan suspected her of being in league with Nigel, and she knew 'twould not take much to convince him to believe Donald. Conspiracy against a noble was a crime punishable by death. The image of an executioner's ax bloomed in her mind.

But Haith worried more for her sister. Surely King William would not enforce a betrothal entered into under false pretenses, and if the betrothal was broken, Bertie would be forever tainted by scandal.

"Answer me now, bitch. My patience grows thin."

Haith raised her eyes to Donald's. "Lord Tristan plans to petition William for release from the betrothal contract." With every word that fell from her lips, Haith felt she sealed her fate.

"How soon?"

"I know not. Perhaps when the village is settled."

Donald glanced away, mumbling to himself for a moment. He turned his gaze once more to Haith. "What else?"

"That is all. There has been no time to learn more."

Donald eyed her as if trying to discern whether Haith spoke the truth. Apparently satisfied, he nodded curtly. "I'll send a messenger from Seacrest seven days hence. Meet him at sunset on the edge of the forest south of Greanly with any other information you learn for Lord Nigel." Donald stepped closer, his hand coming up to once more caress her neck, causing Haith to avert her face and squeeze her eyes shut. "If you fail in this, I'll find you. And when I do, you will wish you had chosen Nigel's bed. Ken?"

Haith nodded, and then the pressure left her throat. When she opened her eyes, Donald was gone. Haith sank to the ground behind the privy, shaking and sick, and she leaned to the side and vomited. All the brave hope for the future she'd mustered before leaving the cottage moments ago had vanished, leaving an aching dread in the empty pit of her stomach.

Now that it was clear to Haith that she would have to aid Nigel for the time being, 'twas all the more important that she make amends with her sister. Bertie must not suspect any of the turmoil that surrounded her sister, her stepfather, and her betrothed until Haith could be assured of her safety.

Haith stood, straightening her skirts, smoothing her hair back, and taking several deep breaths. She made her way along the rear row of cottages, half staggering as she wiped at her eyes, to allow more time to compose herself before approaching the keep. She prayed that she would avoid Tristan until after she'd mended things with Soleilbert.

The hall was nearly empty save for two young lads repairing mail near the hearth, and Haith's spirits rose slightly at her good fortune. She quickly skirted the room and mounted the stairs to the upper level, but when she'd climbed to the top, she faced an unforeseen challenge: a long corridor ran to her left and was lined with identical oaken doors.

All of them closed.

Now, why did I not think of that, she scolded herself and tiptoed down the corridor, pausing to listen at each doorway. Haith knew she could not begin rapping on doors and calling out for Bertie. What if Tristan appeared? Or Ellora?

Her frustration grew as no sounds could be discerned through the thick slabs of wood or the solid stone walls that separated the chambers. She fleetingly wished that Greanly's keep had been built as Seacrest's—you could nigh well carry on a conversation through the thin wooden walls of her childhood home.

Haith's ears strained at a faint sound as she neared the end of the corridor, and she stilled her breathing to better hear. There—Bertie's voice rose in song behind the last door, and Haith rushed to stand before it, only to pause before knocking.

What if she refuses to speak to me, she thought. *What if she hates me?*

"Then 'twill be just what you deserve, you shameful wench," she answered herself in a hissing whisper. "Better to know and get it over with." She knocked.

"Come," Bertie paused in her song to call out cheerfully.

Haith eased the door open and poked her head inside to find Bertie seated, still in her night rail, and brushing her hair.

"Bertie?" Haith called hesitantly. "May I come in?"

Soleilbert's head spun in the direction of Haith's voice, a radiant smile illuminating her face. "Sister!" she cried. "Yea, come in! Come in!" Bertie flung the brush aside and rushed to the door to pull Haith inside by the hand.

"What took you so long? I've been waiting for *hours!"*

Haith was stricken dumb by the welcome as her sister embraced her, but she fiercely returned the hug. She pulled away to peer into Bertie's shining face. "You are not angry with me?" she asked, noting the rosy glow in her sister's cheeks and the sparkle in her eyes.

Bertie laughed and bestowed a hasty kiss on Haith's cheek. "You goose! Of course I'm not angry."

Haith found herself being tugged over to the bed where the two sisters sat.

"But what about yesterday?" Haith pressed.

"Oh, that." Bertie waved a hand and still smiled. "I'm terribly sorry for how I acted—I was simply quite shocked." She giggled. "Here am I, prepared to save you from that hairy beast Donald, only to find you quite safe in Lord Tristan's arms. He is very handsome, is he not? If a bit intimidating."

"Bertie, darling," Haith said slowly, "have you forgotten that Tristan is to be your husband?"

"Yea, well, that is a problem, is it not?" Bertie pulled a face, but then concern flooded her features. "My goodness," she said, touching the bruise on Haith's cheek, "what happened to you? And what is this nonsense Mother has told me of you wedding Donald?"

"You do not wish to know," Haith advised, shuddering at the memories of Nigel sprawled atop her and her recent meeting with the smithy. "'Tis complicated . . . and most unpleasant."

"I am not made of glass, Sister," Bertie said. "Although I admit, in the past my constitution was rather weak. But all that has changed now—I am a different woman."

"I can see that," Haith said, her eyes taking in her sister in wonder. Something dark against the white linen covering the bed drew her attention, and she glanced twice at it as Bertie's words bubbled in her ears.

"So tell me. I'll wager it all has something to do with Nigel, does it not?" Bertie's voice darkened with contempt, not noticing the horror dawning on her sister's face. "That vile creature! Although 'twas his idea for Mother and I to come to Greanly, and I'm so very glad we—Haith? What is—"

Bertie's eyes followed the direction of Haith's gaze to the now dark brown streaks that adorned the sheet.

"Oh my!" Bertie chirped and blushed prettily. "I forgot to take care of that this morning. Up, up, up!" She shooed Haith from her perch and hastily gathered the bedclothes into a bundle, giggling. "I would not want to explain that to Mother this early in the day!"

Haith stood in stricken silence as she watched her

sister happily toss the ball of bed covers into the corner. In her mind, she still vividly saw the reason for Bertie's buoyant mood.

So Tristan is to be with my sister after all, Haith thought, bile churning her stomach. *All those years of dreaming of him, all for naught.* The deed had truly been done, and well, by the looks of Soleilbert. Haith's throat constricted, and she looked at Bertie through blurred eyes.

"Haith?" Soleilbert stopped her chatter to glance worriedly at her sister. "Whatever is the matter? Are you ill?" She reached out to Haith, but Haith quickly stepped away.

"Nay. I mean, yea," she stuttered, the damning vision of Soleilbert's virgin blood clearly etched in her brain. She tried to reason with herself that 'twas for the best, really—mayhap Tristan would grow to love her sister after all, and Soleilbert would be happy.

Then why did she feel as if her heart had been cut out?

"Yea, I'm feeling quite unwell at the moment."

"Goodness, but that was sudden," Bertie fretted and attempted again to snag her sister's hand. "Here, just lie down for a bit, and perhaps 'twill pass."

"Nay!" Haith said, staring at the bed with horror and causing Bertie to retreat a step. "I'll not lie there."

"Haith, what has come over you?" Bertie demanded. "'Tis not tainted. 'Twas an act of love. I would think you would be pleased for me!"

Haith could no longer hold back her tears. "I am, Bertie. Truly," she sniffed. "'Tis just—"

"What, darling?" Bertie tentatively reached for her sister, surprised when Haith let herself be taken in hand this time. "Here, come and sit in this chair then, and tell me. I shall fix it, whatever it is. I only wish for your happiness."

At Bertie's words, nearly verbatim what Minerva had advised, Haith's sobs increased.

"Well, I *do*," Bertie insisted, and Haith wailed.

Bertie rummaged in a nearby trunk for a handkerchief and, kneeling at Haith's side, pressed it into her hand. "Now, dry your eyes, and let me help you. Whatever it is, it cannot be so bad."

Haith sniffed and blew her nose. "Very well, Bertie. I shall tell you the truth." She took a deep breath. "Do you recall when we were girls and I would have those strange dreams every night?"

"Oh, yea." Bertie nodded and smiled wistfully. "I so loved it when you spoke of him: a great warrior on a mighty steed come to save you from imminent peril. The same man, night after night. 'Twas so romantic, and I envied you those dreams." Soleilbert's grin faded. "But you have not spoken of him since the dreams stopped."

"They did not stop." Haith blew her nose quite noisily. "I merely stopped *speaking* of them. Minerva hounded me endlessly with questions, going on about my mother and our father and soulmates and the like." Another great sigh. "She told me over and over that I was destined to be like my parents, and I detested the notion. I wanted to be nothing like my mother."

"But why?" Bertie asked. "I adored Corinne."

"She was an adulteress, Bertie!" Haith cried. "She lusted after another's husband and bore him a bastard without a thought of how her actions would affect others."

"Haith, I still don't understand what that has to do with—" Soleilbert struggled to find the words and, failing, merely gestured to the bed, "—this."

"Oh, Bertie,"—Haith buried her face in the handkerchief in shame—"the warrior I dreamed of for so many years—"

"Yea? Go on."

"'Twas Tristan." Haith's words were barely audible.

Soleilbert's face went slack with shock at Haith's admission. "You're certain?"

Haith nodded, staring down at the handkerchief she was twisting in her lap. "I am so sorry, Bertie," Haith babbled. "I knew not 'twas him, I swear it. You'll never have to worry that I will be as wicked as my mother. I—"

"Haith," Bertie began, the absurdity of the situation clearly apparent to her now, causing her to smile softly.

Just then, Bertie's chamber door burst open with a horrendous crash, causing both sisters to jump. Tristan charged into the room, instantly filling it with his presence. He stopped and fixed his eyes on Haith.

"Oh, nay," Haith moaned and squeezed her eyes shut.

"Lord Tristan!" Ellora's voice screeched as she appeared behind him in the doorway and tried to peek around his impressive width. "You cannot barge into my daughter's bedchamber unchaperoned!"

Tristan's answer was to growl low in his throat, and without turning around, he reached behind him and slammed the door on the woman, throwing the bolt for good measure.

Soleilbert squeaked when she realized she'd been caught in her underclothing by Lord Tristan, although he had not even glanced her way. She hastily dug a robe from one of the trunks.

Haith opened her eyes, but Tristan was still there. His blue eyes mesmerized her with what Haith would have sworn was some power akin to sorcery. Although Bertie stood only an arm's length away, Haith could not help the pull of her heart, the longing she had to be wrapped once more in his embrace. Her thoughts filled her with shame.

Tristan stepped forward and then hesitated, as if only now realizing that Bertie was present. He bowed slightly in her direction. "My apologies, Lady Soleilbert."

"What is this about, Lord Tristan?" Bertie asked not unkindly.

"There is a grave matter I must speak to Lady Haith about," he said with forced patience.

"Say no more." Soleilbert held up a hand and quickly gathered a hodgepodge of clothing from the floor. "I'll attempt to placate Mother and leave you to your privacy."

"My thanks." Tristan bowed again.

"Bertie, nay!" Haith cried, horrified at the prospect of being alone with Tristan. She reached out a hand to stay her sister, who breezed past her to the door. "Please stay!"

"Darling, do not fret," Bertie soothed as she undid the bolt. And because she could not help herself, with a sly grin, she added, "Unlike my mother, I do not feel a chaperone is necessary."

Haith groaned as Soleilbert closed the door firmly. She stood quickly to put some distance between her and Tristan, only to find herself quite suddenly crushed in his embrace.

"Where have you been?" he whispered into her hair. "I have just torn my new town apart looking for you."

For a brief moment, Haith reveled in the strong arms wrapped around her, and her heart sang with relief. She felt as if a physical weight had been removed from her chest, and she sighed, closing her eyes and breathing deeply of his scent.

The temptation to tell him of Donald's threats was nearly overwhelming. Held in Tristan's capable arms, Haith felt that nothing could touch her or harm her, even though she knew the consequences the truth would bring.

Then Haith remembered where she was and what had recently transpired in this very room. She silenced that small voice urging her to tell all and abruptly shoved him away.

"How dare you," she hissed, and the sound of her palm striking his cheek rang out like the crack of a lash.

CHAPTER 14

Haith and Tristan stood facing each other in the tense silence after her blow. Tristan's visage was stony, a twitch in the lean muscle of his jaw the only sign he was flesh and blood and not some granite statue.

Tristan strode around Haith to Soleilbert's window, causing Haith to turn on her heel and follow him warily with her eyes. Once there, he leaned out; scanned the bailey, below; and, finding his intended target, raised an arm. " 'Tis well," he shouted and nodded after a garbled reply from below. When his attention returned to the chamber, Haith involuntarily stepped back.

"Pray tell me, woman,"—Tristan's voice was deceptively calm—"what wrong I have done you to warrant you striking me?"

Haith's nerves jangled under her outrage. "I am no idiot, Tristan. Think you Bertie would not tell me?"

Tristan's brow creased. "I know naught of what you speak, Haith. Cease your riddles and explain. There are grave matters I must see to."

"Oh! So the great lord has matters more important than his intended's honor?"

"Yea, I—what?"

Haith's fury unfurled like a banner in a gale. She charged to the corner and retrieved the bundle of bedclothes, flinging them so they landed at Tristan's feet.

"Are your affections so fickle or your mind so weak that you think Bertie and I would share you?" Haith's entire body trembled, and she stomped her foot with a cry of frustration. "You arrogant jackass!"

"Haith,"—Tristan's voice carried a hint of warning—"I have no hold over your sister's honor, save what William has bound me to by way of betrothal."

"Yea! And marry her you will," Haith vowed and closed in on Tristan, unaware that her eyes had filled with tears, "if I must enchant you myself and cart your great mass to the altar!" She stopped just beneath his gaze, a scant foot away, her breath hitching in her chest.

"I will marry whom and when I please, and no one,"—he leaned down slightly—"be it maid or king, shall force my hand."

"You are not the man I thought you were," Haith breathed, a hot tear sliding down her cheek. "To think that I nearly—" She broke off and turned away. "What if you created a child? Would you be so callous as to discard both mother and babe should they not suit you?"

"Haith." Tristan stepped forward and laid a hand on her shoulder.

She shrugged it off. "Do not touch me."

Tristan turned her with both hands this time and held her firmly while she squirmed. "Answer me this one question, and I will release you."

Although the hurt and anger roiling within her warned against it, Haith stilled and looked at him.

"Did your sister tell you that I laid with her last eve?"

The knot of misery in Haith's stomach threatened to unravel, but she bravely found her voice. "There is the proof," she said, glancing down at the tangle of sheets between them.

" 'Twas not me."

"You lie!" Haith cried, shaking loose from him and backing away. "Bertie knows no one else at Greanly, and my sister is no whore!"

Tristan followed Haith until she had been backed into a corner. He braced an arm on either side of her. "Did she name me?"

Haith squeezed her eyes shut, unable to look at him lest she be overwhelmed by his nearness.

"Did she name me?" Tristan insisted.

Haith's thoughts tumbled. Had Soleilbert said Tristan was the one who'd lain with her? Or had Haith merely assumed? She opened her eyes, shocked to her core to discover Tristan's face, a slight smile on his lips, hovered mere inches from hers.

"There is no one else," Haith offered weakly.

"There is," Tristan said, his hands drawing in until they brushed Haith's arms.

"Who?" she whispered, becoming hypnotized by his eyes, his lips, his breath on her face. She knew 'twas unlikely that Tristan would lie about such a serious matter when 'twould be easy enough to affirm the truth by asking Soleilbert.

Tristan shook his head and said, almost as if he could read her thoughts, " 'Twill be for your sister to tell you, and not I." His hands traveled up her shoulders, then over her neck, erasing all memory of Donald's cruel touch; to cradle her head. "Listen well, Haith," he murmured. "I do not desire Lady Soleilbert. Nay," he amended, "I desire no other woman save you."

Haith's throat constricted. How long she had waited

to hear those words only to now be forced to refuse them. "Nay," she choked, bringing her hands to rest on his forearms and pushing. Tristan's grip was firm. "William will enforce the betrothal, and I will not be an adulteress."

"I will say it once more." Tristan's thumbs lightly stroked the underside of Haith's jaw. "I will marry whom and when I please. Besides, Soleilbert is the one who has apparently cuckolded me, has she not?"

Haith's eyes widened as the reality hit her. *Bertie, nay!*

Tristan leaned his forehead against Haith's and sighed. "There is more—Donald has escaped."

Haith jerked her head away from Tristan's and averted her eyes. "I know."

Tristan obviously mistook her guilt for fear. "Worry not, Haith. He'll not harm you." With a final caress of her face, he turned away from her to pace the room, leaving Haith standing speechless in the corner. As he paced, he talked, and as he talked, Haith's dread increased.

"I will send word to William this day to intervene on our behalf. But until he answers, you must stay within Greanly's walls."

"Why?" Haith asked, stepping forward. If Tristan should forbid her to leave the grounds, she would be unable to meet the messenger from Nigel. She shuddered at the repercussions that could bring. "I am of no consequence to your betrothal."

"But you are." Tristan turned to face her. "After giving the matter much thought, I've realized that your very existence could foil Nigel's plans to see me ruined."

"I don't understand," Haith ventured.

"You are of noble birth, as much related to the house of Seacrest by blood as is your sister," Tristan explained. "If Soleilbert and I were unwilling to wed each other and I instead chose you, 'twould likely be no matter to William. But to Nigel . . ."

"Nigel wishes to hold Greanly," Haith said slowly, realizing the double trap Nigel had laid. "So should William strip you of your lands, he may award Nigel the town, but even if the wedding does occur and Soleilbert becomes lady here, as her guardian, he could still gain the town if you fell."

Tristan nodded. "But were you my lady, he would gain naught at my demise as you would become a ward of the crown."

"'Tis why I was barred from the keep the night you arrived at Seacrest. He wanted to keep me a secret!"

"Yea. And that is why you must stay within these walls."

"But surely I will be safe with Minerva."

"Nay." Tristan stood before Haith and took her hand, bringing it to his lips and kissing it softly. "You will move your possessions within the keep where I can better protect you."

Haith gasped. This was worse than Tristan merely barring her from leaving the grounds. Under his thumb, she might be privy to all sorts of information that she could then be forced to relay to Nigel's messenger. Not to mention the fact that having Tristan so close, day after day, would make it all the more difficult to keep her wits about her.

"I cannot live within the keep, my lord," she said. "Ellora will—"

"Ellora be damned," Tristan growled. "I am lord here, and I would have you within reach of me." He pulled her arm, and she collided with him. Tristan's kiss was like a brand on her lips, leaving her seared and breathless. "You will do as I ask?"

Haith pulled away reluctantly and struggled to calm

her heart's racing beat. "Then we must avoid being alone together."

"Why do you say that?" He pulled her close again. "We risk naught by enjoying each other's company."

Haith disentangled herself and firmly stepped away. "If Ellora grows suspicious, she might send word to Nigel, or even William, and thwart you. 'Tis better we wait for the king's word to ensure all is well." Haith walked to the door and turned before opening it. "She wishes very much for you to wed Bertie, and would do anything to secure it."

"Then we shall be wary, shall we not?" Tristan smiled seductively, the power radiating from him acting as a magnet, and Haith felt as if she were being pulled away from the door by unseen forces. She held firm throughout the assault, though his next words were nearly her undoing.

"Will you come to me in the night?"

Haith shivered under the weight of his meaning. "Nay," she whispered and then spoke louder for the benefit of any eavesdroppers in the hall as she opened the door. "I shall gather my things as you requested, my lord." And she escaped into the corridor.

Tristan turned and strolled to the window to await Haith's crossing of the bailey and disappearance into the hut she shared with Minerva. He would cajole her into his bed, he vowed. If not this night, then soon. His ache for her body was miniscule compared to the emotion he'd felt when Donald had been discovered missing, and Haith could not be found. If she was in his arms every night, he would be assured of her safety, and the dreams of her would cease to torment him.

"My lord?" Soleilbert appeared in the doorway, now fully clothed and wringing her hands. "All is well?"

Tristan turned. "As well as can be for the time, Lady

Soleilbert." He grinned wickedly. "I trust that your first night at Greanly was comfortable?"

Soleilbert blushed crimson and averted her eyes, even though the smile on her face betrayed her happiness. "Yea, my lord. Quite wonderful in fact."

Tristan approached her, glancing past her shoulder.

"Mother is exploring the kitchens, my lord," Bertie said. "You may speak freely."

Tristan ran a hand through his hair. "Why did you not explain to your sister that 'twas not I who visited your chamber last eve?"

"I was about to do just that," Bertie began, "but you arrived, and then Mother—" She shrugged helplessly. "I do not wish her to know—"

"I understand." Tristan saved her from outlining her predicament in detail. "'Tis wise, no doubt. We must tread carefully in the days ahead and trust no one."

Bertie nodded. "Will you marry Haith?"

He cocked his head and smiled. "If she'll have me."

Bertie's eyes widened, and she laid a hand on Tristan's arm. "Of course she'll have you! She's been waiting for you her entire life."

Tristan patted Bertie's hand, unwilling to show how much that knowledge affected him. "And so we must continue this farce of a betrothal until we are safe to make our next move." He peered down into her shining brown eyes. "But what is to become of you afterward, Lady Soleilbert? Have you laid your plans as well?"

Bertie moved away to stand at the window. "Nay, no plans. I've never had a—a lover before." She blushed furiously again but pressed on. "Still, I feel that this is not some sordid affair that will pass." She sighed. "I fear I love him already."

Tristan joined her at the window. "What is there to fear?"

"Although I feel in my heart that he is an honorable

man," Bertie explained, "I know so little about him. We talked of many things last eve, and I told him much that even Haith does not know, but—" Bertie wrung her hands. "He refuses to speak of his home or his family."

"In truth, my lady," Tristan admitted, "I know probably little more than you. His mother was Egyptian; his father, a noble of some sort in one of the smaller courts of India. Phar and his mother fled from there when he was very young."

"His mother's heritage explains his unique name." Bertie smiled, then her face grew serious. "His father was killed?"

"Murdered," Tristan clarified. "His mother contracted influenza soon after reaching Paris. I met him not long after."

Bertie smiled wanly. "And you have been steadfast to each other ever since."

"Yea." Tristan returned her smile. "But that does not mean he has confided in me about his past. Something happened in his homeland that he does not wish to speak of no matter how hard he is pressed."

"It must have been terrible," Bertie ventured, staring out the window and conjuring images of a young boy alone in a foreign city. "Perhaps one day he will allow me to share his burden."

"Perhaps." Tristan turned from the window and made his way to the chamber door before Bertie's words stopped him.

"A question, my lord, if you would indulge me a moment longer."

Tristan half turned. "Of course."

Soleilbert's gaze remained fixed on the horizon as she spoke, her profile that of a remarkably pretty woman with her head held high. "Had you not met my sister, would you have married me?"

"Nay."

Soleilbert took a deep breath. "Why?"

"Were it to mean I would be allied with Nigel, I would refuse the queen herself."

Soleilbert turned to smile at Tristan. "My thanks."

Tristan merely nodded and left the chamber.

Tristan made his way down the stone steps to where Barrett and Pharao awaited him in the hall below.

"Barrett," Tristan began issuing orders before he was among them, "select five soldiers of your choosing to ride to London with Pharao this day and twenty to ride to Seacrest with wagons. Also, send for John the crofter."

"Aye, m'lord," Barrett said and turned to do his lord's bidding.

"A moment." Tristan stopped him and leaned in closely. "No one save us three men, Lady Haith, and Lady Soleilbert can be privy to the goings-on in the keep. Especially," he lowered his voice further, "Lady Ellora. I trust her not. Is that clear?"

Barrett nodded.

"Should you hear any gossip in the village concerning my betrothal to Lady Soleilbert, you are to quell it and relay that the wedding will indeed take place as planned."

"As you wish, my lord." The big man left the hall with a purposeful stride, and Tristan turned to Pharao.

"Is there parchment to be had, Phar?"

From within his voluminous sleeve, Pharao withdrew several pieces of the yellowed paper.

Tristan took the pages and crossed to the lord's table, where a quill and inkstand were kept at the ready. He sat and began to write. The two missives were soon completed and sealed, and Tristan tucked them in his belt. He leaned back in his chair to face his first man.

Pharao's face was stoic, and his eyes were fixed on a place somewhere over Tristan's head.

"Shall we discuss the mysterious activities in Lady Soleilbert's chamber last eve?" Tristan asked pointedly.

"I would rather not, my liege."

"I'm certain of that," Tristan chuckled. "Would that you were more careful in the future, Phar. Your tryst was nearly my undoing with Haith this morning. Ellora must not find out."

Pharao nodded. "The Lady Mother is blinded by her own ambition, and sees only what she wishes. We will not be discovered before the time calls for it to be so."

Pharao's enigmatic statement caused Tristan's eyebrows to rise, but he was prevented from making further comment when Barrett once again presented himself with John at his side.

"My lord." John bowed before Tristan and nodded respectfully at Pharao. "How can I serve you?"

Tristan shook free another sheaf of parchment. "John, some of my men ride to Seacrest today to retrieve the remainder of Greanly's belongings. You know the village and its people well?"

John bobbed his head. "Better'n most, I'd vow."

"Good." Tristan nodded and handed the quill to Pharao. "Name as best you can those villagers and their children who originated from the old Greanly." He stood, and Pharao took his seat. Tristan skirted the table and motioned for Barrett to follow. "Good Sheriff, a word."

Drawing Barrett aside, Tristan spoke to him with a low voice. "I would that you accompany the men to Seacrest with the list Pharao now makes."

"Of course, my lord." Barrett's attempt at a whisper sounded strange coming from a man so large. "What am I to do there?"

"Gather as many of the names on the list as possible. If

the womenfolk are reluctant to leave," Tristan paused and hardened his voice, " 'tis my direct command that you remove the children and all belongings within the dwelling. The women may then remain if they so choose."

"M'lord?" Barrett's eyes widened. "You want me to oversee the snatchin' of the wee ones?"

Tristan's nod was curt. "Yea. Those villagers and their offspring are of Greanly and are, therefore, my property." He paused, his eyes glittering. "I want my property returned to me. Give them one hour to ready."

Barrett looked slightly squeamish at the thought. "I understand yer wish is to have the villagers here, m'lord," he said, wincing. "But 'twill be no easy task. The women will be loathe to let their kiddies go. Are we supposed to use force?"

"I want the bulk of Greanly's residents within these walls by nightfall tomorrow, however it must be accomplished." Tristan studied the stone floor beneath him for a moment, a fist to his chin. "But I see your point. No bloodshed then. 'Twould not aid our plight."

Barrett looked appalled at the very notion but wisely remained silent.

"Make it clear to those who balk that this is a direct command from their lord. Those who disobey me will be forever barred from Greanly, and their families and belongings will be fostered as I see fit. Spouses will make new matches; children will be adopted. I will not compromise on this matter."

Barrett gulped audibly. "Beggin' yer pardon, m'lord, but—"

"Nay." Tristan held up a hand. "This is my word, and 'tis final. Do you understand, Barrett?"

"Aye," Barrett grumbled. " 'Twill not make for pleasant work though."

"I am their lord. It matters not to me that they are

pleased with my commands, only that they obey." Tristan's voice was hard. "They will learn that there are dire consequences for those who do not. Ready the men, and wait for my command." Tristan turned to go but was halted by Barrett.

"Er, m'lord?"

"Yea, Barrett." Tristan's patience wavered.

"'Tis just that I can't read the fine words on your list there."

"You don't read?"

Barrett flushed. "Nay, m'lord."

Tristan sighed and grasped the bridge of his nose. "Well, find someone who can and give them my leave to accompany you."

"Very well, my lord." Barrett hastily left the hall.

At the lord's table, Pharao and John finished up the list of Greanly's unaccounted for villagers.

"'Twill be good to have the village whole again, will it not, my lord?" John ventured with a grin.

Tristan merely grunted. "My thanks for your assistance, John."

The crofter's smile faded. "Of course, m'lord. Good day to you." John bowed slightly and departed, passing Haith in the doorway. "Lady Haith, good day."

"John." Haith nodded, eyeing his departure warily.

Haith crossed the hall, her small sack of belongings cradled in her arms. Tristan watched her advance with blatant lust, the sway of her hips causing her gown to swish softly about her ankles, the fiery red plait lying lovely and long against her breast. His irritation with the day's events had fueled his desire for her.

"What is about in the bailey?" Haith asked as she neared the two men. "The soldiers ready wagons."

"My liege,"—Pharao stood, ignoring Haith's entrance— "I would prepare for the journey."

"Of course, Phar. We shall speak again before you depart."

Haith watched the dark-skinned man leave with a shiver, remembering the role he'd played in her nightmare. She shook the feeling away and faced Tristan.

"He does not approve of me."

"'Tis impossible to fathom Pharao's thoughts," he rejoined, letting his gaze roam her body. A devilish glint lit his eyes. "I approve of you."

Haith ignored his ardent comment and repeated her earlier question. "Where do so many soldiers hie to? Surely you do not send them all to William."

"Yea, some go to London," Tristan replied with a distracted air. "The remainder travel to Seacrest."

"You waste no time," Haith said, and admiration tinged her words. "But why to Seacrest so soon after we just departed?"

Tristan strolled to the ale keg and dipped a draught. He drank deeply, attempting to quench his thirst, if not his lust for the woman so near him. After draining the horn, he faced Haith again.

"Greanly shall be returned to me by the morrow."

"Verily?" Haith looked askance. "Think you they have reconciled themselves to your lordship in so short a time?"

"It matters not that they are reconciled." Tristan approached Haith, lowering his voice before continuing. "Allow me to escort you to your chamber, my lady."

Haith sidestepped his advance and turned to him. "Of course it matters," she insisted. "You cannot *force* them to leave Seacrest."

"I can, and I will." Tristan waved away her concerns like he would an annoying insect. "They will learn to obey their lord." He held out a hand for her. "Now come."

Haith looked at the hand he offered as if it were a red

hot poker. "I will not," she said. *"You* must learn, Lord Tristan, that a people's trust and respect are earned, not owed, and you would be well-advised to do so quickly."

Tristan's face took on an expression of astonishment, and he laughed in disbelief. "Do not advise me on matters in which you are not learned. You above all others should know that a lord's word is the rule and his people follow him without question."

"Why would I know better than some?" Haith asked. "Because my own father was a lord?"

"Yea," Tristan said, obviously pleased that she understood.

"My father," Haith said, "was a kind and just ruler whose people obeyed him because of those reasons. He was no tyrant."

"You were just a babe when your father lived," Tristan scoffed. "You cannot know of his practices." He softened his voice. "Let us not quarrel over this small matter, Haith. I understand that your heart is soft toward Seacrest's villagers because of your mother's blood. 'Tis natural you would want to spare them the consequences of their actions."

"My mother's blood?" Haith's voice was deceptively calm. "You mean because she was Scots?"

Tristan's voice was indulgent. "I know your father laid with a commoner, that you were the fruit of that union. Because he was already wed to Ellora, he cast you both to the village." He smiled sadly. "'Tis no fault of yours though, and I care not about your lineage, Haith." Foolishly, he stepped closer to her. "In truth, my own father discarded me as well, so I am well-versed in your plight."

"You are a fool." Haith's tone was so cool that Tristan's head jerked back in surprise. This time, 'twas she who advanced.

"Perhaps you should know that my *commoner mother*," she half snarled, "was the daughter of Scotland's most powerful laird and that if bloodlines were taken down in a ledger, my station would surely outrank yours by a fathom!"

"Guard your tongue, wench."

Haith ignored his advice, her rage inciting her to put her face mere inches from Tristan's. "Whoever supplied you with the erroneous facts of my childhood should be flogged for spewing such filthy lies!" Once released, her fury would not be dammed.

"My father loved my mother so faithfully that he cuckolded his wife and shared his daughter's title of lady with me. We were *not* cast into the village in shame by my father but lived in the keep as he commanded. Minerva and I were banished to that meager hut in the village by *Ellora* only after your Norman fiends murdered both my mother and father in the same day!"

Tristan was shocked into an uncomfortable silence after being so neatly humbled in his own hall. Haith took his lack of response as an opportunity to further vent her irritation with him.

"And as for those lowly villagers who do not warrant your respect or courtesy, they welcomed me into the village to live among them, yea," she conceded. "But never as a commoner, although 'twas what Ellora would have me branded as. Their respect for my father included me, and they always treated me with the courtesy they showed him."

She paused to breathe. " 'Tis not the bloodline that shows character, but the words and actions of a man that deem him worthy of obedience."

Tristan had regained his tongue and, with it, his wounded pride. "Do not lecture me on my duties, Haith.

Though I desire you as I have no other, I will not pander to your childish temper like some court jester."

Haith's laughter was harsh. "Nay, lord. You need not my presence to act the fool. Your very words brand you as such unaided."

Tristan's breath hissed through his teeth. "Take yourself to your chamber before I act on my anger."

"Why are you angry?" Haith taunted recklessly. "Because my words ring true? Very well then; I'll leave you alone with your greatness. But before I do, know this"—she straightened her spine and pinned him with her gaze—"call me common or bastard as you would, but never liken your trials to my own. Damn your parents to Hell for all eternity if you so desire, but do not sully the names of mine, for they loved *me* enough to sacrifice their own lives!"

Tristan raised his open hand to strike her for her words but halted its downward arc when Haith screamed and turned her head. In the silence that followed the near blow, Tristan immediately regretted his hasty action. Never before had he struck a woman, and his heart cried out at the thought of abusing this particular one. The marks of Nigel's earlier blows stood out on her cheek, as if damning Tristan along with Nigel.

"Haith," he whispered, stepping forward.

She backed away from him toward the door of the hall, her bundle of clothing still tightly clutched to her bosom. "You would have struck me."

Tristan followed, reaching out to her. "Nay. Let me—"

"Stay away from me," Haith croaked. "Do not come near me again." She bumped against the door, and in a flash, had opened it and vanished into the bailey.

Tristan stood in the doorway and watched her run through the crowd of soldiers and villagers, dodging obstacles in her path. It seemed she was always running from him. The eyes of the onlookers turned in the direction from which she ran and landed on Tristan just as he was about to step out after her. Barrett's concerned face was among them, and he regarded his lord quizzically. Pharao sent his liege a look of grave caution.

Tristan retreated into the hall and slammed the door. He would let her go for the time being. Drawing attention to themselves right now would not be wise. Later, when they both had calmed, he would go to her and kiss away the fear he'd caused. For now though, he had to secure his holdings for what he hoped would be their shared future.

"I see you've taught that slut a lesson she's begged for overmuch." Ellora paused in the doorway at the rear of the hall. "'Tis well that you should take her so readily in hand."

Tristan growled under his breath, controlling the urge to tell Nigel's wife to take her praise to the devil. "I have no time to converse with you, Lady Ellora," he said as he made his way to the table to retrieve the list of Greanly's villagers.

"Of course, my lord," Ellora cooed. "You are busy, I can see." Her eyes were bright with interest. "Might I but venture to guess that you've changed your mind with regard to the betrothal?"

Tristan halted at the door of the hall, his hand on the latch. He cast a hooded glance over his shoulder to the woman hanging on the heavy silence.

"There will be a wedding."

Ellora was left alone in the hall after his departure with only the echo of his words and her own shaky smile of triumph for company.

CHAPTER
15

Pharao and Soleilbert sat side by side in the soft green grass outside Greanly's walls. Although they were safely hidden from prying eyes behind the demesne, they did not touch, save for the hems of their garments.

"Must you go today? 'Tis so soon." Bertie turned her head away as embarrassment caressed her cheeks.

"'Tis my duty to my liege," Pharao said simply. Bertie turned to him, and their gazes locked. "I will return, my lady."

"Am I truly your lady?" Bertie whispered. "I cannot bear the thought of waiting for one whose heart I do not hold."

Pharao stared at her for a long moment, the intensity in his brown eyes seizing Bertie's breath. His hands dipped inside the neckline of his caftan, and he withdrew a long gold chain, drawing it over his head. From it dangled a slender, oblong pendant. He held the necklace low, suspended between his hands.

"In my homeland," he intoned gravely, "when a man takes a woman to wife, he gifts her with a *mangalsutra*, a symbol that says she is a married lady and under the protection of her husband." Pharao paused to look down at the delicate chain he held. "It is usually quite beautiful, adorned with many jewels to signify the husband's love."

Bertie's eyes were fixated on the pendant and the strange symbols carved into the gold. A shiver caught her by surprise, and she unconsciously ran the tip of her tongue over her lips.

"This," Pharao continued, indicating the necklace he held, "has been in my family many generations, passed down from father to son. Once, I could have gifted you with all the wealth of my family, but now I have only this to offer."

"Oh, Pharao," Bertie breathed, her eyes welling with tears at his heartbreaking words. "Your wealth is of no consequence compared to what I feel in my heart for you."

Pharao lifted the chain, its length forming a wide, inverted triangle between his hands. "Will you then accept this as a token of my love for you until I return?"

Bertie nodded tightly, her emotion making it impossible for her to speak. She bowed her head, and Pharao reverently slipped the necklace over her head and brought the pendant to rest against the front of her kirtle. His hands remained on the nape of her neck, and he kissed the crown of her head before resting his cheek there.

"You do me a great honor," he said.

"Nay, Pharao." Bertie raised her head and cradled Pharao's face in her palms, staring into his eyes. " 'Tis you who honor me. Never did I even hope that—" She broke off, a sob catching her words for a moment. "I feared I was unlovable."

Pharao mirrored Bertie's hold on him and drew her face close to his. His thumbs gently wiped away the tears from her cheeks, replacing them with soft kisses.

"You are like the most perfect lotus," he said. "Your

form is full and smooth, like the creamiest petals, opening to me. When I am in your presence, I worship in the holiest of temples."

Soleilbert's quiet sobs jarred them both in their embrace. "Pharao, please," she pleaded, "do not leave me. I cannot bear to be parted from you so soon."

"Ah, my flower," he soothed. " 'Twill be for but a short time. In my absence, you will hold my love close to you each moment." He drew away and grasped the pendant that now hung between Bertie's breasts. Bringing it to his lips, he kissed it and replaced it gently against her body. "My Lady Soleilbert." Her name rolled off his tongue like yards of fine silk.

They embraced tightly, and Pharao bestowed on Bertie a kiss that promised her all of eternity. From far away, Barrett's voice called for Pharao, parting the two lovers.

"I will wait for you," Bertie vowed, the tears now vanishing. Her sorrow had been replaced by a spark of resolve that was growing in intensity with each passing moment.

Pharao nodded. A final, gentle kiss he pressed to her lips while their gazes remained on each other. "One day, I will gift you with the finest *mangalsutra* that even God could ever conceive. You will be with me always from that day on."

Bertie smiled and pulled away, her hands sliding reluctantly from his neck. She turned her head to stare over his shoulder to the hills rolling away in the distance. "I beg you then, leave now while I feel I may still bear it."

Recognizing the wisdom of her words, Pharao rose and quickly disappeared around Greanly's wall.

Bertie remained seated in the grass until nearly an hour later, when the small entourage of soldiers bound for London departed on Greanly's dusty road. She watched the band of riders grow smaller and smaller as they crested the nearest hill. A single rider hung back at its peak, his black horse wheeling around to dance impatiently in the keep's direction.

Bertie stood, watching the rider and his horse parade in a tight circle. She raised an arm high in the air.

"Safe journey, my love," she murmured.

The horse reared on its hind legs and then sprung in the direction of the other soldiers.

Pharao was gone.

Haith burst through the door of Minerva's hut, sending it crashing into the wall hard enough to rattle the contents of the shelves that ringed the room.

"Sweet Corra!"

"Christ Almighty!" Rufus, the crop overseer, had been seated at the table, his hands outstretched for Minerva's ministrations for the blisters he'd contracted that morning in the fields. Upon Haith's explosive entrance, he'd leapt to his feet, clutching his chest and smearing the salve Minerva had yet to cover with bandages on his tunic.

"Ye gods, faery!" Minerva said. "I doona want to be treating poor Rufus for apoplexy."

"Lady Haith," Rufus said, a trace of a gasp in his words as he composed himself and glanced down at his salve-stained front. "Sorry, Minerva."

"'Tis no matter." Minerva frowned at Haith and motioned for Rufus to sit once more. "I made plenty of balm."

Haith hurled her bundle, so recently gathered, through the rear doorway with a sharp cry of frustration. She stood in the center of the room, arms crossed over her bosom, her foot tapping impatiently. Her glare alternated between the serenely occupied Minerva to Rufus, who kept glancing over his shoulder.

When Minerva refused to comment on Haith's presence after several moments, Haith growled, "Aren't you nearly finished, Minerva?"

The old woman glanced up, her eyes warning Haith to be still. "Aye, faery. Hold yer rude tongue."

"I can finish wrappin' this meself," Rufus offered, anxious to be away from Haith's furious gaze, which was nearly burning a fiery patch on the back of his skull.

Haith strode to the door to hold it open. "'Twould be marvelous of you, Rufus. Good day."

Rufus quickly stood.

"Sit," Minerva commanded the man.

Rufus quickly sat.

"Haith," Minerva said, "I'll nae have your childish tantrums while I work." She picked up a gauzy length of cloth and began twining it around Rufus's hand. "If you canna control yourself until I finish, then take yourself elsewhere."

Haith rushed toward the table, causing Rufus to duck his head between his shoulders.

"'Tis no tantrum," Haith insisted. "I—"

"Haith," Minerva's voice was as soft as Greanly's spring breezes, but as she spoke, a small crock flew off a shelf across the room and shattered violently on the cottage floor.

"Christ Almighty," Rufus whispered again.

Haith never glanced at the broken crockery when it fell; instead, she stood staring at Minerva with tears of impotent rage in her eyes.

"Very well," she gritted between her teeth in a tight smile. Another crock crashed to the dirt floor. "I shall wait."

Minerva calmly began wrapping Rufus's other hand.

A third jar splintered where it sat, and Minerva glanced up. "You'll fix that," she said.

"For the love of God, Minerva," Rufus whispered under his breath. "Be quick before the next one cleaves me skull!"

A fourth crock wobbled, teetered, and then smashed to the floor.

"Be still, Rufus," Minerva advised. She withdrew her curved knife from her belt and cut the bandages close to the knots. She then grasped both of the nervous man's hands in her own and muttered a short prayer.

A long-handled spoon resting in the brew of a cooling cauldron cartwheeled across the room, flinging splatters of pungent liquid in high arcs before cracking against the far wall.

"Now keep the bandages on through the night," Minerva told Rufus placidly, getting up from the table and crossing the room to retrieve a tiny leather skin from a hook. Her footsteps crunched the earthen shards that littered the floor. She turned to hand it to the man slinking around the perimeter of the room. The fire in the hearth blazed spontaneously. "In the morn, wash the wounds with this water, and all should be well."

"My thanks, Minerva," Rufus said, then jumped with a cry as a large crock directly behind his head shattered in its place. "Good day to you, m'lady" he said to Haith, his voice breaking slightly. He bobbed his head and skittered out the open door, which slammed shut, apparently of its own accord, just as he departed, missing his backside by a thread.

Minerva spun on Haith, her eyes shining merrily. She flung an arm over the mess scattered about the room. "When did you learn you could do that?"

But Haith was not interested in discussing broken crockery, even if her anger was the cause of it. "I want you to cast the stones, Minerva," she said. "Now."

"Oh, nae you don't," the old woman sang in her warbly

voice. "I've been trying to get you to learn your birthright since you were but a wee bairn in your mother's arms. And now here you are,"—she smiled, pride lighting her wrinkled face—"throwing my crockery about in a great fit!"

"Cast the stones." Haith's expression was without laughter. "We shall discuss my *birthright*, as you call it, afterward, if you insist."

"Well, of course I'll be insisting," Minerva scoffed, all but skipping to retrieve a fur sack on a high shelf. She turned to the table, and Haith followed her, clearing away the remnants of Minerva's healing with a swipe of her arm. The supplies crashed to the floor to lie among the broken shards.

Minerva paused, raising a sparse eyebrow at Haith's impatience before pulling out her chair and sitting once more.

"Now tell me," Minerva began after Haith was seated across from her, "what has you in such a blessed hurry that you would have me ask the runes?"

Haith crossed her arms. "I want to know who I shall marry."

Minerva blinked twice, her face screwed into a mask of misunderstanding. "What?"

"Who I will marry!" Haith cried, slapping her palm on the tabletop. "My husband, Minerva! I wish to know his name."

"'Tis Lord Tristan, faery," the old woman said, pulling the drawstrings she'd loosened tight again. "I thought you understood."

"Nay." Haith shook her head and placed a hand over Minerva's to still her from closing the bag. "Throw the stones."

Minerva sat for a moment, her eyes narrowing. Haith's gaze never once wavered. Finally, the old woman sighed.

"Fine! You've never believed a word I've ever told

you any matter." She took another deep breath and blew it out slowly across the fur-covered bag.

> *After rain on the earth,*
> *Wind stirs the fire.*
> *Crone of the ages,*
> *Answer Haith's desire.*
> *Prayers Corra answers*
> *In these stones I shall cast,*
> *Revealing clear truth*
> *To the question 'tis asked.*

Minerva released the bag into Haith's waiting hands. "You remember how 'tis done, lass?" she asked as Haith took possession of the bag.

Haith nodded once, her eyes growing vague. She concentrated her mind on the weighty bag resting in her palm and made her breathing even and calm.

"I wish to know," she said, her voice humming low, "the identity of my life mate. Tell me true; tell me now."

Haith returned the bag to Minerva, and that one loosened the strings and withdrew three stones, laying them carefully in a row on the tabletop. Minerva set the bag to the side and, throwing a rebuking glance in Haith's direction, studied the small symbols intently.

"A young man, fair of color," she said, squinting and leaning closer to the table. She tapped the first rune with her forefinger.

Haith's frown deepened as Minerva continued.

"He's power and heart as well." Minerva looked up at Haith. "'Tis a good mix—a leader of people."

"Go on."

Minerva sighed. "Nay. I'll not go on, for there's nae need." She eyed Haith suspiciously. "Why this burning desire to second-guess your match?"

"Tristan is not my match. He can't be." Haith rested her head on her forearms while Minerva returned the stones to the bag with words of thanks to the goddess Corra.

"Do I have to club you over your thick head?" Minerva stood and tucked the bag between two intact crocks. "Buchanan women have always been possessing of two talents. One is—well,"—she tossed a wry look over the shards that littered the cottage floor— "*this* type of nonsense. And the other—"

Minerva stood over Haith and laid a gentle hand on her head. "Is the ability to see their soulmate." She stroked Haith's long braid. "And you have both, faery. 'Tis nae cause for complaint."

"He nearly struck me." Haith's voice was muffled by her arms.

Minerva's hand stilled. "Now why would he go and do that?"

"We argued. And he said—" Haith's breath hitched. "Oh, Minerva, 'twas awful!"

"Let me see," Minerva demanded. "Look up." The old woman grasped Haith's chin, turning it this way and that. "I see naught but what that viper Nigel gifted you with," Minerva said finally, releasing her. "What did you argue about?"

"Mother and Papa. Greanly's villagers." Haith sighed and shook her head. "Everything."

Minerva raised her eyebrows. "I have trouble believing the lord would be moved to strike you over an argument about the villagers or your parents. What exactly was said?"

"He was being terrible!" Haith cried, standing up and nearly knocking her chair over in the process. "He is *forcing* the villagers to return to Greanly!"

"He's their lord, faery," Minerva said, bending to collect the errant spoon. "He has every right to expect them to serve. Fix that," she said, gesturing to a pile of broken clay near Haith's feet.

Haith scooped the pile carefully in her hands and placed the pieces on the table. "But he's going about it the wrong way to win their trust and respect!"

"Mayhap 'tis nae the *wrong* way, just differently than you would, were you lord," Minerva offered, wiping off the spoon on her apron and returning it to the pot. "Which you are not, I might add." She glanced at the pile on the table. "I said to fix that, not clean it up."

"Papa was a good lord," Haith said, a touch of petulance in her voice. "The villagers loved him, and *he* never acted like a tyrant." She cupped her hands over the pile, then curved them in an arc to reveal the previously destroyed crock now intact.

"Very good, faery!" Minerva crowed. She then flapped a hand around the room. "Now the rest."

Haith moved about the cottage, repairing the damage she'd caused while Minerva continued her reasoning.

"To be fair," the old woman said, "James never faced having to deal with Nigel or bringing a new keep to heel. Your Papa lived at Seacrest since he was a tiny bairn. The villagers knew him well, knew his practices and what he expected from them. Indeed, 'tis well for Lord Tristan that he take a firm hand."

"I disagree," Haith said, replacing the last of the mended pots on the shelf with a thud.

"'Tis not your place to agree or nae. You'll be much happier keeping your opinions to yourself." Minerva gathered bread-making ingredients in a large wooden bowl. "'Twas not why he was angered though now, was it? Because you disagreed with him?"

"Nay," Haith said reluctantly, crossing to the hearth to feed the fire.

"Well? Out with it."

"I—I *may* have implied that his parents abandoned him because they didn't love him." Haith cringed at the ugly words.

Minerva's hands froze in their task, wrist-deep in sticky, brown dough. She slowly turned her head. "You didna."

"Not in those exact words," Haith began. "But he—"

"And she wonders why he got a wee bit upset," Minerva interrupted, eyes raised to the ceiling. "My gods! Such kind words coming from such a sweet-tempered lass! And he was *upset,* you say?" Minerva turned back to her dough, cutting Haith off once more when she would have interrupted. "Sweet Corra, I doona believe it. Had you said those words to another man, I doubt you'd be possessing all your teeth just now."

"Minerva," Haith cried. "You take his side over mine?"

Minerva sighed heavily. "Listen well, faery. I'm nae taking sides. You both were wrong, and hurtful words likely flew from both your lips. However—"

"But—"

"However"—the look Minerva sent brooked no further interruption—"anything that Lord Tristan repeated, more likely than nae, came from Nigel's or Ellora's lying mouths. He canna be blamed for being the receiver of falsehoods."

"You, on the other hand, were deliberately hurtful in your words." Minerva's frown was intense, and she kneaded the bowl furiously until the table danced madly on all four legs. "The poor man, without gentle touches or kind words since he was a boy, always fighting in one war or another, struggling to make his way. Now he's faced with a town full of addlepated villagers, betrothed to one he desires not, and the very one he wishes for his own now tells him he is unlovable and incapable of his duties." Minerva sniffed. "You should be ashamed."

Indeed, shame weighed heavily on Haith in the wake of Minerva's scathing tirade. "I should not have said such things about his parents," she conceded. "I was just so angry!"

"Aye, I know your temper well." Minerva's own heat was beginning to cool, and the table once more rested on all its legs. "But you need to take a moment to see things from Lord Tristan's side before you lash out at him again."

Haith took one half of the divided dough and began kneading. "I have seen firsthand through Ellora what life is like with a man who rules with his fists. I'll not live like that."

"Of course you won't," Minerva scoffed. "Lord Tristan is likely tearing out his hair for what he did, and I'd wager he'd soon cut his own arm off before striking you." Minerva chuckled wickedly. "No matter how much your smart mouth begs correction."

"'Tis not funny." Haith shook her head. "If he thought it once, who is to say he will not again? And follow through? Nay," —her voice held firm—"I cannot take that chance, no matter what I dream or what the stones say."

"We shall see," Minerva said lightly. "You may change your mind."

Haith remained silent, although inside, her mind was quickly assembling a plan. Tristan would not have the chance to change her mind if she did not remain at Greanly.

Haith folded the dough in on itself and gave it a vicious thump as she thought of Donald's threats and Nigel waiting at Seacrest. Haith's mind clicked and whirred with the possibilities, trying to shut out Minerva's merry voice trilling out yet another of her bawdy songs.

Must she always sing while she works? Haith asked herself. *And so loudly! I can barely think over the racket.*

Minerva dropped a cloth over the fragrant mounds of

dough and danced the bowl in a circle before placing it near the hearth to rise. ". . . His arms were braw, and his eyes were blu-u-ue!" Thoroughly enjoying herself, Minerva shuffled her feet in a fancy jig. "My Scotsman lover I loved so true!"

Good heavens, Haith thought, the lively ditty making her mood even blacker. *If I have to endure one more Scots love song today, I shall—*

And it was then that the answer occurred to her.

CHAPTER
16

Nigel fell back on to the bed with an exhausted sigh of contentment, but he was not so tired that he missed the chance to land a quick slap on the bare buttocks of the young chambermaid who scrambled from his bed.

The girl tossed a dirty look over her shoulder while snatching her clothes from the floor and dressing as quickly as her fumbling limbs would allow. Since Lady Ellora's departure, Nigel's lechery had been given free reign over the girls who worked in the keep. The trysts he had instigated only covertly while his lady was in residence were now brazen abductions, likely to occur at any time. No woman within the keep walls was safe.

"Delightful, wench," Nigel praised. "Come visit me again this eve. Bring a friend."

The girl merely glared at the nude man, eliciting a chuckle from Nigel.

"Oh, do be good now." He smiled, and his eyebrows wiggled suggestively. "If I must seek you out, 'twill only be that much more merry for me." He reached a wiry arm over the side of the bed to grasp the wine jug left there and lifted it toward the girl in a mock salute. "I do so love a chase."

Nigel's chamber door slammed shut as the girl exited, and his smile grew wider around the mouth of the jug. He swallowed several healthy gulps and swiped his hand across his mouth.

Too easy, though, he thought as he rose from the bed and strolled to the pot in the corner, wine jug in hand, to relieve himself. The servant girls were a pleasant distraction and a temporary balm for his physical needs, but the one he truly yearned for eluded him.

Haith.

Nature's call answered, Nigel crossed the chamber to dress. He set the jug on a small table and began carefully shaking out the garments he'd laid aside before his most recent frolic.

A montage of visions paraded through his mind as he pulled on his chausses: Haith laughing with that cow Soleilbert; Haith sweeping her long, fiery plait over her shoulder; eyes the shade of a perfect autumn sky, snapping and sparkling with anger; Haith sprawled beneath him, crying out in fear.

Ah, yes, that was his most treasured recollection of all.

Had she now realized what she'd done in her foolishness? Nigel wondered. That bastard D'Argent had fled with his pitiful following of the most gullible villagers two days ago. Surely by now, Haith had seen Donald and had realized the dreadful mistake she'd made. With Soleilbert at Greanly now, Haith's pitiful little conscience was likely getting the better of her, too.

After all, Nigel mused, *her choices are either to betray her sister or to bed a handsome lord and regain her position in Seacrest's hold.* He chuckled to himself. Regardless of her lofty ambitions to catch Tristan's eye, Haith would soon learn, as would D'Argent, that a royal decree was like the word of God. William would not relent, Nigel was certain, especially since messengers from Seacrest had departed for London this morn.

Word from Donald had hinted at trouble with their plans and had also warned of D'Argent's intent to petition William. Nigel knew that information had to have come from Haith. *She may be cooperating now,* Nigel mused, *but I'll wager she will try to disentangle herself from my clutches if the chance arises.*

Even if the wench succeeded in winning D'Argent's favor, it would matter not after Nigel saw the new lord dead and Greanly returned to his own care—permanently this time. He would possess both the grand estate and the woman soon.

But Nigel did not anticipate having to wait for D'Argent's demise for Haith to return. True, her decision to go to Greanly had surprised him, but Nigel doubted the weak twit possessed the fortitude for espionage. Nay, any moment now, he expected a messenger with word that Haith wished to return to Seacrest and Nigel's waiting arms. Perhaps, even Haith herself would come in the stead of a messenger.

And being the gracious and forgiving man that I am, Nigel smirked while pulling his undershirt over his head, *I'll not hold a grudge against her little display of rebellion the night she left. Nay, no grudge at all, once she comes to me repentant and begging for mercy.*

A warning blow sounded through Nigel's chamber window, sending his eyebrows skyward. Perhaps even now, Haith rode through his gates.

Nigel rushed through the remainder of his toilette and, forgetting the jug of wine on the table, departed his chamber while whistling a merry tune through his teeth.

* * *

Donald peeked around the large tree that was his cover. The last of Greanly's soldiers were just disappearing through Seacrest's wall, and he knew that the time to move was now.

He darted from his shelter despite his fatigue and cumbersome form and slid around the wall, slipping into the shadows of the village.

Donald's stump hurt.

He cradled his right arm against his chest, his labored breathing causing the throbbing pain to increase fivefold as he slunk through the darkening alleys of the town. The stench of the wound no longer affected him, although those who followed in his wake would comment on the smell of poultry gone bad. He planned his route as he walked, cautiously avoiding Seacrest's residents as well as Greanly's soldiers, and wound his way through the maze of cottages to end up at the rear of the keep near the kitchens. Donald backed against the wall, his eyes scanning the surroundings for onlookers before disappearing inside.

The sound of angry shouts reached his ears, and he recognized Nigel's voice. Donald had just enough time to crouch behind several casks of wine when nervous servants fled the direction of the hall through the kitchens. He listened closely to the roars distorted by echoes to determine Nigel's whereabouts. 'Twas nearly impossible, and he stretched his neck over the casks, straining to hear.

A faint tickle on the back of his neck startled him so that he jumped up and spun around, banging his head on a shelf and crashing his already screaming stump into the wall. He muffled the shriek as best he could with his good arm and whirled around again with fever-bright eyes seeking his attacker.

There, on a hook above him, hung a shawl and an apron discarded by some maid already gone home to her cottage. The dangling hems had been the cause of his near discovery, and Donald jerked them from the hook and threw them to the ground, stomping them into the dirt of the corridor in his fury.

Then an idea occurred to him.

He picked up the garments and shook them out, then slipped on the long apron and draped the shawl over his head.

"You've come to *what?*" Nigel squawked, sounding quite like the perturbed rooster he resembled.

Barrett remained unruffled by the bug-eyed hysterics and looked on benignly as the prancing lord screeched. "You'll not remove anything nor anyone from this hold! D'Argent had his chance to take what was his two days past." Nigel paraded the hall, flinging his arms about in his choler. "That he could not secure his estate is not my concern, and *you* are not welcome here. Take your soldiers and be gone!"

"You'll not convince me with all yer womanly flouncin' about," Barrett said. He pulled Tristan's directive from inside his vest and tossed it on a nearby table. "But you needn't worry that we'll be back after this—them that don't go tonight is to be barred from Greanly forever."

"If only your brain was as big as your mouth," Nigel growled, stepping perilously close to Barrett, "you would understand my words. *No one shall leave Seacrest!*" A velvet-clad arm slashed through the air to drive his point home. "No one!"

Indeed, no one paid heed to the old woman staggering around the perimeter of the hall save for the few raised eyebrows and wrinkled noses among the soldiers.

Barrett caught a whiff of the stench himself and sniffed, casting a disgusted glance toward the hag. He dismissed the old woman's lack of hygiene as she disappeared up the stairs and turned his attention once more to Nigel.

"Your grievances are not my concern." He stepped closer to Nigel. "I'll carry out the orders given to me, and you'd be well-advised not to refuse a command what's come from William hisself."

"Do not presume to tell me where my interests lie, you ignorant, overgrown stable boy," Nigel said with a sneer. "My word is law here."

Barrett's expression did not change. "Nigel, you interfere in my lord's business tonight,"—Barrett's teeth flashed for a mere second as if relishing his thoughts—"an' I'll cut you down meself."

At those words, Nigel stepped back, his eyes growing wary as if just realizing he was surrounded by soldiers.

"They'll not go any matter," he said, referring to the villagers. "Lazy, stupid cattle. But go on then!" Nigel's laugh was overloud, and he spread his arms wide. "Try to persuade them if you will. It matters not to me."

As Barrett and the soldiers passed out of the hall and into the bailey, Nigel rushed forward—a tardy show of bravado—and cried, "William will see *you* hanged, *and* have Tristan's head for this transgression! Mark my words!"

No one paid any heed to the empty threat, and from the doorway, Nigel saw that while he'd been arguing with Barrett, many more of Greanly's soldiers had been quite busy. Already a score or more villagers were gathered on the green, a line of men quickly loading possessions into several wagons.

"Good people!" Nigel called out to the villagers from the safety of the doorway. "You need not go! If you fear William's Hammer, stay—he cannot harm you under my protection!"

Several of the women looked between Nigel and the soldiers who were herding their children, crying and reaching for their mothers, into a separate wagon. The women looked as if they expected their lord to intervene, and when he did not, they joined their children.

Even the chamber wench who had so recently left Nigel's bed climbed into a wagon as well. She threw Nigel a smug look as she settled her skirts.

"I'll kill him," Nigel muttered and slammed the door.

He heaped vicious curses upon the Lord of Greanly as he stomped around the keep, looking for someone, preferably female, on whom to vent his rage. The lower chambers were empty, most of the servants having fled at the first sounds of imminent conflict. Those who were of Greanly were either hiding or readying for the journey, and those native to Seacrest were too enraptured with the exciting event taking place in the bailey to see to their lord's comfort.

Nigel kicked over a cask with a great yell as he passed back through the hall and overturned a small table holding a draughts game. The pieces clattered around his feet, and he kicked and cursed and skidded his way through them.

He went to the upper chambers in search of prey. He jerked a tapestry that hung over the stairs from the wall and flung it to the hall below. A small stand holding a pretty wooden bowl full of spring flowers met its better in Nigel and lay splintered in his wake as he charged through the upper corridor. He saw flickering light spilling onto the floor —coming from his own chambers no less—and paused, face purple and chest heaving.

So someone is still within the keep, he fumed to himself. *Bloody well right.*

Nigel stormed to the doorway, shoving it open as he

yelled, "I care not who you are, but you'd be well-advised to have your clothes off!"

He was presented with the sight of a short, fat old hag standing at his chamber window with his recently forgotten jug turned skyward. Nigel skidded to a stop.

Holy Christ. I cannot.

Nigel eyed the pear-shaped individual with a sideways look of dread. He shuddered, took a bracing breath, squared his shoulders, and reached for his belt.

"Did you not hear me, hag?" Nigel stepped closer and raised his voice, thinking that the old woman might be hard of hearing. "Today is your lucky—*Holy Christ!*"

The Lord of Seacrest recoiled, a hand clapped over his nose and mouth—the stench was unimaginable!

And then the hag turned to face him.

"Good eventide, m'lord." Donald chuckled. "My thanks for the lovely welcome."

"What are you doing in my chamber?" Nigel retreated further, gagging not only from the odor but also from the fact that he'd eyed the smithy's body with lust. Bile rose higher in his throat.

"The good Lady Ellora freed me." Donald took a swig from the jug, then belched. "Ain't that what you told her to do?"

"Yea, of course." Nigel was slowly regaining his composure, while keeping a fair distance from the odiferous man. His eyes watered, and his nose ran. "But you were to remain at Greanly to receive word from Lady Haith."

"With that great bastard D'Argent huntin' me down? Nay. How was I to defend myself with this?" He withdrew his stub of an arm from beneath the shawl and held it out for Nigel to admire.

Nigel's stomach churned painfully as the air was further stirred by the black and brown sticky cloths that covered Donald's arm. "What happened?" he managed to choke out.

"Oh now," Donald scoffed. "Don't be squeamish, m'lord." He laughed harshly, but the wheeze quickly turned into a racking cough.

"I sent you there to kill Lord Tristan." Nigel's gaze remained steady. "By what is occurring in my bailey at this moment, I can only surmise that you failed."

"I can only surmise," Donald mimicked. He advanced on Nigel. "I got me fuckin' hand cut off! What do you expect me to do? Club him to death with it? The man's the size of a horse!"

Nigel held up his hands to ward off any further advance. "Calm yourself, Donald."

"'Twas me strong hand, too!"

"We shall fix it."

"I'll have to wear a hook!" Donald cried.

"I said we shall fix it."

"That will prove difficult, seein's how they already burnt up me hand!"

Nigel closed his eyes briefly. "I meant," he said with forced patience, "that we shall repay D'Argent for your loss."

"Oh." Donald blinked, his brow creasing. Then his face darkened with anticipation. "How's that?"

"First, you must tell me —what of Haith?"

Donald nodded with pride. "Aye, 'twas her that gave me the information that D'Argent was sending messengers to the king. Since I couldn't very well stay at Greanly with the bloke tearing the village apart searching for me, I told her that you'd send a rider seven days from today for further word."

"Good, good."

"But whether she will heed me or not is another matter."

Nigel's eyebrows rose. "What do you mean?"

"Well, m'lord,"—Donald puffed himself up in a display of importance—"I heard rumor before I escaped that D'Argent fancies the wench. Seems they was caught in a rather . . . *private moment.* He plans to move her into the keep."

Nigel's blood boiled at the thought of D'Argent gaining Haith along with Greanly, and he cursed violently for several moments. When his tantrum was over, he drew a deep breath, stroking his neat beard and thinking. "I will send no rider to meet her."

"M'lord?"

"You must find a way to regain access to Greanly."

"Oh no, you don't!" It was Donald's turn to back away. "I ain't going back there. The lout's out for my blood now, and if he finds me, he'll kill me for certain!"

"Then he won't find you."

"I can't even defend myself!" Donald continued to rant, waving his partial arm about again. "How am I supposed to kill him in this condition?"

Nigel shook his head. "'Tis not Lord Tristan we seek."

Donald's eyes narrowed, and he cocked his head. "Then who?"

"The Lady Haith."

"Go on," Donald prompted, his curiosity peaked.

"If we can abduct the wench and return her to Seacrest, D'Argent will follow."

"Aye?" Donald did not look convinced.

"Yea. The man has an overdeveloped sense of possessiveness. He'll come for the wench, if only to prevent me from having her, and once he comes, I'll kill him myself."

"I like that plan," Donald said. After coming into contact with the Lord of Greanly's wrath once already, the smithy was loath to even be in the same burg as the man. "But how am I to get the baggage here? She won't come willingly, I'll wager," Donald said. "My arm still pains me enough that she might overpower me."

"Good point." Nigel grasped his chin in thought once more and paced the far side of his chamber. "We must lure her here."

"How do we do that?"

Nigel stopped and waved away the repulsive man's concerns. "Details later. First, we must see to your health," he said, indicating Donald's disability. "In this condition, the whole of Greanly could likely smell you from here."

Donald sniffed the air. "I don't smell anything."

"Trust me." Nigel motioned for Donald to precede him through the doorway, at the last minute reaching for a cloth to cover his nose. "Let us seek your care."

Donald passed Nigel, and the two men made their way down the stairs.

"Donald," Nigel asked, his words muffled by the cloth pressed to his face, "what exactly happened to your hand?"

"He cut it off!" the smithy cried in exasperation and hurried ahead toward the kitchens, hitching up his makeshift skirts. He shook his head and muttered, "Dense, ain't he?"

CHAPTER
17

"Tristan, save me," *Haith called.*

Tristan knew she was close, so he ran, searching the alleyways of Seacrest, his breath coming in ragged gasps. He had to find her!

"Tristan!" *She called again.* "I'm here!"

He turned a corner in a sprint and collided with a village woman carrying a cumbersome basket. The woven vessel tumbled to the dirt, spilling its unlikely contents of sparkling blue jewels. Tristan gripped the woman by her shoulders, and she looked up into his eyes.

"Save me, Tristan," *the woman said.* "I'm dying."

Her voice belonged to Haith.

Her face belonged to Tristan's mother.

"Nay!" Tristan bolted upright in bed, his heart pounding as if it would leap from his chest. "Nay," he cried hoarsely again.

"Does a nightmare plague you, m'lord?"

In an instant, Tristan had sprung from the bed and

grasped his sword. He now held the tip mere inches from the intruder's face. "Who dares invade my chamber?"

A candle on a nearby table flamed to life, and Minerva's wrinkled countenance was revealed.

"Fear not, Lord Tristan," she soothed. " 'Tis only I."

"Old woman," Tristan growled, lowering his blade, "you very nearly lost your life." He sighed and ran a hand through his tousled hair before realizing he stood stark naked in Minerva's presence. He snatched a covering from the bed and hastily draped it around his body.

Minerva chuckled. "I'll not assault your form in lust, m'lord. Although a fine form it is."

Tristan threw her a dark look and sat on the edge of the bed, his heart still thumping. "What are you about, Minerva?"

"I've come to speak of Haith."

Immediately, Tristan's stomach lurched, and he sprang once more from the bed to grasp Minerva by the shoulders. "What is it?" he demanded, his thoughts contaminated by his recent nightmare. "Is she ill? Where is she?"

"My, you're a grabby one," Minerva said. "Nay, Haith sleeps and is well, I vow it."

"You are certain?"

"Aye. I left her but a moment ago." She paused when Tristan did not release her. "My lord, you've dropped your blankie."

Tristan glanced down, and indeed, he was unclothed yet again. Disregarding the meager cover as unreliable, he opted to return to his bed instead as his modesty was more likely to remain intact there.

"If Haith is well, then why seek me at this late hour?"

"Think you I would not question her return to the cottage?"

Tristan grimaced. "You know about our argument."

Minerva's eyes narrowed. "Aye. And your heavy hand."

He glanced at Minerva's scowl in a bid for pity. "That woman's tongue is as a blade."

To Tristan's surprise, she smiled. "Aye, her mouth does tend to run away without the company of her brain."

Tristan snorted at the jest, but made no lighthearted reply. Instead, he addressed the old woman seriously. "She loathes me now, does she not?"

"She's willin' herself to," Minerva conceded. "And Haith can be possessed of a hard head."

"What can I do to make amends?"

"I canna answer you that, m'lord."

Tristan's forehead creased. "Then why are you here, if not to advise me?"

"To spin you a tale," Minerva replied. "One that may help you to find your way into our faery's head, although you already have her heart."

Tristan started. "Think you she cares for me?"

"Doona be silly, m'lord." Minerva leaned closer and confided, "She's had the dreams, too, you ken? Since she was a lass of eight winters."

"Since she was a child?" Tristan blinked and then looked to Minerva in earnest. "I would have you tell this tale of yours."

"Very well." Minerva nodded. She rose from her chair and approached the bed, eliciting a wary look from Tristan. She flapped her hands at him. "Move your great mass a bit so that an old woman may find comfort."

"'Tis not proper," Tristan muttered, but heaved himself over to make room for Minerva.

She sat on the side of the bed. "Your honor's safe with me, m'lord. Now, hush your prattle and listen."

Minerva's eyes bored into Tristan's, and as she whispered, the candle flickered, casting mad, dancing shadows along the chamber's stone walls.

From end to end,
The tale begins.
Your ear I'll lend,
From now to then,
And safely bend
It back again.

The candle ceased its fluttering and shone steady.

"That was lovely," Tristan said, his eyes taking on a hazy glaze.

"Thank you. Now be still."

Minerva's soothing voice was low and flowing as she began wrapping Tristan in her words like a soft, warm cocoon.

"Many seasons ago, before William came to this land and while Edward was still king—"

"I was in Paris then," Tristan offered, his eyelids growing heavy.

"How nice. Shall I continue or nae?"

Tristan nodded. "Go on."

"There was a young lass, daughter of the powerful Laird Buchanan. Her father, a wise man, feared for his family's safety while the clans warred amongst themselves. His wife had already fallen to another clan's treachery. He wished to hie his only child away until the unrest was settled."

"The laird knew of an Englishman, friend to Edward and lord of a grand estate. He sent his daughter and his sister to the English lord for fostering. He could foresee troubles that would plague his country for generations to come, and hoped for his daughter to match with a favored lord of Edward's court."

"The laird's sister and daughter cried and pleaded to remain, but he wouldna hear of it. So Corinne and I

journeyed to England at the mercy of James of Seacrest
and his wife . . ."

The wagon wheels clattered over the old Roman road
that led to Seacrest, and Corinne Buchanan clutched her
aunt to her side as the strange manor came into sight. "It
isna too late for us to turn back, Minerva," she pleaded.
"Let us call to the men and return to Da. He needs us."

Minerva patted the nervous girl who trembled beside
her. "Nay, lass. 'Tis the Buchanan's wish that we journey here, and we canna go against him." She smiled at
Corinne, the tiny wrinkles that would line her face years
later just teasing the corners of her eyes. "Doona fear.
Your da wouldna send us to a place unwelcome to us."

"'Tis a strange land," Corinne mused, looking over the
rolling hills that slipped into the sea beyond their intended destination. To her young eye, the countryside was
dismally flat compared to her craggy highland home. She
pulled the bodice of her gown away from her sticky chest
and frowned. "The air is overthick. Like a bog."

"You'll get used to it."

"There's naught that could make me stay here,"
Corinne vowed, tossing her bright, coppery curls over
her shoulder. "I'll nae find a man to suit me either. Certainly nae soft English fop."

Minerva laughed. "Easy, lass. How are you to be
knowin' what an English laird is like?"

"I've heard tales."

"Well, you'll be wise to keep them to yourself while
we're at Seacrest."

Corinne rolled her eyes and sighed. Minerva forever
chastised her as if she were still a child instead of a full
grown woman of ten and seven.

The wagon carried them through the outer walls of

Seacrest and rolled to a stop before the hall. The great doors of the keep swung open, and a pretty blond woman, barely more than a girl herself, burst into the bailey and fairly flew to the wagon.

"Welcome," the woman smiled, breathless in her excitement. Her skin shone with peachy color, complementing her large brown eyes and silky golden hair. "Welcome to Seacrest. I am Lady Ellora." Her eyes flew from the older to the younger woman, and her smile widened. "You are Corinne?"

Corinne nodded, feeling decidedly frumpy compared to the fresh-faced woman beaming up at her. This woman was Lady Ellora? She was only a year, mayhap two, older than Corinne herself!

"Aye." Corinne finally found her voice, and she indicated Minerva. "This is my aunt."

"Minerva! Yea, I remember from the letter. Welcome!" Ellora stepped back to allow the shaggy Scots guards to assist her guests from the wagon. She immediately hooked her arm through Corinne's and led her toward the hall. "I am so glad you are here! I can hardly wait for us to become better acquainted—" She paused and blushed prettily. "Listen to me prattle on when you must be exhausted!"

"I am feeling a bit weary," Corinne admitted.

"Of course you are." Ellora led the women into the blessedly cool, darkened hall. "I'll show you to your chambers and have a light meal and some water sent up. After you've rested, we can visit."

Despite the belligerent attitude Corinne had been determined to keep, she smiled at the friendly, open woman who was her hostess. "I should like that very much."

"Mama!" A small child tottered over to the women, yellow curls bouncing and her nurse chasing after her.

Ellora scooped the three year old into her arms with a forgiving look at the harried nurse. "Soleilbert, say hello to Lady Corinne and Lady Minerva."

"'Lo." Soleilbert held out two chubby arms and launched herself at Corinne, crying, "Me!"

"Oh, my," Corinne laughed, just barely catching the child. "Aren't you a precious one?"

"I'm sorry." Ellora's look was indulgent. " 'Me' is her way of warning you that she wishes to switch keepers. She likes you."

"'Tis quite alright." Corinne tickled the baby's tummy. "I like you as well, pretty lassie."

The nurse stepped forward. "Shall I take her, my lady?"

"Oh, nae," Corinne rushed. "She's nae bother, really."

"You're sure you don't mind?"

"Aye." Corinne smiled and smoothed a marveling hand over her springy curls. "You'd like to come with Auntie Corinne, would you not, flower?"

"Aye," Soleilbert mimicked.

The women shared laughter over the baby's antics, and Ellora led the way up the stairs. Neither Corinne nor Ellora noticed the look of deep sorrow that had washed over Minerva's face.

Within the blurry confines of Tristan's mind, a fortnight passed in little more than the blink of an eye. He witnessed Corrine's and Ellora's friendship growing stronger with each passing day. The visions were dizzying in their speed, and they only slowed on the day Lord James returned as Minerva tried valiantly to engage Corrine's attention outside the keep.

But Ellora was insistent. "Oh, Minerva, she must come to greet him!" the lady cajoled. "He has been away for so long, and I know he will have want to meet the Buchanan's kin right away!"

Minerva's lips were set in a fine line. "Aye, he's been

away for weeks—all the more reason for you to have your greeting in private."

"'Tis true, Ellie," Corinne reluctantly agreed. "I doona wish to intrude."

"We shall have our private time aplenty come nightfall." Ellora grinned wickedly, and the two younger women collapsed upon each other giggling.

Ellora wiped away tears of laughter. "You shall be present at his arrival, and that is my command as lady of the keep."

Corinne pulled a silly face at Ellora's grand attempt at authority, but before the two could lose themselves in merriment again, Corinne stilled.

A warning of riders approaching sounded throughout the village.

"He's come!" Ellora squealed and jumped from her chair to dash from the hall.

A visible shiver shook Corinne, and her stomach suddenly tumbled. She flung off the odd feeling and stood, attempting to smile at Minerva. "Are you coming or nae?" she asked her aunt, who sat by the hearth fingering her smooth telling stones and looking unreasonably sad.

"In but a moment, lass," Minerva said, resignation tingeing her words.

Corinne gave her a puzzled look. "Very well." And she, too, left the hall.

A single tear escaped Minerva's eye as she watched her young niece depart. Through the portal, she saw bright blue skies and fat, billowing clouds. The pure golden sunshine of a perfect summer's day.

Minerva was not at all surprised, however, when a crack of lightning rent the placid air with a sizzle, and thunder rumbled the timbers of the old keep.

"Ah, my precious one," she murmured. "How I will grieve you."

* * *

The candle gutted low in Tristan's chamber, and he started. Minerva's words had enchanted him so that he was certain he had felt the breeze of Corinne's passing through Seacrest's hall, tasted Minerva's salty-sweet tears, smelled the scent of Ellora's hair as she embraced Corinne.

"What happened?" His voice was low and taut.

"The very worst, I fear." Minerva shook her head slowly. "James was my Corinne's soulmate, the one she had dreamed of for many a year, and she was James's as well."

"They fought their love for many weeks. Corinne was determined to remain loyal to Ellora. So much so that she became dreadful ill with the effort. Several months after the lord's arrival, Corrine came to me and told me she would return to Scotland and die rather than betray her friend. I warned her 'twas folly, but she was thick-skulled, my sweet lass."

Tristan's mouth turned up at one corner. "At least we know that Haith is true to her nature." The smile was chased away. "Corinne did not flee?"

"Oh, she tried." Minerva took a deep breath, as if to brace herself for telling the remainder of the tale. "One night in the deep of winter, with only the clothes on her back and a sack of dried venison."

"When James discovered she was gone, he nearly went mad with terror. You see, he'd done his best as well to avoid Corinne, denying his heart out of his duty to Ellora. He and Corinne were never in the same chamber together for any time, but all the same, Ellora had begun to suspect his feelings."

"The night Corinne fled, James gave chase with nary a supply or word of explanation to his wife. It took him two days to find Corinne, and she was nearly dead when he did. She couldna make the journey back to Seacrest right away, and James nursed her for a week before they returned to the keep. 'Twas done then."

"What do you mean?" Tristan asked. The sun had just started to peek over the far foothills, casting an eerie glow in his chamber and giving Minerva's face a wan, gaunt appearance.

"Ellora was no fool," Minerva conceded. "When Corinne and James returned together nearly a fortnight later, she knew that she'd lost him to her only friend. 'Twas a blow not many women could survive."

"Haith was born the following harvest, a seed planted during the time James and Corinne were alone together, and the keep was never the same. James recognized Corinne as a lady of Seacrest equal to Ellora's station and Haith as his daughter, as true as wee Soleilbert. But Ellora never forgave Corinne. I doona think my lass ever forgave herself either."

"You would not think Haith and Soleilbert would be so close," Tristan mused.

"'Tis the way with bairns, m'lord," Minerva smiled. "They cared naught for their mothers' squabbles, for they both loved and were loved by all. Soleilbert delighted in Haith. She had been a lonely little lass before our faery was born."

"Then James and Corinne died," Tristan prompted.

"Aye." Minerva's eyes grew pained. "James cut down at Hastings and Corinne when the hoard invaded Seacrest. The bloody bastards." Minerva trilled off a vicious curse in Gaelic. "They killed my girl while we were giving James the funeral rites. Would have slaughtered wee Haith, too, but they thought her already dead as she walked with the spirits."

"Walked with the spirits?"

"'Tis a tale for another time." Minerva stood from the bed with a creak and a groan. "Haith'll be waking soon."

"Wait," Tristan called when the old woman would have left. "Indeed, I have learned much from you this night, Minerva, but how is it to aid me?"

Minerva halted at Tristan's door. "I canna give you your way, m'lord. I only carry the message. 'Twas time you ken the weight of your and Haith's state."

"You are telling me that fate has decided we shall be together? That we have no other choice?" Tristan's tone betrayed his doubts.

"Aye, there's another choice." Minerva opened the door. "One of you can die."

Minerva left the room, closing the door softly behind her.

CHAPTER
18

Haith sought Tristan shortly after rising the next morning. After their row the previous day, she felt confident of her ability to secure his aid in seeing her to Scotland.

She wandered through the village, loathe to enter the hall, when she spied him in a nearby field. As if he could sense her presence, his head rose from the conversation he was holding with Rufus, and he looked at her.

Her heart lurched at the sight of him standing in the tawny dirt, spring's green finery as his backdrop. In the field beyond, serfs stooped like pilgrims behind ox and plow, rising and bowing as they performed the ceremony of setting Greanly's bounty deep in the fertile soil. His hair was ruffled by the playful breeze, and his strong arms were braced casually on his hips. Haith fancied that she could even see the steely flash of his blue eyes as they assessed her.

Tristan clapped the messer on the back and turned to stride slowly toward Haith. She squared her shoulders and lifted her chin a bit, trying to squash the shiver of need she felt. *I do not love this man,* she told herself.

"My lord," she began before he'd quite reached her, "if you could spare but a moment."

"Lady Haith." Tristan's words were easy, his face carrying neither the anger nor the teasing smirk she was used to seeing. "I'd hoped to speak with you this day as well. Walk with me."

Haith fell into step beside the huge man, her hands clasped calmly in front of her to still their trembling. She opened her mouth to speak but was cut off.

"I apologize for my behavior yesterday," Tristan said. "Never would I wish you to fear me."

Haith was stunned. She had been counting on his anger to further her cause, and his words of regret threw her. She spoke before she thought. "'Twas not my place to advise you on the management of your keep."

Tristan shook his head, his brows drawn down in thought. "Still, 'tis no excuse." He stopped suddenly, so that Haith did as well.

Haith looked up at him, and the regret in his eyes, along with something else she could not name, dented the resolve she'd worked so hard to erect. How could she have said such hurtful things to this man?

"Then we shall not think of it again," Haith said firmly. "'Tis not why I sought you this day any matter."

The hint of a smile teased his lips. "You have done me a great service, Haith." He held out his arm. "Continue on to the keep with me, and ask what you will."

Haith reluctantly took his arm and immediately regretted it. The feel of the warm muscles in his forearm sent shivers to her core, and for a moment, she could not speak. She could smell the musky scent of him through his tunic—he'd been working this morn.

As they wound their way through the village toward

the keep, Greanly's occupants nodded and smiled as they passed.

"Good morn, m'lord, m'lady."

Haith's thoughts became tangled further at hearing the villagers' casual pairing of their titles. How easily they seemed to roll off their tongues!

Haith shook herself. Nay, 'twas not possible. If William upheld his decree, 'twould mean only pain for everyone involved. She must be firm.

"My lord," Haith pressed on, trying to avoid the smile with which Tristan gifted her. "I have a favor to ask of you."

"I will do my best to oblige."

Haith took a deep breath. "I wish to travel to my mother's clan in Scotland."

Tristan halted so suddenly that Haith was nearly jerked off her feet. "Scotland?"

Haith's eyes flew around the bailey, seeking an object to rest upon—anywhere except for Tristan's questioning face. She seemed to have to squeeze each word from her body.

"Yea. 'Twould be best for all. I need your assistance traveling there."

Tristan's mouth hardened. "In truth, you are still angry about yesterday. So much so that you would flee?"

"Nay!" Haith's eyes met his. "Nay. I gave my word that 'twas forgotten, and it is so. My reasons for going to Scotland have naught to do with that."

Tristan crossed his arms over his wide chest and cocked his head. "And those reasons are—"

Haith flushed, and she leaned in slightly to grind out through her clenched teeth. "You know very well the reasons—all of them." She glanced around for prying ears. "'Tis the best solution."

Tristan, on the other hand, seemed unconcerned that they stood in a public place. "Why? Because you say 'tis the best solution?" His voice grew slightly louder. "I fail to see how you cowardly retreating to a land you've never before laid eyes upon will solve anything."

"I beg you, lower your voice!" Haith hissed. She regained some control over her frustration. "If I am not at Greanly when William gives his decision, 'twill make it easier for everyone to make logical choices!"

Tristan growled, looked around the bailey, and then dragged Haith behind a nearby cottage. "You speak nonsense," he began once he and Haith had more of a sense of privacy.

Haith, however, was mortified. Worse than someone seeing them speaking in a public place was being discovered hiding in a back alley. She glanced around nervously as Tristan continued.

"Those involved have already made their choices, or have you so soon forgotten Soleilbert's choice to take a lover?" He lowered his voice and bent his head closer to Haith's. "Or my vow that I would not wed her?"

"'Twill matter not if William decides against you," Haith reasoned, her mouth growing dry at Tristan's nearness. "He is king, and you are his vassal."

"And he is my friend." Tristan's eyes searched Haith's face, and he brought his hand to rest on the side of her head. "Tell me, Haith. What do you fear?"

"Nothing!" Haith said, averting her eyes lest he see the truth—she was afraid of everything. "Would you have me wait here then for William's word until Nigel sends for me to return to Seacrest?" Her eyes met his again. "I've told you before—I'll not go back there."

"Haith," Tristan murmured, "is your faith in me so small that you think I would release you that easily? To

Nigel or to Scotland?" His eyes glinted in the shadows of the alley. "You are hiding something from me."

Haith dropped her gaze. This would be much easier if Tristan would stop touching her, would stop speaking so gently. It made her feel cared for and protected in a way she'd only experienced in her dreams. She found it difficult to lie to him when the warmth of his palm nearly singed her cheek.

"Nay, I hide naught," she said, studying the pebbles under her slippers. "But my presence at Greanly is dangerous. For me and for you as well." She grudgingly looked up, her eyes pleading with him to hear her words. "You don't understand."

"I understand more than you realize." Tristan said, and Haith's breath caught in her throat.

"As long as you are within my reach, you need never fear."

"I cannot stay," Haith whispered on a sigh of relief. "Please release me."

Tristan leaned his forehead against hers, and the pair stayed that way for a moment before Tristan pulled away.

"Let us have a compromise then," he said. "Give me your word that you will stay at Greanly until William's decision is come. After that, should you still have want to go to Scotland, I will aid you."

Haith chewed her lip in thought. 'Twas folly to remain at Greanly with Nigel so near. She had no doubt of the earnestness of Donald's threats should she betray her wicked task, putting the whole of Greanly and everyone she cared about in peril.

But to stay, to be near Tristan with his promise of protection—it was too hard to refuse with the man standing before her. Already Haith's body hummed so that she could barely think, and the headache that had plagued her for days was miraculously gone. Perhaps William would dissolve the edict, and Tristan would be free before Nigel required more information.

But what, then, of Bertie? Would her mysterious lover care for her, or would she be cast back to Seacrest, alone and in shame, to bear Nigel's and Ellora's wrath forever?

"Please," Tristan's murmur interrupted her thoughts, and he brought his lips to the corner of her mouth. "Do not leave me just yet, Haith."

Haith's eyes closed, and she reveled in the feel of him so close to her, his breath warming her skin. "I—I do not know," she stammered, her voice husky. "This is too—you are—" she broke off, unable to find the words to describe how she felt.

"Stay but a while longer," Tristan breathed, moving his lips to the opposite side of her mouth, "and we shall see what we shall see."

Haith's head was spinning, spinning as she turned her face to meet Tristan's lips. And then she soared, all reasoning discarded as Tristan's mouth covered hers. Power filled her body, as if from a deep, ancient spring, and as it welled inside of her, she felt both strong and frightened at the same time.

How would she ever leave him?

A far off rumble like distant thunder filled the alley where Tristan and Haith clung to each other. The sound triggered terror deep within Haith, and she jerked back, eyes wide.

"'Tis only Barrett returning from Seacrest," Tristan assured her with a quizzical frown.

Haith's heart raced, and she tried to steady her breathing. "You must go." She averted her eyes.

"Not until you give me your word," Tristan said, his voice brooking no excuses. "Are we agreed that you will remain at Greanly until my messengers return?"

Haith nodded.

"Say it," he commanded.

"I vow to stay at Greanly until William's word is received," she said and then pinned her shrewd gaze on him. "And then you will send me to Scotland."

"Only if you wish to go." Tristan's smile teased as he pressed his lips to her forehead for a long moment. The sound of the wagons grew nearer. "Come to my chamber this eve," he urged.

Haith looked at him as if he had gone mad. "I will not!"

"I have something for you."

"I am certain you do." Haith said, lifting her nose into the air.

Tristan threw his head back and laughed before dropping his arms and moving away. "Come, Haith. I vow I'll not touch you, do you not wish it."

That is what I fear most, Haith thought to herself. *I cannot help but wish it.*

"What say you?" Tristan asked, still backing away, now nearly out of the alley.

"We shall see what we shall see," Haith said.

"I'll be waiting." Tristan winked and tossed her a wicked grin before disappearing around the cottage.

"Come," Bertie called from beyond her chamber door.

Haith entered to find her sister seated before the window, her chin resting on her fist. Haith noticed the unusual sag of her sister's gown about her bosom and waist as she sat slumped in the chair. Bertie seemed to be shrinking before her very eyes. "Good day, Sister."

Bertie's head jerked around, and she returned Haith's smile. "Thank God, Haith. I thought you were Mother."

"So that's why you hide in your chamber," Haith said, then asked, "Does she plague you of late?"

"Of late, yea. Always, yea." Bertie rolled her eyes, and Haith was shocked and pleased to see the graceful bone structure emerging from her sister's face. Why had she not noticed how much smaller Bertie had become? "She drives me mad with talk of weddings and my duties as future lady of Greanly."

"Hm-m." Haith lounged on Bertie's bed. "'Tis well she does not desire to speak of virginity, is it not?"

Soleilbert blushed, but her smile was dazzling. "I wondered when you would return for gossip."

"Well?"

"Well, what?" Bertie said slyly, getting up from her seat to join her sister across the bed. "What do you wish to know?"

"Soleilbert!" Haith slapped a hand on the fluffy mattress, eliciting girlish giggles from her sister.

"Oh, Haith," she sighed. "I am in love!"

"I surmised as much by the condition of your bedclothes the other morn," Haith said. *"Who is he?"*

"Pharao."

Haith's mouth dropped open. "Lord Tristan's man?"

"The very same."

"Bertie, how?"

"How? I don't know how." Bertie stretched out on her back, her golden curls fanning about her head. "Or why. We seem very different, do we not?"

"A bit," Haith said, still in shock. "You truly love him?"

"Yea. I cannot explain it. 'Tis as if"—Bertie flipped to her side and braced herself on an elbow, mirroring Haith's posture—"as if I had been waiting, searching for something all my life, and the moment I first saw him, I knew I had found it."

"I think I understand," Haith murmured, the memory

of Tristan's warm lips flooding her mind. She pushed the image away. "Does he share your feelings?"

"I think so." Bertie sat up and reached inside the neckline of her gown, withdrawing a fine golden chain on which there dangled an oblong medallion. "He gave me this before he left yesterday."

"Oh, Bertie," Haith gasped, reaching out to finger the pendant with its bold, intricate engravings. "'Tis beautiful!"

Bertie smiled in agreement. "'Tis the only item he possesses of his family." Haith's sister paused hesitantly before confiding, "I believe he plans to marry me when he returns."

"You're getting *married?*" Haith's eyes widened.

"I know not for certain, but he promised to return for me. Where we would go is a mystery—we certainly can't stay here."

Haith clutched her sister to her fiercely. "Oh, my darling, I shall miss you so if you do go." She pulled back, and there were tears in both women's eyes. "But I am so happy for you!"

Bertie smiled. "And I for you."

"What do you mean?"

"If I marry Pharao, Tristan will be truly free."

"Bertie, I do not love Lord Tristan, and he certainly is not in love with me."

"Nay?" Bertie raised an eyebrow. "Then what of your dreams? He wishes to marry you, you know."

Haith's stomach flipped at the admission. "They're just dreams. And he has said naught of marriage to me."

"To me he has." Bertie grasped Haith's hand. "Fight for him, Sister. He needs you so, probably even more than you need him."

"I do not need him," Haith argued. "I need only you and Minerva."

"But I will be gone soon, pray God," Bertie aimed her eyes on the ceiling briefly. "As will Minerva one day. Tristan is your soulmate, Haith. Do not turn away from him."

"You have been listening to Minerva's nonsense," Haith accused and rolled her eyes. "Can I not escape that hag?"

"I do not jest, Haith." Soleilbert's eyes were intense, brown pools. "You have thought of fleeing, yea?"

"Yea," Haith admitted. "To Scotland if William enforces your betrothal."

Bertie gasped and clutched Haith's hand to her heart. "God's mercy, Haith! Never again say such a thing! Do you not know the tale of when your mother fled our father to Scotland?"

"Nay, and I have no wish to hear it now," Haith warned, gently removing her hand from Bertie's grip. "Especially from you. Their behavior shames me."

Bertie eyed her sister carefully but did not comment. "Then 'tis well that I will not be present for Tristan to wed. Open your heart to him, Haith."

"I have an idea," Haith said, changing the subject. "Let us descend and greet the new arrivals from Seacrest. Perhaps they bring word that Nigel's fallen down a privy!"

Soleilbert could not help but laugh at Haith's antics. "Do not worry about me so, little Sister," she said with a warm smile. "I can take care of myself. We're both safe at Greanly."

"Come." Haith scrambled off the bed before she confessed to Bertie the very real reason why no one at Greanly was safe. "Let us go before all the good gossip-mongers are scattered."

CHAPTER
19

Haith and Minerva entered the hall together, summoned to the welcoming feast like all of Greanly by Tristan. Long trestle tables crowded together with benches in every available space, and the din rising from the villagers already gathered was impressive.

Several days had passed since the remainder of the villagers had arrived at Greanly. Haith had done her best to avoid Tristan during this time, choosing instead to spend her free hours reassuring the uneasy serfs and helping them adjust to their new village. Minerva, on the other hand, felt there was no need for comfort or understanding and voiced her displeasure sharply when faced with a weepy peasant woman.

In the midst of Minerva's latest dressing-down, Haith caught sight of Soleilbert beckoning to her from the lord's table and maneuvered through the crowd to join her.

"You did not know of this?" Haith said as her eyes glanced to the hall's entrances, covertly searching for Tristan. To be seen near him by this many of the village people was folly. Haith now knew that she could not trust her own judgment in his presence—a fact that unnerved her greatly.

Soleilbert smiled at the buzzing hall. "Nay. I wish it had been my idea. 'Tis very thoughtful." Bertie clapped her hands together in excitement as servants bearing large trays filed through the rear of the hall. She tugged Haith closer to the lord's table. "Let us sit, Sister. The feast is ready to begin."

"I must find Minerva," Haith said, shunning the notion that she should sit at Tristan's table. "She'll have want to dine with me."

"But there is Minerva, now, Haith—on Lord Tristan's arm." Soleilbert giggled. "And Mother is hanging on him as well. This should be quite entertaining."

Haith groaned inwardly as the trio approached the dais. Tristan's gaze landed on Haith immediately, the twinkle in his eye eliciting a spreading warmth across her cheeks. He halted, graciously depositing Minerva in the end seat before approaching the place where Haith and Soleilbert stood. Ellora scowled openly.

"Good eventide, ladies." Tristan bowed slightly, steering Ellora around the sisters to the chair at the end of the table opposite from Minerva.

"My lord, Mother." Soleilbert curtsied and smiled prettily when Tristan returned to hold her chair. She sat.

Tristan lightly took Haith's elbow, and she jumped at the blatant physical contact. "Allow me to assist you," he murmured.

She barely managed to avoid causing a scene as he led her to the seat next to Minerva, knowing every pair of eyes in the hall was focused on what was occurring at the lord's table. Although Tristan's manners were respectfully executed as he offered Haith her chair, she saw desire flicker just behind his eyes.

Tristan moved to stand behind the only empty seat,

the lord's chair, between the two sisters. He caught Barrett's eye where the big man stood down in front.

"Quiet!" Barrett's bellow seemed to vibrate the very stones in the walls, and the crowd immediately silenced. He turned back to his liege. "My lord."

"Welcome to Greanly." Tristan addressed the hall and raised his arms wide. "I am pleased to have my home filled with the folk who will make their lives here alongside me."

Haith glanced behind Tristan's standing form to Soleilbert and saw her sister smiling regally at the sea of wary faces. *She looks so comfortable,* Haith thought to herself. *As if she were meant to be the Lady of Greanly.*

She is meant for it, a dire voice warned. *By William's own hand, this place is hers.* Tristan's words shook her out of her reverie, and she allowed herself the luxury of his deep rumbling voice washing over her.

"I know the journey here has been a long and weary one. I speak not only of the distance traveled but also of the loss and sacrifice many of you have endured." Tristan's eyes roamed the crowd as he spoke, landing on individuals listening with rapt attention. "I cannot undo the events that have led us to this place, nor would I if I could. We are here now to serve our king, and serve him well we will by constant vigilance to our labors. I vow it."

"I have heard the rumors of my alleged bloodthirst and cruelty." Tristan raised an eyebrow as several villagers looked away. "I will not deny that I have killed, nor will I promise that there will never again be blood shed by my hand. War is cruel but necessary, and the victorious are oft labeled vicious by the conquered."

The crowd murmured nervously at those words. Tristan held up a silencing hand.

"I tell you this only to assure you of your safety at Greanly. You are my people. Greanly is my town as well as yours." His gaze swept the entire room, as well as the occupants of the lord's table. "What is mine, I value and protect—with my life, if need be. I expect no less from you in return." His eyes met Haith's for one brief instant, and she shivered.

Tristan continued.

"You will work here, and your labors shall be rewarded. But take heed because I will not tolerate deceitfulness in any form." Haith's breath caught in her throat. "Thievery, spreading of falsehoods, slothfulness in duty, or word against the crown are all deceit, and will do naught for our town save to destroy it."

Tristan's gaze was sharp, matching his words. "Any person found undermining Greanly's progress in any way will be dealt with swiftly and severely. That includes the villagers as well as those who sit at my table with me."

Haith's blood turned to ice. Could he have found out about her message to Nigel? He had spoken directly about the occupants of the lord's table to either side of him, and Haith knew in her heart that she had committed each act of deceit that he had named. Could she bear the punishment he would mete?

Could she bear the pain her treachery would cause him?

"If any of you have cause to seek me with a concern, do not hesitate, for my duty as your lord includes counsel."

Could she admit all and be forgiven, Haith wondered wildly. She still had two days before she was to meet Nigel's messenger. Perhaps with Tristan's protection . . .

"I have gathered us here tonight for celebration, for on the morrow, our labors begin in earnest. I also come requesting your fealty, although by rights, I could demand it. I wish your loyalty to be given freely or it is useless to me." Tristan picked up the chalice before him and raised it high. "I, Tristan D'Argent, Lord of Greanly, do vow to protect and serve my people in their prosperity and welfare under His Majesty, King William, and God Himself."

The hall was silent for one awful moment while wide eyes took in the sight of Tristan.

Then Barrett rose. "Thusly do I pledge my fealty to thee," he intoned solemnly, chalice raised to Tristan.

Rufus stood. "And I."

John was next, with Mary beside him. "Thusly do we also pledge."

"I as well."

"And I."

Within moments, the entire crowd before Tristan was on their feet, cups raised, echoing the sentiment. The abrupt turnaround in the attitude of the villagers after Tristan's speech was stunning, and Haith felt a pang of bittersweet pride in Greanly's new lord. He had done well.

Minerva stood and turned slightly to address Tristan. "My fealty to you, Lord Tristan, as well as my service and affection."

Haith caught a knowing look between the two.

Soleilbert stood. "In faith will I serve you for as long as I reside at Greanly." Her smile warmed the room, and her wording was not lost on Haith.

Now all eyes turned expectantly to Haith, the only one still seated, save Ellora, who was of another hold and could not swear fealty to Greanly's lord. With fear making her knees weak, Haith rose and faced Tristan, only to find that he regarded her not with suspicion but with a warmth in his eyes and a small, private smile as he waited for her words.

Haith swallowed and then cleared her throat. "I pledge as my sister," she murmured and quickly sat.

A grin tugged at Tristan's mouth as he again turned to

face the hall. His eyes glittered like the gem on the hilt of his sword.

"My people." His words echoed in the hall, and higher still he raised his chalice. "Welcome to Greanly!"

A great roar of celebration erupted, and Tristan gestured to the line of patiently waiting servants to begin doling out the trenchers. He then sat and leaned toward Haith.

"I know the game you play, faery," he murmured.

Haith froze with her chalice halfway to her dry mouth. From Minerva's lips, the endearment was unexceptional, but on Tristan's tongue, the words were a caress. She stammered, causing Tristan to chuckle.

"You think that by pledging loyalty as did Soleilbert that you will be free to leave me and go to Scotland as you choose." He leaned back in his chair and raised his cup in a mock salute. "I commend your effort. However, William's word is not yet come."

"I know that," Haith sniped and gulped her wine to cover her discomfiture.

Tristan was not put off by her tone. "Perhaps we will discuss it further this eve when you visit my chamber."

"I will not," Haith whispered fiercely.

"You will though. If only to hear the news I received." He lifted his eyebrows at her startled expression. "I told you I have something for you."

"What is this news you speak of?" Haith demanded.

"Later." Tristan eyed the trencher placed before him. "Come after midnight when all is quiet."

Haith opened her mouth to press him further, but was foiled when Ellora demanded Tristan's attention, sending Haith a nasty look. She turned to her own trencher to pick at her food, but her appetite had fled. She picked up her chalice instead and took a long swallow.

The temptation to cast a binding spell on Nigel was great, but Haith shuddered at the thought. The Buchanan's curse of talent had brought only tragedy each time Haith had been witness to it, and she could not risk worsening the situation. No, better to muddle through this by mundane means.

Which meant discovering Tristan's news.

Which meant visiting his chamber. Alone.

She drank again, then signaled the serving boy with the ewer of wine to come forth.

Her cup filled, Haith leaned back against her seat and let her gaze roam the room as she thought. The villagers looked happy, relaxed as they talked and feasted, several bursting into impromptu song. Soleilbert conversed easily with Tristan and her mother. Everyone in the room had cause for laughter and lightheartedness, but that would soon come to an end if Haith kept her word to Nigel. When the villagers had been loathe to come to Greanly and Bertie was miserable with thoughts of her wedding, when Tristan was known to her only as William's Hammer, Haith's deceit had been justifiable in her mind. But now . . .

Now, aiding Nigel would result in Greanly being torn apart once again, with no chance of peace. Bertie would be spirited back to Seacrest where her beloved Pharao could not reach her.

And there was Tristan.

If Nigel had his way, Tristan would be stripped of his title and lands. Perhaps even killed.

And all because of Haith's own selfishness. The truth appalled her, and she drank again.

Yea, too many things had changed, and the only one who could right them was Haith. If Tristan hated her for the deceit, then 'twas only what she deserved. Perhaps he would feel differently about sending her to Scotland after all.

Haith's mirthless laughter drew Tristan's attention.

"What amuses you, love?" he asked in a tone pitched for Haith's ears only.

"Oh, a great many things I suppose." Her words echoed into the chalice before she drank.

"Care to share your thoughts with me?" Tristan's grin was heartbreakingly gentle.

"At midnight, I will share all."

"Faery," Minerva pleaded from the doorway of the bedchamber, "let me send word to the lord that you will meet with him another time. Yer in no condition to be making serious talk."

Haith lifted the forearm draped across her eyes and peered down the length of her prone body at Minerva. There seemed to be two of the old healer. "Nay. I would have this matter resolved before dawn." She slowly pulled herself to the side of the bed and paused while she waited for the room to stop spinning.

Minerva's frown told of her skepticism. "No good can come of this."

"Please, Minerva. Be still, I pray." Haith stood, swayed, and then walked past the old woman with great care. "Do I not return by daybreak, 'twill mean he has most likely killed me. Send for my body."

Minerva rolled her eyes. "Oh, go on then."

Haith left the cottage and made her way across the still green surrounding the keep. The sky was aflame with a million stars, and Haith paused to admire them until they began to rotate slowly, spurring her to draw her gaze earthbound once more.

The heavy oaken portal to the hall was obstinate until she persuaded it to open with a mighty shove, leaving her sprawled on the hard, shadow-draped floor within. She groaned and kicked the door closed before awkwardly gaining her feet. Haith's stomach rumbled at the commotion.

"Sh-h!"

Up the dark stairs she went, gently, one hand holding her skirts while the other skimmed the cool, rough stones. The nearer she came to the top, the more resigned she became to the punishment she was certain was imminent.

Perhaps he'll have me whipped, she mused drunkenly. *Or even hung. He may send me back to Seacrest.*

Haith gained the top level and shook her head wildly. Nay, she'd rather be hung than delivered to Nigel's repulsive clutches. Whipped and *then* hung.

The corridor ahead seemed to fork, displaying four walls lined with doors, rather than two. *That's odd,* she thought. *I don't remember there being two passages.*

Haith shrugged, took the corridor on the left, and immediately bounced off a solid stone mass.

"Och! S'wrong run."

She moved to the right this time and was temporarily blinded by a bright light before a massive shadow blessedly shielded her pained eyes.

Tristan's voice sounded oddly sensual from the widening doorway. "I was not certain you would come."

Haith was sure that she breezed gracefully past Tristan, and therefore, she missed the amused gleam in his eyes at her stumbling lunge into his chamber. His hand shot out to steady her.

"Good eventide, m'lord." Haith shrugged his touch away. "I hope the rest of your feast was enjoyable."

"Indeed. 'Twould seem you enjoyed yourself as well."

"I doona wish to discuss such trivial matters." In Haith's mind, she perched on a chair in the corner, "I have important things to tell you. Yea, most dire."

Tristan's grin grew when Haith flopped onto a trunk.

He strode to a pitcher and poured a cup of water. Bringing it to her, he placed it securely in her hands.

"My thanks." Haith gulped the liquid, then sputtered indignantly and swiped at her mouth. "'Tis not wine!"

"I'll wager that after this night, you'll not desire that particular brew for some time." Tristan merely chuckled at the glare Haith shot him. "Drink the water, but slowly. 'Twill clear your head."

Haith set the chalice aside with her nose lifted in the air and then thought better of the angle of her head as she slowly began to lean backward.

Tristan lunged for her and sighed. "God's mercy, but you're pissed." He easily dodged her flailing arms and pulled Haith to her feet. "Come then. I'll see you back to Minerva, and we shall talk on the morrow."

"Nay!"

Tristan put his finger to her lips. "Haith, do you not wish to alert the keep to your presence in my chamber, you'll be quiet."

Haith's eyes widened, and she glanced around as if to spot eavesdroppers. She whispered loudly, "Nay! I must speak with you now! It canna wait!"

Tristan was thoroughly charmed by Haith's accent slipping to mimic Minerva's brogue. She stumbled against him, and he caught her firmly against his chest. Her unfocused eyes swam like the sea, and her face was flushed to the tip of her nose.

Tristan's voice was husky. "What is it, then, that is so important?"

"'Tis my fault," Haith whispered and squeezed her eyes shut. "All your troubles at Greanly. My fault alone."

Tristan smiled at her downturned mouth. From what he'd learned of Corinne from Minerva, he was not at all surprised that Haith had inherited her mother's strong sense of honor. Naturally, she would take responsibility for things beyond her control. Tristan steered her toward the bed.

"I am quite curious as to which troubles you have instigated, my lady. Enlighten me."

"Oh, but there are many." Haith's harsh laughter was interrupted by a hiccough. She flung an arm out and ticked off the list on her fingers. "The villagers! Nigel! Donald!" Tristan gently backed her to sit on the edge of the bed. "Doona even inquire of the lies I've told! And I broke every crockery in the cottage."

Haith peered at Tristan pitifully as he dropped to one knee before her. "Min—*hic!*—Minerva made me fix them though. Will you hang me?"

Tristan's shoulders shook with pent up laughter as he slipped her shoes from her feet. "I'm fairly certain that a few smashed pots do not warrant hanging."

"Oh, but I didna listen!" Haith continued to rant, and her eyes filled with tears. "Nay, the stones warned me, but still I told him all I knew!"

Tristan stood to turn back the heavy coverlet behind her. "Who did you tell what, love?"

"Are you nae listening to me, you great oaf?" Haith snarled as she climbed obediently beneath the covers Tristan held aside. "Nigel knows all." The soft coverings smelled faintly of Tristan, and Haith sighed.

Tristan tucked her deeply into his down pillows. "Do not fear Nigel, love. He cannot harm you here."

Haith struggled to an elbow. "'Tis you I fear for! His greed is fed by my own selfishness, and 'twill burn Greanly alive once more."

Tristan stretched out beside Haith on top of the coverings and mirrored her pose. "With each word from your lovely lips, I become more convinced that you are too drunk to make any sense."

Haith flopped onto her back. "Very well. If you are

too dense to understand what I very clearly explained, then a pox on you. I did my duty and my conscience"— Haith yawned massively—"is cleared."

"Good." Tristan smoothed the riotous locks of hair back from her face, and Haith's eyes drifted shut. "I am pleased that you are concerned with my welfare, Haith."

"Mm-m. I am. Verra concerned."

Tristan smiled. "But you must believe me when I tell you that Nigel is no match for me." His fingertips drifted down the side of her cheek, and he was amazed at its smoothness. He leaned his face close, bringing his lips to hover over Haith's. "I will triumph. There is no other choice."

"I'm sorry, Tristan." Haith's lips barely moved, so close to oblivion was she. "I didna know 'twas you all along."

"'Twill always be me, Haith." His lips brushed hers, and he paused for a moment, gathering his strength before pulling away. "Sweet dreams."

Haith's fingers grasped his sleeve weakly, although her eyes did not open. "Nay, no dreams this night. I beg of you, stay with me."

Tristan was torn between his heart, which lay before him, and his duty, which lay in yonder hard chair. Could he be so near her and not touch her? Especially when she was so willing?

"Stay," she whispered again as if she sensed his indecision.

"Very well," Tristan said gravely, stretching out once more and pulling her closer. "But we cannot make love while—"

Haith's timid snore interrupted his lecture. Tristan chuckled and rested his chin on the crown of her head, prepared to keep vigil over her throughout her sleep.

CHAPTER
20

Haith awoke to a great roar filling her skull, the noise of it threatening to draw blood from her ears. She cracked one eyelid open with care, as it felt rather crusty, but at the first bland rays of daylight, she snapped it shut again.

"Oh, God," she groaned, the two syllables causing her brain to feel as if it were being wrung between two massive hands. She heard stomping in the chamber and a great crash. "Minerva, please."

Tristan chuckled at Haith's wince as he walked quietly to the side of the bed bearing a pitcher, a bowl, and a hunk of bread. He set the tray on the floor before perching on the mattress.

"Good morn, Haith."

At that slight motion and the sound of Tristan's voice, Haith's eyes snapped open wide. With a surprising display of agility for one so ill, she leapt from the bed and instinctively dove for the pot in the corner.

Tristan winced at the painful noises, although his eyes were merry. He did not envy the consequences Haith now faced for her overindulgence, but waking up with her in his arms had been an experience beyond his expectations. At this moment, he should be about Greanly's business, and Minerva or Soleilbert should be playing nursemaid, but he had not been able to resist seeing her in his chamber, his bed once more before handing her care to another.

The first wave of retching had stopped. Tristan poured a cup of water and dipped the corner of a cloth in the cool liquid. He approached Haith bearing these gifts, but he could not keep the humor from his voice at the sight of her with both palms braced on the wall above her hanging head. It was as if she were trying to keep the very stones from tumbling in on her.

"Here, have a drink and a cool cloth."

Haith turned her head minutely to glare at Tristan with red, crackled eyes. "Go away."

"If I do, how will you explain your emergence from my chamber?" Tristan held the chalice closer and smiled when she took it. "Drink slowly, or 'twill set the spasms off again."

His warning came too late as Haith emptied the vessel of its contents. A loud gurgle came from her stomach, and she dropped the chalice with a clang to lean over the pot once more.

Tristan retrieved the discarded chalice and pressed the cloth into her hand when she raised her head.

"Someone has poisoned me."

Tristan fought the urge to laugh and instead helped Haith back to the bed. "Yea," he said gravely. " 'Twas yourself."

Haith lay down with a pitiful mew, but forgot her discomfort as her location occurred to her. "What am I doing here?"

"You do not recall our night of passion?" Tristan chuckled at the glare Haith sent him. He took the cloth from her, rinsed it, and rewrung it in fresh water before handing it back. "I requested your presence after the feast last eve, and to my surprise, you came. Drunk, but you came."

The events slowly emerged from her cramped memory. She groaned softly and covered her face with the cloth as Tristan continued.

"I had news to impart to you, but could not as you seemed desperate to confess some imagined wrong. Then you passed out."

"Not imagined. Real." Haith's voice was muffled through the damp covering.

"Haith." Tristan's voice was indulgent. "You cannot carry the burden of every person close to you, nor can you claim responsibility." He sat down on the bed, ignoring her growl of frustration. "If you will but listen to the news I have, you will see that you are not to blame."

Haith lifted the cloth away to stare warily at Tristan. "I'm listening."

"I have reason to believe that Nigel has placed a spy at Greanly. There is word that his soldiers arrived at William's court before mine and have spread distorted tales of my acquisition of the villagers."

"Oh, my God," Haith breathed, closing her eyes. Now her treacherous alliance was known by the king himself.

"Because some of the rumored events occurred after Donald's escape, I can only assume 'tis someone who resides at Greanly and is in friendly communication with Nigel." Tristan gently stroked Haith's arm. "I believe 'tis the Lady Ellora who betrays us."

"Nay." Haith fought her pounding head and roiling stomach to sit up. "Nay, Tristan. 'Twas not Ellora."

"Is it truly such a shock?" Tristan asked. "Do not try to defend her, Haith. 'Tis possible that she aided Donald in his escape. The woman has motivations only she is privy to. But fear not, I seek her this morn, and she will not contact him again before William's word is come. I vow it."

Haith's hand shot out to grasp Tristan's forearm. "You must listen to me—"

But Tristan carefully extracted himself and moved toward the door. "Rest here a while, and I will send your sister to you."

"Wait!"

The chamber door closed.

Haith struggled out of the bed and stood, the swift motion causing her head to scream and the bile to rise in her stomach. More carefully, she dropped to her knees to locate her thin leather shoes. Quickly slipping her feet into them, she paused for a moment to give her stomach time to settle.

She vowed to herself that she would never drink wine again.

Haith cracked the chamber door open and peered up and down the corridor—empty. She made her way down the stairs as casually as possible, but the commotion below made her entrance unnoticed. She paused halfway in her descent.

Tristan stood in the midst of a group of men, some of whom Haith recognized as being the men sent to London. One of the soldiers withdrew a parchment from inside his vest and solemnly handed it to his lord.

Haith's stomach flipped in on itself, and she clutched at the wall for support. Her eyes met Tristan's as his gaze instinctively sought her over the men's heads. A clatter behind her caused Haith to turn to see Bertie rushing down the stairs.

"They've returned, Haith!" Bertie's voice was excited, and her face shone. "Has Pharao come yet?"

Haith shook her head. "Not yet." She turned back to

watch the proceedings below and felt Bertie's hand slip into her own.

Tristan addressed the guard who had given him William's missive. "Where is Pharao? I would hear his report."

The guard's face was stony, but his eyes flicked to his fellow soldiers. "My lord, your man did not return with us."

Bertie's small gasp was unheard by all except Haith, who squeezed her sister's hand in support.

"Why is this?" Tristan demanded. His eyes met those of each soldier, seeking explanation.

The man who had, unfortunately for him, been elected to speak addressed his lord. "As we departed London, a band of riders dressed in the same fashion as your man approached. Pharao spoke with them briefly before joining them. He did not return."

"Are you saying he was abducted?" Tristan's voice was disbelieving.

"Nay, my lord." The soldier vehemently shook his head. "We would never allow that." The soldier looked around at the other men as if seeking aid when Tristan roared a string of fiery curses. "We would never have marked him a traitor either, my lord."

Tristan spun on the man and lifted the soldier by his chain mail vest before he could blink. The other men quickly stepped back several paces.

"I will cut out your tongue should you ever use it to tarnish Pharao's name again. Do you understand?"

"Yea, my lord. My apologies. I merely—"

"Get out." Tristan released the man, and the soldiers fled the hall. Tristan turned to the stairs where Soleilbert and Haith stood frozen in shock.

Suddenly, Soleilbert dropped Haith's hand and flew down the remaining steps. She crossed the hall and entered Tristan's embrace, her sobs echoing sadly.

"Why?" Bertie cried into his tunic. "Why did he leave me?"

Tristan's and Haith's eyes met over Soleilbert's head, then Haith's gaze dropped to the paper Tristan held against Bertie's back.

"There, now, Lady Soleilbert. Give me time, and I will get to the root of this mystery."

The hall's rear door opened, and Ellora swept into the room, Barrett lumbering several paces behind her. "What is this commotion?" The slim blonde halted in her tracks, and a pleased smile spread over her face at the sight of her daughter in Tristan's arms. "How lovely."

Bertie turned her tear-streaked face from her mother's gaze and, pulling away from Tristan, sped past Haith up the stairs.

"She is moody of late, is she not?" Ellora asked flippantly and turned to Tristan. "From where do the soldiers hie?"

"Act not as if you are ignorant of the soldiers' mission, Ellora." Tristan warned. "Your place here is tenuous at best, and your play of innocence galls me."

Ellora looked taken aback quite convincingly. "My lord, what is it you accuse me of?" Her eye caught the parchment clutched in Tristan's hand, and her eyes widened further. "Do you have word from Nigel? Is . . . is he displeased with me?"

"We shall soon know of his pleasure or no, I'll wager, but until then"—Tristan stepped closer and leveled a finger at Ellora—"you are not to be trusted. Barrett?"

"My lord?"

"Take Lady Ellora to a cell until I send for her."

Ellora looked around, frowned. "What? I pray, Lord Tristan, tell me what I have done!"

Haith finally found her voice to intervene. "Tristan, do not do this. Ellora knows naught."

Tristan did not even glance in her direction. "Stay out of this, Haith," he warned. "And hold your tongue."

"Nay." Haith forced her legs to navigate the remaining steps and came to stand between Ellora and Tristan. "I cannot in good conscience allow this to happen."

" 'Tis not as you think," Tristan growled. "Go to your cottage before you say something you may regret."

Ellora's eyes flew between the lord and Haith. "Does this whore fill your ears with falsehoods?" she asked shrilly. "She lies! *She* is the one not to be trusted!"

"Barrett, take her," Tristan said dismissively and turned to walk from the hall.

Barrett grasped Ellora by the elbow courteously. "Come this way, m'lady."

"Unhand me, dolt!" Ellora tried to shake off the large man steering her toward the rear of the hall.

Haith's cry cut through the hall like a dagger, causing all present to stop and stare. " 'Twas I!"

Tristan paused at the open door, and his brow lowered. "Haith, be silent."

"Nay! 'Tis not right!" She rushed forward and beat a fist on her chest. "I was the one Nigel sent to spy on you, Tristan. I alone."

Barrett gasped. "Lady Haith!"

Haith ignored the sheriff's shock. "I was never betrothed to Donald—'twas a ruse to gain entry to Greanly." Her eyes pleaded with Tristan. " 'Twas before I truly knew you. I took the lies Nigel spoke for truth and feared for Bertie's safety as your wife. I thought I had no choice."

Ellora tried to jerk her arm free of Barrett's grasp to no avail. "You made a pact with my husband?" she hissed. "To ruin Soleilbert's marriage?"

"Say no more, Haith," Tristan's voice was sharp, but she continued.

She turned to Ellora. "Nay, not to ruin her marriage but to protect her! I love Bertie!"

"You love only yourself!" Ellora screeched, and her words made Haith wince. "You are a whore as your mother was a whore, and I hope you both rot in eternal Hell!"

Ellora was ripped from Barrett's hold by unseen hands and flung to the stone floor. Minerva's voice rang true and dire from the doorway where she now stood with Tristan.

"You'll nae sully Corinne's name again, Ellora." Minerva strode over to stand above the shocked woman. "Would you care to hear the other choice your husband gave Haith?"

Haith stepped forward. "Minerva, nay. It matters not."

"Oh, but I disagree, faery," Minerva said with false joviality. "Perhaps Ellora need know that if you did not aid Nigel's perfidy that he would require you to lie with him and bear him an heir."

"You lie!" Ellora whispered, her face crumpling as she looked between Minerva and Haith.

"Nay. I doona lie." The old woman's gaze seemed to burn into Ellora's.

Tristan cursed. "Enough! Barrett, take the lady."

Haith spun to face Tristan. "Why? I have told you the truth! 'Twas I who told Donald of your plans to petition William! I should be imprisoned before Ellora!"

"Very well," Tristan growled. "Take Lady Haith also. Put them in separate chambers lest they kill each other."

Barrett's face held question. "My lord?"

"Now, Sheriff Barrett."

Barrett pulled Ellora from the floor as if she were a child having a tantrum, but Haith meekly offered her arm to be led from the hall. Before they disappeared into the rear corridor, Haith looked over her shoulder.

"I am sorry, Tristan. I tried to tell you."

When they were gone, Minerva turned to Tristan and laid a comforting hand on his arm. She gestured to the parchment. "Do you have your answer yet?"

"Nay, I have not looked." He scrubbed a hand over his face. "Can she never do as she is told?"

Minerva chuckled sadly in answer. "You'll send word to me?"

"Of course."

"I'll be at the cottage." Minerva tossed a rueful glance at the archway to the lower prison before departing, shaking her head as she went.

Tristan walked to the lord's table and collapsed in the chair with a frustrated sigh. "Blasted woman."

He looked at the missive before him, sealed with William's crest. Tristan withdrew a small blade and, with a breath, split the wax cleanly. He unfolded the page to bold, dark words scrawled over the entire piece of yellowed paper.

Lord Tristan,
I have received and considered your petition that your betrothal to the Lady Soleilbert be dissolved. I must be forthright with you in disclosing that Lord Nigel of Seacrest has expressed concerns with your behavior toward the people of Greanly, your refusal of his stepdaughter, and your disregard of Lord Nigel himself as a peer equal to your status. We have known each other well, Tristan, and fought many battles together. I consider you a friend as well as a loyal servant to the crown, and I have always held you in the highest respect. For those very reasons, it is with great regret that I must deny your petition. As king, my priority must lie with the unification of England's lords before all else. As

you are now a lord of high position, you must also adopt the practice of placing England's welfare above your own.

'Tis my command that the alliance between Greanly and Seacrest stand. Unless there is sound evidence as to why this should not occur—evidence indicating a benefit to the kingdom and not personal gain—in my decision I will not be swayed. Defiance on your part will warrant swift reprisal by means that are too distasteful for me to put forth at this time.

'Tis also my understanding that a Lady Haith now resides at Greanly. Until you are wed, this is acceptable, but following the nuptials, she will be returned to her guardian at Seacrest forthwith.

Accept your duty as I know full well your honor persuades you. If you follow this advice, the malcontent of your people will subside, and your position of esteem will again be restored in my eyes.

William

"Dammit!" Tristan's fist slammed onto the tabletop, his rage and humiliation at William's rebuke firing a twitch along the granite line of his jaw.

The ultimatum that William had put forth was clear: do as I command, or Greanly will be yours no more. More so than the king's directive, Tristan's fury was fueled by Nigel's small victory. The vile man's missive had beaten Tristan's messengers to William's ear, succeeding in being first to petition his cause and portraying Tristan's request as selfish and contrary.

Tristan's desire to see Nigel's downfall was ravenous, especially after Minerva's earlier revelation of the position into which he'd placed Haith. The thought of his fiery faery beneath that putrid excuse of a man, her body growing round with his child, sickened him.

And scared him. William's word, however naïvely reached, was final, and the possibility that Tristan could lose Haith was quite real. In addition to this turmoil, Tristan's closest and most trusted advisor, Pharao, was missing.

Tristan flicked William's letter away from him with a toss of his wrist, and it floated to the center of the table. Leaning back in his chair, only one thought circled his mind—Nigel must be stopped. Haith would not be returned to him, no matter the cost to Tristan.

At that moment, Barrett reentered the hall and stoically approached the lord's table. "Both ladies are secured, m'lord," he said. "Is there anything further I can oblige you?"

Tristan could sense Barrett's hostility at the task he'd just performed, and Tristan's regard of the man rose. That the sheriff had shown loyalty to Tristan by following his command, despite his displeasure at Haith's imprisonment, spoke volumes about Barrett's character.

"Sit down, Barrett." Tristan indicated the chair next to him.

The request seemed to unnerve the large man. Never had he presumed to sit at the lord's table, at least not while the lord was in residence. He reluctantly sat.

Tristan paused in thought for a moment before speaking. "You have heard of Pharao's disappearance?"

"Aye." Barrett nodded his shaggy head. "'Tis all the men speak of."

Tristan tapped one long finger on the tabletop and chose his words carefully. "Barrett, I have known Pharao Tak'Ahn for more than a score of years. He is a brother to me, and I know with certainty that he would not depart the men without word to me of his intentions."

Barrett's coolness thawed a bit when faced with his lord's concerns. "What do you reckon happened?"

"In truth, I know not. 'Tis my desire to blame Nigel, as he seems to be the source of many of the trials that plague me, but my instinct says otherwise."

"Aye. Pharao's abduction would be of no gain to the coward." Barrett's eyes were keen. "'Tis my thought that Nigel fears him."

"Mine as well." Tristan's eyes were sharp as they flicked to the parchment between them. "There is more."

Barrett's brows drew together. "William was not favorable to your cause?"

"'Tis as we feared. Nigel has regaled him with half-truths and outright lies in order to secure not only my downfall but the return of Lady Haith to Seacrest as well." It pained Tristan's pride a great deal to admit the setback.

"You'll not allow it, m'lord!" Barrett's cheeks flushed magenta. "William must hear reason!"

Tristan raised a hand. "And so he will. Although William claims to stand firm on his decision, I know he would hear proof of Nigel's misdeeds. I do not think the king trusts him."

"A wise king he is, if 'tis so." Barrett shook his head before meeting Tristan's gaze. "What is there to do?"

"I must journey to London to petition William in person. And since Pharao was taken just outside the city, perhaps I can glean some insight into his whereabouts as well."

Barrett leaned forward. "Of course, m'lord. When do we ride?"

"Nay, good sheriff. There is no 'we' in this matter—I ride alone."

"'Tis too dangerous a journey, m'lord, to make on your own. You'll have to pass Seacrest directly on the London road."

" 'Tis the way it must be," Tristan said with finality. "I can travel faster alone, and attract less attention. Besides, I need you here. With Pharao gone, the burden of Greanly's security rests on your shoulders."

At Tristan's words, Barrett sat taller in his seat as if he now understood the great measure of trust his lord awarded him.

"I'll not fail you," Barrett vowed. "No one shall breach these walls in your absence."

"And neither shall any depart," Tristan added. "I know not for certain who messengers for Ellora betwixt this keep and Seacrest, and until 'tis clear, we can take no chances. 'Twill be nigh impossible to keep my journey a secret from the villagers, and I am certain that once our traitor discovers I've gone to William, she will be eager to relay the news to Nigel."

"Aye. I'll try to quell the rumors as long as possible to give you lead." Barrett hesitated as if unsure of his next words. "What of the, er, prisoners, m'lord?"

"They are to remain imprisoned until my return. The only visitors to the lower chambers shall be yourself, Minerva, and the Lady Soleilbert."

" 'Tis true then?" Barrett asked dismally. "Lady Haith has betrayed us?"

"She thinks thusly," Tristan admitted with a wry grin. "Her only attempt was of no import—Nigel was certain I'd petition William from the night we first met, but he knew not when."

Barrett looked relieved. "She thought to cause your downfall by relaying what Nigel already knew?"

"I was aware of Nigel's game but kept that knowledge to myself until I was certain of Haith's fidelity. Let her go on believing her guilt for now though. Nigel will be furious with her for her lack of communication, and her imprisonment is but for her own safety. Ofttimes, Lady Haith's will outweighs reason."

"You know our girl well, m'lord."

Tristan's face hardened as he spoke his next words. "Lady Ellora's guilt, however, is more easily proven. 'Tis by mere chance that I discovered a missive from her to Nigel. I know not how many of those letters escaped my detection, nor what information they contained."

Barrett nodded solemnly, then looked to his feet as if contemplating a serious matter. When he raised his eyes to Tristan's, they were troubled. "Tell me Greanly will survive, m'lord. I was witness to the heartbreak of all at Seacrest for too many years, and cannot bear to think of the consequences should you be denied."

Tristan clapped a hand on Barrett's shoulder. "Then rest assured, good sheriff. For I am in possession of a considerable will myself." Both men rose from the table. "Ready two horses for my journey, along with only the most meager of supplies. I ride at dusk and through the night."

"Aye, m'lord."

The big sheriff departed, and Tristan headed for the stairs, pausing at the doorway to the cells below. To see Haith once more before he departed was a temptation he could barely resist. After a moment's hesitation though, he continued on to the upper chambers, content with the memory of her in his bed to comfort him on his journey. When he returned from London, Tristan hoped they would have the rest of their lives to spend together.

CHAPTER
21

Haith slumped dismally in the corner of the cool, damp cell in which Barrett had so solicitously interred her. In her mind, her misery was now complete.

As if Ellora could hear Haith's thoughts from her cell across the corridor, she spoke. "I hope you are pleased with yourself."

"Oh, yea, Ellora. I am overjoyed."

"And well you should be." The woman's voice grew louder, and Haith surmised that she had moved to stand at the small, barred opening. "You've gotten what you set out to achieve."

Haith rolled her eyes. "Indeed, I had hoped to be branded a traitor and a whore and then locked away in a cell today. Another chore completed."

"Flippant bitch."

"Do not speak to me."

"Why? Does it displease you? Annoy you? Wonderful! Then I shall do naught but chatter incessantly. What shall we talk about? Hm-m?" Haith heard an echoey ticking, like a fingernail tapping on a metal bar. "Perhaps you'd like to hear all the ways you've made Soleilbert's life miserable? Or we could discuss your lust for my husband and Lord Tristan. 'Twould seem your taste is not picky as long as the man you set your sights on is meant for another."

"Shut up."

"I could tell you how your whore mother threw herself at my husband after I took her and that Scots hag into my home."

"Did you enjoy the way that Scots hag dealt with you in the hall earlier? You were warned to hold your tongue against slandering my mother."

Ellora laughed. "Oh, and what are you going to do? Throw dried leaves at my head? You should know how eager the slut was to spread her legs for a real lord—"

Haith's temper flared white-hot, and in an instant, a sharp flick of her forefinger elicited a shriek and an "oof" from the opposite cell. Haith rested her chin on her fist and continued brooding.

"Witch," Ellora hissed.

"Quiet." Haith needed time to think. The repercussions of her actions were as yet unclear to her, and she felt the situation at Greanly had spiraled wildly out of control.

Foremost in Haith's mind was the welfare of her sister. Word of Pharao's disappearance had devastated Soleilbert, and Haith could only imagine the fear and uncertainty that must plague her now. It was imperative that the two sisters speak and form a plan, but how? Would Bertie even be permitted to the cells, and if so, how would they speak privately with Ellora so near? Haith knew that Bertie's love for Pharao would prevent her from accepting her betrothal to Tristan now even more than before his disappearance, but one woman's will was naught against that of a king.

Haith felt tears swell painfully in her eyes, and she

covered her face. *Had I but remained silent, I could be consoling Bertie this moment.*

But, nay. As vicious as Ellora's words had been to Haith, she could not allow another to be imprisoned in her place. Tristan had needed to hear the truth, and although Haith's conscience was now unburdened, the consequences were bitter. She would never forget the cold stoniness of his gaze when she'd confessed to him, or the way he'd still sought to protect her from blame.

Haith's chest contracted, and she choked back a sob. The stupid curse! Why, why had she been saddled with not only a hex that prevented happiness but also hereditary talents that rained down disaster when used? Haith cursed the lineage that damned the Buchanan women to destroying the lives of the men they loved.

"Oh, sweet Corra," Haith whispered, her head rising slowly as she realized what her thoughts had just confirmed. "I love him."

"Haith?" Ellora's voice was hesitant. "Are you ill?"

Haith struggled to keep her voice level despite the tears that streamed down her face. "Nay, Ellora."

"You are talking to yourself." Ellora's tone turned acidic once more. "I'll not be confined with a mad woman."

When Ellora received no biting retort, she tried a different tact. "Haith, if I ask something of you, can you for once reply with honesty?"

"I'll not lie to you, Ellora." Haith's voice was husky with unreleased sobs. "If I cannot answer truthfully to what you ask, I'll not answer at all."

Ellora seemed satisfied with the response. "If my husband indeed propositioned you as you claim, if he desires you so, why then would he send you away from him to Greanly? 'Twould have been quite convenient to dally with you while Soleilbert and I were away."

"Were you not listening when 'twas explained in the

hall?" Haith scrubbed the tears from her face and pushed her misery aside gratefully to give vent to her rage at Nigel. "Your husband gave me a choice, Ellora. 'Twould seem his greed is equal to his lust."

"Then your explanation is that if he could not persuade you to lie with him, he would enlist your aid to secure Greanly." Ellora seemed to mull this over in her mind.

"Yea. And with either choice I was damned."

"'Tis not you I care about!" Ellora's voice took on a new level of anger that Haith could not remember hearing before. The blond woman took a steadying breath before continuing. "What did he say of Soleilbert's future should Tristan fall into disgrace?"

Haith blinked several times in confusion. "He said only that Bertie would be young enough to remarry."

Language so foul that Haith unconsciously flinched issued from the chamber across the corridor. All was quiet for a moment before Ellora again spoke, and this time, her tone was accusatory.

"Why could you not simply lie with him?"

Haith swiftly gained her feet, sputtering with indignation. She came to her cell window to stare accusingly at the older woman. "So I could prove true your opinion that I am a whore? I would rather die by my own hand."

"Oh, grow up!" Ellora shrieked. "I learned some time ago that life is no joyful tale, Haith, and ofttimes we are pressed to perform duties that are distasteful."

"You would see Nigel's rape of me as a distasteful duty?"

"Yea, if 'twould save Soleilbert from a life like mine!" Ellora's chest heaved. "If you love her as you say you do."

"Ellora,"—Haith's icy blue gaze bore into Ellora's brown—"I am truly sorry for the pain my mother caused you. The memory of her actions shames me every day of my life. But you cannot expect me to spend the rest of my days repaying a debt that is not mine."

"I do love Soleilbert, and the choice I made in coming to Greanly was done with her welfare in mind. Had I the chance to choose again,"—a vision of Soleilbert after her night with Pharao flitted through Haith's mind—"I would do no differently."

"Then you are stupid and selfish," Ellora said tiredly. "He would not have given you a child at any rate—his seed is dead."

Haith's eyes widened in shock. "But he said—"

"I know what he says; 'tis merely a balm for his ego. Think you I am blind to the way he dallies with the servant girls? Or that 'tis any wonder none of them have grown fat with his child in eight years?" Ellora snorted. "My ability to bear a child is moot when he has no seed to plant. The worst fate you would have suffered at his hands would have been a lost maidenhead and bruised dignity. I can tell you true that those are light burdens to bear."

"You know naught of my burdens," Haith declared resentfully.

"And neither do you know of mine," Ellora said as Haith moved away from the window.

Slumped back in her corner, Haith's blood boiled. No matter the course she chose, it seemed she was always at fault. She was weary of the blame, sick with the burden of guilt of her very existence. Fed up with the struggle of seeing to the welfare of those she cared for, only to cause them further misery. It was as if she screamed and screamed, yet no one ever heeded her cries.

Perhaps it was that self-pitying thought, combined with her captivity in the cell, that brought to vivid memory her dream of the empty meadow. Haith froze, and a chill overcame her as the horrific details of the nightmare blossomed in her mind's eye.

'Twas all too eerily mirrored to be coincidence. The stone walls, the feeling of being unheard and alone. Pharao's cryptic warning echoed in her brain as if he had whispered it in her ear.

You cannot stop what is not under your control.

Haith knew she must find a way to speak with Bertie and find out exactly what William's message to Tristan had commanded.

The opportunity presented itself sooner than Haith had hoped when just before dusk, Bertie descended to the cells accompanied by Barrett.

The giant sheriff preceded Haith's sister with torch in hand, setting aflame the sconces that lined the corridor, providing not only light but also a much appreciated warmth to the dank chambers. From Barrett's other hand swung two small braziers. Soleilbert followed closely, a tightly bound bundle in her arms, and Barrett's torchlight revealed her flushed cheeks and swollen, puffy eyes, which darted away from Haith's.

"Good eventide, ladies," Barrett boomed. "We've come bearin' provisions."

The skeleton key clanged in the lock of Haith's cell door, and in a moment, the portal swung open, admitting the two visitors.

"What is the meaning of this?" Ellora's voice called from across the corridor. "I have need of supplies as well."

"I'll be but a moment, Lady Ellora," Barrett replied mildly. He set one of the braziers on the floor and gestured to the bundle Bertie carried.

Haith's gaze flitted worriedly over her sister's form as Bertie unrolled the clutch of items, allowing Barrett to select several objects before departing Haith's cell. She was not at all surprised to hear the lock engage once more. After all, she was a prisoner, no more noble than the vile Donald, and not to be trusted.

Disregarding her sister's aloofness, Haith rushed forward to embrace Bertie, whose only response was to stand woodenly.

"Bertie, my darling, how do you fare?" Haith whispered and leaned back to peer into her face. "Bertie?"

Soleilbert finally raised her eyes. "Haith, I am a fool." Her chin trembled. "How could I have thought for even a moment that he would return?"

Haith drew her sister to her once more. "'Twas not Pharao's choosing to be waylaid, I'll wager. He was on his way back to you when he was accosted. Perhaps his attackers will ask Lord Tristan for ransom."

"Everyone I love is taken from me." Bertie shrugged and pulled away, wiping at the tears on her face. She bent and began sorting items from the bundle: a blanket, a robe, Haith's own comb. She straightened and faced her sister, glancing at the barred window before whispering her next words. "William has denied Lord Tristan's petition."

Haith blanched and placed a palm against the rough stone wall for support. Before she could form a reply, Bertie spoke again.

"Do you plan to flee if you are released?"

Haith nodded slowly. "Yea. To Scotland as soon as can be arranged. I'll not remain at Greanly to complicate matters further, especially now that we know the king is unsympathetic to our plight. And I cannot return to Seacrest." She paused, unsure of how to continue. "Bertie, Nigel sent me here to—"

"I already know, Sister." Bertie met her gaze fully, and Haith was shocked at the calm acceptance she saw there. "Barrett explained the details to me before we came down, but I have suspected as much for weeks."

"I'm sorry," Haith whispered. "I never wanted to lie to you, Bertie. My intentions—"

"Haith," Bertie interrupted again gently, and her face softened, "I know." Those two small words spoke volumes to Haith, and in that instant, she felt absolved. They need speak of it no more.

Then Bertie's mouth became a grim slash as she thought for a moment. "Lord Tristan journeys this night to seek word of Pharao. If he returns without hope, I go with you."

Haith's world tilted. Tristan had left Greanly without word to her. She should not be surprised that he would close his heart to the one who had betrayed him, but nevertheless, the knowledge that he had so blithely departed so soon after her confession left her bleeding. *Well,* she told herself, *'tis truly finished for me now. The curse has achieved its purpose once again.*

"Haith?" Bertie clutched her sister's arm when she did not reply. "Do not say that I cannot accompany you."

"Nay, nay." Haith shook herself and tried to don a smile. The result was watery at best. "Of course you may go if 'tis truly what you wish."

"I will not remain at Greanly to marry a man I do not love, no matter William's command. My heart belongs to Pharao and always will." Bertie glanced furtively at the cell door. "You are my only family now, Haith, and I'll not lose you as well."

Tears filled Haith's eyes, and she nodded sharply. "'Tis decided then. We shall need the time while Tristan is away to plan." The sound of Barrett departing Ellora's cell spurred her to speak quickly. "Send Minerva to me."

Bertie shook her head. "Nay—she suspects you will flee and has spoken of stopping you. We must plan in secret until the time is nigh. Either she departs with us, or we leave her."

Haith was surprised and not a little impressed with Bertie's newfound decisiveness, but was prevented from answering when her cell door swung open.

Barrett entered the small chamber, nearly filling it with his bulk. "Lady Haith, on the morrow I'll be bringin' you some things to make your chamber more comfortable. Hope you can make do for the night."

Haith looked askance at him. She had never before heard of captors eager to make a prisoner more comfortable, but she wisely held her tongue. Perhaps some of the items Barrett would bring would be of use on their journey.

"My thanks, Barrett. I appreciate your kindness."

"'Tis naught of my doing. Lord Tristan bade that you be cared for." Barrett ignored Haith's disbelieving frown and addressed Soleilbert. "Lady Bertie, if you are ready to take your leave?"

"Give me but a moment longer, Barrett." When the man had respectfully moved into the corridor, Bertie leaned close to Haith's ear. "I shall return in the morn. What do I need to do to ready us?"

"A map first." Haith's mind raced. "We cannot depend on Minerva's memory to guide us even if she agrees to the plan. We must know the route."

Bertie nodded. "I'll search the lord's chambers this eve."

"In your own room, ready clothing for the both of us. And coin. Supplies in my cell would appear suspicious, but we will need them close at hand when the time comes."

"Those simple tasks should not be difficult with Mother no longer hovering over me." Bertie embraced her sister. "If only this was not necessary, Haith. Truly, I am afraid."

"I know, Sister. I am afraid, too."

Ellora's voice drew the two women apart. "Soleilbert! I will not be ignored."

"Coming, Mother." Bertie crossed to the door. "Sleep well, Haith."

Haith's only reply was a small smile. Sleep had not been her friend for many months. She sat wearily by the brazier, hungry for warmth.

In the small cottage she'd shared so recently with her niece, Minerva rocked trancelike before the cold, dark hearth. The absence of fire before her belied the visions that had taken hold of the aged healer, for her mind's eye was filled with flames.

From within the fiery wall, faces and shapes emerged, and mumbled bits of Gaelic fell softly from Minerva's wrinkled lips as she concentrated.

"Faery, you must wait." Images of Haith flitted through the blaze, her hair dancing wildly in the inferno. Tristan appeared, a silent scream of rage freezing his face. He wielded a fantastically long broadsword at the flames, as if his blows would vanquish the burning enemy.

Minerva's breath caught in her throat, and then the image exploded into a million tiny embers, realizing Minerva back in her chair at the cottage. Her entire body trembled at the memory of what she'd seen. With her limbs shaking, the woman dropped to her bony knees to ignite a warming blaze but froze when she saw what was scrawled in the ashes of the hearth.

Cunnart.

Danger.

Minerva quickly swiped the offending omen away with a hand that shook as if palsied. She sat back on her heels, fire forgotten, even though the sun was now fully set and the cottage rested in shadow.

When last a fiery vision had appeared to Minerva, her sweet Corinne had died. There was little doubt in her mind that Haith was planning to flee Greanly; therein lay the danger. Away from the keep, Haith could not be protected. Minerva could only thank Corra that she was imprisoned for now and pray for Tristan's swift return. For the first time, the old woman also prayed that Haith would not experiment with her gift beyond the harmless breaking of crockery. If she discovered the scope of her abilities, when combined with her stubborn will, Minerva wasn't sure anything could be done to protect Haith from herself.

CHAPTER
22

Three days had passed since Haith's imprisonment, and although the small area of the cell had been difficult to become accustomed to, she had to admit that it was outfitted splendidly. A small cot had been procured, pushed into the far corner, and piled high with furs for comfort. A tiny table and two chairs for the meals that were brought to her, recently by young Ham, and for the daily visits from Soleilbert. In truth, if it was not for the obvious fact that she was a captive, the cell resembled a typical lady's chamber. Barrett had even fashioned a sort of curtain for the small barred window to offer privacy while changing or bathing.

The days had taken on some semblance of routine. In the mornings, Barrett brought a small pot of warm water for washing; he was accompanied by Ham, who bore the morning repast. Soleilbert and Minerva would appear before the noon meal to dine, Bertie with her mother and Minerva with Haith, but then Bertie would spend the remainder of the afternoon in Haith's cell.

There the two plotted until Ham came with supper, and the next day, 'twould all begin again.

Minerva's demeanor of the past days had left Haith on edge. The old healer questioned her ruthlessly, her sharp eyes seeming to bore into Haith's skull in search of the answers she was denied. Minerva danced around the subject of Scotland almost daily, and when Haith turned the discussion elsewhere, she would be regaled with tales of young women who were lost and never found while traveling. Minerva seemed to want to speak of Corinne and James just as often, but Haith did not need the distraction and heartache that sprung from Minerva's delving into the past.

'Twas the very mistakes of her parents that Haith hoped to set to rights with her and Soleilbert's flight.

While Minerva was abnormally uneasy, Ellora was unnaturally quiet. Her frequent baiting of Haith had nearly ceased altogether, and the only times she could be drawn into conversation was while Bertie visited. When Barrett descended to the cells to see to the prisoners' welfare, Ellora would revert to her usual demanding self, insisting on her release and asking to speak to Lord Tristan. It seemed Ellora was the only one unaware of his absence.

The lady's behavior became more strange late in the morning of the fourth day when a message arrived from Nigel, inquiring of her welfare and when the wedding could be expected. He also asked about Haith's whereabouts—did she still reside at Greanly? Ellora flew into a rage, tearing the parchment into tiny pieces and dropping them into her brazier.

Barrett stared dumbly for a moment as Ellora paced the cell before him, pounding a fist into her palm.

"What is your answer, m'lady?"

"I have no answer for that evil man. Let him sit at Seacrest and wait until he rots."

Barrett shuffled his feet. "His messenger awaits at the gate. You must answer him, Lady Ellora, or mayhap he will journey here himself. We cannot—"

"Of course, you're right." Ellora spun and held out her hand for the quill and parchment Barrett offered. "He must not have reason to come to Greanly until I am ready for him." Ellora sat at her own small table and quickly penned a short missive.

Across the corridor, Haith listened with unabashed curiosity. Never had she heard Ellora rail at her husband in such a manner, and her strange words left Haith uneasy. 'Twould seem that the woman had some plan of her own.

Ellora signed the message and folded it, but when she reached for the candle to seal the fold, Barrett's hand stayed hers. He retrieved the parchment and exited the cell, locking the door behind him.

"Sorry, m'lady," he said. "There can be no secret messages."

"As you wish, Barrett," Ellora sighed. She walked to the opening to twist her signet ring from her finger and hand it to the sheriff through the bars. "If 'tis not sealed, he will become suspicious."

As soon as the ring dropped into Barrett's palm, Ellora left the window, dismissing Barrett quite effectively for one imprisoned. The big man turned to the cell behind him.

"Lady Haith?"

Haith stood at her own window. "Yea?"

Barrett slid the letter through the bars. "Could you read this aloud?" His face pinkened.

Haith took the missive and unfolded it to Ellora's graceful penmanship. She cleared her throat with a glance to the cell across from hers before she began.

My Lord Husband,
*   You need not be concerned—plans for the wed-*
ding are well underway, and all fare well at
Greanly. Of course you will be notified when the
ceremony is to take place. I count the days until
we are reunited.

Your wife, Ellora

Barrett nodded satisfactorily and handed Ellora's signet ring to Haith, who performed the task of sealing the letter. After the sheriff had gone, Haith stared across the corridor, contemplating the wisdom of drawing Ellora into conversation.

"Ellora? Does Nigel's message trouble you?"

"His very existence troubles me," came the reply from the recesses of the other cell. "Do not accost me with your childish questioning, Haith. As usual, I have many burdens to deal with, and I cannot be bothered by your empty prattle."

Haith's face went slack at the cool dressing-down she received. She decided to let the prickly woman be for now, but tucked away the tiny piece of information she'd gleaned from Ellora's bout of temper.

The sound of voices echoed, and Minerva and Soleilbert entered the corridor with Ham, who bore the baskets containing the noon meals. Minerva followed the lad into Haith's cell, but Soleilbert remained in the corridor and leaned close to the bars to whisper to Haith.

"A messenger from Nigel waits." Her face was unusually pale.

"I know." Haith glanced behind her to see Minerva settling herself at the small table. "'Tis well though. Your mother has put his questioning to rest for now." Haith lowered her brows. "Sister, are you feeling unwell?"

Soleilbert shook her head. "Later."

The meal seemed to drag on for an eternity as Haith endured more cryptic tales from Minerva. Haith ate quickly, feeling no hunger but wishing the visit over. Soleilbert had not looked well with her ashen face and tired eyes, and Haith feared that bad news awaited. Minerva, however, seemed content to draw the afternoon out, picking at her stew and rambling on about the many methods of torture highwaymen employed on their victims before slaughtering them mercilessly.

"That's lovely, Minerva," Haith said with a smirk. "'Tis truly amazing how you come by this wealth of information about such vicious brigands while brewing your potions here and at Seacrest."

"Doona be smart with me, faery. I indeed had a life before you breathed on this earth."

"As a highwayman perhaps?"

"Och." Minerva frowned and stood, signaling the end of their visit, and Haith sighed internally. "You're in no temper to humor me today, I see."

"Oh, don't pout." Haith felt a twinge of regret at her sarcasm, as she knew that Minerva's ramblings were her way of trying to warn Haith. However, today's events had already tried her patience.

Haith embraced Minerva and bussed her soft, wrinkly cheek. "You know I love you, *a' phiuthar mo sheanar.* Do not worry so."

Usually, using the Gaelic word for great aunt made Minerva smile, but not today. Her brow wrinkled, and her mouth turned down in disappointment.

"If you weren't so like your mother, mayhap I wouldna." Minerva returned the embrace and shuffled to the door. "Look lively, wee Ham. 'Tis time I departed."

When the portal swung open, Minerva stepped into the corridor and paused at Ellora's window. "Good day, m'lady," she said so sweetly that even Haith cringed.

"Be gone, hag," Ellora muttered crossly, but that was all she said.

Minerva cackled. "Yer no fun anymore, Ellie. Seems imprisonment has killed yer sense of humor." Then she took her leave up the steps, the sound of her amused chuckles fading away.

Ham left Haith's door ajar while he released Soleilbert, risking a considerable amount of skin from his backside should Barrett catch him doing this. Soleilbert exited Ellora's cell and went straight across the corridor while Ham collected the luncheon remains from Ellora's table and replenished her supplies.

"Bertie, sit down." Haith led her sister to a chair after one look at her green-tinged complexion. "Whatever is the matter?"

For the benefit of Ellora, Bertie spoke loudly. "'Tis nothing, Haith. I may have eaten some meat past its prime, is all. I'll fetch a brew from Minerva later." Tears filled her soft, brown eyes as she leaned across the table to whisper to Haith. "I've missed my monthly."

"Oh, my God," Haith breathed. So that explained Soleilbert's pallor. "Bertie, you're with child?"

Haith's sister nodded, and a sickly smile crept across her face. "I cannot help but be happy, although this does not bode well for our plans."

"You cannot go to Scotland," Haith whispered. "'Twould be too much risk for the babe."

"I know, but what will I do if Pharao does not return? I cannot keep the fact that I carry a child secret forever, and I cannot raise an illegitimate child in Nigel's hold. I would fear for his safety."

"Yea, you're right." Haith pressed her fingers to her lips in thought. Soleilbert's baby—Haith's niece or nephew!—deserved a loving home, one where he was surrounded by people who loved him as much as his parents would. That would certainly not occur under Nigel's twisted rule. Soleilbert's life and that of her child would be a living hell.

Haith vowed that she actually heard the sound of her heart breaking as the solution came to her as simply as drawing a breath.

"Bertie, there is a way to secure your child's future. But only one."

"Then you must tell me, and quickly."

"If Pharao does not return with Tristan, you must heed the betrothal contract and marry the lord."

"Haith!" Bertie hissed. "Are you mad? Tristan is your soulmate!"

"Listen to me, Sister." Haith's voice was firm. "I go to Scotland with or without you, for my purpose is not only to escape Nigel. I must seek my mother's family and discover a way to put an end to this evilness that has plagued my women ancestors. I have betrayed Tristan to the point that his heart is closed to me now, and that I cannot change."

"Haith, Tristan loves you!" Bertie insisted. "He—"

"Bertie, please." Haith cut her sister off sharply. "My fate has been sealed, thanks in part to my parents. Now, my concern, and yours, too, must be only for your child. Will you hear me out?"

When Bertie nodded hesitantly, Haith continued.

"Tristan has said many times that Pharao is as his brother. If something has happened to your love, do you not think that Tristan would care for your child as his own? That Pharao would want that as well?"

"Haith, I cannot. You would never be able to return to Greanly—'twould be too painful for you!"

"Once I leave, Sister, I can never return regardless. Nigel will have me killed for stopping his aid." Haith reached across the table for Soleilbert's hand and held on tightly. "Perhaps after the babe is born, Tristan will allow you to visit me. But this is only if Pharao does not return, and well he may."

"I cannot think about this now." Bertie pulled away. "'Tis too horrible."

"You *must* think about it," Haith insisted. "We are running out of time. You know Tristan would care for you." Now Haith pleaded. "Bertie, please. I am going to Scotland and leaving this life behind. Do not give me cause to worry for you when 'tis unnecessary."

Bertie thought for several moments before sniffing and nodding. "But only if Pharao does not return and Lord Tristan agrees."

Ham entered the cell and began gathering the used tableware, causing Haith and Bertie to move away from the table and sit on the small cot.

"When do you go then?" Bertie whispered.

Haith's expression hardened as she steeled herself for Bertie's reaction to the answer. "I think now that I should depart this very night. The moon is full, and 'twill give me light to move by."

"So soon? But Lord Tristan will not—"

"Scotland is far, Sister, and if I am to escape Nigel's clutches, I must go while I have the chance."

Bertie wrung her hands, but did not argue. "Shall I bring the supplies to you?"

"Nay." Haith glanced at Ham and was satisfied with his distance. "I shall come to your chamber after nightfall."

"But how will you escape the locked door?"

"Worry not about that," Haith said absently. "But 'tis important that you not visit me any longer this day, else you be implicated in my escape."

"I understand," Bertie said, her misery plain on her face.

"So,"—Haith took a steadying breath—"go then. I shall see you before the moon sets."

"Go *now?*"

Haith nodded tightly. " 'Tis best."

Bertie stood, and Haith followed her sister to the portal, where the pair embraced fiercely.

"I love you, Haith."

"I love you, too."

Bertie tore herself from her sister and fled the chamber, causing Ham to pause with his full basket. "Is Lady Soleilbert ill?"

"Nay, Ham. She misses Lord Tristan, is all."

"So the rumors are true then? Lady Soleilbert is to marry the lord?"

" 'Twould seem so." Haith returned to her seat on the bed, somewhat annoyed that the boy lingered.

Ham glanced around, then approached Haith, his small tongue darting nervously to wet his lips. "There is a merchant come to peddle at Greanly this day."

"Truly?" Haith picked up her needlework in the hope that Ham would leave her. " 'Tis a treat for the village women then. Perhaps you will be able to wheedle a small trinket from him."

"Aye." Ham glanced over his shoulder again. "I hope to finish the chores Barrett has set me to quickly, for the peddler says he will move on soon." Ham's eyes met and held Haith's. "He travels north from Greanly and speaks Minerva's tongue."

The woman and boy stared at each other in tense silence as Ham's pointed remark hung in the air. Haith chose her next words carefully, her voice lowered.

" 'Tis interesting information you give, Ham. Do you also know when this merchant will take his leave?"

Ham nodded slowly. "At dawn. Says he's in a hurry to return to his family. Perhaps my lady would like to see some of his wares? I could ask Barrett—"

"Nay." Haith did not want a connection to the man if

the plan she was quickly formulating came to pass. "Where does this peddler bed?"

"In the stables with his cart."

"You will come to me if he is to depart before the morn?"

Again, Ham nodded.

"We did not have this conversation," Haith warned. "A loose tongue could put me in great danger. Do you understand?"

"Aye, m'lady." Ham's young face was somber as he turned to go. "Good day."

"Thank you, Ham," Haith whispered.

CHAPTER
23

Tristan's horse danced and snorted on the moonlit cobblestones of the London backstreet. The closely set buildings, nestled against each other like teeth, made the beast nervous, used as he was to roaming open roads and fields. Tristan reined him in lightly and patted his broad neck before urging him further into the inner city gloom.

Tristan's sharp eyes scanned the buildings, all the while keeping his senses alert to his surroundings. The part of town to which he'd been directed was shoddy, and dark characters flitted between even darker shadows—drunkards, mercenaries, prostitutes—all with sharp eyes of their own that were, more oft than not, trained warily on the man astride the fine horse. Tristan flexed the hand that rested on his thigh, ready to deter any would-be thieves. Although the alley was stifling in the muggy night, the miserly breeze was unwelcome, for it carried with it the warm, sticky stench of rot and filth and wet.

The building Tristan sought came into view: a ramshackle, two-story wood frame. The windows on the lower floor were dark, but a light in an upper window indicated that someone was indeed in residence.

He dismounted easily and began to loop the reins around a post when he saw a shadow draw near him. Tristan cautiously turned, his fingers playing lightly on the hilt of his sword.

A scantily clad young woman whose haggard face belied her age approached him with a twisted semblance of a smile. Most of her teeth were missing, and a hairline scar across one cheekbone drew her lower eyelid down slightly.

"Good eventide to ye, milord." She attempted a seductive coo that came out as little more than a gurgle. "Would ye be needin' some company this night?" She reached out a filthy hand to caress Tristan's tunic.

A disgusted dismissal was on Tristan's tongue, but before he could voice it, his horse stamped, calling to mind an idea. He did not relish the thought of leaving his steed on this mean street while he conducted his inquiry. A corner of his mouth drew upward in a sleepy smile.

"As a matter of fact, the offer is most inviting, my lady." Tristan's use of the term caused the whore obvious delight, and she sidled closer. Tristan tried to breathe through his mouth.

"I got's just what ye need," the woman encouraged, pressing her flat bosom to his chest. "Come inside with me an'—"

"A moment, I pray," Tristan interrupted. "I have business to attend to first. Wait for me here, and mayhap when I return, we can enjoy each other's company."

"Oh surely, milord." The whore ran a greedy hand down Tristan's front before he could disentangle himself. As he backed away, the prostitute called after him, "I'll be right 'ere. Don't keep me waitin' now!"

"But a moment," Tristan promised and left her standing guard over his horse.

He rapped soundly on the door to the building and heard footsteps within. A young voice called out from the other side of the door in a language Tristan did not understand.

"I seek a man called Shakir Apom," he tried, hoping the youth understood English. When he got no reply, he tried French. In his frustration, he pounded on the door again. *"Monsieur Apom! Ouvrir la porte, s'il vous plaît!"*

Tristan heard the heavy click of a latch, and the door before him swung inward, spilling yellow light onto the street and revealing a tall, thin man and a young boy, both with dark skin and eyes. The boy glanced nervously between Tristan and the man beside him, and he spoke rapidly in the strange language. The man replied sharply, and the boy fled to the dwelling's interior.

The tall man spoke. "You are Tristan D'Argent, yea?"

"Yea. I am looking for Shakir Apom. Is he here?"

The man stepped back from the door, admitting Tristan into the room. The bolt slid closed, and Tristan looked around the chamber. The walls were plain but plastered. A shrine of some sort adorned one corner, and the tens of candles surrounding it gave the room an eerie glow. Woven rugs of intricately colored designs covered the floor nearly wall to wall, and dark, heavy fabrics hung at both windows, explaining their opaqueness from the street. Tristan's host was barefoot, and he crossed the room to sit on a flat cushion, gesturing for Tristan to do the same.

"If you please," the man said. He picked up a small jug and poured liquid into two clay mugs.

Tristan cautiously lowered himself to the floor and accepted the beverage with thanks, although he waited for his host to drink first. The amber liquid was somewhat bitter, but cool and refreshing to Tristan's parched mouth.

"I am Apom whom you seek," the man said after drinking. "You wish to know of your friend, my countryman, Tak'Ahn?"

"Yea," Tristan said. "He was abducted some days ago outside of London while leading a group of soldiers back to my hold."

Apom shook his head, the serene smile never leaving his face. "Not abducted as you say. Tak'Ahn returned to his family."

"I do not understand. Pharao's mother died of sickness in Paris many years ago, after his father was already long dead. He had no family save me."

"Nay, Tristan D'Argent. Tak'Ahn has many family," Apom insisted. "They search for him these long years. His absence is a great sorrow to them. They feared him dead."

"I do not wish to offend you after you have shown me such hospitality," Tristan began, "but I do not believe my friend would take his leave so suddenly without word. We have traveled far together, and he is a brother to me."

Apom nodded graciously. "Of course. He spoke of you as brother as well." He cocked his head in a rueful way. "I will admit to you that Tak'Ahn was—how do you say?—reluctant at first."

Tristan's anger flared white-hot. "Where is he?"

"Tristan D'Argent, you must be listen to me, if you please," Apom soothed. "Your friend was reluctant to return to his family at first, as I say, but later, he realize his duty. He goes freely and can return if he please."

Tristan was silent for a moment while he digested the information and decided whether to believe this man, Apom. In all the years they had known each other, Pharao had never said he had family other than his father and mother.

On the other hand, Pharao had never said he *didn't* have other relatives—siblings, aunts, uncles—and Tristan had never asked. The country of Pharao's birth and his childhood there were not subjects he was prone to speak of. Since it hadn't seemed important after the two men had become family to each other, Tristan had not pressed for information.

Now, he wished he had, if only for Haith's sister's sake.

"There is a woman," Tristan said, and Apom chuckled.

"Is there not always?"

"Pharao's woman. He gave her the gold chain from his father before he left for London. What is to become of her?"

Apom shrugged. "'Tis our custom that to give a woman a *mangalsutra* is to take her as a wife, but unless the union is blessed by the man's family and priest before our god, there is no bond." Apom shook his head sadly and took another sip of his drink.

Tristan looked skeptical. "Then he left no word for his woman or me?"

"Tristan D'Argent, Tak'Ahn is at his home now. Your heart should be full with joy for him." Apom smiled kindly. "But there is something."

He clapped his hands twice sharply, and the young boy appeared in the doorway, holding a rolled parchment, which he handed to Tristan. Apom dismissed the boy with a short burst of his language.

"If you please." Apom gestured to the paper.

Tristan unrolled the page to see Pharao's precise, heavy script. The sight of it caused a weighty hollowness to expand in his chest.

My liege,
I have been pressed by my honor to return to the land of my birth. There is much that I have not told

*you about my past. Would that I could explain it
now.*

*Tell my lady that I keep my promise to her, and
I pray that one day you will both know all. Until
then, protect her in my stead, I beg you, and seek
your own happiness, Brother. May God bless and
keep you.*

Pharao Tak'Ahn al-Amir

Tristan blew a heavy breath between his lips as he
fought against his constricting throat. His only family,
his closest friend—gone. Perhaps forever. Apom was
correct in saying that Tristan should feel happiness for
Pharao in being reunited with his family, but all Tristan
could think of was the empty place that Pharao left
behind at Greanly.

And in Tristan's heart.

"I thank you for this," Tristan said gruffly, rolling up
the parchment once more. "Without it, I may have set
off to find him myself."

Apom chuckled. "Tak'Ahn said you would require
proof."

Tristan rose, and Apom did as well, escorting him
back to the front door. Before Apom unlocked it, however, he rested a hand on Tristan's shoulder.

"Tristan D'Argent, if you please. You must be knowing that no other would struggle with this choice as
Tak'Ahn did. His family is very rich and powerful in his
land—one would be foolish to refuse them."

"I understand." Tristan averted his eyes.

"Nay. Tak'Ahn named you family. Brother." Apom
squeezed Tristan's shoulder. "He will not forget you."
The door swung open, admitting the slimy fumes of
London into the small, clean room.

"Again, my thanks," Tristan said hoarsely and passed into the night.

He walked in the direction of his horse with his head down, struggling to contain the grief that threatened to consume him. He tucked Pharao's message inside his tunic over his heart. The young boy within him, the one he'd been when he and Pharao had met, needed comfort badly.

"There ye be, milord." The whore straightened from where she had been leaning and plastered the grotesque smile on her face once more. "I thought ye'd forgot me."

Well, he didn't need comfort *that* badly.

Tristan flipped a coin to the sad-looking woman before flicking the reins from the post and swinging onto his horse. He wheeled the stallion around and looked down at the prostitute, who stared in shock from the weighty coin to her mysterious benefactor.

"My apologies, mistress," he said curtly and spurred the horse down the street as if all the demons from hell were at his heels.

"Don't trouble yerself about it," the whore said absently, staring after the handsome stranger silhouetted against the full moon. "I wasn't in the mood, any matter."

Hours away from London under the same yellow moon, another dark shadow was silhouetted as it fled across Greanly's bailey. At the mouth of the stable, Haith paused and glanced up at the glowing disk in the sky as if seeking her strength there. Dawn was soon approaching, and it was now or never.

After a moment's hesitation, she ducked inside.

Seeing a faint light at the end of the corridor, Haith moved silently toward it. When the grumblings she heard affirmed the wiry man spoke only to himself,

Haith stepped into the jagged edges of his torchlight and cleared her throat.

The thin man did not jump at the sound as Haith had expected for someone who had seemingly been alone in the quiet stable. He simply turned and looked her up and down shrewdly.

"There ye are then. Took ye long enough, dinnit?" he barked. "I was ready to leave without ye."

Haith was taken aback at his tone and the fact that he'd been expecting her. She had very clearly forbidden Ham to warn the man of her intent, but since the peddler was apparently ready to leave, Haith was somewhat glad the boy had disobeyed her this time.

The peddler was not a large man, rather thin and short, but the arms that stuck out of his vest were twisted with sinewy muscles. Haith was relieved that she'd tucked her dagger into the bundle she carried, especially after getting a taste of the man's disposition. She decided to forego any attempt at light conversation. He probably wouldn't return the effort, and anyway, he was merely a means to an end for Haith. A fortuitous and unexpected escort to Scotland.

The peddler stopped throwing bundles into the cart bed to turn back to Haith. "Well? Do ye nae speak, lass? Never mind if ye do—just put yer things in the back there, and climb in."

Haith froze in place, looking at the tarp he held up. At his impatient sigh, Haith shook herself and darted forward, tossing her bundle in the cart and climbing in after it.

The peddler lashed the tarp securely at all four corners, enclosing Haith in darkness. She squirmed to move her bundle, which consisted mainly of clothes, bread, and dried meat, under her head in the fashion of a pillow. The wagon rocked violently as the peddler took his seat and whipped the team of two horses, throwing Haith into crates and baskets between which she was wedged. The motion became smoother, however, after the wagon passed out of the stable and into the yard. The sun was nigh risen, as Haith could tell by the thin strip of gray light beyond her feet.

Beyond the tarp, she heard the peddler call to the guards at the gate.

So close, now, she thought. *So close—*

A great rumbling vibrated the floor of the cart, and Haith knew the portcullis was being raised. The wagon leapt forward again, and the echoing drumming of the wheels rolling over the drawbridge reinforced the lurching of Haith's stomach.

She was really leaving.

A large rock under one of the wheels caused her to bang her head on the rough boards of a crate. The cart was picking up speed, and the wind made the tarp flap.

Haith rose up carefully on one elbow in the cramped space and looked down the length of her body to her last view of Greanly in the early morning mist. The dawn's breeze caused the grasses to wave gently, and Haith knew that if she was outside the wagon, the air would smell fresh and clean. The keep and curtain wall were silhouetted against the pearly dawn, and the town appeared peaceful and quiet.

Haith hoped that by her leaving, peace would remain for Bertie and her child. She refused to think of Tristan though, and firmly shut him from her mind.

The escape itself had been easier than expected. Drawing on her experience with the broken crockery in Minerva's cottage, since her imprisonment, Haith had concentrated nightly on using her mind to disengage the locking mechanism of her cell door. Her first attempts had been futile and unpleasant, for no matter how hard she concentrated, she was unlearned in the inner workings of the lock and only succeeded in giving herself a splitting headache for her efforts.

The cart hit another rut, jarring Haith's skull and reminding her in full of her failed attempts to open the door. She cursed under her breath with a spiteful look toward where she guessed the merchant to be sitting.

Only when she had begun envisioning the large key that Barrett kept and the sound the lock made when the key was used had her manipulations become successful. Haith had refined the trick with practice, and soon she could unlock the door with little more than a glance.

So although the escape had occurred without much effort, the leaving itself had proven intensely painful. Bertie had been awake in her chamber as planned, and was nervously pacing the floor when Haith had slipped into her room.

Haith's sister looked in better health than she had earlier in the day, but her face was drawn with worry. She'd tried one final time to dissuade Haith from leaving.

"There must be another way, Sister," Bertie had reasoned. She stood by the bed as Haith rifled through the supplies gathered there. "I feel something could go terribly wrong."

Haith did not pause to assuage Bertie's fears as she quickly tied her provisions into a tight bundle. "You sound like Minerva, Bertie, with your talk of feelings and omens. 'Tis merely nerves. I have them as well, but we've discussed this, and we agreed that there is no other way to assure the safety of your babe."

"But Haith—"

"Nay." Haith faced her sister and spoke firmly to stave off the tears that threatened. "'Tis decided. I shall send word to you once I reach my mother's clan." She withdrew a small piece of parchment from her bodice and handed it to Bertie. "Minerva will rise at dawn.

Give this to her, and try to ease her worry. I will send for her as soon as I am able."

"I cannot read this," Bertie said, glancing at the foreign scribbles on the page.

"'Tis Gaelic, the only written word Minerva understands." Haith gathered her bundle under one arm and, with the other, drew Bertie to the door. "Besides Minerva, no other is to have knowledge that you aided me."

Bertie nodded, a heavy cloud of resignation darkening her usually sunny face.

"I must go." Haith touched her sister's cheek in a loving gesture. "We will see each other again, Sister— Papa swore it."

The women embraced tightly, both holding their emotions in check. And then Haith was gone into the corridor once more.

Now, lying on the hard wagon bed and feeling more alone and burdened than she ever had, Haith could let her sorrow overtake her for a bit.

"Ye should stay down a bit longer, gel," the driver called. "I doona know the vision of the guards."

Haith laid her head in the comfort of the bundle that still held her sister's scent and sobbed.

CHAPTER
24

Tristan rose before dawn had truly broken, the few sleepless hours he'd spent abed only serving to increase his restlessness.

He dressed in the guest chamber given him by William and made his way to the hall below to send word to his liege that he departed London this day. While he waited for the servant to return with word of whether William wished to see him or no, Tristan's thoughts turned once more to Haith.

He wondered what her reaction would be when he told her of the news. Would she be pleased that William would hear testimony of Nigel's treachery? Or would she remain steadfast in her resolve to avoid him? William had given Tristan his oath that should he find Nigel guilty, Tristan would be free to marry whomever he chose. Tristan hoped that Haith would see that he'd secured their future by his visit to William and, furthermore, that her imprisonment was for her own protection until Nigel could be brought before the king.

The thought made him grin—she'd been unusually

docile when he'd ordered Barrett to take her below, but Tristan surmised that she had lost all traces of her repentant meekness after a few nights in a cell. She would be glad of his return, he wagered, after she finished threatening him with physical harm.

The vision of Haith in a fury had Tristan still chuckling when the somber footman reappeared.

"Lord Tristan, His Majesty entertains a visitor now, but he wishes to see you immediately."

"Of course." Tristan unfolded himself from the gilded chair and followed the prissy manservant to the ornate double doors of William's private receiving room. He knew it was unusual for the king to interrupt a private audience, especially when Tristan was merely taking his leave. He wondered who in William's court would be keen enough about seeking royal advice to rise before dawn.

The footman preceded Tristan into the room to stand by the door and announce, "Your Highness, Lord Tristan of Greanly, at your request."

Tristan entered the room casually to see William relaxed in a large brocade chair, his portly frame attentive to the blond woman on a settee to his right. The footman exited discreetly.

Tristan bowed. "My liege, I am honored that you would see me, although truly, 'twas unnecessary. I merely wished to bid you *adieu*, I was unaware you were otherwise engaged."

William stroked his chin. "'Tis no matter, Tristan. I would have summoned you this morn regardless." He leaned his bulk heavily on one arm of the chair, but his gaze was alert. "I have reason to believe you would also be interested in meeting my guest."

Tristan's eyebrows rose in interest and his attention was drawn to the heretofore silent woman. Her faded blond hair was intricately dressed atop her bowed head, and her gown appeared costly. Even from the distance at which Tristan stood, he could see that she trembled. What would this lady of obvious status want with a fledgling lord of a new estate?

William waved a hand to the woman. "My lady, may I present the man you seek—and my good friend—Tristan D'Argent, Lord of Greanly." William spoke to the woman as if in warning, but looked to Tristan with keen interest. "Tristan, the Baroness of Crane."

Tristan stepped forward and bowed slightly. "Baroness, 'tis a pleasure to meet you."

The woman's head rose slowly as Tristan spoke, and faded blue eyes met ones of a brighter hue. Her voice was husky when she spoke.

"Bonjour, Tristan. Do you remember me at all?"

Tristan's eyes narrowed. Something about her was indeed familiar. He should know this woman, some part of his memory warned. "Forgive me, but I—"

The baroness tilted her head to one side with a sad, little smile, and the movement caused a twinkle to emanate from the jewel adorning the woman's necklace. 'Twas a large sapphire identical to the one gracing Tristan's sword hilt.

"Mother?" he rasped.

Genevieve's smile widened, and her blue eyes, so similar to Tristan's, filled with tears. She rose from the settee and glided to Tristan, her arms held wide. "Oh, my darling son, I have found you at last!"

Tristan stood rigid as a stone statue as his mother's arms wrapped around him. His shock at seeing the woman who'd abandoned him so long ago left him momentarily speechless, but the young boy inside him exploded with rage and pain. That child longed to lash out at Genevieve.

"The king tells me that you are soon to marry."

Genevieve squeezed him once more before holding him at arm's length to beam up into his face. "'Twould seem I am just in time."

Slowly, the woman's words penetrated the roar in Tristan's head. He stepped back stiffly, causing his mother's arms to fall away. "I beg to differ with you, Baroness." Tristan's voice dripped icy venom. "Indeed, you are most definitely too late."

"Tristan?" Genevieve's eyes widened in confused hurt. "Why do you—"

"My liege," Tristan interrupted, addressing William and dismissing the woman completely. "I thank you for seeing me on such short notice and for your indulgence with regard to the matter which we previously discussed. I hope to have the proof you require shortly after my return to Greanly. However, I have a lengthy journey before me, and I must beg your permission to be excused."

"In but a moment," William answered. He turned his head to address Tristan's mother. "Baroness, 'twould seem your appearance has left our man at somewhat of a loss. You'll understand, I'm certain, if we speak privately?"

"But I—"

"Merci." As if on cue, the receiving door opened, and the footman appeared. William commanded him, "See the baroness to her chamber."

Not bothering to hide her frustration, tears spilled down the woman's cheeks as she curtsied, then stiffly followed the servant from the room.

Tristan's breath left him in a rush, and he fought off a wave of dizziness.

"Sit down, Tristan," William said not unkindly. "You've had a shock, *oui?*"

Tristan took his king's advice gratefully. "Indeed, my liege. You did not know of her identity?"

"I suspected as much when she explained that she

sought you, but I did not know for certain until this morn. Like you, I thought her dead." The king stroked his chin again and cocked his head. "You favor her."

"Yea, I suppose I do," Tristan murmured. After a moment, the memory of the title William had addressed her by surfaced. "You called her the Baroness of Crane."

William nodded. "'Twould seem your mother came to England years before either of us. She was, until recently, wife of Lord Richard FitzTodd, Baron of Crane. He died not more than six months ago."

"She is an English widow."

"*Oui.* Perhaps you would be more accepting of her had her husband's death made you a baron?" William's eyebrows rose expectantly as he waited for Tristan to catch his meaning.

Tristan's gaze rose to meet William's. "The baron had an heir?" he asked slowly. "A child of my mother?"

William nodded. "A son. Nicholas."

"I have a brother," Tristan said as if in a daze. "I have a brother called Nicholas."

"Will you now hear the lady out, Tristan?" the king asked. "I feel she has been running from some trouble or another and that by hearing her story, many of your shared ghosts will be laid to rest."

"Nay." Tristan shook himself, and his voice hardened once more. "I beg your pardon, my liege, but I have no lingering ghosts nor any wish to pander to more lies from that viper. Unless 'tis your express command that I do otherwise, I would forget this meeting ever occurred." Tristan looked away. "To me, she remains dead."

William thought in silence for a moment, the corners of his mouth drawing down. "And your brother? Have you no wish to know him?"

"In truth, I cannot answer that now."

"I understand. 'Tis much to comprehend with the

recent obstacles you've faced in securing Greanly."
William sighed. "You will think on it though?"

"Yea." Tristan stood. "If it pleases you, my liege, I
would go now."

"Of course. I'll be expecting word from you soon."

"In but a few days' time," Tristan assured him and
then turned to go.

The receiving doors swung open again as if by magic,
the faithful servant ever attendant, but before Tristan
could pass through the portal, William's voice called out
once more.

"Lord Tristan, would you humor me a moment longer?"

Tristan halted and half turned. "My liege?"

"Why this animosity toward the mother you lost so
long ago? 'Twould seem this reunion would only bring
you happiness."

"'Tis simply because I never lost her," Tristan said
smoothly. "She lost me, for a purpose."

"There was no caregiver as she says, then?"

Tristan's memory recalled the gnarled hag who had
thrown him into the streets moments after his arrival,
and he shook his head.

"Very well." William waved him away. "We shall
meet again when you bring me your witnesses."

Tristan bowed curtly once more and left the room, his
backbone stiff.

After Tristan's departure, William sat tapping at his
lips and contemplating seriously his young lord's
predicament.

The Lord of Greanly was certainly ambitious and re-
sourceful, William knew, else he could not have gained
all he now held on his own. But ofttimes, his pride made
him overly rigid, and not without a thirst for vengeance
if he perceived he had been wronged. William almost
pitied Lord Nigel if Tristan's accusations proved true. He

admired his young vassal's strong adherence to his personal code of honor, and had never had reason to suspect its origins.

But what if this overdeveloped sensibility stemmed from a wrong that had never been intended? And what if this wrong had been dealt by a loved one and had resulted in the abandonment of a young boy? 'Twas possible that Tristan's inability to yield would only cause him needless suffering and damage his future.

William sighed. Matters of the heart confounded him. War was so much simpler.

The king called out to his servant.

"Send the queen to me," he commanded. "I have need of her advice if she is not already occupied in her day and can spare me an hour from it."

After what Haith surmised had been more than two hours, she was all cried out, and the tarp-covered wagon bed had turned stifling beneath the morning sun. She struggled to the most upright position she could achieve—propped on an elbow—and swiped at the sweat and tear-dampened curls stuck to her cheeks. Surely they were far enough from Greanly now that she could emerge from this oven. She also had need to seek some bushes, whether from her nerves or the bumpy road, but certainly not from an overindulgence of water. Her throat was parched.

She knew not the surly peddler's name, so she strove for politeness in her request.

"Sir? Good merchant," she called loudly over the rumbling wheels, pressing her face as close to the top of the wagon bed as possible. "'Tis safe for me to be out from here, is it not?"

Several seconds ticked by with no reply, so that Haith

cleared her throat, preparing to voice her request more loudly. Perhaps he was hard of hearing.

"*Sir!*"

"What?" The peddler's voice was much closer and louder than Haith had expected, and she jumped, banging her head once more.

"Might you stop the cart? I have need to seek a respite."

Haith felt the wagon slow, and she sighed her relief while the driver mumbled crossly about "damned water-making females." In a moment, the tarp was thrown back, admitting the blinding sun onto the cargo. Haith threw a shielding arm above her eyes as she scooted the length of the wagon on her bottom. She hopped to the ground and smiled hesitantly at the merchant, who scowled back at her.

"Well?" he said, crossing his arms. "Do ye have to go or nae?"

"There's no need to be nasty about it!" Haith snapped, but then cringed inwardly. 'Twould be unwise to anger the man. It could make for a rather awkward journey, or worse, he could grow tired of her company and set her on the side of the road to walk the rest of the way to Scotland.

Her desire to save her feet still overpowered her pride at this point, so she revived the cheery smile and tried again.

"I apologize. I think we may have started on a sour note, and I'd like to remedy that. You are very kind to stop." Haith nearly gritted her teeth to keep her smile as the driver merely stood before her, looking disgusted. "My name is Haith. You are . . ."

The driver spat in the dust not far from Haith's slippers. "I know who ye be, an' the less ye know of me, the better for the pair of us. Now, if ye've got business to attend to, do it now." The driver stalked off to some bushes on the far side of the cart, leaving Haith and her demanding bladder no choice but to seek her own comfort.

Haith walked swiftly into the dense shrubbery on the opposite side of the road and lifted her skirts, careful to keep an eye on the wagon lest the driver decide to be off without her. While she relieved herself, she noted the sun still shone from somewhere over her shoulder in the east, and she was satisfied that they traveled north. Although why she would bother to note that was unclear to her—considering the driver's brogue, if anyone would know the direction they should be traveling, 'twas he.

Haith dropped the hem of her gown, and was attempting to shake out the wrinkles as she emerged from the copse. She walked to the front of the wagon, but a voice startled her.

"What do ye think yer doin'?" The peddler stood at the rear of the cart, a corner of the tarp in his hand.

"You cannot expect me to ride the whole way to Scotland in there!" She pointed to the cargo. "I'll smother! Surely we're far enough from Greanly now that there is little chance I'll be discovered."

The merchant shook his head vehemently. "Nae. If anyone sees ye up top, 'twould be too easy to call those red locks of yers to memory."

"Then I'll wear a scarf over my head."

"Nae."

"Why not?" Haith cried in frustration.

" 'Tis too dangerous. Now get in." The man shook the tarp pointedly.

"Good merchant," Haith tried again, "I hie to Scotland to seek my relatives, my mother's clan, the Buchanans. Perhaps you know of them? Should I arrive there in good health, I am certain they will repay you generously."

"I care not a cock's peck who ye seek, lass, nor will I

be tempted by these riches ye hint at," the driver growled. "If they be so concerned about yer arrival, then they should've come and fetched ye themselves. Get in."

Haith dropped her head in her hands and massaged her temples with her fingertips. If this blasted ache in her skull would only subside, perhaps she could calmly talk some sense into the stubborn man. She was slowly reciting the Lord's Prayer to herself when she noticed the oddity on the ground beneath the wagon.

Wheel tracks and hoof marks clearly defined in the fine dust seemed to have made an irregular circle. Haith shifted her eyes to the right, past the nags that pulled the cart. A definite path had been made by a vehicle coming from the north, according to the sun's position. She could not remember hearing another wagon pass theirs.

Haith's eyes shifted to the left, where the man still stood impatiently at the rear of the cart. The dirt that lay in the direction from which they should have been coming was completely unmarred by tracks.

Should she mention that they had strayed off course? Surely, 'twould further incite his anger, but better to arrive in Scotland with an angry driver than not to arrive at all. Haith raised her head and opened her mouth to speak, but closed it just in time.

The horses and cart faced north.

The peddler *knew* they were traveling south, and had turned the cart in a wide circle before Haith had emerged in the hope that she wouldn't notice.

But why?

Haith spun on her heel and walked calmly back into the bushes, her heart racing.

"Ay! Where're ye goin' off to?" the driver demanded.

"If I must ride back there, I want to be sure you needn't stop again right away," Haith called over her shoulder. "Just a moment longer!"

"Bleedin' Christ," the man groaned. "Hurry it up!"

At his words, Haith burst into a run, trying to put as much distance between her and her abductor before he realized she had fled. Each breath seared her already dry throat, and the twigs and branches she flew through whipped her tender face and snagged her hair.

From behind her, Haith heard a muffled shout and knew her flight had been discovered. She mustered strength from an unknown source and sped even faster through the sparse undergrowth. The pounding of hooves reached her ears, and Haith marveled in fear at the notion of the merchant unhitching one of the nags to retrieve her.

Why did he want her so badly?

She chanced a glimpse over her shoulder, and her worse fear was confirmed—some distance behind her, a rider did indeed give chase. Haith knew 'twas only a matter of seconds before she was caught. She cursed herself for leaving her dagger in her bundle, but the peddler was a smaller man, she reasoned. Perhaps she could fend him off with some other weapon.

Haith continued to run, but now her eyes scanned the forest floor, searching for any object that could be used to defend herself.

The rider drew nearer, and Haith could feel the reverberations of the hoofbeats even as she spied the smooth, fist-sized rock ahead. She reached out to seize it, shrieking with both frustration and fear when she was jerked out of its proximity. An arm around her middle hoisted her through the air to the forward part of a saddle.

"Let me go, you filthy bastard!" she screamed, flailing her arms blindly at her captor.

"My, my, Lady Haith. Haven't we found a temper of

late?" the smooth voice without a trace of Scots brogue chuckled.

Haith's struggling ceased, and her gaze flew upward to meet Nigel's black orbs and amused smile.

Haith promptly fainted.

CHAPTER
25

Haith felt herself surfacing from the black abyss into which she'd escaped but, hearing voices nearby, gathered enough self-awareness to keep her eyes closed. From the unyielding hardness beneath her, she surmised that she lay once more in the cart bed, this time face-down. The strain on her shoulders indicated her arms had been restrained behind her, and her ankles ground cruelly together within their own tight confines.

Someone had trussed her like an animal. She fought the urge to struggle and writhe against her bindings only by concentrating on the conversation going on outside the cart.

"I told ye I could handle the gel." Haith recognized the voice of the peddler.

"Yea, I can see how allowing her to dash into the forest alone is in keeping with my instructions." Nigel's words were rife with sarcasm, but his tone was quite amused.

"She wasna *runnin'* 'til ye charged after 'er. I'm tellin' ye she didna suspect a thing!"

"You are a bigger fool than I gave you credit for if you truly believe that."

"She's awake," a third voice advised, and Haith's dread increased. 'Twas Donald. Haith concentrated on remaining perfectly still.

"She doosna look it t'me."

"How do you know?" Nigel asked.

"Her breathing." Donald's voice amplified, and Haith imagined him leaning over the cart bed to peer down at her. "Me old woman used to try this trick. I'll show you . . ."

Haith could not help but scream as the tender flesh on the side of her breast was twisted viciously. Her eyes flew open, and she jerked away to see Donald grinning above her.

"I told you she was awake."

"It matters not," Nigel said, irritation clipping his words. "And do not touch her in that manner again, you scaly buffoon, or I'll have your other hand. The only one to touch her shall be me."

"Release me," Haith ground out between clenched teeth.

"I think not, sweetling." Nigel turned to the peddler. "The bonds will hold her well enough to continue on to Seacrest."

Haith writhed onto her side, and leaned up to glare at Nigel and his two cohorts. "Tristan will kill you for this. He shall see each of you dead by his own hand."

Nigel sighed and rolled his eyes heavenward as if seeking patience. "Haith. My dove. Tristan will think you in Scotland. After all, 'tis where that cow Soleilbert thinks you travel to at this very moment." His eyebrows rose. "Is that not so? I doubt young Master Ham would have the forethought to lie to our good friend here," Nigel said, indicating the shamefaced peddler beside him.

When all Haith could do was glare at him, he continued. "Now, do be quiet and lie down, or I shall have to see you gagged and strapped to the cart itself. You don't want that, do you? Hm-m?"

Nigel's voice waned in volume as he and Donald made their way to the fore of the cart. The jingling of tack sounded as they mounted their horses. "Old man, if anyone sees what is beneath that tarp before my belongings are delivered to me, you die."

The sound of horses galloping away gave Haith some measure of relief until the peddler stepped into her line of vision, tarp in hand.

"Please don't," Haith pleaded. " 'Tis so hot, truly I shall smother."

"I'll leave a corner loose," the peddler said curtly without meeting her eyes. Half of the tarp was soon secured over the cart bed.

"Do you have any water, then?"

"Yer goin' ter get me killed," the man muttered and headed toward the front of the cart. He returned in a moment with a large skin.

Haith looked toward her restrained appendages with frustration. "You'll have to loosen the ropes."

"Nae." The peddler uncorked the skin and held it to Haith's lips. Her eyes burned with humiliation, but her thirst overpowered her pride and she drank deeply, cool rivulets running down the corners of her mouth.

The peddler withdrew the skin too quickly for Haith's relief, but her mouth was less parched and her throat soothed for now.

"My thanks."

The man merely grunted as he recorked the skin, tossed it up on the seat, and once more began fastening the tarp. Haith lay down obediently as the covering was lashed over her, one corner left slightly askew as promised for air circulation. Even with the vent, the cart bed was pitch black.

The wagon rocked and then lurched forward as the driver circled back to head south. Once the motion of the vehicle took on a less jarring gait, Haith began to shimmy within her confines. Her wrists were secured at her lower back, and she tried to bring her hands under her bottom to pull her legs through the loop made by her arms, but she was wedged too tightly amidst crates and baskets to allow such movement. Straining against her foot restraints was of no use either, and she only succeeded in deeply bruising the thin skin covering her ankles.

Haith made a frustrated sound in her throat and tossed her head, trying to fling the loose tendrils of tickling hair from her face. Already, sweat was beginning to trickle down her forehead and back. She tried to relax slightly, breathing in and out in a soothing rhythm, and then set to gingerly moving her wrists to try to determine the nature of her bonds.

'Twould take the slow-moving cart several more hours to reach Seacrest than it would Nigel and Donald, who traveled on horseback. The thought of those two awaiting her arrival nearly sent her into a panic once more, but she fought it and won again. She knew she must remain calm and use the time in the cart to attempt escape, and the only way she could see to do that was to use her mind to loosen the ropes on her wrists.

Unlocking the cell door at Greanly had taken several nights of trial and error before she had realized success. Closing her eyes, Haith prayed that she could free herself once more with only a few hours in which to practice.

"Oh, sweet Corra," Minerva breathed as she read the words Haith had penned. She read the entire note through twice before closing her eyes and leaning one hand against the table for support.

Soleilbert sat in a chair by the hearth in Minerva's cottage, sobbing silently. One palm was braced against her forehead, and the other lay protectively over her belly.

"Did you know of this beforehand?" Minerva finally asked.

Soleilbert nodded.

"Why? Why would you aid her in such a foolish scheme?" Minerva hobbled to the young woman and grasped her by the arms, shaking her. *"Why?"*

"Because I am with child, Minerva!" Bertie cried. "And my babe's father is gone from this place! There is no one to provide for him save Lord Tristan!"

Minerva drew back as if slapped and stared at Bertie in shock.

" 'Tis true." Soleilbert lowered her voice and wiped at her face with her sleeve. "I helped Haith to flee so that my child would have a chance to live."

"The father of your child is the dark man, is he not?" She hesitated. "Yea."

"And you think he would not return for you now that you carry his babe?"

"He knows not," Soleilbert said. "He was taken before even I had knowledge of my condition. I only realized after Lord Tristan set out for London."

Minerva made a sound of disgust. "So 'twas convenient for you to assume Lord Tristan would take over your care and foster your child without a cross word? How arrogant you are, lassie, to do as your mother accuses Haith and claim your sister's man. You know they are soulmates!"

Soleilbert bolted to her feet. "You yourself told me you suspected she would flee to Scotland, so do not blame me for this, Minerva!" she yelled. "I was leaving for Scotland *with her* before I discovered I was with child! She is tired of this curse of your kinsmen haunting her, and she seeks your clan to learn of a way to break it!"

Minerva blanched. "Bertie, lass, what curse?"

Soleilbert groaned in frustration. "You've spoken of it yourself oft enough to know!" She took a deep breath. "Buchanan women are cursed to find love only with the one man they dream of, the soulmate. But when they meet, only tragedy follows!"

"Nae," Minerva whispered, horrified. "'Tis not a *curse*—'tis a blessing! A gift passed down from mother to daughter in order that the Buchanan line continue through the strongest bonds—true love."

Bertie blinked. "I do not understand."

Minerva sat down heavily in the chair Bertie had vacated, as if her legs did not possess the strength to hold her. "In my faery's mind, the blessing is a curse because of all your father and Corinne endured. Because of the hurt it caused Ellora. When Haith discovered her soulmate was your betrothed, it only made her belief stronger that she was destined to cause disaster because of her dreams."

Bertie's face was ashen. "Like Corinne."

"Aye." Minerva looked up. "'Tis fear that drove Haith, not desire. Should we nae find her, she'll grow weaker and more ill with each passing day. Her soul longs for Tristan. He's the only one who can save her."

Soleilbert dropped heavily in another chair, her face a ghostly pallor. "And I've aided her in fleeing to her death on foot."

Minerva's cottage door flew open, and a small bundle rolled across the dirt floor and skidded to a stop at Minerva's feet.

Barrett filled the narrow doorway. "Nay, not on foot." His murderous gaze was fixed on the bundle, which began unfolding itself as a teary-eyed Ham. "Go on, tell 'em, you little bastard, an' I hope Minerva turns you into a mouse and feeds you to Willy for what you've done."

"Barrett!" Soleilbert scolded and pulled the shaking boy from the floor and into her arms. "What is it, Ham? Do you know something?"

Ham nodded, but only looked at Minerva in fear.

"I found him blubbering in Lady Haith's cell this morn," Barrett accused.

Minerva's voice was low. "Tell us, lad."

The boy was wild-eyed. "W-w-when the m-messenger came—"

Bertie stroked the boy's hair. "Yea, Ham. We remember the messenger. Go on."

Ham gulped. "I was h-helping Rufus in the f-field, and the peddler passed through the g-gates. He s-stopped and talked to us. S-s-said he was going north from Greanly." The boy leaned further into Soleilbert and looked at Minerva. "He talked like you."

Minerva sat back in her chair and regarded the boy. "You knew Lady Haith wished to journey to Scotland?"

Ham nodded. "I heard her and Lady Bertie talking, and I told her of the peddler."

Soleilbert looked over the boy's head to the seething sheriff. "So she flees to Scotland by cart. In a way, 'tis better." Her eyes widened with hope and sought Minerva. "Is that not so?"

Minerva's brow wrinkled. "Aye, it could be. She'll nae be alone and on foot, and pray gods, she'll reach my clan faster to care for her. But—"

"But what?" Barrett asked.

The old woman looked to the sheriff. "If Haith travels by cart, 'twould mean it will take longer for Tristan to reach her."

Barrett took a menacing step toward Ham, who cowered on Bertie's lap. "How did she get out, you little rat?" he demanded. "Did you steal the key and unlock the door yourself?"

"Nay, Barrett! I swear!"

Minerva intervened. " 'Tis alright, Ham. I know you didna unlock the door. Barrett, Haith accomplished that on her own."

"How?" the big man insisted. "There are but two keys. I have one, and the other is with the lord."

Minerva looked at the boy on Bertie's lap. "Ham," she said gently, "if you doona want to be frightened, you'd do well to close yer eyes." The boy immediately complied.

"This is how our faery escaped," Minerva murmured to the two adults. She swept an arm in a wide arc, and the cottage came instantly to life.

The stew over the hearth stirred itself; a trunk lid opened and closed repeatedly; a large basket unraveled its reeds and then rewove itself into two smaller vessels. A flower from a bowl floated through the air to tuck itself behind Bertie's ear. The broom in the corner hobbled across the floor on its brittle straws right up to Barrett. It was still for a moment, weaving hypnotically before whacking him soundly on the shin, then bobbing over to lean against the wall once more.

As quickly as the commotion had begun, it was over, and the contents of Minerva's home behaved normally again.

Soleilbert merely had a small, wondrous smile on her face. "You may look now, Hammy."

The boy cautiously raised his head. "You've a flower in your hair, Lady Bertie."

Barrett, on the other hand, seemed to be in shock. His eyes bulged, and he hunched over, rubbing his abused leg. "Lady Haith can do this as well?" he asked Minerva.

" 'Tis possible, although I doona think she kens her

talents. I believe they've only started to show since she's been at Greanly."

Bertie nodded. "'Twould explain why she would not tell me how she planned to escape the cell. She was ashamed to be using her talents as Corinne did."

"What do we do now?" Barrett asked, still eyeing the renegade broom warily. "I cannot set out for Scotland and leave Greanly unguarded with Nigel about."

"We wait for Lord Tristan." Minerva stood and retrieved a biscuit, which she handed to Ham. "He's the only one who will be able to convince her to return any matter. Unless Haith figures out the truth for herself beforehand."

"He'll have me flogged," Barrett said dismally. "No one was to enter or leave Greanly, and only you two ladies was permitted to visit the cells." The sheriff looked quite ill. "I admitted Ham and his loose tongue, as well as the means for Lady Haith's escape."

Bertie set Ham from her, as he was done with his biscuit, and he scrambled from the cottage. "I'll wager Lord Tristan will not be concerned with your error right away, Barrett," Bertie reasoned, and then her voice turned wistful. "I only hope he does hurry, and that he brings good news with him."

CHAPTER
26

Nigel lounged in the hall at Seacrest after returning from his meeting with the peddler. Save the wench's poor attempt at escape, things could not have gone more smoothly with Haith's abduction. Nigel knew that in but a few short hours, the remainder of his machinations would be set into action, and the mere thought of this brought a smile to his face.

The chit had betrayed him by not upholding her end of the bargain, and for that, she would pay. But Nigel had expected the weak-willed girl to renege on her word the very night she gave it. 'Twas a good thing Nigel had been wise enough to protect his interests by sending his ninny of a wife to chase after D'Argent. How fortunate for Nigel that Seacrest lay between Greanly and London. His plan had been made all the more effective by knowing the value Lord Tristan placed on Haith's head, and the king now knew it as well.

"Oh, yea, William," Nigel murmured aloud and raised his chalice in a mock salute. "'Twas a crime of passion indeed. D'Argent could not have her, so he was determined to see that no other would." Nigel clucked his tongue, then drank.

Of course, I must concentrate on perfecting my air of regretful sorrow at having to cut down one of his lords, Nigel thought. He knew nothing would give him more pleasure than dealing that deathblow. In the meantime, he would enjoy Haith at his leisure. Perhaps he would even let her live.

Nigel's musings were interrupted by one of his guards. The overweight man rushed into the hall, his face red from exertion. He bowed quickly, gulping to regain his breath.

"My lord," the man wheezed. "Visitors arrive at Seacrest."

Alarms went off in Nigel's head. Surely D'Argent had not figured out the girl's whereabouts so quickly! The peddler had not even arrived. Nigel sprung from his chair. "Who comes?"

"A lady. Her forerunner announced her as the Baroness of Crane, and she wishes an audience with you immediately."

Nigel relaxed a bit, although this woman was unheard of to him. "Very well. Give her welcome, and show her to me."

The guard hurried from the hall in his galumphing gait, leaving Nigel to ponder the reason for this unexpected visit from a stranger, a baroness at that. He called loudly for a servant, and a young girl came running.

"My lord?" The girl cowered and winced before him.

"Fetch refreshments. I have guests."

The girl's relief at the command was apparent, and she hurried to do his bidding.

"Stupid twit. Why am I forever plagued by ignorant women?"

* * *

The Baroness of Crane swept into Seacrest's hall with a manner befitting her station. Nigel was suitably pleased with her elegant beauty, if not the fact that she outranked him.

"My lady, I don't believe I've had the pleasure," he said as the woman glided to stand before him. "I am Nigel, Lord of Seacrest. Welcome."

"My apologies for arriving unannounced," the baroness said with a small smile. "But I think you will look upon this visit as fortuitous—perhaps for us both."

Nigel's eyebrows rose steeply. "Oh? Please sit, my lady, and enlighten me."

The noblewoman smoothed her skirts and accepted the chalice offered by Nigel. "I have just come from William's court where I learned some valuable information regarding my son."

"I beg your pardon. To my knowledge, I am not acquainted with any members of your family." Nigel sipped at his own chalice.

"Oh, but you are. My older son is none other than Tristan D'Argent, Lord of Greanly."

The wine in Nigel's throat took the uncomfortable paths of his nose and lungs, and he scrambled for a kerchief while he gasped and choked.

"My lord, are you alright?" The baroness leaned forward in her chair. "It must be quite a shock."

"Indeed, my lady," Nigel wheezed. He coughed and cleared his throat several times before drinking again. He watched her warily over the cup's rim. "Forgive me, but I was unaware that any of D'Argent's family still lived."

"We have been estranged for some time, 'tis true. I only discovered his whereabouts through a coincidental reunion at court this very morn." She scowled prettily. "'Twould seem my wayward offspring has done well to be awarded a demesne such as Greanly. Why he is still so intent on causing upheaval is beyond me."

At the lady's words, Nigel cautioned himself to tread carefully, although his heart pounded. "My lady, are you saying that Lord Tristan was in audience with the king this day?"

The baroness nodded. "And because of his behavior toward me, I now seek his home to regain an item in his possession that is very valuable to me—the jewel that adorns his weapon."

Nigel recalled the large sapphire on D'Argent's sword hilt as his eyes caught sight of the gem's twin gracing the lady's neck. Why had Ellora not informed him that D'Argent had departed for London? That wretch would pay now as well. He turned his attention to the baroness once more and continued his lightly veiled interrogation.

"I hope you are successful in your task, my lady, but I fail to see how this matter concerns me."

"Patience, my lord Nigel." The baroness's eyes flashed. "William spoke of some dissension between my son's household and your own. A betrothal Tristan wishes to see dissolved and a common wench he desires in place of your stepdaughter, true?"

"Yea." Nigel chose not to elaborate.

She shook her head sadly. "'Tis not enough that he disgraces you by refusing the betrothal contract, but now,"—her eyelashes fluttered—"he has personally petitioned the king for your arrest on the grounds of treason."

Nigel sat dumbfounded, not only by the news of D'Argent's cunning attempt to destroy him, but also by his mother's generosity with the tale. "This does not please you, my lady?"

The baroness huffed. "Not at all. That boy has been naught but a burden to me. His very birth caused my downfall in Paris. I was willing to forgive him, but Tristan's attitude toward me before the king was deplorable! His own mother!" She held out a hand beseechingly. "I was humiliated! And now I learn he wishes to sully the names of the innocent—your family, Lord Nigel—in his hurry to gain this one called Haith."

The frown on the lady's face deepened, and she leaned forward. "Tristan's actions these past months disgrace my family, my *true* family," she amended. "Lord Nicholas FitzTodd, Baron of Crane, is my son, and his connection to Tristan could prove damning in William's favor. Tristan's antics must be stopped—I will not have further scandal attached to me."

"I see." Nigel's mind was awhirl with the possibilities of laying D'Argent low with the aid of his own mother. "You have my deepest sympathy, my lady, for your trials."

The baroness flicked an imaginary piece of lint from her gown and looked at Nigel through her lashes. "Do you know of this wench? This common slut he desires? I would seek her as well."

"Indeed. She is . . . being returned to me as we speak."

"Wonderful!" The lady's eyes narrowed, and she openly studied the man before her. "Perhaps you would be so kind as to allow me access to her when she arrives? I have a thing or two I'd like to say to her."

"Of course, my lady. I expect her within the hour." Nigel paused, returning the baroness's stare and stroking his beard in thought. "My lady, perhaps you would be interested in my plan if you truly seek to reprimand this disrespectful son of yours."

"Very interested, actually." The baroness leaned back in her chair with a satisfied smile. "Do tell, and let us see if we cannot aid each other's plight."

* * *

Haith felt herself being dragged from the bed of the cart, and the next moment, Donald was setting her hard upon her feet in the dusky twilight. She promptly collapsed to the ground. The last half of the journey to Seacrest had been a living hell, and now she lay on the dirt outside the keep's walls, soaked with sweat and nearly delirious from the pounding in her skull and the rivers of pain in her limbs.

"Please," she managed to croak. "My hands."

The peddler rolled her over with a scowl and found the young woman's hands purple and gnarled below the ropes that bound them. "Bleedin' Christ," he gasped and quickly drew his knife to cut the bonds. "Yer laird is a cruel one, is he not?"

"He didn't bind her so tightly," Donald said without concern. " 'Twas her tryin' to escape that tightened the knots."

Haith screamed in agony as the ropes were removed, the sound coming out broken and jagged before she again passed out. The peddler moved his blade to the bonds that held her ankles.

"You're not supposed to do that, you great git," Donald growled at the old man.

"I doona think she'll put up much of a fight in this condition, even for ye." Disgust wrapped the peddler's words, and he left Donald sputtering as he dragged a large, rolled tapestry from the wagon and unfurled it in the dust alongside Haith's still form. "Now, help me get her on here so's I can get me coin and be done with this business."

The two men rolled Haith loosely into the woven covering and replaced her in the bed of the cart, Donald being of little help with only one hand. The peddler regained his seat behind the nags, who pulled the conveyance through the gates, leaving Donald to slip in behind. The merchant drove through Seacrest's dusk-cloaked village, waving off the few alert serfs who called to him to stop, seeking to peruse his wares.

Through shortcuts and alleyways, Donald arrived at the rear of the keep at the same time as the wagon. Together, the men wrestled the cargo that was Haith into the rear corridor, and Donald left the peddler to announce their arrival to Nigel. The Scot stood in the darkened passageway, staring dismally at the still package.

"Och, lass. 'Tis sorry I am of yer plight," he whispered. "But if I doona gain the coin this task pays, me family will surely starve." He ran his hands through his thinning hair and eyed the cart through the doorway.

No one should be treated in this manner, the man thought, *least of all a pretty and spirited maid such as this.* Perhaps those she fled would have the coin he required if he returned her, for surely the intentions of the devilish Lord Nigel could be naught but deadly. If he could get her in the cart by himself and be off quickly before Donald returned . . .

The peddler reached down, grasped the end of the tapestry, and pulled, only to feel the roll lifting into the air easily. The peddler looked up, startled to see Donald at the other end of the burden.

"What?" the scarred troll growled. "Let's go."

The Scotsman felt he had no choice but to continue. He followed Donald through a maze of claustrophobic passages and up a narrow rear staircase, taking as much care as he could with the package he carried. The lumpy Donald kicked a door open and backed through the portal.

The peddler entered a small chamber to see the evil one, Lord Nigel, and a well-dressed older lady, obviously of nobility, already within and watching the tapestry with interest. He and Donald set their burden down, and to the merchant's horror, Nigel approached the rolled bundle and kicked it forcefully with his booted heel.

The tapestry unfurled and spit the girl out against a far wall, where she groaned softly but did not move. Nigel swept an arm gallantly over Haith's still form.

"My lady, may I present Haith of Seacrest."

The baroness blanched. "This is the girl then? The one my son risks all for?"

Donald, who was caught up in the excitement of the kidnapping, overstepped his bounds by answering the lady himself. "Aye, what's left of her," he chuckled. "Stupid twit tried to escape them knots you made, m'lord. I'd be surprised if she don't end up like me for it." Donald held up his stump as if in example, but he lowered it, his grin fading, when he saw the woman's horrified expression.

Nigel's glare was murderous. "You two, move her to the cot." The lord pointed to a narrow bedstead against the wall of the tiny chamber. When that had been done, he ordered, "Now get from my sight, both of you. Donald, your work here is done. I'll send for you should I need your assistance further."

Donald flushed with embarrassment at his *faux pas* in front of the baroness. He bobbed politely before sidling out of the room.

The peddler, however, shuffled his feet.

"Are you deaf, old man?" Nigel demanded

"Er, beggin' yer pardon, m'lord. I just need me coin. Me payment."

Nigel sighed and removed a small, weighty pouch from his belt and tossed it to the relieved merchant. "Now go."

The lord slammed and bolted the door after the peddler, leaving himself and the baroness alone in the room with the unconscious Haith.

* * *

Night had truly fallen when the peddler wound his cart back through the village of Seacrest as quickly and quietly as he could. His part in the nasty business had left a bitterness in his heart, and he wished to put as much distance between himself and the home of the maniacal lord as possible. That a village eager to purchase from him lay unsampled did not deter him. Coin did not matter to him now. Indeed, the pouch that lay within his leather vest, resting on the edge of his belt, nearly seared his skin with its guilty weight.

Little more than an hour away, but far enough that the peddler could not be chastised by the sight of Seacrest, he stopped and made camp. Setting out his meal of bread and meat by the fire, the man fished the pouch from his shirt to count his tainted spoils.

At first, the Scot thought the objects he poured from the pouch were twisted by the flickering firelight, but as he held them closer to the flames, realization dawned on him.

He'd sent a young woman to her death for the price of two coins and a handful of broken links of chain mail.

His fist closed over the duplicitous payment, and he cried out in rage and guilt, calling for the revenge of his ancestors to be heaped on Lord Nigel of Seacrest. First, he indulged in tears and self-recrimination, but after that initial wave of emotion, the peddler's mind cleared.

Perhaps the town of Greanly had been no more kind to the lass than Nigel, but the Scot knew of the powerful Laird Buchanan. Although 'twas unlikely he'd reach the clan in time to save her life, he had to try. He would travel immediately to the girl's kin and alert them to her whereabouts. Lord Nigel would then pay.

While the peddler hoped for the sake of his own family that he would not be killed for his part in the lass's abduction, he felt in his heart 'twas just what he deserved.

The Baroness of Crane leaned over Haith's seemingly lifeless body and peered into her face. "Oh my."

"She's not dead, is she?" Nigel asked from behind the lady. He scurried to her side to see for himself.

"Nay, but nearly so," the baroness said, straightening and turning to Nigel with a haughty look. "I would hope you take better care with your hostage in my absence, Lord Nigel, if you wish the girl to live until Tristan arrives."

"Of course, my lady." Nigel's voice was matter-of-fact. "I should have known better than to set that bumbling peddler to such a task. And Donald is not known for his subtlety."

The baroness let her eyes fall back to Haith. "If we are to lure my son to Seacrest, we must act quickly. Send for my personal servants to give this girl a modicum of care. If any here should see her in the keep, she must appear to be in good health or 'twould seem suspicious."

"As you wish." Nigel bowed and walked to the door. "I shall await your—my lady?"

Nigel paused with his hand on the latch when he saw the baroness leaning over Haith with a small, but deadly looking dagger in her hand.

The baroness's laughter trilled merrily when she saw Nigel's shocked expression. "Fear not, my lord." She grasped a long, curling lock of Haith's hair and severed it cleanly with her blade. She straightened, dangling the swatch from her fingertips. "I am sure my son will require proof of the girl's presence at Seacrest as he is hardly likely to take my word. I have seen few wenches in this part of the country with hair of such bright hue, wouldn't you agree?"

Nigel smiled and shook his head. "You surprise me, my lady, with your cunning and intellect. 'Twould be a dire situation, indeed, should one find oneself on your bad side."

Genevieve's smile was dazzling as Nigel left the room, but as soon as the door closed, she sat heavily on the cot beside Haith, her body racked with tremors.

"Oh, my God. My God," she breathed, her shaking hands fluttering over Haith's face and upper body. "Hold on, darling. I will fetch Tristan to you, no matter what I must do to convince him." Genevieve took massive, steadying breaths to calm herself and stave off the horrified tears that threatened.

Genevieve drew one of Haith's tinged and twisted hands between her own and rubbed vigorously, trying to restore circulation. The girl groaned pitifully in response.

"I know, darling. 'Tis painful." She switched hands for a moment and then slid to the end of the cot to remove Haith's slippers, but the feet inside them were too swollen. Genevieve had no recourse but to again draw her dagger and carefully cut the shoes from Haith's feet. That task done, she set to massaging the girl's discolored ankles.

"I have made many mistakes in my life, Haith," Genevieve murmured, talking more to herself than to the unconscious girl. "Things I have done with the best of intentions have ended in tragedy. Perhaps this is my last chance to set things aright."

Genevieve returned to Haith's side and smoothed the hair back from her damp, pale face. "Mayhap he will never forgive me, and if 'tis so, then I must live with that. But for now, I will try with all my strength to give him what he most desires—you."

Haith turned her head restlessly, and her voice came out as a cracked moan. "Tristan."

"Yea, darling. I shall bring Tristan to you." Genevieve's eyes filled with the tears she had tried to prevent, and she blinked rapidly.

"Tristan, save me. I'm dying."

"Nay, nay—you mustn't say such things. You're not dying," Genevieve assured her, a bit of panic tingeing her tone. She knew that if the girl was not seen to promptly, her death was a very real possibility. The baroness's heart broke for this beautiful girl and the son she'd just begun to know before he was taken from her. "Hold on, darling."

The door opened, and two of Genevieve's personal attendants, Rose and Tilly, entered, carrying a large tapestry bag between them. Both young women gasped at the sight on the cot.

The baroness nodded. "I know, dears. 'Tis horrible, but you must be strong and do your best to save her." Genevieve's eyes misted as she looked at Haith. "She is most important to me."

Genevieve gave the servants strict instructions as to Haith's care and then departed the room in search of Lord Nigel. She found him once more in the hall. Steeling her face into a mask of aloofness, she entered.

"The girl sleeps. She will be cared for by my servants, and none should trouble you."

"Good, good. I'll see her later this eve then."

Genevieve froze for a split second before taking a seat across the small table from Nigel. "I'm not sure that is wise, my lord," she offered hesitantly. "I have given my girls instructions to keep her sedated, but if she awakens to your presence, she could become alarmed. We do not wish for her to attempt an escape."

Nigel sat for a moment, stroking his beard, and his

eyes narrowed. "Forgive me this impertinence, my lady, but how am I to be certain this is not some elaborate scheme against me?"

Genevieve's heart stopped, but she drew strength from her love for her son. She rose regally to tower over Nigel, her chin lifted and her eyes cold. "Am I correct to assume that no others know of Haith's abduction, save your two inept lackeys?"

Nigel shrank slightly in his chair. "Yea, my lady. But—"

"Then answer me this: why would I have reason to come to this hellish, paltry hold of yours to aid a lesser noble in his harebrained scheme if not to my own benefit? You forget that my involvement in this trickery is at great personal risk."

"My lady—"

"My very *lifeblood* whom I have not laid eyes upon in more than a score of years has humiliated me and refused me before the king himself, and you have the *audacity* to question my motives?" Genevieve drew a deep breath as she glared at Nigel, and he sank even further down in his chair.

The baroness prayed her next ploy would work.

"If that is how you repay a kindness, Lord Nigel, then I hope you fail miserably!" Genevieve turned and stalked to the stairs.

Nigel sprang from his chair. "My lady, where do you go?"

"To collect my attendants and ready them to depart for Hartmoore," the lady said, not slowing her pace. She had mounted the bottom steps by the time Nigel reached her.

"My lady, please! A thousand pardons! I should never have questioned you. Please forgive me—I cannot express how truly grateful I am for your assistance." Nigel tentatively reached for Genevieve's hand. "I beg you, stay and see this thing through to the end."

It took Herculean control for Genevieve not to breathe a sigh of relief. She turned and stared coolly at the supplicating fop below her. "Very well, Lord Nigel," she acquiesced. "But you would do well not to question me again."

"Of course not, Baroness."

"Now release me so that I may prepare to depart."

"But I thought—"

"To *Greanly,* Lord Nigel," Genevieve said in exasperation.

"So soon? My lady, 'tis nightfall, and unsafe for travel." Nigel smiled. "Dine with me this eve, and depart in the morn when you have rested."

The baroness pretended to consider the suggestion, then shook her head. "Nay. I wish to catch my son off guard. He should have returned from London by now as he departed before I did. He will be distracted by the girl's absence. I must act quickly."

"When do you return?"

"If you receive no word from me, plan for my arrival three days hence; four at the latest." Genevieve put a finger to her lips as if in thought. "'Twill give me time to convince him and time to travel."

"And you will bring D'Argent?"

Genevieve's smile, this time, was sincere. "Yea. I swear to you, I will bring you my son."

Less than an hour later, the Baroness of Crane rode north from Seacrest with her entire entourage, save the two girls she'd left behind to care for Haith. She called one of her guards, and he approached his lady's side on horseback. Genevieve handed him a note with a dire look.

"Ride hard to Hartmoore, and deliver this message to the Baron. It must be in his hand by morning."

Without a word of question, the guard took the parchment and wheeled his steed around to race westward. Genevieve watched him go with an apprehensive heart.

"Be swift, Nicholas," she murmured to the night-draped horizon. "Your brother needs us, even if he knows it not."

CHAPTER
27

Tristan entered the great hall at Greanly before day-break with mixed emotions. The relief at being at a place all his own and the prospect of seeing Haith soothed him. He was filled with new hope for their future together and was eager to share with her the news of his meeting with William. Although he was exhausted from his journey and the ordeal at the king's court, being surrounded by the solid walls of Greanly comforted him and made it easier to push the shock of seeing Genevieve aside.

On the other hand, it was still at the forefront of his mind that the friend—nay, brother—dearest to him was no longer within these same walls. Amidst the growing familiarity of his home, there lurked also a sense of loss.

Tristan crossed the dimly lit hall with a weariness that echoed in his footfalls. 'Twould be his responsibility to inform Lady Soleilbert of Pharao's return to his home country. He did not look forward to the task, which would force him to relive the pain of the message.

His desire to see Haith was great, but he knew that because of the late hour, she would be lost in slumber.

Tristan also needed whatever rest he could steal before the tasks looming in the days ahead demanded his energy and full attention. The damned nightmares had plagued him since he had departed for London, and he longed for deep, dreamless sleep.

He swerved from the doorway that led to the lower cells and had nearly reached the stairs when a voice called to him.

"My lord."

Tristan halted and squinted through the hall's murkiness to see Barrett sitting at a rear table. A single candle threw shadows on his long, shaggy face, making him appear more beastly than usual. The sheriff grasped a large tankard in his hands, both forearms resting on the tabletop.

"Barrett, what has you about so late? Surely you do not await my return?"

Barrett nodded, never taking his eyes from the candle's flame before him.

Tristan chuckled, then looked more closely at his town's sheriff. He would have to speak to Barrett about the limitations of his duties. But not tonight—Tristan was too weary.

"Well, I have returned, good sheriff. I beg you, seek your bed."

Barrett shook his head and raised his eyes to meet Tristan's inquisitive gaze. The sorrow and fear was apparent in the sheriff's haggard face, and his tone betrayed his regret.

"Lady Haith has fled."

For a moment, Tristan stood with leaden limbs and a loud buzzing in his ears. He shook his head to clear it. "You released her against my command?"

"Nay, m'lord. She escaped with help from Ham and a

traveling merchant." Barrett seemed to wait resignedly for the recriminations and vows of punishment from his liege.

But when Tristan finally spoke, his voice was low, almost thoughtful. "Do we know where she hies to?"

"Aye. She left Minerva a note, and Bertie knew of the scheme all along. She goes to her mother's clan in Scotland."

Finally able to command his legs, Tristan recrossed the hall to join the sheriff at the table. Barrett reached down the darkened length and fetched another tankard, which he then filled from the jug beside him on the bench and slid to his lord. Tristan drank deeply, then replaced the tankard on the tabletop with unnecessary care.

Barrett broke the unsettling silence. "I didn't follow her because 'twould have meant leaving Greanly unguarded with both you and Pharao gone." Barrett raised his gaze. "Any word on his whereabouts?"

Tristan nodded. "He's not coming back, Barrett. He's returned to his homeland." Almost as an afterthought, he added, "You did well in staying at Greanly."

Tristan's grim thoughts were reflected on his countenance. On his last night in London, sleep had eluded him with the return of the familiar nightmare that had plagued him for so many years. Just as he would slip into slumber, snippets of the dream would startle him awake, and leaving him tossing in his bed.

Tristan, save me. I'm dying.

Try as he might to discount it as fanciful imagining, the hard conclusion he was slowly reaching was that the nightmare could only mean one thing.

Tristan raised his gaze to Barrett's. "She is in danger."

"You are certain, m'lord?"

A shadow emerged from shadow, revealing Minerva in close proximity. "Aye. He's as certain as I." Barrett jumped at the old woman's appearance, but Tristan merely turned to her calmly.

"You have seen it as well?" he asked.

"Nae." Minerva moved closer to the table. "The runes have been silent to me. But I felt it this night and last. Did you dream?"

Tristan nodded. "Mayhap I am already too late."

Minerva laid a hand on the lord's shoulder. "I think not. If it were so, she couldna have reached out as she did. She is weak though."

Barrett did not take time to question how Tristan and Minerva were garnering their information; instead, he sought direction. "What do we do, m'lord?"

"We depart for Scotland within the hour. Barrett, wake the soldiers, and ready them for the journey." Tristan's orders were given with an authority that belied the desolation in his face.

Barrett paused in rising. "Do I go as well?"

"Yea," Tristan said. "I care not if Nigel comes to claim every stone at Greanly. 'Tis only Haith that matters. Make haste, Barrett."

Minerva took the seat vacated by the sheriff. "My lord, I have felt that perhaps 'tis nae Scot—"

Her words were interrupted as the hall door crashed against the wall and Barrett reentered, this time struggling with another, much smaller individual.

A female.

A *blond* female who threatened to wake the entire village with her shrieking. Tristan shot to his feet.

"Let me go, you witless brute!" the woman screamed. "I must see my son immediately! I know he is here!"

"You daft cow! The lord's mother is dead!" Barrett looked to Tristan in bewilderment. "I found 'er lurkin' just outside the hall, m'lord. She's got at least two score riders beyond the walls."

At Barrett's address, the woman ceased her struggles and looked around wildly. "Tristan!" she nearly sobbed. "Thank God!"

"Release her, Barrett," Tristan said. His face was devoid of all expression, but a small tic had appeared at his jawline.

"M'lord?" Barrett seemed unsure of his lord's decision to loose the mad woman.

But Tristan nodded, then addressed Genevieve as she stumbled across the hall. He held out a commanding arm, preventing her from embracing him.

"Stay where you stand, Mother," he warned, his words eliciting sharp gasps from Minerva and Barrett. "You should not have come here. I haven't the time nor the desire to deal with your lies."

Tears ran unchecked down Genevieve's face. "Tristan, you must listen to me! I have word of Haith."

Tristan was upon her in a blink, seizing her arms. "What? How do you know of Haith?"

"I have seen her!"

"Sweet Corra," Minerva breathed.

"You lie." Tristan thrust the woman away as if she were afire, a vicious snarl emanating from him. "Haith flees to Scotland."

"Nay!" Genevieve approached her son again. "She is imprisoned at Seacrest Manor."

Tristan pointed a long, deadly arm at the woman. "Stay. Away. From me." To Barrett he said, "Take her to a cell. Then send the archers to the wall walk, and give them my order to kill all who wait outside for her." He strode to the stairs and began to ascend. "I will not be delayed by their questioning when we depart."

"Nay! Tristan!" Genevieve shrieked and strained against the sheriff's massive grip. "She shall die if you do not heed me! Look at me, I beg you!" The baroness wrenched a hand to her belt and withdrew the lock of red hair, tied with a leather strip.

Tristan did not turn at his mother's pleadings, but paused at Minerva's exclamation.

"My lord, she speaks true!"

Barrett releascd his hold on Genevieve and snatched the lock from her, studying it carefully. He looked up at Tristan.

"Aye, m'lord. It looks as though it belongs to Lady Haith."

Tristan's tone was demonstration enough that he had once been William's Hammer. His voice dripped with the threat of death as he descended the steps. "What have you done to her, bitch?"

"I have done naught, I swear to you!" Genevieve said, heedless of the murder in his eyes and the hand that gripped the hilt of his sword. "She was abducted by a peddler sent by Lord Nigel of Seacrest. He wishes to lure you to him."

"A peddler?" Barrett said, looking to Minerva, then to Tristan.

Genevieve ignored everyone but Tristan as he approached her with a measured step. "Once you are at Seacrest, he plans to murder you and seize Greanly for himself!"

Tristan came to stand directly before Genevieve, and each step he took forced her to stumble backward. "How do you know this unless you have been included in Nigel's plan? It sounds to me like a trick."

"I *was* included, and it *is* to be a trick!" In her frustration, Genevieve turned and seized the lock of hair from Barrett and then turned back to her son, showing no fear in the face of his rage. She grasped Tristan's hand and pressed the lock into it, closing their joined fingers around it. "Tristan, Nigel trusts me to return with you to

Seacrest three days hence so that he may kill you and claim your love. If we hurry, we can return before he expects us with your men and my guards."

Tristan's stony visage did not yield the slightest at his mother's admissions, so she continued.

"She is not well, Tristan. I have left two of my servants to tend her, but I fear we have little time to waste." Genevieve squeezed Tristan's hand. "Please. I know that I have hurt you terribly, perhaps beyond my ability to salvage, but you must believe me when I say that I shall explain all once your Haith is safely returned to you."

"I promised her I would bring you, Tristan, when she called out for you."

A muscle in Tristan's cheek twitched, and he looked down into the tear-streaked face of the woman who pleaded with him. When he spoke, his voice was little more than a murmur.

"Why were you at Seacrest? You have no acquaintance there."

"William sent me to confirm your suspicions," Genevieve whispered. "He thought perhaps 'twould redeem me in your eyes. I now know the whole of Nigel's plot and can attest to his guilt by his own tongue."

Tristan's entire system was in such shock that he was having difficulty thinking. He looked over his mother's head to Minerva and Barrett. "What say you, friends?"

Minerva spoke first. "I had it in my gut that Haith would not gain Scotland. The lock of hair seems likely enough."

Barrett nodded in agreement. "Aye, m'lord. And the description of the peddler seems more than coincidence."

Tristan returned his gaze to the frightened woman who still grasped his hand.

"Very well, Baroness," he said gravely. "I will indulge your tale and journey to Seacrest prepared for battle.

But mind you,"—he jerked his hand and the lock of Haith's hair free from Genevieve's—"if you lie, if Haith bears but a scratch because of you, believe me when I vow that I will kill you slowly and with relish."

Genevieve's gaze did not waver. "My men are at your disposal, and they await your word."

Tristan addressed Minerva. "You and the baroness will remain at Greanly to comfort Lady Soleilbert when she awakens. Surely she will seek you when she finds the hall empty. 'Tis also necessary to see to Ellora's care." Tristan looked to Barrett. "Assuming that she has not escaped as well."

Barrett flushed crimson. "Nay, m'lord."

Genevieve spoke up. "Tristan, Nigel expects me to return with you. He—"

"The slime also expects me in three days, not this day. I will waste no time nor any lives other than those who are willing and able to do battle." Tristan's eyes glittered like deadly blue flames. "And I trust you not. I would have you as far as possible from Haith, if she is indeed at Seacrest."

"Very well," Genevieve whispered. "Have a care, Tristan—Nigel is devious and desperate."

"Do not fear, *Mother*," Tristan sneered. "I have faced worse deceit in my lifetime and conquered it." He dismissed her by turning to mount the steps once more. "Commence to stirring the men, Barrett." He paused, addressing Minerva. "If you would see to the baroness's housing, Minerva, I would be grateful. She has earned no place within my home." At the old one's nod, Tristan continued on without a glance toward Genevieve.

Minerva approached the deflated woman with a gentle hand and a kind smile. "Come with me, my lady. I have many questions."

* * *

Haith was lost in the silent meadow of her dreams once more. She felt as if she'd been there for days, walking through the still grass under a perpetually blue sky and calling, calling endlessly for Tristan. The dream and reality were so enmeshed that her thoughts were jumbled like the tiny multicolored panes of a stained glass window—sane thought warring with the fantastic.

Haith's hands throbbed and hung like dumb weights. Her feet screamed silently with each step. Her ears were keenly aware of her drumming heartbeat, slow and heavy in her chest.

Was she walking north? Would Scotland lay waiting on the edge of this maddening world?

And where was Tristan? Surely he would search for her here. She tried calling to him again.

"Tristan! I'm here!" Her own voice threatened to shatter her skull with its intensity. She paused and clutched at her offended head with a low moan. A thought occurred to her then: the first time Haith had found herself in this meadow, 'twas only the dark man—Pharao's—voice that she had heard. Perhaps . . .

"Pharao! Can you hear me?" Haith turned slowly in a circle, scanning the bland horizon. She tried again, this time cupping her hands around her mouth. "Pharao, I need your help!"

Haith gave up hope that any could hear her voice, and she had begun walking once more when the grass and sky ahead began shimmering like steam over a cauldron. A tree sparkled into being, its gnarled, ancient limbs growing in an instant and flowering with lush, verdant leaves.

Beside the tree, a figure stood.

Haith ran, ignoring her clublike feet, and as she neared the landmark, she saw the figure's long robes in blinding contrast to the stale surroundings. She halted breathlessly before him.

"Haith." Pharao's voice again seemed to speak from inside her head, and his lips did not move. "Why do you call me here?"

"You are the only one who can hear me," she said, unsure if she spoke with her mouth or her mind and unable to differentiate between the two. It seemed to matter not. "I must find my way back to Tristan."

"You do not need my assistance, here of all places."

Haith's forehead wrinkled. "I don't understand. I am trapped in this meadow."

"You are only trapped because you believe yourself trapped." Pharao sank gracefully to the ground and motioned for Haith to do the same. After she had sat, he continued.

"This place, this meadow, as you call it,"—Pharao gestured to the ocean of grass surrounding them—"is your perception. You created it, and therefore, you control it. You have been here before, perhaps long ago?"

Haith shook her head. "Nay. Only when I dreamed of it and you some weeks ago."

"You have forgotten." Pharao stretched out an arm, bringing his hand inches from her temple before pausing. "May I?"

"Go on."

Pharao laid his palm gently along Haith's face, and his other arm he stretched out toward the meadow before them. To Haith's utter amazement, a scene began to unfold before her very eyes.

Trees sprung up as if their growth cycles were only mere seconds, and a breeze raced through the meadow like a pup let out to play, tossing the grasses wildly. The sun arced up from its hiding place over the horizon and dangled overhead.

And then a man and a young girl were walking across the meadow. Tears filled Haith's eyes as memories flooded her consciousness.

James and Haith—she still a young child—walked and conversed before them.

"Oh. My God."

Pharao dropped his hand, but the scene continued, sustained by Haith's remembrance. Sound was added to the meadow, and the rumbling roar of thunder and the sizzle of lightning filled the empty air. Seacrest appeared in the distance, and suddenly, the younger Haith ran toward the town.

Haith knew that the child did so on her father's command.

Corinne appeared at James's side, and the couple watched sadly as first their daughter disappeared, then the keep. Finally, they themselves were gone, leaving only a sunny, calm meadow in their wake.

Haith turned to Pharao. "I still do not understand."

Pharao looked at her intently, thinking for a moment. "You created this place out of your needs as a small child, perhaps to contact your father. Am I correct in guessing that worse disaster followed his death and your return from meeting him here?"

Haith nodded, unable to voice the details of what she'd awoken to in the hall when she'd come out of her trance those many years ago. Her small body had been hurled across the room to land atop Corinne's, who had been killed by a sword through her chest and lay covered in blood. The hall was filled with terrified screams. Ellora and Bertie were tied together and sobbing, both already having been beaten. Minerva lay near them, unconscious but alive.

And everywhere, everywhere, huge Norman soldiers

and foreign mercenaries wielded bloodied weapons over dead or dying villagers.

"Seacrest was nearly destroyed," Haith whispered.

Pharao nodded. "In your young mind, you likened your talents and abilities with tragedy, and forever linked this place you'd created to death and sadness." He paused. "You do not acknowledge the gift of your people, am I correct?"

"Yea." The pieces were beginning to fall into place for Haith now. "So much loss—I could not comprehend the reason for it. Perhaps I felt at fault."

"Ofttimes, there is no reason behind the actions of men. Your guilt these many years has prevented you from experiencing your potential. It also has prompted you to take on the responsibilities of those around you."

Haith blinked. "As you warned me before. You said I cannot prevent what is not under my control."

Pharao nodded.

Haith started as a bird flew into the tree above them. "But why do I keep returning to this place when it frightens me so?"

"Perhaps 'tis your soul's way of trying to access your gift, the ancient knowledge you locked away as a small child."

"I've forgotten how to use it," Haith realized. "And so it frightens me."

Pharao smiled and stood, drawing an anxious look from Haith.

"Where are you going?"

"You have your answers now and do not need me." Pharao's form took on a shimmery appearance. "We will meet again soon, Haith."

"Wait! How do I—"

"You have your answers . . ." Pharao's voice faded away along with his presence, leaving Haith alone under the tree.

She felt looser, freer than she could ever remember. Although Haith's feet and hands still pained her, the sensations faded behind a flood of rushing, white energy that filled her. As it poured through her and out, the grass became greener, the sun's warmth more intense. Haith unfolded her legs and stood tall, taller, reveling in the simple beauty her younger self had created so many years ago. Her troubles, while still grave, no longer seemed insurmountable. Her vision was cleared, the preciousness of the ones she loved squashing the doubts and fears she'd previously clung to.

Tristan, my love.

Haith closed her eyes in the meadow and *felt* her way back to her body.

She came to consciousness as if she had been dropped from a great height, starting violently and eliciting a shriek from the attendants who waited on the other side of her eyelids. The pain she now felt, blazing from all her extremities as well as her skull, was agonizing, and she moaned.

"My lady!" a girl's hushed voice called to her. "My lady, can you hear me? You must awaken!"

"W-where am I?" Haith's eyes fluttered open to see two strange faces peering down into hers. "Who are you?" she croaked.

"You are at Seacrest Manor, and we are the personal attendants of the Baroness of Crane," a different girl supplied. "I am Tilly, and this is Rose."

The memory of the torturous wagon journey burst into Haith's consciousness, and she struggled to sit up. She looked around the room and realized she lay in her childhood chamber at Seacrest.

"The Baroness of Crane?" Haith asked, but before the girls could answer, a great crash shook the walls, and all three women flinched. "Never mind that. Where is Nigel?"

"We know not, m'lady," Rose offered. "But we believe this castle is under siege, and our mistress has not returned for us!"

Another impact rocked the room, and the two girls shrieked and fell together. Haith pushed herself to the edge of the cot.

"We must get out of here," she told the girls calmly. "Help me to see if I can stand."

"Oh, nay, m'lady," Tilly gasped, her eyes wide. "You have been sleeping since last eve, and are very weak. We have strict instructions from the baroness that you are not to leave this room for your own safety!"

Rose chimed in as well. "Besides, we know not what manner of barbarians threaten the keep!"

"The only barbarian at Seacrest is its lord," Haith snarled and pushed herself awkwardly to her feet. Weak indeed. "The one who challenges the keep is of no danger to us. I know these passages well, and we will escape unseen."

The servants looked at each other in terrified indecision. Tilly spoke, "I do not know, m'lady—"

"Very well then. Stay if you wish. I know no baroness and hold her no allegiance." Haith hobbled toward the door on feet that felt lined with shards of glass. She turned to the trembling girls as another crash shook the walls. "Where are my slippers?"

The one called Rose held up a handful of leather strips. "The Baroness had need to cut them from your feet, m'lady."

Haith sighed and looked down—the bandages would have to suffice. What manner of woman was this who cared for her under Nigel's roof? She addressed the maids. "Stay in this room, throw the bolt, and *be quiet.* I shall send someone for you, but I vow 'twill not be

Lord Nigel. If he tries to remove you though, do not struggle, for he is cruel and dangerous."

"Not to worry, m'lady." Tilly withdrew a wicked-looking blade from her belt. "Our mistress has provided for us."

Satisfied, Haith opened the door a crack and poked her head into the corridor. Although horrific reverberations could be felt and shouts heard coming from below, the upper corridor was empty. Haith slid from the room and made her way to the back stairs as quickly as her shrieking feet would allow.

She eased her way down the first few steps, listening for approaching footfalls. When none came, her confidence grew, prompting her to increase her pace. Haith could see the bottom of the stairs and the doorway beyond, and was so intent on her escape that she did not see Donald snake around the corner.

He grabbed her around her waist with his stubbed arm, and he clamped his hand over her mouth. Hot, foul breath hissed in her ear.

"Hello there, m'lady. Lord Nigel sent me to fetch you. Seems we have visitors."

CHAPTER
28

Tristan and his men, including Genevieve's small entourage of soldiers, awaited dusk on a forested knoll overlooking Seacrest and the sea beyond. The tension that hung over the group was palpable. It took all of Tristan's warrior's training to hold on to his patience and wait for the opportune moment to strike, instead of charging ahead. He longed to tear Seacrest's very walls to splinters with his bare hands.

Indeed, it looked as if Nigel had prepared for a misstep in the plans he'd laid. The tall wooden gates were shut tight, and guards stood along the wall walk at regular intervals. Tristan let a vicious grin slide over his mouth at the thought of Nigel trying to prevent him entrance if he indeed held Haith captive.

His mind went to his mother, and then quickly dismissed the woman. This was not the time to try to wade through that one's cryptic motives. He was still more than a little shocked at her arrival. If she proved trustworthy in this campaign against Nigel, he would listen to the explanations she offered.

And then Tristan would reject her as she had him.

Barrett moved his horse next to his lord's and spoke, though neither man's eyes strayed from the town below.

"'Tis nearly time, my lord?"

"Yea, Barrett. Once we gain entrance to the gates, I will lead half the men to the hall while you and the others fend off Nigel's soldiers and surround the keep. None who follow the bastard shall have the opportunity to escape with Haith."

"Aye. And when—"

The sheriff's words were abruptly silenced as all the men took notice of a great rumbling coming from the west.

'Twas the sound of many riders approaching.

"My lord," Barrett said uneasily, "Nigel could not have hired mercenaries to defend the town, could he?"

"I know not, Barrett. If my mother has spoken true, he does not expect us so soon."

The sloped shoulder of the knoll was soon crested by a line of soldiers crowding the small rise—more than two hundred it seemed. A lone rider broke away from the pack and galloped toward Tristan's army.

"Stand ready, men," Tristan warned in a low voice. "He rides alone, but be wary of a signal to attack."

The man approaching rode a massive silver destrier, and his battle armor was immaculate. Clearly, he was of noble station to be wearing such rich armaments. The man was large, that was apparent by the size of his steed, and younger than Tristan. As he drew closer, he pulled off his helmet, revealing curling black hair and eyes of icy blue. His jaw was set determinedly when he slowed his mount to a halt several paces in front of Tristan's.

The two men stared at each other without words and then both dismounted in the same instant. The dark-haired man approached Tristan, his arm extended as he spoke. "I came as quickly as I could ready the men. When do we strike?"

Tristan took his brother's arm in a firm grasp, and their eyes met and held as did their grips on each other. "At dusk."

"I am Nicholas FitzTodd."

Tristan nodded and swallowed, but was unable to speak with the furious emotion that filled him. The only outward sign of his discomfiture was the muscle that twitched along his jaw. His expression was mirrored by that of the younger man before him.

Nicholas spoke again through clenched teeth. "You are Tristan D'Argent. My brother."

The words were Tristan's undoing, and he roughly pulled Nicholas forward into his embrace.

"Yea," Tristan choked gruffly as he pounded on Nicholas's back. "I am your brother."

Barrett tore his eyes away from the reunion with a constricted throat, as did most of the men.

The two brothers finally withdrew from one another and cleared their throats to cover their embarrassment.

"I'll signal my men to join yours," Nicholas said and turned to give the orders.

Within the hour, both sets of troops had merged, and the plan of attack had been described so that all were in accord. The guards atop Seacrest's wall had no trouble discerning the intent of the now massive number of riders assembled so near the keep. The line to defend Seacrest had been fortified.

Tristan looked to the men who flanked him: his brother, Nicholas, to his right and Barrett on his left. Although he felt Pharao's absence like a gaping wound, Tristan drew comfort from the memories of the hundreds of battles they'd ridden into together. In his heart, he felt Pharao was still at his side.

In a fiery burst, the sun began dipping behind the foothills, casting Seacrest in a bloody haze and putting the light at the troops' backs.

"Ride." Tristan's voice was low, but was followed by the battle cry of nearly four hundred men in a deafening roar as they charged down the knoll toward their intended target.

As they neared Seacrest's wall, arrows loosed by the guards rained down on Tristan and his companions. Although many of the brothers' men were spared because of the blinding sun at their backs, the sheer number of missiles released insured that some would find their marks.

The sea of soldiers charged the outer wall with a mighty impact, shattering the old wooden gate with an explosive crash. The first wave of avengers flooded into the bailey, Tristan and Nicholas riding its crest together.

They were met by a wall of defenders, and the hand-to-hand combat commenced with a collective roar. Swords clanged, and screams of the fallen filled the air with a macabre melody that spurred the righteous on. Seacrest's soldiers were afoot and unused to battle, having had no one challenge them in the years since Nigel's acquisition of the town. They were no match for Tristan's battle-seasoned warriors and Nicholas's strictly disciplined group. Fattened, complacent men were laid low in the unequal fight, and many now lay strewn about the bailey, causing the soldiers astride to pick their way among the dead as they fought their way to the keep.

Tristan's blood coursed rich and thick in his veins, his thirsty revenge feeding on every soft body run through on his sword and every fat head severed. He chanced a glance at Nicholas, who battled near him, and was shocked to see the man swinging his own mighty broadsword with relish and actually laughing at the carnage.

His most recent challenger easily dispatched, Nicholas

wheeled his horse to join Tristan at the doors to the great hall. Soldiers from Nicholas's outfit appeared, bearing a heavy oaken battering ram with crude pegged handles adorning both sides.

"Stand back, milords," the soldier manning the front of the log advised.

Tristan and Nicholas exchanged looks, then sheathed their swords and dismounted to take a place on either side of the front of the missile.

"One, two, ho!" the soldier cried, and the ram crashed against the barrier, jarring the doors, but leaving them still closed.

"Ho!"

Again, the portal withstood the mighty blow, although a groaning splintering was heard.

"Back!" Nicholas waved the men further to the reverse and then looked at Tristan with a gleam in his eye.

Tristan nodded and tightened his grip.

"HO!"

The ram surged forward on the swift feet of the men who bore it and slammed into the doors with a fury that blew both slabs away. The two massive doors cartwheeled into the hall in a thick cloud of wood shards and dust and landed with a ground-shaking crash.

The men were carried into the keep by the force of the blow, prompting Tristan to release his hold and step away from the projectile. He drew his sword and veered away from the soldiers, adapting a readied stance.

Before him, seated casually at the lord's table with a chalice clasped between his fingers, his tormentor beckoned. Nigel looked down upon Tristan and his invading army with amusement, for between him and Donald sat Haith, a knife held to her throat.

* * *

Haith's heart leapt as the doors to the hall blew inward, revealing Tristan at the fore of the attack. His front was awash in crimson, and she prayed that not one drop of the blood he wore had flowed from his veins.

The cold blade at her throat pressed cruelly, and Donald leaned closer, forestalling any hopes of escape.

"Lord Tristan," Nigel said as if delighted at his appearance. "How lovely of you to call. I was expecting you of course, but not so quickly."

The hiss of armor was nearly deafening as Tristan's men flooded the hall and surrounded the table in a semicircle, stopping several paces away. Tristan stepped forward.

"Release her now, Nigel, and I will still give you a chance to fight with honor," he advised. "Just you and I."

"Oh, I think not." Nigel reached out a finger and ran it lightly down Haith's breastbone, tugging at her bodice. "Is she worth all this? I suppose I shall find out soon enough, eh?"

Haith squeezed her eyes shut and whimpered at Nigel's touch and Donald's encouraging guffaw. "Tristan, stay back. He'll kill you." Her eyes opened to see a man who looked oddly familiar restraining Tristan.

"Hold your tongue, slut!" Nigel's temper flared, and he grabbed Haith by her hair. He jerked her head near his, causing Donald's blade to nick her milky throat. Blood welled forth, beaded, then trickled down her chest.

Nigel swiped at the drop with one slim finger and tasted its warmth. "M-m-m—sweet."

Tristan roared, the veins standing out clearly on his forehead, and he lunged against the grip of the man who held him. Barrett approached to assist in his restraint.

"I suppose I am a fool for trusting your mother, Tristan." Nigel thrust Haith toward Donald once more and stood, gesturing with his chalice. "I should have known that all women are liars and fools and that the baroness was no different."

"Our mother is no fool," the dark-haired man spat. "She took your measure well enough."

Haith's eyes widened as the resemblance between Tristan and the man fell into place. The Baroness of Crane was Tristan's mother, Genevieve D'Argent! The dark-haired man was Tristan's brother! Even in her fear, Haith's eyes filled with tears at the sight of the two men side by side.

Nigel's eyebrows rose. "'Our mother,' you say? Hm-m-m. Well, that would make you Lord Nicholas, Baron of Crane, then." Nigel bowed with a chuckle. "Welcome to Seacrest, my lord."

"You are finished, Nigel," Nicholas gritted.

"Release me, Brother!" Tristan roared, his voice cracking with intensity. His chest heaved, and Haith could see the strain of the muscles in his neck. How the two men continued to hold him, she did not know.

Nigel looked upon the men before him with an expression akin to curiosity. "Yea, 'twould seem my plans have indeed gone awry. There are too many witnesses against me now to gain my desires through the crown. But that will not prevent me from seeing that those who hindered me suffer as well." He gestured to Tristan with his chalice. "How does it feel, Tristan, to know that even after all of this, you will never have her?"

Haith felt Donald's blade ease away from her neck slightly as he sat mesmerized by Nigel's words. With her eyes on Tristan, she took her chance.

Using both bruised hands, she shoved at the table's edge with all her might, sending her chair toppling backward. Donald lunged through empty space to land heavily against Nigel, causing Nigel's chalice to go tumbling from his hand. Wine splashed across the table and ran onto the floor like blood.

Hell broke loose in the hall as Tristan tore free and dove at the table and the soldiers rushed forward. Haith scrambled on her hands and knees along the rear wall, but her escape was short-lived. She screamed as Donald's meaty palm closed around her bruised ankle and jerked her facedown on the rushes.

Haith cried out again as the smithy's boot found purchase in her side. He seized her hair and pulled her upright. Haith was whirled around in front of Donald as a shield, his knife once more pressed to her throat, this time, not so gently.

"D'Argent, you great bastard!" Donald called. "Look here what I caught!"

Haith saw that Tristan had Nigel pinned against the wall, the tip of his broadsword dimpling the man's abdomen. At Donald's cry of triumph, Tristan glanced out of the corner of his eye.

"Call your men off an' step away," Donald advised, "or I'll slit her throat this instant."

"Do not, Tristan!" Haith cried. "Kill him now!"

Tristan looked from the knife at Haith's throat to Nigel's pasty grimace. "Hold, men!" he called over his shoulder. "Nicholas, hold them back!" He began lowering the tip of his sword.

"Nay!" Haith screamed.

The events seem to unfold in slow motion before her. As Tristan drew back, Nigel pulled a long, slender dagger from his belt and arced it toward Tristan's chest. Tristan deflected the blow with his forearm, sending the blade flying through the air, harmless. Without so much as a blink, Tristan plunged his sword into Nigel's gut with a ragged cry of triumph.

Like the kiss of an angel, something brushed Haith's

cheek, and then Donald's grip was no more as he sank to the floor behind her.

Haith rushed forward to throw herself into Tristan's arms just as he lunged for her. He crushed her to him, and the two looked down to where Donald lay.

An iciclelike projectile protruded from Donald's eye, the ball on the end of the thin shard the shape and size of a small egg. Both Haith and Tristan looked across the breadth of the hall from whence the weapon had been hurled.

His great black horse prancing impatiently atop Seacrest's breached doors, Pharao swung his leather sling idly. A small smile played about his lips, and several heavily armed young men dressed in similar fashion surrounded him.

"Son of a bitch!" Barrett shouted, a smile spreading across his shaggy face.

Haith felt Tristan's shuddering intake of breath, and she gently pushed him away through her tears. "Go to him."

"You're certain?" Tristan's eyes searched her face hungrily. "I do not wish to leave your side, even for a moment."

"We shall have our entire lives together," she assured him, and her heart sang when he smiled at her. "Go and thank him for saving my life." *Twice,* Haith thought to herself as she watched Tristan stride across the hall.

The men guarding Pharao parted for the large Englishman, and Pharao dismounted. " 'Twould seem that I arrive just in time, my liege," Pharao said.

"As always, Phar. As always." Tristan reached him, and the two men embraced, laughing and clapping each other's shoulders.

Across the hall, Haith saw Nicholas look away with

an expression of disappointment. He called to the soldiers still standing about.

"Look lively, men. Let us begin collecting the bodies and burying the dead." His voice was subdued, and his wide, strong shoulders slumped.

"Nicholas!" Tristan called and motioned to him with the arm that was not about Pharao's shoulders.

Nicholas straightened and approached.

"Phar, this is my brother, Lord Nicholas, Baron of Crane."

Pharao's smile was broad. "Your brother, my liege? How fortunate and joyful you must feel!" Pharao extended his arm, and Nicholas readily took it.

"Nicholas, this is my *other* brother,"—Tristan's eyes met and held Pharao's—"Pharao Tak'Ahn. Without the both of you, I am not certain this day would have been so easily won." Tristan looked across the hall to where Haith stood, and she laughed aloud as the love in his eyes raised gooseflesh on her arms. Suddenly, his eyebrows drew downward, and he started forward.

"Haith! Behind you!"

Haith spun to see that Nigel, sword still embedded firmly in his abdomen, had grasped a lit torch from its sconce on the wall. With a crazed grin of triumph, he tossed the flaming stick onto the alcohol-soaked table before her. With a sizzling whoosh, she and Nigel were surrounded by a circle of flames.

Haith screamed as the impaled man staggered toward her, one hand trying to still the bobbing skewer that pierced him. Beyond the crackle of the flames, Haith could hear shouts for water to be brought and Tristan calling her name.

"'Tis just you and I now, wench," Nigel rasped, blood bubbling at his lips. "We die together."

The smoke roiled within the fiery circle, causing

Haith to choke and cover her nose. She held out a hand to ward off the approaching Nigel, whose arm, he'd failed to notice, had caught fire.

"Come perch upon this blade with me, love," Nigel said deliriously. "And come to your death as your mother did—willingly."

His admission rocked Haith, and suddenly, all the anger and guilt and fear she'd felt since the day of her parents' death welled up inside her. The energy expanded in her, shattering her doubts and leaving in their place a power so great and old that it sparkled from her eyes and fingertips like white threads of lightning. Her hair fanned wildly around her face as if she stood in a fiery gale.

Nigel fell back a pace at the transformation before him, and Haith saw a hint of terror light his deluded gaze. She raised her arms high, mindless of the hungry blaze that licked at her but did not singe. Pinning him with her stare, Haith spoke words from deep within, words that were instinctually hers by right of birth.

> *By fire I damn thee!*
> *By blade I damn thee!*
> *By purity of soul I damn thee!*
> *Three times three times three!*

The sword in Nigel's gut twisted of its own accord, eliciting a hellacious shriek from the man. The flames on his arms and torso rose up to engulf his head with a satisfied sizzle and pop. Haith's gaze on him never wavered, and Nigel fell screaming to the ground as images shimmered in mind-numbing succession in the air between he and Haith: Haith and Soleilbert as young girls, playing under the indulgent eyes of their mothers; James, working side by side with the serfs in Seacrest's fields; Tristan, raising a toast to his subjects at Greanly; the trinity of brotherhood of Tristan, Pharao, and Nicholas; Haith wrapped protectively in Tristan's arms; Bertie, Pharao's golden pendant glowing against her breast; Minerva, clasping Nigel's wrist in Seacrest's bailey and calling down the wrath of the ancients.

Nigel writhed on the rushes long after his heart had exploded in his chest, and Haith stood over him, greedily watching as the flames devoured him in the midst of the tempest.

'Twas over.

CHAPTER
29

They rode away from Seacrest's bloody aftermath as quickly as Tristan's horse could carry them. The cold night air moaned in Tristan's ears as they raced northward, its chill reminiscent of Haith's cool, damp skin when he pressed his lips to her cheek. His arm was hard around her middle, and his breath ragged as he urged the mount onward, and Haith sagged against him, limp and frighteningly silent. From the moment after sending Nigel on to Hell, when the fiery cage about her lay shattered in a smoldering circle, she had spoken not a word.

The moon, but two nights past full and silvery ripe, had begun to wane. It hung halfheartedly over the blackened forest which swallowed the road ahead, as if there were nothing more it cared to see and it was turning away, going home.

Tristan reined their mount to a canter as they entered the wood, then to a walk. Intricate lacework of shadows lay on the road, and through the soft hush of the trees, he heard the playful night chatter of a stream. He slowed the horse to a halt.

Holding her steady, Tristan slid from behind Haith to the ground. She seemed to weigh nothing as he urged her down after him, as if she might float away or disappear altogether. Her knees did not lock when he tried to set her upon her feet, and so he lifted her into his arms and walked away from the road, his horse obediently following them into the trees.

He came upon a tiny clearing, a shoulder of ground sloping down to the moon-rinsed stream. He knelt, placing her so very gently with her back against a wide old beech. He peered into her pale, smooth face, frowned at her vacant eyes. She looked into a place somewhere deep in the dark beyond him. She was shivering.

"Haith," he called gently. "Haith, love." He grasped her chin, forcing her quiet gaze to his. "I'm going to collect some wood for a fire. I'll not go where you cannot see me, ken?"

Her eyelids fluttered into a blink, and her gaze became slightly more focused, as one who is just waking from a deep sleep.

"Faery, can you hear me? I need to start a fire."

She blinked again and dropped her head in a single nod.

Tristan gave her a smile and cradled her cool cheek in his palm for a moment before gaining his feet in search of fuel. True to his word, he never strayed from Haith's range of vision, if indeed she even saw him at all. She never stirred from her seat against the tree, save for her trembling. Tristan had seen this before in soldiers after their first battle—the shock. Some came out of it on their own; some needed urging.

Some never returned from the brink.

When the close clearing was bright and warm, he hurried back to her side. He slipped off his belt and sword, placing them within reach. Kneeling, he began to examine her inch by inch, touching her to reassure himself she was there with him. To try to bring her back from that dark place to which she'd gone.

"That's better, is it not?" he cajoled, smoothing his hands over the crown of her head. He brushed his thumbs over her dry, parted lips. "Warming up a bit?"

She did not answer, and Tristan drew a deep, silent breath. He skimmed his fingertips down her throat, over the crusty wound from Donald's blade, and the air escaped his lungs in a shudder. Her bodice was torn, the thin, dingy material of her underdress sagging.

"I fear this gown is worse for the wear, my lady," he said, striving for a light tone. If she would only speak to him, Tristan could be free of his terrible fear.

His palms eased down her slender arms to her hands, and he lifted them toward the firelight. 'Twas then that he saw the deep gouges on her wrists, the splotchy bruises splashed across her pale skin.

"My God," he said hoarsely. "My God, love, what did he do to you?" He moved to her feet, pushing the hem of her skirts away, and saw the spider webs of burst vessels, the bruises on her ankles where she'd obviously been bound.

And Tristan could take no more. He felt the silent sob deep in his chest, felt it move up the tight cording in his throat. He bowed himself over Haith's injuries and let it come, shaking furiously with the fear of what might have been. How easily she could have been taken from him forever, and how much worse than death itself the consequences would have been. He made no sound there in the dirt, and yet he cried like he had not since he was a young boy, abandoned and alone.

Oh, how he loved her.

"Haith," he said, a hitch in his breath. He leaned further down and kissed the marred flesh of her feet once. Then again. "Come back to me. Please."

Haith heard his cry. She had no recollection of how they had come to be in the quiet forest clearing, but in truth, she cared not the how of it. 'Twas as if she blinked and Tristan appeared at her feet, his blond head bent over her legs, his wide shoulders shaking. The back of Tristan's neck was exposed above his mail shirt and tunic, and Haith raised a throbbing hand to brush his skin lightly.

Tristan stilled at her touch and raised his head. Her heart clenched at the wet streaks on his cheeks, to see this proud, strong warrior so raw and humbled before her. She thought he would turn from her in embarrassment, but he met her gaze honestly, and she felt his hands caressing her calves.

"Haith," he whispered, "have you much pain? What can I do?"

Her palm slid from his neck, and she shook her head, her heart swelling with such emotion she felt it likely to burst from her chest. His query echoed their first meeting when he'd found her crying in Seacrest's stables. It seemed as though years had passed since she had asked him to hold her, to take her in his arms and protect her.

But she would not ask that of him now. Not yet.

"Nay," she finally replied, her voice raspy. "Not much pain."

He moved to her side, dragging his hands up her outstretched legs as if unwilling to lose physical contact with her. His calloused fingers caught the snags in her worn, dirty kirtle, and she could feel the heat of him through the thin cloth. She followed him with her eyes, so filled with joy was she to be able to look upon him.

"Are you cold then?" he asked. She could sense his

uncertainty, and her love for him doubled. "Shall I fetch a blanket?"

The night breeze was indeed crisp, but Haith had yet to feel its chill. Her trembling had all but ceased in this calm, warm space Tristan had made for them in the wood. But Haith had preparations of her own to attend to.

She let her lips curve. "If you would, my lord."

He nodded and made as if to rise, but then hesitated. Tristan raised his hand, and she could see its slight tremor before his palm slid behind her head. He pulled her cheek to his, his scratchy stubble warming her skin when he turned into her and pressed his mouth hard to her temple. She covered his arm with her hand and closed her eyes, smiling to herself.

Then he rose and walked to the edge of the trees and she watched him, studied the way he moved, the heavy grace of him. His form was but a vague outline as he robbed his mount of its covering, but she could see him when he paused in his task as if listening. Haith heard it, too.

He returned, a dark wool blanket crushed in one hand. Crouching at her side, he shook the folds out to cover her legs.

"I hear riders approaching," he said quietly, tucking the blanket around her. "'Tis most likely Phar and the others, thinking to follow us on to Greanly." He met her eyes. "Can you continue?"

Haith would have loved to see Bertie's face when Pharao returned to Greanly, to witness Tristan's reunion with his mother and brother, to embrace the old Scots healer and thank her. To tell them all how very much she loved them. But not this night.

All that she wanted most this night was in this little clearing.

"I am not certain I have the strength just now," she

lied. "Would that we rest here a bit longer, should it please you, my lord."

"I'll tell them to continue on to the keep," Tristan said immediately. "We can rest for as long as you desire." He caressed her face again before rising. "You'll be alright alone for a few moments?"

She nodded, and her smile followed him into the dark.

When he had gone, Haith gingerly gained her sore feet, snatching the heavy covering up in her hands. She threw it into the air with a giggle, and it snapped open and floated to the thick forest floor, covering the rich moss and stirring up the delicious perfume of decaying leaves. She looked at the fire, and it doubled in size.

She turned toward the sound of the laughing water and made her way down the easy embankment. At the water's edge, the icy current bubbled just over her toes, soothing them. The wet mineral smell made Haith's mouth water, and the silt beneath her feet began to hum.

Haith pulled her fingers through her tangled locks, stretched tall, and then bent to grasp the ragged hem of her kirtle. She pulled it up her body and over her head. Tossing the gown and underdress to the soft grass, she stepped into the metallic streak of moonlight that crossed the stream like a bridge.

Tristan hurried back through the forest toward the clearing, a small sack in one hand and a skin in the other, gifts from Pharao to sustain him and Haith in their respite. They would rejoin the party at Tristan's home when Haith felt well enough to travel.

Home. He ducked around a low hanging evergreen bough, and his heart skipped a beat. The word held such promise.

The small fire he'd built seemed to have doubled in

size, becoming a roaring blaze in his short absence. It beckoned to him through the black slashes of forest, and he stepped faster, already craving the sight of Haith, longing to hear her voice speak the words his ears ached for. He cautioned himself that 'twas perhaps too soon to press her for her vow after the horrific ordeal, but Tristan wondered how long he could wait.

Fear struck him cold as he stepped into the empty clearing. The firelight flickered happily on the spread blanket, but Haith was nowhere to be seen. The skin and sack of food fell from Tristan's hands as he charged toward the stream.

"Haith!" he roared, swiping at branches. His running footfalls crashed through the undergrowth. "Haith, where are you?"

He caught the shimmer of water through the trees, and his mind grasped the possibility that in her state of shock and confusion, she'd fallen into the stream, perhaps hitting her head. Macabre images of her lifeless body floating facedown, away from him, in the swift current paralyzed him for an instant.

"Haith! Answer me!"

His eyes strained, searching the inky loam for any sign of her passage, when they fell upon a jumble of muddy cloth at the water's edge. His head jerked up, scanning the water.

And then he saw her, and his breath seized in his chest.

She stood naked in the stream, her hair hanging down her back, long and black with water. Her skin glowed and sparkled, radiating the silvery luminescence, glistening wetly.

Tristan braced himself with one palm on a fledgling trunk as the sight before him nearly drove him to his knees. Haith's arms were outstretched as if to embrace that far away, glowing moon, the profile of her breasts pushing against the night. The swell of her hips and buttocks, the gentle curve of thigh, twisted his guts as she bent at the waist to scoop the water over her pearly body once more. She stood again, flinging her hair in a wide arc and sending tiny diamond droplets flying about her.

And then she turned toward where Tristan stood on the bank, her lips parting in a smile of invitation.

Tristan heard his own growl of desire coming as if from some forest wolf. He splashed into the stream, the cold water rushing around his boots and caressing his calves, and stood before her. He panted not with exertion, but with a wild hunger and need. He wanted to touch her so badly he shook, but he had no wish to frighten her with his desire.

Haith looked up into his face, droplets dancing on her lashes and cheeks. Her blue eyes were clear and snapping, her lips full and curved. Tiny dervishes of steam spun up from her skin, and her body hummed at him until Tristan thought he could stand it no more.

"Good eve, my lord." She smiled and at last stepped to him, placing her palms on his chest and running them up to his shoulders. Tristan vowed he could feel the whorls of her fingertips through his mail.

He swallowed, not trusting himself to speak. As if afraid she would evaporate into the moonlight she resembled, he raised his hands slowly to her bare back, brushing the smooth bumps of her shoulder blades. Her skin was cool and damp, but not cold, from the water. She radiated inner heat like a brazier, and Tristan feared he would boil in his clothes.

"My lady," he finally managed to croak. She pressed herself to him, searching his face with her eyes, and everywhere she looked, Tristan's skin tingled. Nay, blazed. "I could not find you."

"But you did find me," she sighed. Her hands swept up to his face, behind his ears, and into his hair, dragging his head to hers and claiming his mouth as any rightful victor claims a battlefield sorely won. She sucked at his lips, found his tongue, and held him to her with a strength Tristan knew could not be solely physical. Thunder rumbled in the distance.

She drew away, leaving too little of her taste with him, and looked so deeply into his eyes that Tristan felt her in his very soul.

"You found me, and you saved me," she insisted.

His restraint broke then, and this time, 'twas he who played the victor. He pulled her against him once more, allowing his hands to hold and press that precious flesh. Her fingers tugged at his heavy mail shirt, pushed it and his tunic up away from his belly. When their bare skin met, Tristan felt the sizzle of lightning in the length of his spine, tasted the tangy current in Haith's mouth, saw the ghostly traces on his eyelids.

He parted from her for an instant—an eternity—while he helped her jerk his clothing over his head. The tunic and chain shirt fell into the stream with a splash of applause, and then his bare arms were around her body once more. He kissed her mouth, dragged his lips over her face to her cheek, her jaw, the sweet curve of her neck. She breathed his name, and Tristan felt he was in very real danger of coming loose from the earth when he felt her hands at the laces of his chausses.

Haith rolled her head under his chin, ran her mouth over his chest, her tongue leaving a blistering trail across his skin. She tugged at the knotted cords at his waist and whimpered at their stubbornness.

He stopped her struggles with gentle hands and took

a step back from her. Tristan had to draw a ragged breath at her naked beauty, the fire in her eyes. He bent and splashed the cold water onto his own body, scrubbed it through his hair, sluiced it down his chest, ridding himself of the filth of battle. Haith boldly watched him as if daring him to resist her a moment longer.

In a splashing arc of water, he swept her into his arms and treaded the current toward the shore, to their clearing and the blanket by the fire.

Tristan's deep breaths lifted his chest rhythmically against Haith's own bare skin as he carried her near the fire. She pressed her mouth to his shoulder, bit down on the warm flesh. Her body throbbed with his heat such that the rush of air between them when he laid her gently on the blanket sent gooseflesh racing over her. She watched him brazenly, wantonly.

He stood over her, his gaze licking at every inch of her as he jerked at the laces of his chausses. The wet leather ties snapped in his grip, and she could see his arousal through the slick material. He kicked his boots away, and they tumbled down into the darkness. And then he, too, was naked.

Haith was not afraid when Tristan lay down beside her, the glow from the fire caressing that face so familiar to her. She gave not a thought to the probable pain their physical union would bring her. She had no worries for the future, no regrets about the past. Tristan's touch was a promise on her skin as he moved over her, his lips a holy seal when they pressed against her collarbone and then her breasts and lingered there. His hand swept down over her stomach, cupped her buttock, pulled her against him. She ached for his touch—from his touch—and nearly shrieked aloud when his hand moved between her legs.

Tristan was panting at her side, murmuring unintelligible words over her skin between kisses. Haith's world was a jumble of warm darkness and physical sensation so intense the pleasure closely mirrored pain. Her moans sounded feral to her own ears. His hands played her body like a mad drum, with an insistent, unrelenting beat. His body shuddered with his own desire, and Haith felt as though she were on the verge of something so ecstatic, so frantic, that if Tristan did not hold her very tightly she would shatter.

Now, now—she had to tell him now.

"Tristan," she gasped, tugging at his damp hair. "Oh, Tristan."

He raised his face, the intensity of his passion clear and thrilling in his eyes. His teeth flashed in the light. "Yea, my love?"

Any moment now, Haith knew she would break, for surely her body could not contain this mad pulsing much longer. But she held one sweet breath longer.

"Tristan," she cried, *"I love you."*

And then she did shatter, into tiny points of light behind her eyelids, a sky full of stars, a dark ocean of fulfillment. She called out for him—her man, her warrior—again and again as she was buoyed along on those warm waves. And Tristan answered her, moving between her thighs while she was still fantastically adrift.

The stab of pain was like a cold spray of water, and Haith opened her eyes at the shock. But seeing Tristan over her, his brow creased and dotted with sweat, his nostrils flaring; seeing the wide curve of his shoulders above her, feeling his arm hard and steady under her back, she trusted him to pull her down into the warm surf again.

She felt whole, full, and she clutched him to her. Burying her face in his damp neck, she whispered to him, telling him of her love between kisses.

"I love you, Haith," he moaned. "Oh, God, how I love you."

She clung to his slick back, her heart and body singing as his movements became more furious, more wild. She arched into him and dropped her head back to the blanket, gazing at the bright circle of night above the trees.

Tristan moaned her name again, and again, louder. Then with a hoarse shout, he tensed, his body thrumming into hers. She felt his tears on her cheeks as surely as her own.

And a single star blazed over the darkened forest, kissing Haith and Tristan with sweet light.

EPILOGUE

New Year's Day, 1077
Greanly Manor, England

Haith rose from Tristan's side with a weary sigh when the babe cried again, demanding her attention once more. Tristan's wide hands slid lingeringly down his wife's arms as he reluctantly let her go. He propped himself up in their bed and waited for her to return with their daughter.

Haith peered over the crib and smiled at the wriggling child. "You must not be left out of anything, is that it, little Lady Isabella?"

A gurgling coo was the babe's reply, and with a chuckle, Haith scooped her up and skittered back across the cold floor to ensconce them both within the warm bed.

Tristan smiled as he held the coverings aside. "She is like her mother then, no doubt."

Isabella settled comfortably to nurse, the red curls of mother and daughter tangling together against Haith's creamy breast. She leaned back against Tristan's shoulder and craned her neck to grin mischievously at her husband. "And you are one to mind your own business?"

Tristan shrugged and kissed her mouth lightly. "I fear any answer I give would only implicate me further."

"Hm-m." Haith smoothed the baby's short curls from her small face. "Think you Bertie is angry with me for not coming to visit her as of yet? She and Pharao always come to Greanly."

"Nay, she knows 'twill be some time before you can bring yourself to return to Seacrest. I expect she and Phar will be along again soon." Tristan smiled indulgently. "I received word from him yesterday—your sister is with child once more."

"Oh, Tristan!" Haith squealed, causing Isabella to squawk in offense. "How wonderful! Now, wee Jamie will have a brother or sister to play with!"

Pharao and Soleilbert's firstborn, James, or Jamie as he was called, had arrived nearly a year ago, to everyone's delight. The child was a gorgeous combination of his mother's fair beauty and his father's darkness, with soft, tawny curls; creamy skin, and deep brown eyes.

Ellora's turnaround at the birth of her first grandchild had been nothing short of miraculous to all who knew her. William had given Tristan leave to punish Ellora as he saw fit for the lady's part in attempting to destroy his life, but in the end, it had been Haith who had stayed her husband's hand from banishing Ellora from the land, citing that the woman had suffered enough in this lifetime. That had proven to be a wise piece of advice, for Ellora doted on the child shamelessly, all the while deferring to Bertie and Phar as Lady and Lord of Seacrest. Now Ellora was a productive member of her daughter's hold, not to mention the mother-in-law of royalty.

"I wonder," Haith mused, "if at times, Pharao regrets not returning to his country to rule, as was his right."

"I have asked him as much," Tristan admitted. "But he assures me that his home is here now, with us and

Soleilbert. I believe he was away from his people too long and still held much resentment toward them for the overthrow and murder of his father. Thank God he realized where his true family lay before getting on that ship."

"A prince," Haith mused. Isabella had fallen asleep once more, and she snored softly. "'Tis no wonder William granted him Seacrest after he aided us so faithfully against Nigel."

"Yea,"—Tristan winced—"but 'twas also a political move, love. William seeks foreign allies, and one way to assure Phar's people's allegiance was to hold him in esteem as one of his own lords."

Haith snorted. "Always the devious one, our king."

A rap sounded on the chamber door, and husband and wife drew the covers higher. "Come," Tristan called.

Genevieve, Baroness of Crane, poked her head inside the room. "Blessings on this first morn of the new year, darlings."

"And to you, Mother." Tristan smiled. "Come in."

Genevieve approached the bed on Haith's side with her arms extended. "There is my granddaughter!" Haith handed the drowsy baby to her. *"Ma petite chéri!"* Genevieve looked to Haith and Tristan. "If you like, I can dress her and take her to the hall while you prepare yourselves."

"Thank you, my lady. We shall be down soon," Haith said. When Genevieve had gathered clothing for Isabella and glided out the door, Haith sighed and snuggled closer to Tristan. She wrapped her arms tightly around his lean waist. "She's wonderful."

"Yea, I can hardly bear to think of the years that were wasted." Tristan spoke with regret of the terrible separation from his mother in Paris years ago.

After Nigel's death, Tristan had kept his promise to hear his mother's explanation. He soon learned that shortly before his abandonment, Genevieve was to wed a wealthy French lord who was displeased with the fact that she had borne an illegitimate child. Telling Genevieve that his family would not accept Tristan, he persuaded her to hide her son away until their marriage was final. She did not love the French lord, but as a young woman tainted by scandal, she felt she had little choice if she wished to marry and provide a home for her son.

Genevieve had agreed to the foster care—only for a few short weeks, she was promised—and she sent Tristan to an acquaintance of her fiancé's with half of the only valuables she owned, the D'Argent sapphires.

Genevieve had barely been able to form the words when she'd explained to Tristan that after the marriage ceremony, her new husband had blithely informed her that he'd sold her son. Not believing him, Tristan's mother had taken to the streets of Paris immediately in search of the hag who traded orphans for slave labor. When she'd found Tristan missing, Genevieve had returned to her husband's suite and struck him in the head with his own heavy iron coin box, killing him in his sleep in revenge for the loss of her only love—her son, Tristan.

Fearing now for her own life, she'd emptied the murder weapon of its contents and bought passage on a ship bound for England before word of her misdeeds could spread. Once in London, she'd quickly caught the eye of and married the Baron of Crane, and her French persona had faded into obscurity. She grew to love Lord Richard dearly and delighted in Nicholas's birth, but in those years, she still searched for Tristan relentlessly.

After the old baron's death, Genevieve heard rumors about the new lord of Greanly so she sought an audience with William. The king heard her entire tragic tale the same day Tristan met Genevieve at court and absolved her of her crime. William vowed that she would never be forced to return to France.

Now that mother and son had reunited, Genevieve had stayed at Greanly to witness her son's wedding and then aid Haith in the birth of Isabella. After the baby's christening, she would return to Hartmoore to find Tristan's brother a suitable bride.

"We should rise," Haith murmured into Tristan's chest. "The Buchanans arrived late in the night, and will be expecting us."

"M-m-m. They can wait." Tristan pulled her closer and trailed his fingertips down her warm, naked back.

Haith pulled away to laugh up at him. "Do you not remember what happened the last time they were made to wait?"

After Haith and Tristan's loving interlude in the forest, they had returned to Greanly—Tristan shirtless and wearing only one boot, Haith wrapped in the blanket—to find not only the rest of their victorious party in residence but also three score Scots warriors.

And one very nervous traveling merchant.

Haith's Grandda, Corinne's own father, still lived, and he had been the honorary host of the festivities that had taken place in Tristan's absence. Tristan and Haith had arrived in the hall to much revelry, with Angus Buchanan later telling them that he had dreamed of the granddaughter he thought dead after Hastings. He had foreseen her victory over Nigel and had gathered many of his clan to make the long, dangerous journey south.

The Scotsmen had run across the peddler on their way and, after hearing his tale, had forced him to return with them.

"Just in case," Angus had said while glaring at the wiry man.

Minerva had been elated at the reunion with her

brother, Angus, but a look of wistfulness had passed through her eyes all the same. When Haith had queried her aunt about her melancholy, Minerva had merely replied with a sad smile, " 'Tis but an old dream, lass. Mayhap I will tell you of it one day, but not now."

The drinking and merriment had lasted for days.

"You're right." Tristan pretended a giant, horrific shudder. "Do we not descend soon, there shall be no ale left to celebrate Isabella's christening."

Haith laughed out loud and pulled her husband even closer to kiss him deeply. She then leaned back, blue eyes looking into blue eyes. "Minerva was right. 'Tis a blessing, this."

"Yea," Tristan agreed, his smile fading as he basked in the warm glow of Haith's magical love. "We are blessed indeed."

"I love you, my warrior."

"I love you as well, my lady wife."

Haith leaned forward to kiss the corners of his mouth, his cheeks, his eyelids. When Tristan rolled atop her and pinned her to the bed with a wicked grin, Haith laughed, and the sound tinkled through the chamber.

"Perhaps we *could* stay abed a while longer."

Atop a knoll not far from Greanly, two shimmery figures, a man and a woman, faced the keep. Their hands joined as the sound of Haith's laughter wrapped around them, and the man smiled.

"My faery," Corinne whispered, and the hushed sound echoed over the frozen, silent land with no more volume than the sound of falling snow. "My blessing."

James pulled Corinne closer to his side, and the couple lifted their faces toward the heavens as their figures faded away.